THE TOWER
of
THEO

Sasha Zeiger

ISBN: 978-1-7923-7966-6

This book is dedicated to you.

Table of Contents

PART ONE   vii

  Chapter One   1

  Chapter Two   13

  Chapter Three   25

  Chapter Four   37

  Chapter Five   49

  Chapter Six   61

  Chapter Seven   73

  Chapter Eight   85

PART TWO   99

  Chapter Nine   101

  Chapter Ten   111

  Chapter Eleven   123

  Chapter Twelve   127

  Chapter Thirteen   139

  Chapter Fourteen   147

  Chapter Fifteen   151

  Chapter Sixteen   161

  Chapter Seventeen   171

  Chapter Eighteen   183

PART THREE   193

  Chapter Nineteen   195

  Chapter Twenty   207

  Chapter Twenty-One   219

  Chapter Twenty-Two   229

  Chapter Twenty-Three   241

  Chapter Twenty-Four   255

  Chapter Twenty-Five   265

  Chapter Twenty-Six   279

PART ONE

PART ONE

Chapter

One

Demetrius, an enemy to no one, roamed the world of Platanis with child-like light steps, but with the heart of a man who has loved and most certainly has lost. His tall stature, consistently draped in loosefitting, bright yellow linens, ensured his ever-warm presence. The world to him was a perfectly painted masterpiece, to which he fully immersed himself in vivid colors.

To not see Demetrius smiling equated to seeing a shadow upon the sun's surface. His patchy beard, accompanied by his wild dark curls, only added to his overall charm. His gratitude toward life had shielded him from most turmoil throughout his thirty-eight years, except for two of his darkest days.

Today was the second of those days.

Demetrius sat at a triangular wooden table in the three-sided room in his home. The bare room accommodated only a sundial, the table, and its chairs, leaving just enough room for sitters. Demetrius ran his hand through his messy hair as he pushed his chair onto its rear legs, resting his head on the wall behind him. He squinted as the sunlight from the glass ceiling poured over him and his attire, splashing shades of yellow onto the blank grey walls.

Across the table sat Leander, his friend since childhood, whose formal posture and clasped hands were hidden under an oversized dark blue robe. His matching headwrap elongated his upright posture. The blue material absorbed the sunlight, refusing to interfere with Demetrius' magnifying appearance.

Leander's long, pale fingers, one weighted by a silver, sapphire ring, reached for the box of pencils beside them. He offered one to Demetrius who smiled wearily and accepted the offer. The gesture was more of a formality, as Demetrius was not one to take notes. He'd place the pencil behind his ear, but today, he held onto it.

"I sense your anticipation," Demetrius said, rolling the pencil anxiously between his fingers as his smile faded.

"Time is not on our side, my friend," Leander responded, returning his hands to the clasped position. The pencil protruded from his fingers. "It is not I who pressures you." Leander tilted his head as much as his headwrap would allow toward the sundial in the corner of the room. Brightness reflected off its surface, imprinting itself onto Demetrius eyes, imparting Leander's urgency.

Demetrius' leg bounced and he exhaled defeatedly. The bags under his eyes darkened as he bowed his head. Even his bright yellow attire appeared duller, as if a giant cloud of misery had swallowed him. Demetrius sat forward, resting his head upon his arm for support as he stared blankly at the tabletop.

"I'm not ready," he admitted.

"You are as ready as you will ever be."

"No!" Demetrius retorted, pounding his fist on the table. "What a hopeless thing to say. Commemorating someone's death when the cause of it remains unknown, well, I don't know how to do it. And it's not just any death, but a… a murder. It was a murder, right? It's still unfathomable. But let me assure you," Demetrius continued with a lowered voice, pressing his index finger against the table, "I *will* find out who did this. One day."

"Twenty years have passed since the fatal incident of your father," Leander said, treading lightly. The sadness Demetrius exuded was too much for Leander to mend immediately, but not enough to deter him from the task at hand. "Your acquisition of that knowledge should have no effect on your responsibility to celebrate his legacy. I am not minimizing the pain you experience from this uncertainty; you must know. But the time has come to build the statue upon his grave."

"That's the last step, isn't it? To cover his grave with a vague representation of what he stood for. I can't do it, Leander."

"If you are expected to do something, then you *can* do it," Leander said. "You have a responsibility as his son. Every son, at some point, buries his father. I buried mine when I was still a boy. And my mother."

Demetrius shoulders tightened as he strenuously shut his eyes to erase the memory of a young Leander rolling up his sleeves and patting the last bit of soil upon his parents' graves. He had long hair at the time, which had conveniently curtained his tears from those around him. Leander, however, upon recollection, had not budged an inch.

"Also," Leander continued, "dear friend, must I remind you that building the statue upon his grave does not make him more or less gone?"

Demetrius pressed his lips together. The sternness in Leander's blue-grey eyes, those eyes which had always looked protectingly at Demetrius over many decades, reinforced the seriousness of Leander's statement.

The statue must be built.

A *snap* broke the momentary silence, and Demetrius opened his fist to see the pencil had cracked under pressure.

"Sorry," Demetrius said, rolling the remains to the side.

"An apology is not necessary. I simply need your blessing to proceed. I am willing to sacrifice any amount of pencils for it."

Leander put his pencil aside and reached under the table, grabbing the canvas bag propped against one of the wooden legs. He retrieved a sizable blue sketchbook with a small "L" drawn on the cover. A torn piece of paper bookmarked his current project.

Leander opened his sketchbook and reclaimed his pencil, placing it flat on the table. He pointed the graphite tip toward the sketch. As he raised the pencil, the illustration on the paper likewise rose. He stopped once the pencil and sketch had reached eye-level.

Tears congregated on Demetrius' lower lashes as he faced a sketch of his late father; he tilted his chin upward to restrict the tears from falling. He shared many similarities with his father: the contagious smile, the chiseled jaw, the jet-black curls. His father's body had been the result of decades devoted to athleticism, something Demetrius couldn't achieve no matter how hard he tried.

Leander rotated the sketchbook, showing Demetrius a complete view of the drawing. The rotating stopped when his father's outstretched hand was inches away from Demetrius face. As if hypnotized, Demetrius raised his finger toward the sketch.

"Touching it will smear the graphite," Leander said. Demetrius noticed the dark smudge that covered the tip of his index finger.

"Sorry about that." Demetrius wiped his finger with his thumb, spreading the graphite further. Leander handed him a tissue from the canvas bag. "Thank you. I didn't mean to touch your work. It's just so…" The tears grew fuller, but Demetrius maintained his composure. "So realistic."

"I used every memory I had." Leander placed the pencil behind his ear to ensure the sketch remained erect, since the pencil controlled the three-dimensional stature.

"These details are all from memory? Not even from a written account? I wish my memories were this vivid. I'm more nostalgic of feelings than visuals. Your work is spectacular, Leander."

"Thank you. I think it will fit in the Garden very well. The outstretched hand will be the most animated part of the statue, waving to those who approach."

4

"Wonderful. He was always so welcoming to those around him," Demetrius said, rubbing his freshly cleaned hands against his chin. He imagined what it would be like to visit his father's grave once the statue was complete; the glooming feeling of dismay, of longing, that typically accompanied visits to the Garden would perhaps be buried, too. "How long will it take to build?"

"We do not have much time," Leander repeated, glancing at the sundial again. "I will have to work overnight to ensure the piece functions properly for the ceremony tomorrow evening."

"That's right," Demetrius said, sitting back in his chair, covering his face with his hands. An audible frustration escaped his lips. "I can't express how much I don't want to do this."

"My friend, you must stop blaming yourself for what happened."

"For the hundredth time, I don't blame myself for what happened," Demetrius mumbled behind closed hands. "I blame myself for not vindicating his murder, for not finding a mere clue pertaining to the identity of the murderer. How, Leander? How? I just gave up somewhere along the way, and now, somehow, twenty years have passed."

"I understand your frustration, however—"

"You understand this means the murderer still lives among us, right? We are a small community. Not too small, but small enough that no such catastrophe could remain as mysterious as it has. And no one travels outside our Forest. No one. Well, except for one person…" Demetrius peaked through his fingers and stared blankly at the third chair beside him. The chair faced outward, as if someone had forgotten to push it back in, or as if its sitter would soon return.

"Enough!" Leander exclaimed. "He, too, has been gone for quite some time, and yet one would think he remains forever present given how often you recall his existence!" Demetrius lowered his hands and lifted his eyebrows at the sound of Leander's raised voice. Leander took a deep breath, though a protruding vein in his neck had already emerged. "You need to forgive the past and live in the present, Demetrius."

Demetrius bowed his head in understanding. Leander avoided two subjects with everyone, those being of his parents' untimely deaths and of the man who once sat in the abandoned chair. Demetrius reached over to place his hand on Leander's.

"Leander, how can I forgive the past if I don't *know* the past? How can you expect me to face anyone and give a speech about my father, knowing everyone awaits an answer to the inevitable question?" Demetrius pulled at his hair in frustration. "Will they even listen to anything else I have to say? I know I wouldn't."

"They will," Leander replied, pulling his sketchbook closer to him, returning it to the bag. Leander grabbed the sharpened pencil behind his ear and laid it beside Demetrius' broken pencil. "Remember, I will be by your side, dear friend. Always. You need not worry. You are expected to reflect upon Myron's life, not his death."

"I'm not sure I can separate the two, life and death," Demetrius confessed, leaning on the table, keeping his eyes on the two pencils. Leander now reached across the table to place a comforting hand on his friend's shoulder.

"Tomorrow, on the twentieth anniversary of your father's passing, you are providing closure. For yourself and for those who need it. You are strengthening and insuring the loving memory of your father into the hearts of everyone whose lives he had enriched tremendously. What an honorable position in which you find yourself."

"I hope everyone is too amazed by your incredible statue to listen to anything I have to say."

Leander shook his head, flaring his nostrils.

"My art is not a distraction," he stated through tightened lips. "And you have no reason to seek distraction. You need this closure as much as the rest. By tomorrow, we will wash away our impending curiosity of this heinous crime to rejoice in the loving memory of your father. Every moment, Demetrius, is like clay. Embrace the moment and shape it how you would like before it permanently dries as a memory in your mind."

"I see there's no point arguing with you," Demetrius sighed. He clenched his fist and placed it on his stomach. "I just have this gut feeling—perhaps it's hope—that the answers to my questions are accessible." Leander placed the canvas bag's strap over his shoulder and rose from his seat.

"You must act with what you know and nothing else."

"A bit strange coming from an artist, no?" Demetrius teased, as color slowly returned to his face. "Don't you all express your emotions?"

"Are our emotions nothing more than the product of our actions?" Leander asked. "I will go to the Garden immediately and begin my work. I assume you will begin writing your speech?"

"I suppose," Demetrius said, also rising from his seat. As Demetrius walked past Leander toward the door, Leander warmly patted Demetrius' back.

"Everything will be alright," he assured.

Upon opening the door into the hallway, a splash of scarlet red consumed Demetrius' vision. He blinked feverishly until he noticed a scarlet envelope placed directly below him, its edges perfectly aligned with the doorframe. As Demetrius bent to retrieve it, the envelope's redness washed over him, swallowing him with its hue.

Demetrius peeked into the hallway, searching for the messenger. The sunlight beamed rays of reflected scarlet into the deserted corridor, establishing its eerie omnipresence. Demetrius turned to Leander, clutching the envelope to his chest. The room's grey walls were set ablaze as Demetrius' yellow linens blended with the cherished letter.

"Please," Leander said in a low tone, "assure me you will not entertain the contents of that letter." His heavy robe expanded and compressed as he steadied his breathing.

"After all these years," Demetrius mumbled to himself. Leander kept his bag on his shoulder as he reclaimed his seat at the table.

"Demetrius," Leander said, pointing his boney finger with the sapphire ring at the sundial, "we simply do not have time for this. The most we can do is leave that... thing here and revisit it another time."

"I knew he'd be back."

Leander pinched the bridge of his nose, took a deep breath, then braced his palms on the table.

"Have you not been listening?" Leander asked. Demetrius tilted the envelop forward, peering over it to acknowledge Leander. Leander's nostrils flared as he saw the reflected scarlet color in Demetrius' eyes. "Must I repeat myself? You need to act with what you know, not how you feel."

"What I know," Demetrius said, waving the envelope, "is that Theo is back." He smiled as he glided his hand across the surface of the envelope.

"You know no such thing. What you know is that you have twentyfour hours before the ceremony of your father's passing and the unveiling of the statue. What you also know," Leander said, pointing at the rectangular source of his misery, "is that you do not have time to engage with whatever this... man has to say. Look simply at its surface: the color, the 'T?' A changed man he is not! Since you last heard from him all those years ago— nineteen? Eighteen? Ah yes, nineteen years ago, he suddenly decides to insert himself back into your life in typical fashion— disruptively and carelessly. And based on what he was like back then, what good can you expect from him now?"

"Why won't you say his name?"

"He is dead to me," Leander answered without hesitation, peaking at the third, unoccupied chair at the table. "I wish to never speak of him again. I look forward to the day where you, too, share my view."

"You shouldn't be so quick to judge. Let's at least see what he has to say before any further condemnation."

"Do you find the time of this delivery to be a coincidence? Of course not. I cannot, I *will not*, reason another intent except malice. Pure malice, Demetrius. If you do not believe me, I am sure Aluna could be a source of reason. Please, allow her to remove whatever it is currently blinding you."

"You're right," Demetrius said, heading quickly toward the door. "Let us go to her."

Leander held his headwrap as he hastily rose to follow Demetrius into the hallway. As Demetrius rushed out the doorway, the walls lost their eccentric colors, returning to their neutral grey state.

A single window insufficiently lit the hallway, just enough to reveal a faint floral design engraved onto the stone floor. Specks of dust floated through the air, stirred from the crevices of the curvy chiseling. Demetrius charged past it, but Leander stopped in the center of the spotlight as the sunlight turned his navy-colored garments an electric royal blue. It seemed his robes' colors could only be projected if Demetrius' clothing weren't in direct competition.

"Demetrius, please wait," Leander said. Demetrius halted but did not look back. "You must know that I have no ill will toward you. I never have. The excitement and adrenaline I am sensing from you: I cannot place nor understand it, but I will caution you of it. Have you even pondered how the letter was delivered? The man no longer lives among us, nor even close to our proximities."

"I hadn't thought about it."

"Exactly," Leander said, pointing his index finger upward. He paused to let the question sink deeper into Demetrius' mind. "The Tracoses Forest surrounding our community is filled with trackers, poisonous plants, and other obstacles to prevent intrusions, remember? I am sure Aluna has told you about it. My parents risked their lives ensuring the forest would protect us." Leander made a fist and firmly closed his eyes.

"I didn't think about that either." Demetrius tapped the corner of the envelope in contemplation. "We can ask Aluna if there has been any alarming botanic interference in the past couple of days." Leander dropped his formal posture into a defeated shrug.

"I pray Aluna revives your rationale, takes the letter from you, and persuades you to prepare for the ceremony. I also pray there are no signs of invasions. Building the statue now with my persistent paranoia will be very difficult. What it would take to reconstruct the precautions my parents built throughout the forest if that man had somehow infiltrated…"

"I can't even recall the last time you were this worried about something, my friend. I can assure you; I married the best botanist in the world," Demetrius said, putting his arm around Leander with a smile. "I have always known Aluna to have a solution. Trust me. And if your paranoia persists, I'm sure Aluna has a remedy for that."

Leander had no choice but to step out of the rectangular spotlight and shadow Demetrius down the hallway into Aluna's herbaceous nursery.

～

Behind Demetrius' house was an expansive garden, and in the middle of this massive greenery was the foundational framework of a greenhouse. Myron had begun to build it for her prior to his untimely death, and Aluna refused to temper with the nostalgia engraved in the wood's crevices. The massive wooden beams and the abundance of overlapping plants made finding Aluna challenging, but once Demetrius' eyes landed on her, color flushed to his cheekbones. Aluna's profile was visible as she hunched over an oval glass table, taking notes on a potted plant. For a moment Demetrius watched in awe as Aluna bit her bottom lip to focus on the plant's examination, tucking her light brown curls behind her ear to reveal a heavy golden hoop. Her emerald green, loose-fitting bodysuit helped her blend into her surroundings. Her hazel eyes, however, would always stand out.

"Aluna!" Demetrius called from the back door. He kept the letter behind his back. Leander remained hidden, standing outside the narrow doorway until Demetrius' departure from the doorway exposed him.

"Come, sit," Aluna said, gently pointing at the nearest chair. "Oh, Leander, so good to see you! Apologies for the mess. This new harvest has kept me busy. The sun seems to be traveling across the sky quicker these days." She cleared the table in front of the two chairs beside her. "I'm raising these new water lilies. You see them, over there? A stubborn bunch, they are. But who isn't stubborn upon their arrival to this world? They're still babies, in my eyes."

Aluna referred to this space as her nursery due to her motherly nature toward all the plants. She knew everything about each one, showering them with love and attention. Her garden was filled with ancient and newly blossomed plants, making her nursery the perfect balance between botanic antiquity and modernity.

Aluna's bare feet dug into the soil as she stood on her toes, reaching for the clay jug hanging from one of the wooden beams.

"Would you like some water?" she asked.

We would love some, the vines wrapped around the beam joked. She winked at them as an acknowledgement of the jokes' telepathic delivery, then turned her attention to her guests.

"I will never cease to be perplexed as to how you drink warm water in this weather," Leander said, blocking the sun's rays with his hand. He clutched his canvas bag in his lap to ensure it wouldn't fall into the soil.

"No water for either of us," Demetrius said. Aluna nodded and replaced the clay jug onto the fixture. She scanned her periphery in search of her already filled cup, and once she wrapped her fingers around the cylinder, she seated herself at the head of the table.

"Gentlemen, to what do I owe this honor?"

Chapter
Two

In the middle of a grassy respite in the forest, twenty-one-year-old Damian sat beneath a tree; his arms were propped behind his head for maximum comfort. A flask of water and a stack of unused notebooks amidst a handful of reading materials, everything he had cleared from his desk at the Academy, rested haphazardly beside him. When he saw Caterina approaching from across the field, he hastily fixed his light brown hair, tugged at his shirt, and reorganized the pile.

He couldn't take his eyes off her as the sunlight shined over her brown skin. The gentle breeze graced Caterina's silky, braided black hair, in dire contrast to her off-white dress. She carried a large canvas bag over her shoulder, the way all artists did. Damian's heart beat rapidly as he stood to greet her.

She smiled and stretched out her hand.

"Formal, are we?" Damian asked with a raised eyebrow.

"And why not?" She reached in her bag for a neatly folded blanket, much the same color as her dress. With Damien's help, they laid the sheet over the grass and sat across from each other.

Caterina tucked her crossed legs under her dress so that the ends of the linens blended into the blanket beneath her, giving the illusion she herself had blossomed from the fabric. Her delicate hand again reached into the tote bag and pulled out two apples: one red, one green.

"Which would you like?" Caterina asked.

"Green, please. A little sour never hurt." He bit into the fruit with pleasure. "You're not hungry?" he asked, watching Caterina rotate the apple in her hands.

"I have a lot on my mind."

"Don't," Damian said, flashing her a charming smile with his notorious dimples. She rolled her eyes though she couldn't help but smile. She was drawn to him not for the affinity but for the dissimilarity, for the unfamiliar.

"I thought you would empathize with me, Damian, especially as a student."

"What if I told you I wasn't a student anymore?" Damian asked, taking another bite of his apple. Caterina furrowed her brows as Damian tilted his head toward the stack of books and journals beside him.

She reached for the journals one by one, expecting filled pages of notes but instead met with blank pages. The books beside him were in too pristine condition to have ever been opened.

Damian happily bit into the apple again.

"Seems like you mentally left a while ago," Caterina started, flopping the final notebook atop the pile. "What sparked the final departure?"

"Now I'm freer than ever to practice philosophy. Real philosophy. *And,* I have more time to get to know *you.*"

"Real philosophy?" Caterina asked. "Without any guidance?" Damian scooted closer to Caterina, accidentally dragging the blanket underneath him. Caterina opened her mouth to point out the unevenness of the blanket, but Damian responded before she could utter a word.

"Philosophy is a love of *wisdom,* Caterina. Not knowledge. The Academy, once a space filled with insatiably curious minds has dissolved into a… I'm not even sure what to call it. A room of narrowminded egos, I suppose. The discipline has become a semantics game, where everyone wants the last word. To ask a question is to show weakness, in their eyes. 'How dare you question us!' They'd say. 'Perhaps if you listened more, you'd ask less!' That's not philosophy! That's nauseating."

"All of philosophy sounds nauseating to me. You could've chosen a less detestable field, if that's really how you feel. No one forced you into philosophy."

"You see, any other discipline would be a force," Damian replied. "Philosophy, real philosophy, is and requires *ultimate* freedom." Damian cocked his head back and extended his arms, dramatizing his point.

"You say that," Caterina said, "but surely you don't think you can practice philosophy on your own?"

"Life will be my mentor."

He returned to his original closed-eyed position leaning against the tree as Caterina restituted the pile of notebooks. Damian adjusted his leg until his ankle touched her knee. He didn't want to make too big of a gesture, as she was never receptive to those. His eyes jolted open as he felt her leg move toward him.

Ensuring the dress still covered her legs, she stretched her leg until they were parallel to his. Damian again closed his eyes, hoping to hide his excitement. The side of her lip curled upward, sensing it anyway. Caterina put aside her uneaten apple and leaned onto the palms of her hands.

Damian sparked Caterina's curiosity in a paralyzing way, where she found joy in his insights but turmoil in the endless questions which would soon after arise. Unlike Caterina, Damian loved surrounding himself in a sea of inquiries.

"Speaking of life being my mentor," he continued, opening one eye to meet hers, "I had a question I've been meaning to ask you."

"Hmm?" She flipped her braid to the other side, smoothing it out as it fell to her hips. She looked deep into Damian's eyes, noticing for the first time how long his eyelashes were. She must have previously been too distracted by the green speckles scattered among shades of blue in his eyes.

Her eyes stayed glued to his as he sat up, bringing one knee closer to his chest while keeping the leg nearest to Caterina locked in place. He placed an arm over the knee and dug his chin into it, bracing himself.

"Do you know anything about the ex-artist?" Damian asked. The side of Caterina's lips flattened. She nodded and returned her braid to its original placement, resetting her formality. Damian's eyes glistened with excitement, though Caterina let out a disappointed sigh.

"I can't say I know too much about him, and I can't say I want to know too much about him either. He's referred to as the ex-artist for a reason; no one knows his real name. Why do you ask?"

"I think he was a philosopher," Damian said, rubbing his chin. "I was hoping you could share with me what you know. You being an artist, and all."

"I don't know a lot," she repeated, shifting her leg away from his.

"In some ways that's good," he said, immediately bringing his foot closer to hers, reinstating their proximity, "because I didn't come here to take copious notes." His smile appeared again, but Caterina was not amused.

"You brought plenty of empty notebooks, though."

"Forgot a pencil," he joked, shrugging his shoulders. Caterina leaned over and playfully pushed Damian's shoulder.

"I've never met anyone who thirsted for knowledge but refused to write a single thing down. But, if this helps in any way, the one thing I know is the ex-artist was the only student to have ever dropped from the Academy, right before graduation. I'm not sure what he was assigned or what he created, but typically the final assignment for art students requires the student to replicate and improve a current artist's most recent work. I'm getting anxious just thinking about it."

Caterina reached for her apple and rotated it in her hands again.

"Hey, hey, hey," Damian said, placing a hand on hers. "What are you afraid of?"

"Everything."

"Don't be," Damian said, pushing her apple out of the way and interlocking his hand with her graphite-covered fingers. "There's no one in this world quite like you; ergo, your art is incomparable to the works of others. You have no competition, except for yourself it seems."

"Did you really just say 'ergo,' Damian?" Caterina asked, letting out an involuntary laugh.

"Rewarding me with that vibrant laugh of yours enables this sort of vernacular, Caterina. Ergo, I will continue using ergo." He paused briefly to stare at his hand in hers, imprinting the memory into his mind. "Tell me though," he continued excitedly, "what did this exartist do after failing the final assignment?"

Damian released his grip from her hands and gently glided his hand down the side of her leg as he fell back against the tree. He kept his fingers lightly wrapped around her ankle where the ends of her dress met her bare skin.

"Hmm, I'm not sure. He was banished from the community a year later— but I don't know what kept him preoccupied during his final days."

"Final days! You make it sound like he died once he left the community? Surely this world isn't that unmanageable for an artist? Is there something hiding in the shadows of life we're not seeing?" Damian jokingly looked left, right, and over his shoulder, scanning the trees around them.

Caterina humored him, examining the forestation surrounding them, squinting and pretending to search for the answer among the trees. She returned to face him and gently shook her head.

"Interesting," Damian said. "This ex-artist became mad, failed the Academy, then left Platanis never to return again?"

"You're making many assumptions, but I have no reason to believe otherwise."

"You never need a *reason* to believe."

"Don't use your philosophy on me," she warned, wagging her finger in disapproval. Damian put his arms up, defending himself from her accusations.

"I think the ex-artist was a philosopher who happened to have artistic means of expression," Damian said, lowering his arms and his tone. "I don't believe he went mad at all." Caterina scrunched her face in perplexity, contemplating Damian's hypothesis.

"You should share your thoughts with Leander. He was the exartist's supervisor, you know."

Time passed as the two conversed; the clouds above them glided as effortlessly as their words, floating through the sky with gentle ease. The distance between them lessened throughout the conversation until Caterina glanced at her tote bag. Damian paused mid-sentence with a look of despair.

"Don't tell me you have to leave so soon."

She gently placed her hand on Damian's cheek. He held his breath.

"I have my lesson with Leander," Caterina said, standing up. "I stayed as long as I could."

"Funny, how time flies," Damian said as he brainstormed ways of asking her to stay. "What are you working on with him?"

"Since when are you interested in my work?"

"Is that your sketchbook in there?" Damian asked, pointing to her bag doubling as a weight to ensure the picnic blanket's placement. Without waiting for a response, he tugged the blanket closer, bringing the bag within arm's reach.

"Hey!" Caterina protested, crouching to reach for her belongings. Damian snatched the sketchbook from her bag and raised it above his head. She pressed her hand on his chest and reached across his body for it. She could feel his heart pounding, as was hers.

We've never been this close before, Damian thought. Caterina again lost herself in the speckled green parts of Damian's eyes. Damian gazed into Caterina's dark brown eyes until he could clearly see his reflection in them, like a window showing the world from her perspective. His focus lowered to her lips.

Caterina blushed and retreated. She held out her hand, waiting for him to return the book.

"Sorry," Damian said, handing her the book. He could still feel the warmth from her hand, and he cursed his shirt for the barrier it created between his skin and hers.

"No, I'm sorry, I didn't mean to—" she stuttered, pointing at his chest. "Anyway, I was just surprised that you were curious. You've never asked before."

"It's no secret I'm an idiot," he said, chuckling. She smiled and nodded. He stretched his arms out in a pleading position. "Please, Caterina, free me of my ignorance! Tell me about your sketches." *Anything for us to share another minute*, he thought.

"I really can't be late."

"I'll clean up. Tell me about your project." Damian stood and grabbed the edge of the picnic blanket.

"I shouldn't be shocked by a curious philosopher," Caterina joked. "I'm glad you asked, though. Thank you." Caterina stood to help fold the blanket, grabbing the corners and pinching them together neatly. "It's really quite fascinating, what Leander has been teaching me. Last week he showed me the anatomy of a human hand. It's so complex, Damian! Leander can draw a hand in ten minutes, and when he lifts it from the canvas, each part moves like a real hand. Ten minutes! That's all it takes him. I think it would take me days, if not weeks, to accomplish something like that."

"That's incredible," Damian said, taking the folded blanket from her, "and a little unsettling."

"Unsettling?"

"I wouldn't want to see a random hand just laying somewhere, twitching."

"It's not a real hand. Even the painted subjects that *look* realistic would never *feel* entirely real, unless you're one of the Greats like Leander."

"Ah," Damian said, rubbing the back of his head.

"Plus, I'm not really interested in human subjects. I'd rather draw animals. If you want, I can show you my most recent sketch. It's this bird that—"

A group of birds screeched from the other side of the respite. Caterina spun, her braid whipping her face as it followed.

In the distance, from the same place where Caterina had earlier emerged, a young woman with flaming red unkempt hair trudged forward. She wore a tattered and faded white dress. Her head tilted forward, as though the weight of her thoughts burdened her posture. Similarly, her shoulders were hunched, and her arms hung loosely at her sides.

At first, she didn't seem to notice them. Though she walked in a perfectly straight line, she moved with no definitive purpose, failing to react to her surroundings. Her demeanor mimicked a sleepwalker's, with the dark bags under her eyes accentuating her exhausted expression.

Caterina held her breath, discomforted by the advancement of this stranger. Damian held his too, but in the hopes of remaining undetected. As he leaned back to hide his face behind Caterina's, he accidentally snapped a branch beneath his weight.

The wandering woman immediately glared in their direction, pushing aside fallen strands of hair.

Damian muttered profanity.

"That's Gabriella," he whispered to Caterina through the corner of his mouth. He waited for her to come closer, though he didn't want to make a formal introduction.

Gabriella remained motionless in her white dress, while the breeze blew her red hair to the side, like a wild flame on a composed candle.

"Aren't you going to say hi?" Caterina asked, though she too leaned away.

Damian motioned for Gabriella to come closer. While her eyes followed his body's movement, the rest of her remained still.

"What're you standing like that for?" Damian asked with a raised voice, ensuring his words reached Gabriella.

"Damian," Caterina whispered as she nudged him, "Don't aggravate her."

The sound of Caterina's voice faintly reached Gabriella and ignited a spark within her, powerful enough to stimulate her legs, one after the other. She walked so lightly, like a whisper, gliding toward the picnic with her shabby dress skimming the blades of grass.

She stopped within a few feet of the two. Her hair was much brighter up close, glistening from its natural oils indicating she hadn't washed her hair in days. Her long nails, though beautifully shaped and curved, were also dirty. The most apparent feature was the sadness in her round blue eyes. A redness surrounded her irises. Her pale lips remained closed, frowning.

"I'm surprised to see you during Academy hours," Damian said, aching to cease the discomfiting silence. Her pale, sunken eyes remained fixated on him, expressing more with her glares than with words.

"You look like you need some rest," Caterina noted gently, extending her hand. "Sit down for a moment. Here." She unfolded the blanket she had returned to her bag.

Gabriella's nostrils flared as her chest expanded and collapsed.

"No," Gabriella said dryly, her lips barely parted. Her voice was deep and groggy, as if she hadn't spoken in days. It hardly resembled that of a human's.

Caterina nodded to herself, her lower lip protruding. She sensed Gabriella's heightened sadness and rage and packed the remaining items around her, reaching lastly for her unbitten apple.

"Wait, no," Damian said, exchanging glances between the two women, uncertain as to with whom he was supposed to engage.

"It's alright," Caterina said in a whisper, though she pressed her lips together. "You clearly have some unresolved matters to attend to."

Caterina shyly nodded her head once more toward Gabriella, unsure of how to depart when no formal introduction had been made. She stood to leave, avoiding Damian's attempt at an embrace. Gabriella dug her nails into her skin as her limp hands made fists, the fire within her slowly rising.

"Are you *happy*?" Damian asked, as Caterina faded beyond the trees. Gabriella's arms shook. In Caterina's presence, Damian hadn't noticed how disheveled Gabriella truly appeared. Without her bright red hair, she would have been unrecognizable. "I'm sorry. Clearly, you're *not* happy," Damian added.

"Is, this, what, you, do?" Gabriella asked, each word separated by a heavy breath. She inhaled deeply before continuing, "You bring women to this spot, to this tree, and make them fall in love with you?" She extended a shaky finger toward the tree. A half-hearted chuckle escaped Damian's lips, and Gabriella's pointed finger shifted directly to Damian. "You! You're a monster."

"That's a bit of an exaggeration, don't you think?"

"It's an understatement," Gabriella said as her head fell into her hands, tears streaming down her face. "I gave myself to you, entirely. And you... you left."

"You gave yourself to me? How do I give you back, then? You'll forgive me if this comes off insensitive, judging by how fragile you look I suppose I should choose my words more carefully, but Gabriella —" She looked up, her blue pupils conflicting with the red swelling. "Help me understand how that makes sense? Giving yourself to another?"

He held out his palms, displaying their emptiness.

"Love, to you, is an illusion," she whispered in her raspy voice. "I surrendered myself to you, because I thought you had surrendered yourself to me."

"I don't follow."

The clouds above them darkened and hung still.

"You... You said..." Gabriella's tears soaked her cheeks as she gasped for air. "You said you loved me!"

"And I did."

"Love is supposed to be forever, Damian."

"Ideally, perhaps," Damian said, pocketing his hands and straightening his posture. "But realistically, all we have are these tiny moments. In those moments we shared, I did love you."

"No!" Gabriella rejected. "No! What changed? You never gave me an explanation!"

"Gave you an explanation? I see. You're more giving than I am apparently," Damian joked as Gabriella continued sobbing. "What's worse, Gabriella? Me not explaining how I feel, or you turning yourself into… whatever you are now? I'm sorry—no, listen—I'm truly so sorry. If I knew how much me living—er, leaving—would hurt you, of course I would've stayed a moment to explain."

"You've moved on," Gabriella said, sniffling.

"It's just a new moment," Damian said, shrugging. "And it's just as new and pure for me as it is for you." He held out his hand, though he didn't know exactly why. Instead, Gabriella wrapped her arms around herself for comfort.

"I gave you my heart," she repeated, staring emptily at the ground. Damian exhaled in frustration.

"*Gave*, sure," Damian said. "But you have it back now, alright? It's yours. Not mine. I don't want it, or anything, from you anymore."

The grey clouds hovered before the sun, extinguishing any lingering light between them. Gabriella's rage boiled over, and she charged at Damian, pushing him with all her might. Damian lost his balance and tripped into a bush behind him, breaking his fall with his forearm.

"I hope you *never* find love again, you awful man!" Gabriella screeched, tears falling from her face.

"Again?" Damian grunted from the ground. "Surely if you loved me, you wouldn't have pushed me over like that?"

Gabriella leaned down until her face was close to his, restricting Damian from seeing anything else around him. She stared deeply into his eyes.

"You haven't learned what love is," she whispered through gritted teeth, "and at this rate, you never will." He watched her lips deliver the message, and a smile came over his face.

"Perhaps you're right. Or, just maybe, I'll find a better teacher one day."

Her eyes burned redder from tears and anger. She dug her nails into the dirt beside her and hurled a handful of soil into Damian's face. Damian lied stunned on the ground, brushing the dirt from his eyes.

Gabriella hastily rose and stood over him, a vengeful grin stretching across her face as she watched Damian sputter the lingering soil from his mouth. Her smile faded as Damian chuckled the last bit of dirt away.

Her lower lip quivered as she took her final glance at Damian, and with heavy shoulders and a sunken head, Gabriella retreated along the line she had imprinted in the grass, leaving Damian alone in the bush with the sound of fading cries.

The clouds continued their way across the sky, allowing the sun to reemerge.

He took a deep breath and blinked repeatedly, replaying in his mind what had just transpired. A sudden burning sensation on his arm captured his attention; a rash surfaced on his forearm, and he jumped to his feet.

"Not again with this poison ivy," he grunted, hanging his head. He looked around for the flask he kept his water in, and when he couldn't find it, he realized Caterina must have taken it as she rushed away. His muscles relaxed, excited for a reason to run into her again. The elation of seeing Caterina once more exceeded the pain of Gabriella's emergence.

The burning and itching on his forearm immediately erased the joyous daydreaming from the forefront of his mind. He had no choice but to visit Aluna and ask for the cure, and luckily for him, Leander's studio was across the street.

"Everything happens for a reason," he reminded himself, looking up at the sky. He then scanned the reddening bumps and scrapes on his arm, hoping they were mild enough to abate the frustration Aluna always felt when he reported another altercation.

He rolled his sleeve tight around his bicep to ensure it wouldn't further irritate the rash. He picked up his books with his other arm and rushed into the forest.

Chapter

Three

"Gentlemen, to what do I owe this honor?" Aluna crossed her legs and placed her interlocked fingers around her knee, shifting her head from Demetrius to Leander. The sun was lower in the sky, directly behind where Demetrius sat, casting his shadow over the table. He felt the sun's rays heating his back, particularly on his fingertips, which still held the sealed red envelope.

"Demetrius has something to share with you," Leander said. Beads of sweat condensed along his head wrap as he shuffled his seat into the shade, closer to Aluna.

Demetrius gradually revealed the letter. Aluna's eyes immediately widened when she saw the envelope's scarlet corner. He showed it to her in its entirety, positioning the letter so the sun created a glowing aura around the scarlet rectangle, igniting its presence.

Aluna froze, clutching the table for support. Her intense stare at the ornate "T" sketched a semi-permanent imprint on her vision. Leander straightened his spine and unfolded his arms, relieved that Aluna did not share Demetrius' excitement.

"How…" was all Aluna could muster. She released her grip from the table and pressed her left palm to her cheek.

"We do not know," Leander answered. "He somehow infiltrated our community to deliver this. If he did not deliver the letter himself, we have a message with no messenger." A stinging sensation traveled throughout Aluna's body as she turned to the vines beside her. "He couldn't have entered Tracoses," Aluna said.

Aluna, the vines beside her said telepathically, *we would have informed you of any disturbances.*

Check again, she responded. *Please.* Her eyes traced the plant's stem down to its roots, hoping the message traveled to the furthest parts of the land with the utmost speed. She closed her eyes.

This may take a moment, the vines said in unison.

There are no other means by which this letter could have been delivered, if it truly came from Theo, Aluna emphasized. *I need to know from where he, or anyone else, entered.*

This may take a moment, the vines repeated. Aluna nodded to them and returned to her guests, who watched her puzzling behavior.

"Are you alright?" Demetrius asked, lowering the envelope as a worried expression washed over his face.

"I will be, yes. Well, then? What does he want?"

Though birds chirped merrily, and neighboring children giggled in the distance, nothing could silence the accumulation of perilous thoughts flooding the forefront of Aluna's mind. Her gold bracelets slid down her wrist as she rubbed her temples. Demetrius placed his elbows on the table and rotated the envelope in his hands, contemplating its contents.

"You haven't read it yet?"

"Leander thinks now is not the time," Demetrius said. "But—"

"Of course it's not the time," Aluna interjected. She saw Leander nod in her periphery. She felt oddly comforted by the solidarity, something that she and Leander rarely experienced together. "Frankly, love, I'm not sure there will ever be a time." Leander gave another single nod.

"Don't say that," Demetrius said, frowning. He stopped rotating the envelope and placed it on the table, clasping his hands upon it. He tilted his head and asked, "Why are you assuming the worst?"

"I know how much he meant to you, but you have to understand that there are no coincidences with Theo." Leander shuddered at his name while Aluna continued, "He must know tomorrow is Myron's ceremony, and I have no doubt that letter will deter you from proper preparation. Have you written your speech yet?"

"He has not," Leander responded, "which is another reason we need to put this matter aside."

His pale boney fingers slithered from the crevices of his sleeve, extending toward the envelope across the table. His heavy sapphire ring hit the table as he opened his palm, hoping Demetrius would hand him the envelope. Demetrius kept his interlocked hands pressed heavily upon it, refusing to budge.

"My friends," Leander continued, bracing the glaring sun as he faced Demetrius, "speculation is a waste of time, and time is not something which we can spare. A man must always be remembered as he was. From prior experience, we know not to trust this man. Demetrius, are you even listening?"

Demetrius hung his head, weighted by the contradicting thoughts circling his mind. Aluna shook her head disappointedly.

"He won't listen until he reads it, Leander."

"Demetrius," Leander pleaded, leaning closer to his friend, "Please, please hear me. Or, if you prefer not to hear me, then speak to me. Help me understand why you prioritize this message over preparing for the speech about your own father."

"You both are right," Demetrius said, keeping his head down. "I don't presume the timing of this delivery to be mere coincidence. However, is that not reason enough to open it? I haven't heard from Theo in so long…" Again, Leander winced, returning his outstretched hand into his lap. "If the letter was meant to be delivered today, its message was supposed to be delivered as well." Leander and Aluna exchanged defeated glances.

"Perhaps he's right," Aluna whispered to Leander. "Maybe we don't have anything to fear."

Aluna, the vines said, *we're sorry, but...* Aluna closed her eyes as she braced herself for the news she didn't want to hear. *...there weren't signs of an intruder.*

It simply can't be. Check the Eastern side of Tracoses; that's where Theo had left twenty years ago. Perhaps he memorized the maze and its obstacles. That was the last disturbance, the vines replied.

Though the vines weren't capable of lying, Aluna was unsettled by what had to be a missing piece of information, for even if Theo had somehow come back years ago and stayed hidden, he would have had to disturb the plants which were coated in markers, sending signals to all the botanists. *There's no way he entered through Tracoses,* she concluded.

As Aluna grew silent, so too had Leander sunken into introspection.

The sound of paper tearing snapped Aluna and Leander back to the present; Demetrius tore the short end of the envelope and reached inside to pull out the letter. He stopped mid-way as rustling in the nearby bushes diverted his attention.

A man half their age with dirtied clothes, a pile of books under his arm, and a rolled-up sleeve upon the other arm emerged from the bushes with a hesitant, crooked smile.

"Sorry, Aluna," Damian said, stumbling out of the wedges clumsily. He quickly scanned the setting, and the tension in the air piqued his curiosity. "I didn't mean to stop by unannounced, and it seems like you're busy. I'll just be going then."

Though Damian motioned toward the bushes from which he'd come, he didn't move, hoping Aluna would permit him to stay. She didn't say a word. Leander rested his elbow on the chair and leaned his temple against his forefinger, taking a deep breath.

"No, son, don't apologize," Demetrius said with a sudden smile. "Have a seat, won't you?"

Leander gripped both his armrests, resisting the urge to bury his head completely beneath his hands. His headwrap absorbed his sweat until what remained rolled down the sides of his face, dripping down his sunken cheekbones.

"I'll gladly join you."

Damian placed his books on the table and sat directly behind them, assuring he would sit comfortably in the shade. He had never met Leander before, though Caterina had told him plenty about her beloved mentor.

"Hello, Leander," Damian said, flashing his charming smile. "How are you?" Leander straightened his posture and turned to Demetrius with stone-cold eyes ignoring Damian entirely. Unpleased, Damian continued, "You're Caterina's mentor, aren't you? Speaking of which, don't you have a class with Caterina?"

Though his face remained still, Leander's blood boiled as he recognized that time had indeed escaped him, and more time was being wasted trying to convince Demetrius to set the letter aside. He quietly stood and placed his fingertips on the table as he glanced over his shoulder toward the backdoor of the house.

"Never have I been late to an appointment, and I will not be starting now, especially not due to these circumstances," he said. He turned to the newly arrived guest, and through forced civility said, "Thank you for the reminder."

Leander, though typically not affectionate to anyone except Demetrius, for the first time, lightly placed his hand on Aluna's shoulder.

"Aluna," Leander said, "I thank you for your hospitality and your efforts. Demetrius... I hope you do the right thing." He adjusted his headwrap which had loosened during the strenuous conversation, secured his tote bag over his shoulder, and walked away, with his blue robe trailing behind him.

"What a fascinating man," Damian said, placing his arms on the table, one of them on the red letter. Demetrius slid the envelope back into his possession before Damian continued. "I've heard so much about him, but I must admit, he's not as incredible in person as you I have heard him be. I don't see what you see in him, Demetrius. He seems to be the opposite of you. Quite a character." Demetrius chuckled and rubbed his sweaty forehead.

"Well, you stay true to your character, don't you, Damian?" Aluna interjected, pointing to Damian's wound. "How have you yet to learn your lesson about tussling in the poison ivy? You were in the Northern part of Tracoses again, weren't you?"

"I didn't go there to fight," Damian said.

"You must have been up to no good," Aluna said as she left the table in search of her medical kit. Damian nudged Demetrius with his other arm.

"I was on a date."

"With Gabriella?" Demetrius asked.

"No, with an angel." He said this in awe, elongating each syllable and reveling in it. "Caterina." Her sweet name slipped off his tongue like melted honey.

"Caterina!" Demetrius exclaimed, patting Damian on the back. The strong patting caused Damian to jolt forward, hitting his wounded forearm against the table. He grimaced as the pain intensified.

"Caterina didn't do that to you, did she?" Demetrius asked, using the envelope to point at Damian's ever-growing reddish rash.

"No, no. We were... interrupted."

"As were we," Demetrius said, rotating the opened envelope in his hands again. "I'm not sure about yours, but my intuition tells me *this* interruption was a good one." Demetrius poked his fingers inside the envelope and gripped the parchment again.

The parchment was as vibrantly red as the envelope, folded perfectly into fourths. Demetrius placed the envelope and the letter on the table. The parchment was too thick to remain completely flat; the letter slowly unfolded itself, just enough to augment their curiosity while keeping the contents concealed.

"Who's that from?" Damian asked.

"An old friend."

"Doesn't look like it," Damian noted, pointing at the letter. "Why the hesitation?"

At that moment, Aluna came around the corner with a handful of paintbrushes and a crate of jars, each filled with a different colored substance. Her curls fell over her eyes as she rushed to the table. She stopped abruptly as she saw the folded scarlet letter resting near Damian's outstretched arm. She blew her hair away from her eyes with a single puff.

"To whom do I tend first?" She asked. The unyielding uncertainty made her fingers inch toward the letter, but instead, she dragged a chair beside Damian and reached for his arm. She twisted and turned his forearm to inspect all aspects of the wound. Damian firmly shut his eyes to resist the pain.

"What's the hesitation, Demetrius?" Damian repeated, begging for a distraction from the burning irritation.

"You still haven't read it?" Aluna pulled out a jar with a clear liquid substance and dipped a paintbrush into it. She then traced each bump with the bristles, looking at her husband with anticipation between each brushstroke.

"I'll read it now," Demetrius said. Demetrius held the scarlet parchment gently, though he seemed more fragile than the paper. His eyes darted back and forth along the letter. The letter's redness reflected onto Demetrius' face as the setting sun's rays now fell directly upon the parchment. Aluna caught herself holding her breath while Damian eagerly awaited the reveal.

A smile gradually grew across Demetrius' face, and a sigh of relief escaped from the corner of his mouth. Aluna reached for the next jar, ironically filled with a substance whose color closely resembled that of the letter.

"Well?" Damian asked. "Is it a secret, or are you going to tell us?"

"Wait," Aluna said, dipping a clean brush into the new jar. "Let me finish applying this layer first. I can't be a nurse and a therapist at the same time." Damian groaned as she continued layering the wound with organic pastes.

Demetrius stood, unable to contain his alleviation.

"You know," Damian said, longing for discourse, "I never understood why botanists gravitated toward medicine as opposed to the arts. You both basically use the same tools." He motioned toward the pile of paintbrushes and jars beside Aluna.

"All art is useless," Aluna said, taking the bait. She moved her paintbrush in circular motions across the wound. Damian felt a cooling sensation and finally relaxed his muscles. "It's not about the tools you use, but why and how you use them. Some people lean toward the theoretical; others, toward the practical. I would rather heal someone now than sketch a memory of them once they've passed. I say that with the utmost respect to artists, though," she said, looking at her husband apologetically. "Speaking of artists…" Her hazel eyes awaited recognition from her husband.

"It's an invitation," Demetrius said, excitedly shaking the letter. Aluna sealed the last jar shut and returning it to the bin.

"An invitation? To what exactly?"

"Can I see it?" Damian asked, reaching for the parchment.

"Hold still," Aluna said, gripping Damian's wrist and wrapping it with gauze.

"He's inviting me to make amends. It's right there, in black and white. Er— black and red, I suppose. He wants to come back, Aluna. He finally wants to return."

"There's nothing on here," Damian said as he frowned, turning the parchment over and over. Demetrius frantically retracted the letter. He then rolled his eyes, pointing to the center of the letter.

"This isn't a time for jokes," Demetrius said. He held out the paper so the two could read it together. Aluna tilted her head to the side and looked worryingly at Demetrius.

"My love, there's truly nothing there." Aluna placed Damian's arm on the table and walked over to Demetrius, placing the back of her hand on his forehead to check his temperature. She wiped away beads of sweat and cupped his face in her hands. "Are you feeling alright?"

"Aluna!" Demetrius exclaimed, pointing aggressively at the letter. "Are you really telling me you can't see what's written?"

"Have I ever lied to you? Take a deep breath. Perhaps this is one of those silly— not silly, unique— art techniques, where only certain things are made visible to certain spectators." She turned to Damian and continued, "This is another reason botanists tend to stay away from art."

Damian nodded. Demetrius raised and tilted the letter in every way possible, hoping the angle was to blame for their inability to see the writing.

"This invitation is just for me, then."

"What's it say?" Damian asked.

"If it was meant for others, he would have created it that way."

"You're not going to tell us?"

"Like I said, he's inviting me to make amends, and he needs my help. And as you said, Aluna, he might need to tell me something right now. That's why this letter appeared so randomly, but it's not random at all." Demetrius sprang from his seat and paced as he reread the letter. Damian accidentally used his wounded arm to push himself up to join Demetrius, but the instant pain humbled him back into his seat.

"Don't make it worse, and don't encourage this," Aluna muttered to Damian. "Stay here." She walked to Demetrius and ran her hand across his shoulders, soothing him and returning him from a trancelike state. "Are you really considering leaving after the ceremony to go see Theo?"

"No," Demetrius said.

Aluna let out a deep, relieved sigh.

"I'm going to leave right now."

"What!" Aluna exclaimed, releasing her hands from his shoulders. Damian shifted uncomfortably as Aluna listed multiple reasons Demetrius was acting impulsive and irrational. "How can you be okay with leaving Leander to prepare for *your* father's ceremony? Don't you see how disruptive Theo is being? Isn't that the reason he left in the first place?"

Damian's ears perked up. *There was only one person who has ever left Platanis.* And now he had a name.

"I'll be back before the sun comes up," Demetrius said with a single nod. "Plus, I can prepare for the speech during the journey. And Aluna, what if Theo has information about my father and what happened? Don't you think I should know about it? Don't you think that's why he's written to me today, of all days?"

"Don't *you* think he would have written the information about your father in the letter if he wanted you to have it? Why must you leave *now*?" Aluna said, fearful tears sprouted in the inner corners of her eyes. "I don't think it's safe. What if something happens?"

"I'll go with you," Damian said, raising his hand. Aluna pressed her hands against her forehead, pushing away the emerging headache.

"I'm not letting you miss your classes."

"Can't miss them if I dropped out!" Damian gestured toward the pile of books beside him. He walked over to Demetrius and placed his hand on his shoulder. "Mind if I come along?"

The sun had set a little lower, at an angle where Aluna was entirely covered in Demetrius' shadow. She knew the instant she saw the letter, her words would be no match against Theo's. A stinging pain ran through her body as fears of Demetrius' journey ahead flooded the forefront of her mind. She lowered her head as she weaved her hair into a ponytail, reminding herself to stay strong.

"I can't stand to watch this," Aluna said, raking the final hair strands into place. She packed up her jars and closed the crate, lifting it with one arm and pressing it against her side. "The least you can do is notify Leander of this." She softly kissed Demetrius' cheek, and he saw the tears in her eyes. "Then come back here, and I'll give you what you and the horses will need for the journey. I can't believe, after all these years… Still…" she said the last part quietly to herself, wiping away a fallen tear and disappearing further into her garden.

Demetrius squinted as he held his hand above his eyes, guarding them against the sun's rays.

"She's right," Demetrius said, folding the parchment and placing it on the table. "Time's running out, but I have to talk to Leander I'm leaving."

"I can come along though, can't I?" Damian said, restraining his voice from showing too much excitement.

"Did you really abandon the Academy?" Demetrius asked. Damian sat back and grinned, pointing again to his books. Demetrius shook his head. "The only reason Aluna isn't yelling at you right now—"

"Is because she's probably more worried about you," Damian interjected. Demetrius' nostrils flared, but Damian was right.

"She thinks of you as a son," Demetrius said.

"And she will always be like a mother to me. However, I'm a grown man now. I can make my own decisions." He turned to stand beside Demetrius as they both stared in the direction of the sun. "Besides, I have a feeling I will learn more on this journey than I ever learned in the classroom. Who is this guy anyway? You said his name was Theo?"

"He's an incredible man and a wonderful friend," Demetrius said, staring down at the letter. "He just had a couple loose screws, is all."

"A couple loose screws?" Damian asked, brushing off some leftover dirt on his pants to portray an aura of nonchalance, though he was deeply intrigued. "What happened?"

"I'll tell you about it once we're in the desert," Demetrius responded. "First, I need to talk to Leander."

"What desert?"

"Past Tracoses is an expansive desert," Demetrius explained, stretching his arms out as far as he could. "Theo lives on the other side of it. We'll take our best horses, ones that can handle the journey, that way we get there and back as soon as possible." Demetrius leaned closer to Damian and whispered, "You need to keep all this a secret, understand? From this point forward, what you see and hear must remain between us. Promise me."

"I promise."

"Good." The sundial beside them showed almost an hour had passed. "Leander should be done with his class any minute now."

"Caterina, too," Damian responded, his cheeks softly reddening.

Chapter
Four

Caterina sat on a bench outside Leander's studio, across from Demetrius' house. She cupped her oval face upon the arm rest, anxiously tapping her cheek.

Surrounding her were tall, clay homes painted a brilliant white, decorated extravagantly by a variety of hanging vines and flowers, lined perfectly with neatly trimmed hedges. Mumbled conversations from nearby neighbors traveled down the main path, though Caterina could only hear the echoing of her worrying thoughts.

In search of a distraction, she observed the exterior of Leander's studio. Its lack of greenery provoked an icier blue shade to its bare, white walls, delivering a cold, unwelcoming presence. The front door was painted Leander's signature shade of blue, gleaming radiantly in the evening's glow.

Caterina blocked the setting sunlight with her hand until the familiar blue robe and headwrap appeared in her peripheral. She stood eagerly, catching her bag's handle before it fell off her shoulder.

"Am I late?" Leander asked, quickening his steps. Caterina shook her head, and Leander sighed in relief. He unlocked the front door with a silver key and held it open as Caterina squeezed past him.

The walls were dull and off-white with tints of light blue and purple, creating a pearl-like reflection depending on the light's direction. In the evenings, the walls would turn a deeper blue with hints of white, mimicking the sensation of being underwater. The floor was made of reflective glass, enhancing and amplifying the studio's atypical ambiance.

Having an open floor gave Leander plenty of space to fill the room with artwork, but instead, each wall showcased a single canvas. Three walls exhibited recent works of Leander's, while the fourth depicted a serendipitous waterfall, filling the space with the tranquil sound of water crashing onto stones that acted as a barrier between the downpour and the glass floor.

The two descended a blue carpeted staircase to a lower level where Leander had allocated space for his four students, each granted one side of the square room. Though the glass floor was reflective on the main level, it was transparent on the lower level, allowing students to reference Leander's work from below, while permitting students privacy if someone had come to visit the studio. Sound also traveled to the lower level, as the tranquility emerging from the waterfall poured into the student's work area.

Across this work room was a second staircase, much narrower and painted black, which led to the basement, a space no one except Leander was permitted to enter. Caterina's station was closest to this second staircase, though she had never paid mind to it.

"Please, have a seat," Leander said, gesturing to her chair as he stood next to his, waiting for her to be seated first. Each station was composed of three things: a table for supplies, another table for sketching and meeting, and an easel upon which to work. Her station was the neatest and most organized compared to his other students. Caterina noticed Leander had placed a blank sheet canvas onto her easel, one the size of her torso.

"I must admit, I'm very nervous."

Caterina released her twitching fingers from playing with her braid and clasped her hands in her lap, keeping the tote bag weighing on her tensed shoulder.

"Good," Leander said with a slight smile. "Nervousness appears when preparedness is faced with the unknown. And you, Caterina, are more than prepared." Leander bent beside his chair into his bag, reaching for his sketchbook, until Caterina surprised him with a question.

"Do you ever get nervous?" Caterina asked. The image of Aluna's sundial flashed before his eyes. *I should be heading to the garden*, he thought to himself. *I am running out of time.*

"Art does not make me nervous," he responded. "I believe one day you will feel the same. Now," he said, placing his sketchbook before her, "over the past five years, your art has come as a result of an assignment. You have always exceeded my expectations for each assignment, so by now, you have become accustomed to receiving instant gratification upon completion. I suspect the nervousness you are experiencing derives from the contingency of this expectation—this anticipation—of gratification."

He opened his notebook to a page where he had written the subjects Caterina had successfully painted each year of her program: landscape, still-life, portrait, movement, and darkness. Her cheeks rosied as the fond memories blossomed before her; she noticed that the line next to "sixth year" was left blank, and she pressed her lips together as the nervousness returned.

"I'm not so sure I seek that gratification, Leander, for that means I've completed the program. I can't even imagine what it'll feel like," Caterina said, her posture slightly drooping, "to be finished with art school. This is the only life I've ever known."

"Allow me to relieve some of this anticipation and anxiety from you. Hear what I am telling you now: You will *never* feel that sort of elated gratification again."

Caterina's mouth dropped. She studied Leander's face closely, in search of any exaggerated signification. But, as always, Leander remained poised and serious. He continued, "Life becomes the ultimate test, and if gratification ever arises, it will only show its face at the very end."

Caterina swallowed the lump in her throat as her heart beat faster.

"That's quite some insight," she said, taking a deep breath. "I wasn't prepared for such bad news." She raised her eyebrow as she noticed the faintest smile upon Leander's face.

"I say this not to discourage you, but in the hopes of opening your eyes to new sorts of gratification, one that does not rely on the validation of others."

He tore the paper from his sketchbook as Caterina winced, feeling as though he was removing her from his life. He noticed this change in her face and softly handed her the paper, which she gladly accepted.

"Are you releasing me from seeking your validation?" She joked.

A chuckle finally broke Leander's stoic demeanor.

"Caterina, you never sought my validation. What you sought was a path, guidance, toward meeting the artist that has always been inside you. On that piece of paper is a list of everything you have accomplished. But the paper, the paper itself, is nothing to you. Rip it."

"What!"

"Rip the piece of paper."

At first, Caterina ripped only the corner of the paper and looked embarrassingly at Leander, knowing this is not what he asked. She scanned the paper one last time, tracing Leander's stellar handwriting, until she focused again on the blankness following her sixth-year assignment.

Leander put his hand to his chest. "Take a deep breath, and as you exhale—" he mimicked the act of tearing the paper. Caterina held the paper up in the air, gradually ripping the paper perfectly down the middle.

"There is only one last thing I can ever ask of you, and that is the final assignment," Leander said. "Before I share it with you, I must remind you of the three parameters by which you must abide." Caterina shoved the ripped paper in her bag as she hurriedly shuffled through her belongings in search of a pencil and unripped paper. "You are aware the final assignment requires you to raise a sketch from the canvas, one that fully functions on its own. Yes? Good. First, the externalities of the piece must not exude a single brush stroke. The common spectator should perceive the piece's liveliness as opposed to its constructiveness."

Caterina's pencil skidded across the paper, writing Leander's instructions word for word.

"Second, your piece should not extend past arm's length. The canvas behind you will suffice. I will observe your attention to detail in the *anatomy* of your work. In other words, I am interested in how you build the piece, not how large it is. Once you have mastered the interior's framework and construction, the possibilities for the exterior's grandness are endless."

Leander put his hands together on the table and leaned over it. In a lowered tone, he asked Caterina, "Do you see the canvas of the lamb behind me, on the opposite wall?" Caterina squinted her eyes and saw a shelf-like object disguised as a rock protruding from the wall, with a fluffy white sleeping lamb perched on top. Caterina had trouble seeing the object from far away, so Leander retrieved the sitting lamb, placing it in his lap as he returned to the table.

"Did Marina make this?" Caterina asked.

"No. A second-year student could never achieve such high detail. I created it many years ago, for the sake of demonstration. I cannot say I am too proud of its construction."

"How can you say that?" Caterina asked, admiring every detail of the piece, running her fingers through its cloud-like wool. "It looks like at any moment its eyes will open, and it will come to life." She playfully tapped the little sleeping lamb on the nose and smiled.

"Things are never as they seem, Caterina."

Leander wrapped his boney fingers around the lamb's head, his sapphire ring placed exactly where its eye would be. The lamb's face was completely hidden by Leander's palm, and with little effort, Leander ripped off its head. Caterina gasped, covering her gaping mouth with her hands.

"Why would you do that?"

"Please, peer inside." Leander tilted the hole in the lamb's neck toward Caterina. Cautiously, Caterina looked inside and frowned. She was expecting to see torn muscles and tissue, a protruding spinal cord, all covered in blood-like paint. Instead, there was nothing. She leaned closer and saw the wool had simply been painted upon a lamb-shaped foundation.

"You see," Leander continued, "this lamb will never come to life, for it is nothing but a three-dimensional traditional canvas, or a shell. There is nothing impressive about this kind of art, which is why I only use it for demonstration. For second-year students, this demonstrates the importance of a multi-textured piece. For you, well, tell me, what does this demonstrate?"

"That you are willing to sacrifice a canvas to get your point across."

Caterina shifted her hand to block the beheaded lamb from her view. Leander approached Caterina's working station with the broken object. He dipped the nearest paintbrush into a jar of a thick, black liquid and balanced the head in its proper position. With circular motions that mirrored the curly pattern of the lamb's wool, Leander moved the paintbrush along the torn edges, securing the head back onto the body. The paint dried clearly, eradicating the damage.

"One would hardly call an object sacrificial if its reparations are feasible," Leander said, reaching for a piece of paper he kept folded in his sketchbook.

He unfolded the parchment to show another sketch of a lamb. This one was two-dimensional and extremely detailed. The darker lines stemmed from the center of its body and faded as it reached its furthest points. Leander retrieved the pencil from his bag and pointed it toward the sketch. As he raised the pencil, the lamb rose from the paper in perfect, three-dimensional form. When Leander's pencil had reached shoulder length, he stopped.

"This is called *constructus*," he said.

Caterina's heart raced as her fingers gripped the edge of the table. Before her was the most precious little lamb, with button eyes and the smallest nose. It didn't move, but its eyes were captivating. She had seen other *constructus* creations before, but never directly rising from the paper.

"Your pencils and paintbrushes will become *constructus* tools as well. Your art will no longer be a prison to the paper. I will teach you how to animate them." Leander lowered the pencil until the lamb flattened. "A bright mind like yours does not need to be warned of the risk such abilities pose. That is why we assign young artists this final assignment, to judge their character." Leander paused as he pushed an unfavorable memory from his mind. "Are you ready for the third instruction?"

Caterina grasped her pencil.

"I expect you to create something completely of your own imagination."

The color in Caterina's cheeks faded as the pencil fell from her hand. She reached for it on the floor, noticing in her bag her untouched green apple.

"I don't understand," she stuttered, suppressing her stomach growling. "I thought I had to improve the work of another contemporary?"

"If your previous work had any similarities with the artists of today, that assignment would be yours. Fortunately, you outshine them."

"Leander, please," Caterina begged, her eyes darting back and forth as she processed this new information. Damian's voice entered her mind as she recalled what he said about her being unlike anyone else, but the thought brought her no comfort.

Leander reached across the table and placed his hand near her folded arms.

"I would not assign you something you could not achieve," Leander said. "In a week's time, you and I will be sitting here admiring your final assignment— the key with which you will enter the art realm as an independent entity." With his other hand, Leander retrieved the silver key from his pocket and put it on the table. Caterina saw her miniature, distorted reflection in it.

"Did I hear you correctly?" She asked. "I have only a week to complete this?"

"Something tells me you will not need all that time." Leander flinched as he uttered the word *time*. He pocketed his key, knowing he'd be leaving his studio soon.

"What do you mean?"

"You have developed the artist glow," Leander said. "I know not how to describe it except as a specific sparkle in one's eyes, a developed mental image raging to break free from its captivity, transitioning from potentiality to actuality. If I know you well enough, I would be correct in assuming you already have an idea, possibly even a sketch, for your final assignment."

Color returned to Caterina's cheeks as she pulled out her sketchbook. As Caterina looked down, her braid coiled onto the table in a circular, sundial shape. Leander once more pressed his lips together at Time's nondiscriminatory lack of mercy. Leander removed his arms from the table to make room for Caterina, who had flipped the pages to her latest sketch.

Leander's pale complexion turned an eerie iridescent blue as he faced Caterina's sketch of a bird, its wings outstretched with its head turned to face the spectator. Its beak was slightly parted, as if about to say something, but its piercing eyes said enough.

"Are you alright?" Caterina asked, looking back and forth from her sketch to Leander. "Is it not good? Do you not like it? I know it's a little unoriginal for me, to work on another animal, but this one is different. I thought my final assignment would require me to improve upon another artist's work, and I was quite taken by the collection of birds you showed me, the ones you created as musical symphonies. If I remember correctly, that was your final assignment as well? I wanted to create a bird that served an instrumental purpose, but this isn't just a bird. It's an—"

44

"Owl," Leander whispered.

Caterina clapped her hands in delight, mistaking Leander's observation as acceptance. She finally noticed Leander's still composure and unblinking stare at the sketch, and her fingers began nervously curling the end of her braid.

"Yes," she said. "I thought, why simply recreate an existing being, when I can create a more evolved version? This owl isn't like the ones of which we already know. I am already quite fond of the owl, and I was asking myself, how can I make it more magical?"

"Mhm."

"Mysticism permits this sort of exaggeration, no?" Caterina asked with a slight hesitation. "This bird can be constructed to sing every note, perhaps notes outside a human's range. Or maybe, I can construct it to learn how to speak. Am I saying too much? Is this all absurd?"

I fear to imagine how much more absurd today can be, Leander thought to himself.

"I do not approve this project," Leander said after a moment's hesitation.

Caterina bottom lip quivered as she straightened her posture and forced herself to keep composure. She closed the sketchbook and placed it in her lap. Leander sighed in relief as the owl left his sight.

"Caterina, please do not let this upset you, and listen to the words I speak. My disproval of the project is of no sentiment to you or your artistry. I am not surprised that my work has inspired you. I, too, am quite fond of the musical birds I created years ago."

Caterina retrieved her green apple and began rotating it in her hands. Leander gently placed his hand on hers, stopping her from perpetuating the anxiety.

"Rarely do I have the honor of training a student such as yourself: one who does not need the work of others to spark your inner fire. I have been painting my whole life, Caterina, so please, trust me when I say, only you know what your work will look like once you seek inspiration from within. Never, in all my years, would I have guessed that an… owl… would pique your interest. Residing within you is a island of *your* ideas, waiting to be discovered."

"I'm afraid I don't understand," Caterina said, pressing a fingertip to the corner of her eye. Leander asked for her sketchbook and ripped out the last sheet of blank paper, placing it on the table in front of her.

"This is all you need to be inspired," Leander said, pointing to the blank page. "If you stare at it long enough, it becomes a mirror, reflecting the images in your mind eager to escape." Caterina placed the apple aside and pressed her fingertips to her temples, staring intensely at the paper.

Leander grinned and shook his head.

"The image already exists, Caterina. You need not force it. Relax your shoulders, your breath, and your mind." Caterina followed his instructions for several seconds until her nostrils flared.

"I can't do this!"

"I know you can," Leander said, rising from his seat. "Perhaps my presence is distracting."

"No, never!"

"My dear, the presence of another is always distracting for an artist, who already exists as a duality." Leander smiled softly, relinquishing a bit of Caterina's anxiety. "I need to go downstairs to… prepare for a project and will return momentarily. In the meantime, enjoy your time with the infinite space of possibilities before you. Fasten the space between your mind and your hand, until they become one."

The basement was not lit, though it also had a semi-transparent ceiling, enough for light to trickle in. The overall darkness magnified the feeling of entrapment. Rows of various sized cabinets covered the walls, filled with documents, sketches, rolled canvases, books, and other products of years of artistry. None of the drawers were labeled, yet Leander never misplaced a thing.

His face remained motionless and unyielding as he crossed the floor to the other side of the room, where he kept some of his previous students' works.

The row of cabinets stationed at the furthest point from the staircase was designated for one particular student. Leander stopped before the bottom drawer, as if he had stumbled upon the gravestone of an enemy. He fought a nostalgic rage as he pulled the drawer open.

"Where is it?" Leander asked through clenched teeth as he shuffled through numerous sketches. He looked over his shoulder, though he knew Caterina would never trespass. Once his privacy was ensured, Leander threw the sketches on the floor like a mad man, searching for the one.

Every sketch he threw to the side had the symbol, the bane of his existence, drawn in the bottom right corner. He shuttered at the sea of papers, the waves of the ornate "T," that had compiled around him.

He mumbled something as he reached the bottom of the drawer, empty. He collected the sketches around him and threw them back into the drawer haphazardly.

He shut the drawer and placed his hands behind the cabinet to push it forward, as he sometimes left larger canvases hidden behind the furniture if they did not fit into the drawers. A scarlet folded note that was pressed between the cabinet and wall fell onto Leander's sandal. His heart sank with it as his eyes met with the symbol that ensured its permanence in his life, regardless how hard he fought to erase it.

The whirlwind of thoughts completely faded as Leander's heart beat faster and louder. His fingers wrapped around the edges of the folded parchment; he thought of Demetrius, particularly the advice Leander had given about there not being enough time to entertain malice.

The letter was larger than a regular piece of paper, but the note itself, and the writing, was very small. Leander repositioned himself to hold the letter under the little bit of light shining from the floor above. He read the single sentence:

"What you seek has been returned to her original owner.

-T"

A wave of conflicting emotions rushed over Leander. He reached for his pocket, fumbling to find his silver key, the only admittance into the studio, which he always kept on himself. He traced the key's imprint in his robe. *How did he get in here?* He thought to himself, panicking. He breathed heavily, sensing the details in his periphery fade.

"Leander?" Caterina called from above, returning his consciousness back to the present. "Our time is up, and I don't want to overstay my welcome."

Those who are welcome never want to stay, Leander thought to himself, gripping the letter. *But those uninvited will never leave.*

Leander pushed the cabinet back to its place and pocketed the letter. He ascended to the second floor and greeted Caterina with a forced smile. Her worried expression gave away Leander's unsuccessful attempt at hiding his feelings, so he quickly spoke.

"You, dear, are more than welcome to remain here as you envision your next project." A sudden, overpowering cough surfaced from Leander as he clutched his chest to reduce the pain. Caterina rushed to him, though he continued. "Has the paper spoken to you, yet?"

"I'm afraid not."

"I see," Leander said, rubbing his chest. He noticed Caterina staring at his pocket, where a scarlet corner had suddenly made an appearance. Leander shifted his body to hide it, and Caterina immediately locked eyes with Leander, pretending her curiosity hadn't been sparked.

"I should go, if you're sure you're alright," Caterina said, taking the piece of paper in her hands. "Will I see you before the assignment is due?"

"You will not need to. The answers to your unasked questions reside within you. Trust yourself." *And no one else*, he wanted to add. Caterina nodded, ascended to the first floor alone, and walked toward the exit.

Leander pressed his hands together and brought them to his lips, closing his eyes in deep thought. He felt his heartbeat increase against his forearm. He had no choice: it was time for him to find Theo.

Chapter

Five

amian awaited Caterina outside Demetrius' house. He pressed his back against the wall and repositioned his wounded arm, contemplating whether he wanted Caterina to notice. He defaulted into his most comfortable position, sitting on the ground with his good arm propped against a knee. He picked at the grass beside him before he heard the door opening across the street.

Caterina hastily stepped outside and closed the door behind her. The setting sun blocked Damian's ability to accurately read her facial expression, but gaging by the unbitten green apple in her hand, she was still nervous.

"Caterina!"

She jumped in surprise, pressing her hand against her chest. Her immediate instinct was to smile, but upon recollection of the incident earlier, she thought better of it.

"Can I help you?" She asked, swinging her braid to block the part of her face closest to her companion. Damian caught up to her and flashed that crooked smile of his, though she remained poised and unbothered.

"Yes, please. Can we sit somewhere and talk?" He pointed to the bench closest to the studio.

"I don't have anything to say."

Damian held out his hand and motioned toward the bench anyway. She curled her lips in contemplation, but as soon as his fingers touched hers, she figured she could spare a few minutes.

The two walked to the same bench where Caterina had waited for Leander. Damian gestured toward the closest part of the bench, motioning for Caterina to have a seat. As soon as she did, she noticed Damian's bandages.

Caterina immediately dropped the apple beside her and reached for his arm to examine it further, though Aluna had thoroughly covered the entire wound.

"I'm fine," Damian said, clenching his other fist to resist the pain he felt from Caterina tugging and twisting this arm. "No, really, I'm fine." He repositioned his arm to ensure it wouldn't be within her reach.

"What happened?" Caterina focused on the bandages as her mind explored the various possible causes of injury. "Is this what you wanted to talk about?"

"Absolutely not," he said with a slight chuckle. "I actually don't have much time, and the last thing I would want to do is waste it." She snorted at his sentiment.

"Caterina, I'm serious," Damian said, turning his whole body to face hers. "What happened in the forest was… unfortunate."

"Unfortunate?"

"Truly." He pushed his hair back with his wounded arm, and sympathy washed over Caterina again. He noticed her eyes soften and mistook it for pity.

"Are you going to tell me what happened?"

"Someday, yes," he said.

"I suppose we'll speak then," she said calmly, readjusting the strap from her bag as she prepared to leave. He placed his hand on her knee.

"I only said someday because right now is not the time. I'm headed on an expedition with Demetrius."

A group of distant children squealed in delight as they chased one another, eventually running past the two, mirroring the excitement Damian felt inside. Caterina furrowed her brows in perplexity.

"This is what I was telling you about, in the forest, Caterina. Life… Life is the wisest teacher of them all, and I'm about to embark on the greatest journey of my existence. Thus far." His pupils dilated with elation, and the green speckles within them, Caterina's favorite, seemed to glow wildly brighter as he spoke.

"Did you injure your head as well? You sound mad." A giggle escaping her lips. He beamed.

"You remember how I asked you about the ex-artist? Well, turns out, he has resurrected. *Today,* of all days."

"Resurrected? Resurrected how? When?"

Damian related the news to Caterina regarding the scarlet letter, from the joy Demetrius felt to the message written in invisible ink which only Demetrius could read. The information stunned Caterina, as she dropped her posture and leaned against the bench. She tapped her fingers rhythmically beside her as she analyzed the story.

Since she previously didn't know anything about the ex-artist, she never inquired about his life. Suddenly, with this tidbit of information, questions poured into her mind like a waterfall, though more vigorously, and less tranquilly, than the waterfall in Leander's studio.

"And his name is Theo," Damian concluded.

"Theo," she repeated. "Leander has most certainly never mentioned his name before."

"I'm not surprised. He seemed very pale at the table, very upset, about this whole situation."

"You met Leander?"

"In the most basic sense, yes," Damian said, rubbing the back of his neck. "I might have said two words to him, though he said none to me. Or none that I can recall, really. I tried to seem personable, but..." His voice trailed off as his insecurities surfaced.

"Just *be*, Damian," Caterina interrupted, suddenly grazing her fingers along his arm comfortingly. "You try too hard to seem."

Struck by the gentleness of her touch, Damian didn't have a response. He reveled in the moment of closeness, before she lifted her fingers and returned her hand to her lap.

"I wouldn't take Leander's cold shoulder personally," she said, staring off into the distance as she allowed her thoughts to consume her. "Not that he is particularly a friendly person, but today, I noticed something heavy must be weighing upon his genius mind."

Caterina took a deep breath and stared at the blank piece of paper she had placed beside her, secured from the breeze by the green apple. She took the paper in her hands and squinted, as if waiting for an answer in invisible ink to surface.

"Is that your final project?" Damian joked, pointing at the paper.

"Part of it." She tilted her head, wondering why Leander had so vehemently rejected her owl sketch. "Damian?"

"Hmm?"

"Did Leander see Theo's letter?"

"No. Demetrius opened it after Leander left." Damian paused for a moment and chuckled. "You know, I can't even imagine what Leander's reaction would be, as he comes off very… stoic. Unemotional."

Caterina's mind started racing. She thought back to how Leander had immediately excused himself when she showed him the sketch of her owl. She closed her eyes tightly as she tried to recall another time Leander had excused himself from their lesson, but no such memory arose.

A sense of guilt crept inside her, as she had never questioned Leander to any extent. This was not due to any blind faith she had toward him, but more because there was never a suspicion about her beloved mentor.

"He would probably just walk away, don't you think?" Damian interjected. Caterina snapped back to reality, glancing at Damian through her periphery.

"I suppose. But you, Damian, do you really want to lean into this venture?"

"You mean this *ad*venture? How could I not? I want to know everything there is to know about this ex-artist, about Theo."

Caterina readjusted her dress as she crossed her legs and faced Damian. He raised his eyebrows in surprise, wondering what he had said to have gained her undivided attention.

The same group of children ran past them once more, though this time neither noticed.

"How do you do it?" She asked.

"Do what?"

"How do you…" she paused, muting all the other questions her mind conjured as she searched the clouds for the right words, "How do you allow yourself to chase your curiosities?" The question sparked an intensified intrigue in Damian. His eyes locked on hers, refusing to give away everything about which he was curious. He understood her question to be theoretical in nature, but their close proximity, and the opportunity to see her the slightest bit vulnerable, made him wish he could permanentize the moment.

"I suppose that's all I know how to do," Damian whispered. He reached for the side of her face and tucked a stray hair behind her ear, bringing her attention from the clouds to him. "The way I see it, life is a cat and mouse game of questions and answers. We don't have a choice but to be curious, to seek explanations. What made you ask such a question? Are you finally brave enough to practice philosophy?"

He intended for this to be a joke, but her eyes showed an extraordinary earnestness, which only enticed him more. He waited for her to look away and blush, the way she usually did in these kind of moments, but not only did she remain resolute, her eyes lowered to his lips, and Damian seized the opportunity.

Caterina pressed her soft lips against his as they melted into the moment. She felt his hands brush against her cheeks and push away her stray hairs again, as he gently held her face. She didn't expect this level of tenderness from someone who portrayed himself as unbothered and free-spirited. The longer they kissed, the more questions assembled in the confines of her mind, as if his inquisitive spirit was entering hers. Or perhaps, he was extracting her filters.

When they finally parted, Damian pressed his palms together and looked up toward the sky, unable to hide his smile. Caterina blushed and playfully pushed him away.

"You see," Damian said, his voice cracking, "when I'm curious about something, about someone, I yearn for answers."

"Did you get the answer you were looking for?" Caterina interlocked her fingers with his.

"No," Damian said, as Caterina frowned. Damian kissed the back of her hand, smiled, and said, "I now have many, *many* more questions, all of which I can't wait to answer."

A tingle ran down Caterina's spine as her heart filled with fire. She now understood what he meant, about being driven by these questions.

The blank paper that had been beside her was suddenly lifted by the wind and flew hastily down the path. Damian stood to chase after it, but Caterina placed a hand upon his shoulder, beckoning him to remain beside her.

"But, your final project…" he joked again, pointing his thumb behind him in the direction the paper had flown.

"I've got my final project already sketched out," she responded, tapping against the sketchbook in her bag. The flying paper caught the attention of the nearby children, and they gleefully chased it. She watched the paper disappear beyond the scope of her vision, and she relaxed her shoulders. The piece of paper was nothing more than an obstacle in her way of delivering her final assignment, which she had concluded must be the owl.

Damian noticed her slight smirk and immediately straightened up. He flexed his muscles and cocked his head to both sides, clearing his throat as well, trying his hardest to maintain composure.

"Don't seem, Damian," Caterina reminded him, laying her head upon his shoulder, watching his chest expand and compress as the sun sank lower in the sky in front of them, covering their surroundings in a golden and purple hue. "Just be."

"I suddenly don't want to go on this adventure." He pressed his head against hers as he chuckled nervously. She immediately sat up and placed her hand upon his arm.

"You must go!" She exclaimed. "Yes, we must both pursue our curiosities. Even if it leads to more questions." Damian raised his eyebrow, curious as to what Caterina was referring. He assumed it had something to do with her final assignment, but before he could ask, they heard a door opening beside them.

Caterina immediately turned to Leander's door, accidentally whipping Damian's face with her braid. She bent over and reached her neck as far out as possible, waiting to see the familiar blue robe appear. However, Leander never emerged.

They exchanged questioning looks until they heard a voice from the other direction. Demetrius had poked his head out from the front door, and upon seeing Damian, shuffled over to them.

"Good evening, Caterina," Demetrius said, bowing his head. She stood to greet him properly, but he shook his head as he pointed toward the studio. "Forgive me for interrupting. Is Leander still inside?"

"He definitely hasn't left."

"Wonderful."

"I should go," Caterina said, noticing she was still leaning on Damian.

"Wait!" Damian said, loud enough for even Demetrius' eyes to widen with alarm. "I just…" Damian turned to look at Caterina, rummaging his mind for a viable excuse to again extend their time together. He suddenly remembered what he was going to ask her from the beginning. "I was just going to ask about my flask!"

Caterina tilted her head in confusion, as Damian asked her if she had accidentally packed his flask from their time in the forest. She scoured her bag until her fingers skimmed the familiar piece of cold, hard clay.

"I'm sorry," she said, returning his possession.

"I'm glad," he said, leaning toward her subtly and whispering, "Otherwise it would have been harder for me to find an excuse to see you again."

"You don't need an excuse," she said, cradling the side of his face. A redness presented itself upon his cheeks as she stood to leave.

"Do you want to come with us?" Damian asked, his words spilling out of him in desperation and infatuation. Demetrius hid a smile, astounded by Damian's fixation. A sudden sadness washed over him as he thought of Aluna, reminiscing the beginning of their relationship, and how hard he too had fought for her attention. How he wished he had her blessing for this journey.

"I have my own adventure to go on," she said to Damian, grabbing her apple and taking a bite out of it. She winked at Damian as she walked away. Damian sat on the bench stupefied.

"Son," Demetrius said, walking over to Damian, "you don't have to go with me if you don't want to."

"A man can want many things at once," Damian said, keeping his eyes on Caterina until her silhouette disappeared, "but I want nothing more than to explore beyond the borders of Platanis." He exhaled deeply and burrowed his head into his hands as Demetrius patted his back. The pain returned to his forearm, and Damian winced.

"I'll just have a quick word with Leander, and then I'll meet you at the stables," Demetrius said. "You can leave your books on the table outback. I assume you won't be needing them?"

Damian chuckled and shrugged.

"Did you leave the invitation on the table, too?" Damian asked. Demetrius shifted uncomfortably before answering.

"No, I brought it into the house, somewhere where no one would see it."

"Not that anyone else *can* see it," Damian reminded him. "Take your time with Leander. I'll be at the stables."

Damian left the bench, seeming to walk on clouds as he faded from view. Demetrius on the other hand sat for a moment, still as a rock. He couldn't understand the anxiety trembling within him.

56

With a forceful exhale, Demetrius walked over to Leander's front door. As he reached for the doorknob, he frowned, noticing the door was already slightly opened. His eyes rose to see a sliver of Leander's face peeking from within. Though his head wrap shadowed the majority of his face, he seemed paler than usual.

"Leander?"

Leander opened the door wide enough for Demetrius to see his beloved friend but not wide enough to permit entry into the studio.

"How long have you been standing there?"

Leander paused before responding, "Long enough."

"May I come in?"

Though again he hesitated, Leander opened the door. The sound of water crashing upon rocks intensified as Demetrius entered. He hadn't visited Leander's studio in several years, though upon recollection, he remembered the sound of water seeming much more relaxing and less turbulent.

Demetrius' bright yellow linens usually lit up rooms as he entered, but Leander's studio was different. He was consumed by the overwhelming blue, so much so that his attire looked a shade greener, matching the queasiness he felt within.

"How interesting it is to see the two of them together, no? Damian and Caterina?" Demetrius asked, staring at his feet.

"Quite."

Leander stood by the door, barely moving, while Demetrius nervously shifted his footing. His shoulders stiffened, unsure how to navigate the sudden shortness of Leander's discourse. He looked around the room for something upon which to sit.

"I heard you read the letter," Leander said. Demetrius pocketed his hands and resumed his downward stare. Though his robe concealed it, Leander reached for his pocket too, feeling the secret letter Theo had left just for him in the basement.

"I had to," Demetrius said, almost pleadingly. "I simply had to." The vein on Leander's forehead reappeared as he clasped both hands into fists, hiding them underneath his giant sleeves. He remained silent, giving his friend the space to explain himself. However, Demetrius remained silent.

"I am surprised you came here, Demetrius, since my advice evidently means nothing to you."

"What makes you so sure? About Theo?"

The water behind Demetrius poured significantly harder as Leander's eyebrows furrowed and lips tightened.

"You will respect my studio and not say his name here." His cough reemerged, alarming Demetrius though Leander refused the compassion. "If my word is not enough for you, after all these years, then there is little left for me to say." He paused for a moment, closing his eyes as he continued, "To be honest, I doubt I will sympathize with your reasoning. I asked earlier you to explain your dedication to the traitor."

"He is not a——"

"He is," Leander said as his anger resurfaced, this time more calamitous. "And—somehow, beyond my understanding—the words he wrote you had a larger impact than the words I say as I look at you. Should I write my words down for you, Demetrius? Should I betray and abandon you, wait several decades, and write to you from afar? Will you listen to me then?" Leander paced the room as the roaring waterfall grew louder. Demetrius panicked as the water leaked onto the main floor, beyond the parameters of the rocks.

"Leander, please," Demetrius said, pointing nervously at the water, though he didn't know specifically what to ask. But Leander continued.

"Did I overhear correctly, that you are on your way, *now*, to see him?" Leander squeezed his eyes shut, restraining his impatience. "Respectfully, have you lost your mind? Have you lost track of time? On the eve of your late father's ceremony, you decide to leave? For *him*?"

"Make it stop!" Demetrius shouted, trying his best to avoid the water spilling onto his exposed feet.

Leander strode across the room until he was inches from Demetrius' face, as the water pouring more heavily around them. The water stopped before it touched Leander's robe, always keeping a dry circle around the artist. Meanwhile, Demetrius' feet were soaking wet.

"I will only believe it if I hear it directly from you," Leander said, speaking just loud enough for Demetrius to hear his voice over the rushing water. "Are you really leaving?" Leander's stoic expression flattened into an incapacitated state of anger and anticipation. He already knew the answer, but the little bit of hope which resided in him was the seed of his anguish.

"I'll be back soon."

Leander closed his eyes. With one powerful motion, he retrieved a pocketed paintbrush and struck his arm out toward the waterfall to stop the flooding. Instantly, all the water evaporated, and the room became eerily silent. A little bit of yellow returned to Demetrius' clothing, though his own skin seemed to lose some color. Leander walked to the front door with heavy steps. He pushed the door open and gestured toward the setting sun.

"Leander, please, just let me explain," Demetrius mumbled, recovering from the shock of witnessing Leander's abilities. Leander, however, kept his eyes glued upon Demetrius, lips pressed together, refusing to speak a single word. He saw Demetrius open his mouth in attempt to further reason with him, but Leander firmly raised his hand, commanding silence.

With a sunken head and wet feet, Demetrius trudged out the studio. He had barely stepped foot outside before Leander immediately slammed the door, refusing Demetrius the opportunity to say one more thing.

All that remained in the studio was the artist's pounding heartbeat.

A narrow stream of water trickled from the ceiling onto the rocks, as a single tear ran down Leander's face. He reached into his pocket and retrieved the red envelope Theo had left just for him. His fingers burned as he grasped the scarlet letter.

He thought for a moment that if he had shown Demetrius the letter, he could have convinced him that this was all some elaborate scheme the ex-artist had orchestrated. "But then I would have revealed to him the secret," Leander said to himself, as if hearing it aloud would solidify his decision to hide this bit of information. His eyes, though slightly blurred from the tears, re-read Theo's message: "What you seek has been returned to her original owner."

Raging anger immediately replaced his sadness as he recalled the impending doom beclouding him. He gripped his ears, attempting to silence his roaring anxiety.

Demetrius was leaving to see Theo.

Caterina had decided to pursue the owl project.

He didn't have enough time to build the statue.

Theo had stolen one of Leander's canvases.

Theo had stolen Leander's biggest secret.

As fast as he could, Leander ran down to the third floor and grabbed his cloak, blowing off some of the dust that had settled upon it. He threw it over his robe and adjusted the hood as he ascended back to the main floor. The bottom of the cape trailed down to the floor, hiding his brilliant blue robe completely. The black cloth reflected none of the light from the room, swallowing Leander into nothingness.

Every artist had this hooded shawl; it was given upon graduation and was required to wear if the artist desired to visit the Artist Residence, a secret meeting location along the mountainside. The artists typically traveled at night, and the cloak provided them the necessary privacy to protect the whereabouts of the Artist Residence.

While the sun had not completely set, time was no longer a reliable alibi of Leander's, and he decided to make the short trip to the Residence immediately. If he planned to recover the stolen canvas, he would need to be properly equipped.

He opened his front door just a little, enough to hear whether anyone he knew was nearby. Assurance met his ears, and he locked the door behind him, securely pocketing his key.

The boisterous children innocently skipped by him, as though he was but a shadow on a wall. One boy raised the blank sheet of paper he'd caught and wrapped it around his head like a hat.

Leander fixed the hood of his cloak and sulked to the studio's posterior.

Chapter

Six

Behind Leander's studio were green hills and a chain of mountains, in between which the sun had cozily settled. Leander secured his hood over his eyes as he once again ensured his solitude. The sun was higher than eye-level, indicating Leander's all-black attire wouldn't provide him the expected form of camouflage for another two hours.

He lifted the bottom of his cloak and his robe until the sun bathed his pale leg in a golden orange. He used his sandal to draw an "X" in the dirt beside him. He immediately heard galloping in the distance.

Leander squinted until his beloved horse came into sight. Her shiny black coat reflected the setting sun's hues as she sped across the hills. Leander pressed his finger to his lips as his horse arrived, and the horse nodded in understanding.

"Hello my Mesa."

Mesa brushed her snout against Leander's outstretched palm, and for a brief moment, Leander smiled. He brushed his pale, bony fingers through Mesa's jet black mane before mounting her.

"We are headed to the Residence," Leander said, bracing himself for the sudden momentum. Mesa bent her ear backward and turned her head.

Leander looked toward the sun, then back at Mesa. "You heard correctly," he assured her.

Mesa raced toward the mountains in the distance as Leander's eyes wildly scanned their surroundings. As the two ascended and descended the hills, the towering trees, almost vertical to a fault, accentuated the grasslands' steepness. Mesa avoided the adamant trunks with ease, zipping between them like a darkened wind.

Their town faded in the background as the smell of purified air and greenery filled their nostrils, and although Leander could hear Mesa's hooves crushing the twigs beneath her, the wooded hillside was peacefully quiet. The loudest sound was his own heartbeat, ringing in his ears.

The last hill which Mesa had to conquer had the thickest shrubbery and trees. She steered toward sideways in attempt to perforate only the outskirts of the wooded area, but Leander redirected her toward the center.

"Time is not on our side," Leander explained, though the treetops blocked the view of the sun making it impossible to know exactly what time it was. His intensifying heartbeat confirmed his declaration, and he continued, "We must take the shortest route."

The scenery around Leander blurred as he withdrew into his mind. He hadn't visited the Residence in several years— so many years, for even someone as particular as Leander had lost count.

The Artist Residence was an underground lair where artists, patrons, and exclusive guests gathered for social and professional matters. Leander, as the Director of the Arts at the Academy, didn't have the flexibility in his schedule to make recurring appearances. Though he was visiting the Residence for an unfavorable reason, he couldn't deny the excitement luring at the pit of his stomach to reunite with his colleagues, and one in particular.

"Mesa, do you remember the last time we were here? I must have visited at least once since… Well, I suppose the exact date is irrelevant. Though art surpasses time, we, this human flesh, know nothing *but* time. And though we know it well, we have yet to find a way of controlling it. I am afraid time flows fastest in spaces like the Residence."

Nostalgia flowed through his body as the mountainside came into focus. The sinking sun, who Leander deemed to be his favorite artist of them all, shone on just half the mountain, honoring it with her golden paint. The glimmering stone enticed Mesa, but Leander kept her on the shaded trail as they neared the darker side of the mountain.

"The Residence is an entrapment of its own, and I believe this must be the reason as to why I have not visited. A darkened room, beautiful art and guests, food of every variety, why would anyone desire to leave? Why would anyone voluntarily track time? It undoubtably is a world of its own, and that is why I cannot afford to enter under regular circumstances."

Though Leander wore a heavy robe and cloak, he shivered as a chill found its way to his core. His fingers trembled as he held on to Mesa, the metal of his silver ring feeling colder than usual.

Mesa slowed down at the sight of glowing blue rocks, no larger than the size of one's palm. They faded in and out synchronously in a hypnotizing manner, painted with a material that, when it detected the presence of an artist, would glow to guide the artist to the entrance of the Residence.

"Please, wait here," Leander said, pointing to a shaded area of bushes as he dismounted Mesa. "This will not take long. I hope." He clutched his heart as he inhaled deeply. "I should return before the sun extends her last ray of light. Enjoy the beautiful sunset, particularly how the evening sun coats the world around her." Before leaving Mesa, he retrieved his paintbrush from his robe and kneeled toward Mesa's hooves. Leander rubbed the paintbrush again the nearest glowing rock, and with the gentlest touch, pressed the paintbrush along the top of Mesa's hooves, transferring the material.

He wasn't planning on staying at the Residence for an extended period of time, but he also wanted to take every precaution. If he were to leave after the sun had set, he'd want to ensure that Mesa would still be visible to him, and only him.

Leander pocketed the paintbrush and traipsed toward the entrance. The glowing blue light faded from Mesa's hooves as he left her among the shaded trees.

Leander ensured the security of his cloak, though he knew he was entirely alone. The last glowing rock was a couple steps before him, and he braced himself as he stomped on it. A jagged, rectangular rock carved into the mountainside, like a poorly engraved outline of a door, slid silently to the side, inviting Leander to enter a dimly lit hallway. Glowing blue rocks caressed the borders of the path beneath Leander's feet as he entered the Residence.

The aroma of damp, rich soil filled his nostrils as he heard the faintest drips of water falling from the earthy ceiling somewhere in the distance. Though the sliding rock behind him didn't make a noise as it closed, he noticed the hallway significantly darkening, trapping Leander in an echoing silence grander than before.

"Nothing has changed," Leander noted as his vision traveled down the hall.

The walls of the hallway, if one could call them walls, were made of dirt with some silver-striped rocks scarcely protruding. There was nothing impressive nor aesthetically pleasing about the Residence's entrance, except the glowing rocks beneath him. At the end of the hallway, he turned to a wall made entirely of stone. Again, he stomped on the closest glowing rock, and the rectangular stone along the wall slid sideways, revealing Leander's presence to the crowded room.

"Do my eyes deceive me? Is that my favorite student?" A familiar voice reached Leander's ears as he stepped forward, lifting the hood from his eyes and observing the room. It was just as he remembered. He sighed in relief.

The room was a large open space, split into different levels and lit by dull purple orbs floating near the ceiling. Each level had its own arrangement of couches and tables, offering different compositions for various purposes. To his right was a long counter where wine was offered. Someone, or something, was playing an unrecognizable tune in the background.

Only one significant difference about the room's design caught Leander's eye: a giant sundial emerged from the other side of the room, though there were no windows through which sunlight entered. *It must be a canvas,* Leander thought, his throat tightening.

An unrecognizable group of people walked past the sundial, careless of its bulging presence. He couldn't identify anyone, except for the husky man running to greet him.

"Hello, Zotikos," Leander said, extending a hand. Though Leander was rather tall himself, his mentor was much taller, and wider. He pushed Leander's hand to the side and hugged him tightly, burying Leander's face in his bushy beard, which had greyed since the last time they had seen each other. He was dressed in dark linens, though not even the darkest material could hide the stains splashed along the folds.

"Surely, we can put the formalities aside, Leander! Everyone refers to me as Zo now, if they refer to me at all," Zo said, grinning widely and patting Leander on the back. "It's more modern: Zo. You know how popular modernity tends to be."

"Would you mind lowering your voice a bit? I am not here to stay, so I would like to avoid as many greetings as I can." His focus returned to the sundial's haunting vicinity. Beside the sundial were three women, all of whom had stopped conversing to look directly at Leander. He couldn't see the details of their faces from where he stood, but their gazes were uncomfortably felt. "How did so many people find themselves here?" Leander asked.

"Fascinating, isn't it?" Zo asked, putting his hand on his hip as he scanned the room, nodding. "So many non-artists are interested in what we have to offer. They have no talent themselves, poor souls, but they're eager to learn, to *experience*. For example, look over there— you see that sundial?" Leander gulped as Zo proceeded, "It's mere decoration now."

"Mere decoration? Does it not tell time correctly?"

"Oh, no, it most definitely tells the exact time. But no one cares! It even sings every hour, yet I can't remember what it sounds like. The sundial has become its own work of art, where we can admire it without feeling any obligation to it."

The three women who sat beside it whispered to each other, keeping their gaze on Leander, whose irritation caused him to turn his back toward the group and face Zo directly.

"You will have to tell me all the changes the Residence has undergone the next time I visit. For now, I seek your assistance in an urgent matter." Leander lowered his eyes to the wine in Zo's other hand and added, "If you are not too busy." Zo grabbed his large stomach and laughed heartedly, raising his glass to Leander's face.

"Leander, no duty, nor pleasure, would *ever* deter me from assisting you in anything. How long has it been since our last reunion? Why must you make that face? When was the last time I saw you? Oh, that's right... You, me, and..." Leander's body tensed as he braced himself, but Zo thought better of it. "Well, regardless, I am ecstatic to hear how I can be of service."

"Thank you," Leander said, relaxing his muscles only a bit, as he still felt the trio's unnerving gaze. "I need to access my study."

Though the Residence was mostly used as a common space, each artist had access to their own study. The doors to their rooms were along the furthest walls, and most visitors didn't notice anything particular about them.

"Is yours the one covered in cobwebs?" Zo joked, throwing his large hand upon Leander's shoulder. Leander steadied his headwrap, recomposing his balanced position from the weight of his mentor's gesture.

A blue door waited for Leander behind the sundial and beside the women of whose attention he'd captivated. The purple orb above the door gave the impression that it was black, as filtered lighting always distorted the truth.

"Do you still have your key?" Zo asked.

"Of course." Leander felt the imprint of the key inside his robe's pocket. Zo raised his bushy eyebrow and frowned.

"If accessing your study isn't what you need help with, what is? I thought you maybe you needed me to charge through your door and knock it down. I would've been flattered, really, that you'd have thought of me capable of such strength."

"I will tell you once we are inside," Leander promised. "But for now, please, help me cross this room."

"Just like the old days, huh?"

"Precisely," Leander said, hiding his hands in the sleeves of his robe, reducing his exposure as much as possible. Zo's ability to redirect everyone's attention to himself, freeing Leander from people's peripheries, remained one of the pillars of their sacred friendship.

The two walked across the room, and a wave of silence followed behind them, as artists and their guests muted their conversations in observation. Zo casually put down his cup of wine on the nearest table, smiling politely at those whose conversation he'd accidentally interrupted. A trickle of sweat formed upon Leander's forehead, as he quickened his pace.

"I see some women have their eyes on you," Zo whispered behind Leander, eyeing the trio.

"Let us save them from disappointment," Leander said dismissively, though their insistent stare penetrated his attire and burned his skin. Leander wondered how these feminine strangers recognized him, even from across a dimly lit room.

He mistakenly shot a glance in their direction, noticing the one closest to him who had the most smoldering eyes. The woman's skin was a glowing white, like snow, contrasted by her short black hair. Her lips seemed to be painted black too, or conceivably any dark color, as the purple lights overhead made it impossible to detect colors accurately. She wore the tightest linens, leaving very little to the imagination, drawing Zo's interest immediately. Leander refused to look her directly in the eyes, returning his focus to his door.

Zo, unfortunately, didn't do the same. He winked and smiled at them, an infallible gesture for him.

"*Who* are you?" One of the women asked. The elongated "who" mimicked the way an owl hooted, and her question struck Leander's ear. Fear swam through this blood as he slowly turned to her. Her eyes resembled those of an owl's as well: large, round, and dark, with a slither of a lighter color, golden brown, circumventing the pupil.

Leander tried to uphold his stoic composure but ultimately failed as his knees buckled, requiring Zo to immediately stabilize his friend. The woman blew a satirical kiss at Leander as he fumbled feverishly for the key in his pocket, jamming it into the lock.

Leander walked into the darkened room and motioned for Zo to hurry inside. He quickly shut the door behind his friend. Leander's boney finger reached for the paintbrush in his pocket, the one he used to transfer the glowing paint onto Mesa's hooves.

In the silence of the darkened room, Leander hastily pressed his paintbrush against a panel beside the doorway. The room instantly brightened before them, enough to cause both men to squint in irritation. For the first time since arriving, Leander removed his cloak entirely, hanging it on the door behind him.

The room was a perfect circle, like a bubble, cut in half by the carpeted floor. The parameters of the room resembled a pearl, similar to the walls of Leander's studio, though this time the room mirrored the shape as well. This pearl was greyer, with shimmers of blue, white, and black glistening in and out of focus every once in a while. The floor was carpeted a navy blue, the same shade as Leander's robe. Once Zo's eyes had adjusted to the new light, he frowned.

"This isn't what I expected," he admitted. "Now I understand why you never visit. Why, there's nothing exhilarating about this space. Leander, what is this? A storage room?" There wasn't a single piece of furniture in the room. Rather, scrolls of various colors and sizes were piled around the room, resembling the honeycombs of a beehive but instead with perfect circles.

"You have nothing to fear," Leander said. "This may not be what you had in mind, but we are safe here." Zo looked behind him before deciding to lean against the door, the only flat surface.

"Were we not safe earlier?"

"I believe you will understand once we find the source of my misery," Leander said, wincing at his choice of words, convinced he had shared too much.

"Misery?"

"The past has come back to haunt me. And when the past involves art, art which rises from potentiality to actuality for that matter, well, the stakes rise, do they not?"

"You mean you've drawn something destructive?"

"Not I," Leander said as he crossed the room. "Not ever. That which I am about to share with you, you must promise to keep between us. The scrolls you see around me are a combination of my own sketches, my parents', my beloved mentors—yes, your work is back there, and some of my students from long ago. You will notice that the bottom of each scroll, that which is facing you, is lined with a specific color." He bent down and reached for a scroll rimmed with black ink.

"I know now is not the time, but I have so many questions." Zo chuckled, though stupefied, as he continued, "I've yet to treasure anything in my life, Leander. Anything tangible, I should say. Seeing your collection here, well, I've never felt this level of inadequacy as an artist." Leander gripped the scroll and made his way to his friend across the room, who had made himself comfortable, cross-legged on the floor.

"Zotikos, I was just explaining to my student—I believe you have already heard of her, Caterina?—yes, a prodigy indeed, I was explaining to her that adequacy and artistry do not exist on the same plane. To feel one is to lose the other entirely." A shudder ran down Leander's spine, as he had just spoken to Caterina less than an hour ago, though it felt like a distant memory.

He felt the cumbersomeness of not having furniture, as there was nothing upon which he could lay the paper. He had no choice but to join his companion on the ground.

He mimicked the way Zo had crossed his legs, readjusting his robe accordingly. He rolled out the scroll, displaying a very detailed sketch of the human body. Zo glanced at Leander as though he was staring into the eyes of a stranger, in awe of Leander's talent.

"I know this is not something which I necessarily need to share with you as a fellow artist," Leander started, staring at the paper, "but please, bear with me." Zo's smile bore the weight of fond nostalgia as he nodded eagerly, watching Leander reach for the pencil he carried with him and pointed directly to the center of the sketched human, the belly button.

"As you know, most artists begin a portrait with the eye, for symbolic and practical reasons. The size of the eye determines the proportions for the rest of the body, yes? Well, I ask my students to begin in the center of their work instead. You will notice that the darkest parts of this sketch are around the stomach area here, as this area required the most focus," Leander continued, touching the tip of the pencil to the belly button and tracing the line that extended toward the face, "And the further you depart from the center, the lighter the graphite becomes."

"Why do you do it this way, Leander? No one's chest is more defined nor prominent than something like the face or the hand."

Leander took his pencil and pointed it toward the opposite side of the room, directing Zo's attention along with it. "I assume the first thing you noticed about this room was at eye-level. We train our eyes to address that which attracts us, as you said, faces and perhaps hands. These, faces and hands, are all *extensions* of things. The *source*," Leander said, as he lifted his pencil toward the ceiling, "is where the truth lies. This room would not appear as a dome without the construction of the center, as the center is the truth of the dome, the source of the dome. The face is but a mask, extending from the skin, extending from the skull, extending from the mind." Leander lowered his pencil and redirected it to the sketch's belly button.

"That's one way of looking at it."

"Creation is no different than destruction," Leander continued. "If one knows the point of creation, the source of creation, one simultaneously understands the target of destruction."

"Yes, presumably. But I'm not quite sure I understand. What are we destroying? And why?"

"I will tell you more once we find the particular sketch," Leander said, lowering his voice hesitantly. "We need to recover this sketch quickly."

"Which color are we looking for?"

"Scarlet," Leander said, quickly rising and turning away from Zo.

"Did you say… Scarlet?" The color from Zo's jolly cheeks faded as he stood with his mouth agape. Upon closer inspection, Zo noticed quite a few scrolls marked in a scarlet rim scattered around the room.

"Leander…"

"We need to go through each one in search for the sketch of an owl."

"These are Theo's?" Zo asked. The immediate tensing of Leander's shoulders sufficiently answered his inquiry. He suddenly realized the number of red scrolls before him, bewildered by how many works Leander had collected over the years.

Zo scratched his head as he counted at least twenty scrolls just to his left. Most students complete less than ten assignments at the Academy.

"What happened to Theo?" Zo asked. "You might as well tell me. I promise not to tell a soul."

"He failed the final assignment."

"Yes, this we know. However, I can't imagine failure from the Academy results in excommunication," Zo said, pulling out a scroll and returning it with a disappointed frown. Leander froze.

"Excommunication? My friend, who told you such nonsense?"

"Even you, Leander, can't convince me that someone willingly chose to leave Platanis! Surely he was forced?" A scowl appeared on Leander's face as his nostrils flared.

"I know not why everyone thinks so highly of… him. He was *not* excommunicated. Demetrius gave him a choice, he could either stay under a certain condition, or he had to leave. Where there is choice, there must be accountability. We cannot, *should not*, consider… him a victim." Leander's cough interrupted his response, but Zo's curiosity could not be curbed.

"So it was Demetrius who banished him!" Zo exclaimed, accidentally dropping a scroll. "I must confess, I don't know Demetrius well, but those two were inseparable. I thought they were brothers. My goodness, I can't imagine banishing a brother."

"For the last time," Leander said, taking a deep breath and pronouncing each word slowly, "he chose to leave."

And now he has chosen to return, Leander thought to himself.

"Where's he now?"

"We should focus on finding the sketch," Leander asserted.

After several minutes, the two had checked every scarlet scroll, without an owl in sight. Leander grasped his headwrap as he paced anxiously, wracking his brain for the answer as to where he'd find this sketch. He stopped as the red envelope in his pocket suddenly felt more prominent.

"Was he here?" Leander asked dejectedly, as if he was in a trance.

"Was *who* here?" Zo asked, replacing the last scroll. The stressed "who" led to an image of an owl flashing before Leander's eyes, a scarlet owl this time, and he closed his eyes tightly, pushing the image out of his mind.

Leander remained motionless, unable to speak.

"Oh, was *he* here?" Zo repeated with a laugh so blaring it shook Leander, enough to return his mind to the present. Zo patted Leander on the back, as if the two had shared a joke. "Leander, his arrival would be the news of the decade. The past two decades, right? I don't think any other news would travel as fast as that one would, were it true."

"How can you be certain?" Leander asked, his eyes darting back and forth in search for clarity. His breaths shortened as he hyperventilated.

Zo held Leander by his shoulders and said to him directly, "Because I haven't seen him here in years. In fact, I don't remember the last time I left the Residence, Leander. I live here now. Most of the other artists do as well. I don't think anyone would have kept his return a secret— especially not from you, my friend."

"Why— why has Fate turned from friend to foe!" Leander cried, his protruding vein returning to his forehead. He released himself from Zo's hold and collapsed to his knees, burying his head in his hands. His cough deepened his descent to the ground as he gasped for air.

Chapter
Seven

Demetrius entered his home, his soaked sandals slipping on the stone floor. He steadied himself as he bent over, taking the ruined shoes into his hands. Silence surrounded him before he forcefully threw the shoes against the wall. Mud splattered everywhere. His shoulders loosened, as though he'd also discarded the hurt Leander had caused him. The mess wasn't the desired consequence, but he'd attend to it once he returned. He dashed to his bedroom with a renewed elation in every step.

"Aluna?" He asked before opening the door, though he assumed she was still in the nursery outside.

He entered his bedroom and was momentarily disorientated, as he couldn't recall the last time he had seen how the evening's sun washed over his room.

The bedroom wasn't extravagantly furnished. The walls were of white painted clay, protecting a large bed on one side, and a tall, narrow window on the other, where a table and chair had been placed underneath. Aluna had draped some vines around the frame of the window. On each side of the bed was a wooden nightstand, both carved by Aluna, and Demetrius' was on the furthest side.

Light penetrated the window and created a sliver of gold directly onto his nightstand, like a sparkling, destined path encouraging Demetrius to retrieve the item which he sought.

His bare feet walked along this path, the floor beneath him warmed from the sun. The yellow from his linens as usual reflected against the walls, as though the sun herself had entered the room. He bent down to reach the lowest drawer, and upon opening it, his eyes were immediately blinded by a shiny object.

Red sparkles now dazzled across the yellow-washed walls. In the drawer was a silver ring with a giant ruby protruding from the center. This ruby was covered by two thin, silver bars: one stretching from top to bottom, the other left to right, creating a "T" across it.

Demetrius held the ring in the palm of his hand, feeling the band's coldness, accentuating two decades of abandonment. He turned toward the window and tilted his palm forward, watching as the sun shone directly on it. The red sparkles around him danced as he moved the ring back and forth, admiring its beauty. His eyes were glued on the "T" as he thought back to the moment Theo had gifted it to him.

❧

They were both eighteen, walking along a winded path toward the lake closest to Demetrius' father's home. Demetrius wore a loose, yellow shirt and white bottoms, both muddied by the errands he had that day. Theo wore all black, which was peculiar, given their tropical surroundings. His dark brown hair, though thick, stuck to the edges of his round, freshly shaven face. His brown cheeks were flushed with excitement as he grinned, patting Demetrius on the back.

"You must share every detail with me," Theo said. "I knew she'd say yes, but you know me— I want to know everything!"

"I wish I had a thrilling tale to tell, but I just asked! I didn't plan a thing."

"Ah! There's no escaping who you really are, is there?" Theo asked, pressing his palm against his forehead as he continued laughing. "You knew she was the one from the beginning, though. And that accounts for more than some elaborative arrangement. Was she happy? Did she like the ring?"

"You won't believe this—" Demetrius started, but Theo stopped in his tracks and placed a hand on his friend's shoulder.

"You brought a ring, didn't you?"

"I didn't!"

The two howled as Demetrius revealed everything he hadn't done. Theo wiped a tear from his eye and nodded heavily, saying, "You, my friend, are a gem." They continued down the path as Demetrius raved about how lucky he felt to have found the woman of his dreams.

The lake finally appeared in the distance, and they hurried to it. The breeze from the water relieved them from the blistering sun that summer day. The Tracoses Forest in the background reflected onto the lake's glassy surface, with only the faintest ripples breaking its perfect stillness. They took off their sandals and rolled up the bottoms of their pants, feeling the water wash over their ankles, the fresh, salt air entering their nostrils.

Theo listened to Demetrius daydream aloud as they walked along the edge of the lake. Demetrius retold the story of how he had met Aluna, with Theo interrupting now and then to finish sentences he'd heard countless times. The sounds of birds chirping in the distance accompanied their pleasant walk. An old paintbrush and a newly acquired item in Theo's pocket clung to his legs as water splashed higher than expected.

"Now we need to find someone for you!" Demetrius said, shielding the sunlight from his eyes as he jokingly scanned the view in search for a partner.

"None for me, thank you. I get bored too easily."

"Leander was telling me about that."

Theo turned quickly, eyes widening as Demetrius continued.

"You know I have nothing but love for you, Theo, but you really, really need to start focusing. Leander goes on these never-ending rants about how talented you are, and how you just need to apply yourself more." Demetrius straightened his posture as he lovingly mimicked his stoic friend. Theo chuckled.

"The problem is," Theo said, ripping a blade of grass, "when you focus too long on one thing"—he held the grass before his nose—"you lose sight of all the other wonderful things around you." He slowly moved the grass away from his face until his arm reached its limit, then he watched the sliver of green fall gently to the ground. He continued walking, ensuring he applied extra pressure as he stepped over the befallen.

"Where'd you come up with that?"

"I must've read it somewhere," Theo said, twisting the corner of his mouth and kicking the water.

"Well, stop reading and start drawing!"

Theo walked away from the water and laid down in the grass, rubbing his face aggressively with his hands.

"It's *such* a commitment," Theo groaned.

"You have one more year left at the Academy," Demetrius said cautiously, sitting down beside Theo. "Finish the program and obtain the utmost freedom."

"Ha!" Theo said, sitting up. "Freedom? Let me show you something." Theo reached into his pocket and pulled out a silver ring with a ruby jewel glistening atop. Demetrius tilted his head to that side.

"What's that?"

"It's an Artist Ring, one of ten," Theo said, twirling the ring between his thumb and forefinger. "Only the 'Greats' are awarded one. You've seen Leander's sapphire ring, haven't you?"

"Sure, sure."

"It's a strange little thing. The whole exchange was very strange. After one of my lessons, Leander and I were talking about age. Age— at our age! But Demetrius, you should've heard him, the way he spoke, as if we weren't born in the same year. 'You are destined,' he said. Or better yet, 'You are a young man with the soul of an old artist.' I couldn't stand it!"

"Sounds like Leander," Demetrius said, smiling with fondness.

"I understand our arrangement is bizarre, having a mentor the same age as myself. But if anyone's soul is older than his body, it's Leander's, not mine!" Theo stopped twirling the ring and threw it beside him. Demetrius reached for it and observed it closer.

"Then what happened?"

"He could tell I wasn't happy. I pushed back against his declarations. How can he know my soul better than me?"

Demetrius shrugged, while Theo rolled his head back, looking up at the sky in agony. A raindrop fell onto his face, right between his eyes.

"I was about to quit the Academy in that moment— don't look at me like that! I'm *bored*, Demetrius. Art doesn't excite me. I don't care if I have some miraculous power or understanding. I don't care if I'm 'Great.'" He used his fingers as air-quotes, sticking out his tongue in disgust.

"I assume Leander didn't take the news well," Demetrius said, wiping a raindrop from beside his nose. Theo nodded toward the ring.

"He most certainly didn't. First, he called me names—ungrateful, childish, stubborn. A moment prior, I was everything. Then, nothing. You could see how his name-calling, both the praiseworthy and blameworthy, have no effect on me."

Demetrius closed one eye as he observed the minute details of the ring. Engraved elegantly in the inner part of the ring was the number "2." *Probably out of ten*, Demetrius thought to himself. He shifted the ring slightly and noticed another line, a curved one, which intersected the "2," though it wasn't as deeply engraved. *Is that an eight? No, no... it looks like an infinity symbol.* Demetrius twisted the ring once more, and this second curved line disappeared.

"He tried a bunch of different tactics," Theo continued, watching the grey clouds roll in faster. "I saw the desperation in his eyes, and I'll admit, I felt bad. I don't want to hurt Leander, but…"

"But you don't want to be an artist," Demetrius finished, wrapping his fingers around the ring. "Why did he give you this ring?"

Theo sat in silence for a moment as he bit his lip. A raindrop landed near the corner of his eye and ran down his face before Theo rubbed it away.

"He was looking for commitment from me. He said he was going to give it to me once I graduated. Not every student gets one, but the others who have a ring agree that the ring should belong to me. You know Zotikos?"

"He's a friend of my father's, yes."

"He's also Leander's mentor, and he has the opal ring. I'm not sure who has the others. And do I care? Absolutely not. You ask why Leander gave me the ring? It was a baiting gesture into some elitist nonsense."

"But you accepted the ring," Demetrius said, grabbing Theo's hand and placing the ring back into it. Theo shook his head.

"Leander said 'It is yours, and when the time is right, you will wear it.' Demetrius, if I ever begin wearing red, you know that I've succumbed to an insignificant existence."

"I can't remember a time you wore anything but black, except when your mother was still dressing you. Do you even remember wearing all white? Ha! Some color would be nice on you. I do think you should return the ring, though. Don't give Leander false hope."

Theo bounced the ring from hand to hand as a chuckle escaped his lips. The drizzle slowly transitioned into a harder rain.

"I told Leander if I leave with the ring, I'm throwing it into the lake."

"You're not serious."

Theo's dark eyes darted to Demetrius as a mischievous smile appeared on his face. In one quick motion, he leaped to his feet and rushed to the lake. Demetrius sprang up and charged at Theo, tackling him to the ground.

"Are you insane?" Demetrius yelled, retrieving the ring from Theo. "Leander probably thought you were joking. *Return it*." Theo faced the lake, opening his palm toward the ring in Demetrius' hand. Demetrius rolled his eyes. "Nevermind. I'll return it for you."

"I wouldn't return it if I were you," Theo said, raising his voice above the pouring rain. "He said if he ever sees it again, it should be on my hand." Theo tilted his head back and breathed a sigh of relief, as if he had washed away some irritable thoughts. He pushed his hair back and returned his attention to Demetrius, his eyebrows rising in excitement.

"You should have it," Theo said. "Consider it a gift from me, aside from the gift of me listening to you instead of fulfilling my promise to Leander."

"I can't... I couldn't..."

"Just don't give it to Aluna," Theo laughed as he started making his way back to the winded path from which they arrived. Demetrius stood like a statue, too scared to put the memento in his loose pocket but too unsure to put it on his finger. He covered the ring to protect it from getting wet, though its sentiment was more fragile than its physicality.

"Theo! But it's engraved... Surely you can just keep it somewhere safe?"

"It's engraved?" Theo asked, turning slowly. "What does it say?"

"Just the number two," Demetrius said. Theo turned his back again, but Demetrius continued, "But then when I twist it, I think it shows an infinity symbol." Theo's stopped abruptly. The rain poured as his hands turned into fists. He stormed toward Demetrius, grabbing the ring into his possession. He raised it above his head and squinted up at the sky as he furiously twisted and turned the silver band until the infinity symbol was visible to him. He lowered the ring and snickered. The snicker avalanched into a fit of laughter, leaving Demetrius alarmed.

"What's it mean?" Demetrius asked, placing both his hands on his head and keeping his eyes secured on the ring.

"It means Leander is full of lies," Theo said. He drew a *constructus* paintbrush from his pocket and pointed it at the engraving, carving a line directly through the symbol. "This," he said, holding the ring to Demetrius' face, "is finite. Everything we— *they* make, their art, is finite. That fool has his head stuck in the clouds, and that's not where I want to be. This solidified it for me."

Theo used his brush to draw two metal bars over the ruby, one from top to bottom, the other left to right. He took the newly crafted ring and again held it to Demetrius' face. The rain poured over the edges of the ruby like tears falling from a darkened heart.

"You see this ruby, trapped in the metal like that? That's what being an artist is like. And I want no part in it." He took his paintbrush and flung it into the lake. The paintbrush spiraled like a windmill until it plopped into the lake, joining the endless ripples from the pouring rain. Theo grabbed Demetrius wrist and placed the ring in the center of his palm before he walked away. Demetrius sighed in relief, wrapping his fingers around the ring.

~

More than two decades later, Demetrius opened his hand to see the ring reflecting its scarlet sparkles upon his skin. A slow and steady smile spread across his face as he nodded to himself. He opened the top drawer to retrieve the scarlet invitation he hid earlier. He pocketed the ring and left in search for Aluna. As he closed the door behind him, the vines hanging around the window all turned to one another.

Aluna… They reached out to her, briefing her of what had transpired.

Demetrius stepped into a fresh pair of shoes and left through the backdoor. Aluna came around the corner at the sound of someone approaching.

"You're not taking anything with you?" She asked with a raised eyebrow, seeing that Demetrius only held the letter. He rushed to embrace her, shifting his wait to ensure she didn't detect anything in his pocket. He pushed through her voluminous curls to hold the back of her head as she wrapped her arms around him.

"I'll be back by sunrise," he whispered, pushing a curl away from her face, behind her ear.

"You promise?" She asked, pulling away and giving him a stern look. He nodded and flashed his warm smile that made her melt. She hesitated, contemplating if she should share what the vines had told her, but she couldn't help but smile too. "I prepared this mixture for you," she said, dismissing her previous thoughts. "Well, not for you, but for the horses. The Tracoses Forest is filled with traps and poisons used to detect intruders. They're scattered among the shrubbery. If you coat your horses' hooves with this, it will protect them and you two, too." She handed him two jars filled to the brim with green liquids, along with two paintbrushes. "It doesn't have to be evenly distributed or perfect, but use everything to the last drop."

"Thank you, love."

"I hope you receive whatever it is you're seeking."

"I have no doubt that I will," Demetrius said, grinning. "I knew this day would come, Aluna. I wish we had more time; I want to tell you everything I'm feeling. And I see that insatiable look in your eyes, that you want to know more. I promise, when I return, I'll tell you every detail." Her cheeks rose as she beamed with joy before Demetrius continued. "The three of us will return, and we'll pick up right where we left off. Time heals all wounds."

The smile from Aluna's face fell as she placed her hand on her lower abdomen.

"Not all wounds," she said in a lowered voice. Demetrius immediately cupped her face in his hands and looked into her eyes as she fought back tears.

"*All* wounds," Demetrius assured her. "We'll keep trying."

"And you know how to get there?" Aluna asked, quickly changing the topic while she still had control over her composure.

"Not exactly, but don't worry. No, don't! Theo informed me and Leander where he'd be going, based on some map or tale he read in a book. I remember Leander nodding, and that's all the assurance I need." A shiver ran down Demetrius' spine as memories of his final minutes with Theo flooded his mind. "I do wish Leander would join us. He just needs more time, I suppose."

"Hey Demetrius!" Damian yelled from beyond the bushes, freeing Demetrius from his flashbacks. "The sun is almost gone! We should get going!"

Aluna nodded and stole a quick kiss. Demetrius tightly embraced her a final time before winking at her and speeding off in a hurry through the shrubbery. Excitement jolted through his veins.

"Wait!" Aluna yelled, reaching for the scarlet letter. "You forgot—" She waved it in the air above the bushes, hoping Demetrius had turned to look back. After no response, she growled at the blank letter and threw it back onto the table.

"I hope it rains," she said.

≈

Demetrius and Damian rushed to the stables. The barn was entirely covered in vines, and without the massive open door, differentiating the structure from its forested backdrop was near impossible. A woman with long white hair emerged at the sound of visitors.

"Ah, Demetrius!" she exclaimed, rushing to pinch his cheeks as if he was a child. "I'm so happy to see you. Look at you, so handsome! So handsome!" Demetrius smiled and hugged the older woman before introducing Damian to her. He explained they needed two horses that could withstand an overnight journey.

"Yes, of course! Just make sure to bring them back. I saw a man earlier today, less than an hour ago, well I didn't really *see* him as he was wearing a black cape. Anyway, his horse was black, too. And my instinct was to yell 'Hey! Where are you going with my horse!' But, that wasn't my horse! I just worry— a lot!" Demetrius laughed to appease the older woman. He didn't know who the man was to whom she referred, but there wasn't much time to ask additional questions.

"Be sure to prep them in secret," she whispered to Demetrius as she noticed the jars he carried. "Otherwise, the other beauties in there will get jealous. They'll cry all night! And I'll cry if they cry!"

He promised to abide; Damian nodded a farewell as they rushed to their horses. Damian's horse had an off-white coat with speckles of brown, marginally resembling Damian's soiled white shirt. Demetrius' horse was a rich brown, with her mane as dark as his. Demetrius handed Damian one of Aluna's jars and a paintbrush, and the two began coating their horses' hooves. Damian looked over to ensure the other horses couldn't see, but they paid him no mind. He dipped the brush fully into the jar and whipped it out, splashing the green minerals haphazardly onto the first hoof.

"Be gentle," Demetrius suggested as he saw Damian's horse resisting.

Damian thought of Caterina as the brush moved back and forth across the hoof. *Be gentle*, he repeated to himself but in Caterina's voice. His horse shifted her hoof to help him apply the mixture at a better angle. He looked up at her and smiled.

"It isn't too late to turn back now," Demetrius said as he closed the lid on his empty jar.

"It *is* too late," Damian said, standing up as well. "The spark of curiosity has been ignited, and its roaring flame is inextinguishable."

The two mounted their horses and left from the back entrance, leading directly into the Tracoses Forest.

The sun had reached her final hour in the sky, and her golden curve touched the horizon. The sky was a raging pink and orange, fighting against its darkened counterpart seeping through. The last ray of light hit the back of Demetrius' bright yellow linens, momentarily washing the entrance of the Forest in a lemon-gold before the trees had swallowed him whole.

Chapter
Eight

Zo crouched over Leander, who rocked back and forth in dismay. Zo pushed Leander's sketch of the man to the side and sat beside his friend.

"Do you remember the last time you collapsed?" Zo asked gently. Leander made no response. The scrolls around him suddenly seemed like eyes of his past, scrutinizing his weakness. "It was the night before your graduation. I'd spent six years teaching you everything I ever knew, and yet you were convinced you knew nothing. Your self-doubt was extraordinary. I mean *really* extraordinary. Do you remember what I said to you then?"

"Yes," Leander muttered between shaking fingers.

"I gave you that ring," Zo said, pointing to the sapphire which was directly placed over Leander's eye, "and I said, 'Leander, you are undoubtably one of the Greats. Welcome.'" Leander groaned and fell further to the floor until only his hands blocked his face from touching the carpet. His mumbled groans turned into painful coughs.

"That was not the last time I collapsed."

Zo's eyes squinted before they widened, immediately recollecting the cursed day over twenty years ago. He solemnly hung his head for a moment, recentering his mind after the intrusion of dark memories.

"Now, now," Zo said, pulling Leander up forcefully, "I'm afraid I must inquire as to what's happening. You, the most rational man I know, well— this just isn't like you. And although we're friends, I'm ultimately your mentor. It's my responsibility to protect you. Please, Leander, share with me what's troubling you so deeply."

Leander's pale face had sunken into a heavy frown as he twisted his ring. His paranoia strained his posture, and the whirlwind of thoughts buzzing through his mind was only momentarily silenced by the increased thumping of his heart.

"I understand I may not seem rational in this moment," Leander said with a tense voice, "but please, believe me, it is reason that has convinced me my life will never be the same."

"Life was never the same to begin with! You should know this by now, Leander. We can only depend on life changing." Zo stood up, extracting Leander from the floor as well. "Look at these scrolls around you. This collection you have. This *evolution* you've witnessed, of so many different people."

"My life from this moment forward will be a devolution," Leander said.

"The Greats don't devolve."

"Perhaps I was never..." Leander started, but Zo held up his finger, forcing Leander's silence. He pointed to Leander's ring and said nothing more. Leander retrieved his sketch and carefully rolled it back up. He returned the scroll to its original place before facing Zo.

"I had considered... *him* to be Great," Leander said softly, twisting his ring again. "I still cannot fathom why you permitted me to give him the ruby ring."

"I remember that day! How could I forget? At first, I thought it was a joke or an exaggeration of how talented you thought he was. Don't mistaken me, I knew he was talented beyond words, but no one in their right mind would offer an award before the accomplishment. But your eyes… There was so much certainty in them. So much faith."

Leander clenched his hands as the recollections resurfaced. The past clouded his mind like a storm approaching, swallowing the present in its tumultuousness.

"And the way you spoke about him, well, let's just say I never heard you speak that way about me!" Zo laughed again, but Leander had lowered his head. "You once said he was so extraordinary, even mirrors would sadden when he walked away, for reflecting Theo meant reflecting something other-worldly. Did you give him the ring, Leander? Now that I think of it, you never told me what happened."

"The ring was given."

"Wonderful, wonderful."

"I was mistaken," Leander said, feeling his knees start to buckle but refusing to come face to face with the floor again. "I believe the ring is at the bottom of a lake now."

"Ah, well, that's easily replaceable. Better there than in possession of someone who doesn't deserve it."

Leander stared at Zo in disbelief.

"The ring is not what makes one great. You do know that?"

"*Nothing* is replaceable," Leander said firmly, scanning the room once more for the missing scroll. "For this reason, and this reason alone, I must accept my fate." Hearing his thoughts aloud relieved the pounding in his chest.

"You expect me to believe that a sketch, a sketch of Theo's at that, was the piece of string that held your life together? Leander, how tight is that headwrap of yours? You're delusional! I won't stand another minute of this. Tell me how you equate the foundation of your life to a piece of paper made by another. I'm very interested in hearing this."

"If you think these rings to be replaceable, you will think the same of this sketch. The peril lies beneath the surface. That is where the truth resides."

"So what's the truth behind this owl canvas?"

"One that can never be shared," Leander responded, his palms sweating.

"With *whom*?"

"Demetrius."

Zo pressed his hand against his forehead, trying to piece the puzzle together. The pearly dome grew darker, its blue streaks fading in and out less prominently.

"And you think Demetrius took the sketch?"

"I do not know who stole it," Leander lied as he felt the presence of the red letter in one of his pockets, "but I know I cannot rely on the truth remaining a secret for much longer."

Zo walked over to the door with long strides, placing his hand on the knob. He faced Leander and said, "Then go to Demetrius first. Tell him the truth, before someone else does. I don't know what the truth you're hiding is, and I don't need to know. But my intuition tells me it's not the secret you fear, but its messenger. Be the messenger, Leander, and you'll have no one to be afraid of. Treat this the way you treat your art: do you let a mistake linger on the canvas, ruining it? Or do you actively fix it? If you had the power to keep the secret, you have the power to reveal it as well. Be the source of truth, just like in the sketch you showed me. Go, tell Demetrius! Even if it's on the night before the ceremony. Did you forget? Yes, though word travels fast, how could I forget that day? Don't mind that now!"

With a single swipe, Leander wiped away his tears. Leander contemplated Zo's logic and wearily smiled. Leander reached for the cape he had hung on the door. Before Zo twisted the doorknob, Leander, for the first time, gave him a hug. Zo happily hugged back, patting Leander on his shoulders.

"Thank you," Leander said, raising the hood until it fell just above his eyes.

"You can thank me by coming to visit more often," Zo said with a chuckle, to which Leander assured him he would. "I'll see you tomorrow, then?" Leander nodded.

He touched his *constructus* paintbrush to the panel beside the door, burying his scrolls in darkness. Zo pushed the door open, bathing the two in a warm purple glow. Leander immediately locked the door behind him, securing his silver key back into his pocket.

The sundial greeted him once more, though this time less alarmingly.

"Be safe," Zo whispered as Leander made his way across the room. His cape and robe trailed behind him like an elongated shadow as he focused on the exit, refusing the emergence of distractions.

The three women were still sitting below the sundial, eerily silent and still, mimicking the staticity of furniture. As soon as Leander had reemerged from hiding, one stood to approach him, but another placed a hand on her companion's knee, shaking her head. As the main door slid behind Leander, removing him from their view, the three stood simultaneously. In a single file line, they headed to another door, located on the left side of the room.

Zo leaned against Leander's door with crossed arms, watching the trio move in unison. The leader took off her earring and used it to unlock the door. The three exited the main room without a word to each other, silently closing the door behind them. Zo raised an eyebrow as he made his way to the door, wondering which artist had given them a key. He smiled and waved to people as he crossed the room, avoiding any suspicion.

A purple orb hung above this door as well, making it difficult for Zo to see the color of the door. He had only one choice, and he had to act fast to dodge unnecessary attention. He discretely pulled out his *constructus* paintbrush, holding it against his chest as he faced the door. He directed the paintbrush upward, directly at the purple orb.

The purple quickly vanished, replaced by a bright white light, one that blinded the whole room. In that split second, before the orb turned back to its original violet hue, the door appeared in its true, yet severely faded, scarlet form.

Murmurs flooded the room as everyone looked at one another, panicked by the sudden flash. Zo played along after pocketing his paintbrush, asking those closest to them what had just happened. He looked longingly at the exit from which Leander had left and closed his eyes, shaking his head. He placed his hand on his heart for a moment before inserting himself in the conversation of those in closest proximity. Zo returned to his boisterous self externally, but internally, the uncertainty amplified.

Leander stepped outside the Residence, the cooler, evening air filling his lungs. The golden arch of the sun had just touched the horizon, and the night sky gradually pushed away the day. The fading warm purple and orange hues coated the trees, in dire contrast to the sorrow rising in Leander's chest. He followed the blue rocks to where he had left Mesa. For fear of losing more time, he hurriedly drew an "X" in the soil with his sandal, and moments later, his beloved Mesa arrived.

"Did you enjoy the sunset?" He asked, patting her snout before mounting her. "You certainly must have enjoyed your time more than I did. Let us head to Demetrius' to extinguish this tedious misery. Perhaps I can watch tomorrow's sunset with you in peace."

Leander took a second to adjust his hooded cape before Mesa sped off. Though she was proficient in navigating nightfall, Mesa's hooves raced against the sun to arrive at Demetrius' before the golden contender disappeared.

"Zotikos was right," Leander reminded himself. "I simply have to tell Demetrius first. Surely, he will understand. Oh, but how can he? Would I?" Leander lowered his head closer to Mesa's, partly to help shield him from the wind, and partly for comfort. As he dropped his head, his stomach fell too, as the thought of Demetrius having already left entered his mind.

The forest's darkness gave Leander's vivid memories a blank canvas upon which to replay. He recounted that tragic day, how grief had strangled Demetrius, refusing to release its grip for months, if it ever truly left at all. Leander swore to himself he'd ensure Demetrius' happiness and safety from that moment on, and he winced as he hoped Demetrius could handle the truth.

Wind powerfully rushed past Leander, roaring over his thoughts and paranoia. He squeezed his eyes shut as he braced the wind, gripping onto Mesa as tightly as he could. With his eyes closed, his attention could only be drawn to two things besides the wind: the coldness of his ring, and the corner of the red letter in his pocket, jabbing consistently into his leg. He briefly considered hiding the letter in his studio before confronting Demetrius, in fear of its exposure.

His heart sank as his lack of control rose.

Mesa slowed down as they reached the end of the wooded area, with only a handful of hills separating them from Demetrius' home. The last rays of sunlight brushed the tips of the grass in a fainted orange. Demetrius' smiling face, enhanced by the bright yellow he always wore, entered Leander's mind. A scarlet silhouette attempted to creep into this thought, but Leander forcefully pushed it away.

His stomach rose and fell with each hill.

"Here we are," Leander said hesitantly. Mesa stopped behind Leander's studio, exactly where she had met him earlier. He ran his fingers through her mane in gratitude before dismounting her. She brushed her snout against his arm then took off, effortlessly blending into the shadows of the scenery.

He removed his cape and left it neatly folded by the wall facing the hills. He contemplated running inside to hang it properly but dismissed the idea as his favorite golden artist disappeared behind the horizon.

A single candle flickered in one of Demetrius' windows as Leander turned the corner. A wave of relief flowed over him. While crossing the street, Leander straightened his posture and took a deep breath. Though he didn't know exactly how to tell Demetrius the truth, he felt certain that their conversation would swing the pendulum back to equilibrium, restricting the chance for Theo to cause any more disruptions.

And perhaps there was a way Leander could still keep part of the truth to himself.

He knocked on the door, watching a moving candle flame fade from the window as someone traveled down the long hallway to the entrance. The door opened, and Aluna stood there holding a cup of water in one hand and a candlestick in the other, her head tilted to the side.

"Is everything alright?" she asked, then suddenly chuckled. "That's a silly question to ask given today's series of events, isn't it?"

"I apologize for disturbing you. I just need a quick word with Demetrius," Leander said, sliding past her. He noticed Demetrius' muddy sandals beside the door, and he further relaxed his shoulders. He peered down the hallway, waiting for his friend to peek his head from around the corner and greet him. Aluna scrunched her face.

"Didn't he say goodbye to you? He already left. About an hour before the sunset."

Leander stood motionless, his nerves paralyzed with fear. The dim candlelight from Aluna's hand bounced off the embroidered patterns of his robe, the way the winter's sun glistened through the cracks of an immovable glacier.

"Didn't he say goodbye?" Aluna repeated, a little louder, now closing the door to prevent the wind from extinguishing the candle.

"May I sit down?" Leander asked slowly, treading toward the next room.

The common room, similar to the bedroom, was minimally furnished. Again, a string of vines bordered a single, narrow window. In the middle of the room was a wooden table, upon which a candle rested in its handle, the same candle Leander mistook for a sign of Demetrius' presence. Accompanying the table were two couches, one slightly larger than the other. Leander sat facing the window.

He placed his hands to the side and stared emptily ahead. Aluna hurried to the kitchen to concoct an herbal remedy for Leander.

He traveled quite a distance to get here… the vines told Aluna.

Wasn't he just in his studio? Aluna asked.

No, the vines responded. *He visited the Artist Residence.*

Aluna walked over to Leander and gently put her hand on his shoulder, to which he jumped in surprise. She placed the cup in front of him and nodded toward it. He used what little energy remained to lift his hand as a no-thank-you, but Aluna insisted anyway. He took a sip, his ring clanking against the side of the cup.

The candle transferred sapphire sparkles onto the cup's clay like the accumulation of tears Leander refused to cry.

The sweet smell of Jasmine enticed him as the hot beverage rush down his throat and through his veins. He looked suspiciously at Aluna.

"Don't worry, I didn't poison you," Aluna said with a laugh. "It's all natural, I promise. You don't look good though, Leander."

"My appearance has never been a priority," he said, hesitating between returning the cup to the table or taking another sip, "and it certainly is not a priority now. I have failed many times in my life, but not to this detrimental extent. He did say goodbye to me, though I suppose I thought my reaction would have redirected his intentions."

"Really? Demetrius has all the admirable qualities, except for one: compromising something he's passionate about."

"He compromised quite a lot," Leander said with a scowl. As he pressed the cup to his lips, Aluna walked over to the other couch, sitting in its center.

"There is no reason for me to stay here," Leander said, staring past Aluna, through the window. She crossed her legs and placed her interlocked fingers around her knee, leaning forward.

"At least finish the drink."

Leander sighed as his boney fingers wrapped around the cup. A soft smile spread across Aluna's face. Behind her, a fragment of the moon appeared. When she sat back, the moonlight magnified Leander's paleness.

The bags under his eyes were prominent and blue. Even the warm, yellow glow from the candle had no effect on Leander's skin. He closed his eyes as he took another sip, and Aluna noticed the veins on his eyelids, as blue as his robe and headwrap.

Aluna crossed her arms and snickered. Leander lifted his head, waiting to hear what caused the amusement.

"I just realized," Aluna said, pushing her hair behind her ear before crossing her arms again, "this is the first time I've ever sat down with you. It's just us."

"I should be leaving," Leander said, tilting the cup as far as possible to get every last drop. As he reached down to place the cup on the table, Aluna put her hand over his, concerned by how cold his hands were compared to the drink he'd been holding.

"Can you tell me about Theo?" Aluna blurted out. Leander winced at the name but calmly sat back, placing his clasped hands in his lap.

Is this where I reveal my truth? he asked himself, looking at the night sky behind Aluna. His eyes suddenly widened. *If I cannot control the truth with Demetrius, perhaps I can with Aluna. He would always trust her.*

"I assume Demetrius has shared with you everything there is to know." Aluna's eyebrows rose slightly in surprise of Leander's compliance.

"Quite the opposite, I'm afraid. And you know me, I rarely pry."

"I am bound by the Artist Code to not share details about my mentorship."

"Thankfully, my question concerns what happened *after* your mentorship."

Leander placed his hands at his sides, bracing himself for what Aluna had up her sleeve.

"Why did Theo leave?" Aluna asked. Several thoughts overwhelmed him: *Did Demetrius truly not tell her? Is she testing me? How much does she already know? Why is this information relevant to her?*

"Demetrius approached him with the ultimatum."

"Impossible."

"You are not the first to think that," Leander said through gritted teeth, "but it remains the truth."

"You must have told him to do it," Aluna said, the candlelight setting her hazel eyes ablaze as she intensely studied Leander's face. He nodded, impressed. Aluna scoffed. "So, it is your fault."

"I would say it was my victory," Leander said, keeping his composure. "Respectfully, to both you and Demetrius, you two did not know him to the depths I did, and likely still do."

"Why couldn't you deliver the choice to him then? Why did you use Demetrius?"

"I could not deliver *anything* to him," Leander said, suddenly sensing the weight of his ring. "He would toss everything away, deeming it useless." The candle in front of them burned brighter as the anger within Leander rose. "I promise you, Aluna, my intentions are grounded in protecting that which is sacred, and what is more sacred than art and friendships? All by the Artist Code, of course."

"It seems you forfeited your friendship with Theo."

"What we had was not a friendship," Leander said with flared nostrils. "I did that which was essential to preserve my friendship with Demetrius. Please, believe me."

The moon had shifted across the sky until it was perfectly behind Aluna, creating a halo around her. She rested her chin upon her hand and leaned forward again, troubled with growing suspicion.

"Would telling you the ultimatum suffice?" Leander asked. Aluna nodded, pressing her fingertips against her cheek as she listened intently. "Demetrius asked him to either forfeit his writings or leave Platanis."

"His writings? I thought he was an artist?"

"He was a Great Artist," Leander responded too quickly, "but his art suffered as he focused more on writing. He settled for that which was two-dimensional. The subjects on which he wrote were destructive, to say the least." Leander steepled his fingers as he continued, "Without a mentor, without a beacon of light, how can one expect himself to navigate complete darkness? The darkness of which I speak is not of the unknown, but of true, complete, endless darkness. One which is accompanied by a sinking feeling, until all that remains is numbness."

"Oh my…"

"I was terrified for him. Thoughts become words, and words become actions. This succession is undeniable. Demetrius was the only one who could intervene, before the man's words became actions. I cannot tell you how long I waited, hoped, pleaded, that a return to art would be made. That the writing would be forgotten, as mistakes are bound to be made, and I was all too ready to forgive. However, when a man makes a choice, and the choice was made autonomously, I must respect it. No one wished for his departure, nor his fall. The decision was made to leave. For what? I know not."

Aluna pressed her back against the couch, contemplating.

"There's something I'm not understanding," she confessed. "How could Demetrius, after all these years, be just as— if not more— elated by the thought of Theo returning, if you claim him to be so dangerous? Why does he not share your sentiment?"

"If I only knew," Leander said, shoulders sinking.

"I remember you said earlier today, that you couldn't understand the excitement he felt. You should've seen him as he left the house to meet Damian at the stables. There was a boyish charm to him. With every step he took, he seemed more and more eager to leave."

Leander felt a knife pierce his heart. Having heard enough, he pressed his palms against the cushions as he stood to leave. Aluna remained seated, staring at the candle as she processed all the new information, piecing it with that which she already knew.

"So excited," she repeated. "He even forgot to take the letter." Upon asking her for clarification, Aluna told Leander the letter was still on the table in the nursery. "I've been hoping for rain. Anything to wash away this uncertainty. This waiting."

"Would you mind if I took a look at it?" Leander asked, though he didn't wait for a response. His steps were quicker than the cough forcing its escape, and he rushed to the back door.

The cold air washed over his pale face, though no color returned to it. The silence of the night weighed upon the scene as the folded scarlet parchment stood out like a bloodied wound upon the table, its stillness glowing in the light of the full moon. Leander's vision tunneled as he hurried toward the letter, blurring the surrounding greenery and Damian's pile of books beside him.

"You won't be able to read it," Aluna shouted as she propped herself against the doorway. He couldn't hear her. With trembling fingers, he grabbed the corner of parchment, unfolding it gently. The ink appeared dark and jarring. Leander's heart stopped as sentimental wistfulness flowed over him at the seeing the familiar handwriting once more.

"My dearest, closest friend—"

The nostalgia intensified resentfully as painful tears formed in Leander's eyes. He started breathing heavily, forcing himself to continue reading.

"If you could hear my agonizing cries, you would rescue me, wouldn't you? I've been buried for years under the Truth, and I've finally pushed a single hand through the dirt, enough to write this letter. Will you come retrieve me from my grave? I'm afraid I can't bear the weight or gloom any longer.

Yours,
Theo"

Leander's hands shook as the signature burned his pupils. The two o's in "gloom" had dark circles in them, and Leander immediately recognized them as the inescapable eyes of the haunting owl.

He wanted me to see this, Leander thought to himself as a tear strolled down his nose, landing directly beside the signature.

"Leander?" Aluna called. "There's no point in staring at a blank piece of paper."

Without a word, Leander pocketed the letter and rushed through the shrubbery, out of Aluna's sight. She held her hand out to call out his name, but he was already gone. She closed the door behind him, rubbing her temple to eliminate the oncoming migraine.

Leander held his head wrap as he ran across the street. He turned the corner behind his studio and picked up the hooded cape where he had left it. He threw the garment over his head and drew an "X" with his foot. He saw four glowing blue hooves traveling rhythmically toward him.

Mesa's coat shined brilliantly under the full moon, and given any other circumstance, Leander would've acknowledged it. Instead, he quickly mounted her, so forcefully that he almost fell off the other side.

"To the desert," he ordered, locking his eyes on the Tracoses Forest lingering on the horizon, the border that separated security from danger.

He braced himself as the two embarked on the journey into dark uncertainty, with a reignited flaming passion acting as his only guiding light for keeping the truth buried forever.

PART TWO

PART TWO

Chapter
Nine

A stone tower protruded from a swirling, silver fog, basked ominously by the full moon. A freshly lit candle's glow peered through a semicircle window, like a half-closed eye judging the world from its risen seat. A steady hand emerged from a scarlet sleeve to remove the curtain, permitting the night's breeze into the bedroom.

The square room's furnishing and dim lighting amplified its emptiness. The man, dressed in an embroidered, lazily secured scarlet robe, baring his chest, inhaled the cool air as he limped into his seat below the window. He brushed away his unkempt black hair, permitting the moonlight to creep into the deepened wrinkles above his contemplative brows. A large bed hid in the shadows across the room, too far for the candlelight's reach. A rectangular item draped in a black covering rested against the bed frame.

Between the bed and window was a massive bookshelf, twice the occupant's height. The books were not organized, nor were they adequately stacked against each other. Some were hanging off the edge, others crammed horizontally in the margins. Only the books sitting upon the table before him had somehow drifted from the sea of untidiness.

Three knocks reverted the man's attention to his bedroom door.

"Hello, Theo," a woman said as the door creaked open. Her body dwelled in the darkened entryway as she stretched out both arms, one further than the other, revealing a cup in each hand. Theo gestured to the chair opposite him, though his focus returned to the window. She shivered as the night's breeze brushed against her skin. "I see you only lit a single candle tonight." Her voice was as delicate as she was.

The woman was dressed in a loose, off-white shirt and oversized pants, tied at the waist by a single string. Her light hair was pulled back in a tight bun, exposing her pale complexion. She took a seat and instantly adjusted the chair, ensuring the candlelight only showered half her body with its golden glow while the other half hid in the curtain's shadow. She placed Theo's cup before him, then quickly retracted her hand into her lap.

"It is a beautiful wonder, no? How the moon always sets the tone perfectly for what will come. A fortune teller in her own right." His voice was deep, perfectly matching the depth to which he usually spoke. He leaned toward the window, smiling. The fog captured the moon's shine, twirling below the tower as Theo wrapped his wrinkled fingers around the cup's handles.

"What makes it beautiful?" the woman asked, keeping her body stiffly positioned.

"The same thing that makes everything beautiful. The light. And tonight, the full moon graces everything with her brilliance." The woman shuddered, shifting further into the shadowed corner. Theo smiled. "Why do you hide, Janus? Your beauty is alluring, delicate, stunning…"

Janus sunk further into her seat, her youthful glimmer masked by uncertainty.

"I wish you wouldn't," Theo continued, lowering his head. "But I shouldn't say such a thing. I would be upset— devastated— if you adjusted to anyone's wishes. There's nothing beautiful about submission. And you are beautiful just the way you are. Please, forgive me." Theo raised his cup in her direction before taking a sip.

Janus traced the top of her cup with her finger. A faint *hoot* from the corner frightened her, almost knocking her drink over.

"I see—er, hear— your prized possession was delivered. Is there a reason it's still covered?"

"She'll free herself when the time is right," Theo said, clearing his throat. "I must warn you: she doesn't like strangers. Uncovering her now, with you here, well, she might not react kindly. And after all these years, I just hope she recognizes me at the very least." Janus raised her eyebrows in surprise, but since she was half-hidden, Theo saw only one raised eyebrow. "It was a joke," he explained, though with a defeated chuckle. "I know she'll recognize me."

The quivering candlelight only reached the middle of the room, teasing Janus' curious eyes by emphasizing its limitations.

She brought the cup to her parted lips, squinting at Theo, unamused. The flame flickered wildly against the sudden gust of wind, highlighting Theo's dark eyes which paled in comparison to the heavy bags underneath them. The wrinkles around his face, particularly on the sides of his eyes, sagged considerably lower than Janus remembered. Even his black hair seemed different: lighter, greyer, near the roots.

"Are you alright, Theo?"

"My dear, of course! Why wouldn't I be? I have... all that I need. And soon, I will have all that I've ever wanted." He placed his fingertips on the edge of the table, tapping them rhythmically.

"Do you expect your guest will be arriving soon?"

Theo stopped tapping as the corner of his lips rose. He gave a single, deep nod.

"You must be very excited," Janus added.

"There are no words to describe how I feel. And you? How are you feeling?"

"Oh, I don't know," she responded, nervously tucking an invisible hair behind her ear. "Does it matter?"

Theo rose from his seat, eyes opened wide, clutching his chest.

"Does it matter? Janus, what else matters? Our emotions make us human. Without them… Well, the world would be quite blue, wouldn't it?" The scarlet threads in Theo's robe radiated brightly in the candlelight as he approached Janus, keeping one hand on the table to offset his limp. For most, the sight of such a vibrant red would signify a warning or danger. For Janus, his presence was like a ruby: rare and beautiful, though she could feel that this evening, the jewel shined less brilliantly.

"How am I to feel about a man I don't know?" Janus asked. "I've heard you speak of Demetrius in the greatest of words, but to me, he's just an idea. I'll feel something once he arrives. I'm sure."

"What about the *anticipation*?" Theo asked, clenching both hands passionately. He started to pace as adrenaline rushed through his veins, though his left leg made it difficult. "You can't be a mere reactionary!"

"It's all the same to me, really. Things either are, or they're not. Anticipation is in the category of that which is not, so please excuse my lack of a reaction to something which has not yet occurred."

A handful of books fell from their unstable placement, falling to the ground one by one, joining those with similar fates.

"Things either are, or they're not, you say? My dear friend," he said softly, "you, of all people, should know that the world is not so easily… divided." His eyes darted to the shadowed part of her face. Janus' nostrils flared.

"I hear what you're saying," she started.

"But you don't agree," Theo finished, softly patting her shoulder before returning to his seat. "You might have more in common with Demetrius than I thought."

"How so?"

"You asked me earlier if I expected him to be arriving soon. The reason I responded affirmatively is that Demetrius sees the world categorically, just like you do. People who see things as either one thing or another become predictable. This predictability you two have, accompanied by good faith, is a dangerous combination."

"Ah," Janus said, although she rubbed her temple. "Wouldn't that make all art dangerous? The ones you raise from the canvas? Are they not highly predictable subjects acting in good faith of their creator?"

Theo leaned into his chair as a smile spread across his face, and the wrinkles beside his eyes creased. He reached for his cup and hung it in the air. "We'll see!"

Theo grinned from ear to ear, raising the cup as high as he could before bringing it to his lips. Janus' brows furrowed.

"The owl is yours, isn't she?" Janus asked, extending her cup toward the sealed canvas. "Doesn't she act the way you designed her to?" A *hoot*, this one louder than before, traveled across the room, taking Janus by surprise. "Guess not," she mumbled.

"Perhaps there's some part of me hiding between the brush strokes, yes," Theo admitted. "I can't deny she resembles me in some way. Ultimately, however, she is her own being. Any comment of mine regarding her would be a form of criticism. And no one loves a critic now, do they?"

"Criticism? An artist *describes* his work, no? It's only a critique if it's from a spectator, I thought."

"Once an artist places the canvas down for the last time, he becomes a critic of that piece. It becomes its own subject, and therefore objectified by everyone else, you see? A finished piece has no artist. But an artist, a *real* artist, never truly finishes a piece. Perhaps that's why you rarely see artists at peace!"

Janus rolled her eyes, though a smirk escaped her lips. She tapped her finger against her cup as she continued listening to Theo describe the difference between an artist and a critic, a subject and an object.

How animated he is, Janus thought to herself, *when he speaks for his passions. How lifeless he becomes when he doesn't.*

"The bird is no better than the egg from which she hatched," Theo said, interrupting Janus' train of thoughts.

"Sorry, what?"

"What separates an artist from a critic, my dear. Artists," Theo said, observing his shadow on the wall, "are like birds. They live in this vicious cycle... how can I describe it?"

Theo's eyes glazed over as his attention shifted to the starless midnight sky. Janus held her breath as Theo stood once more, placing his hands on the windowsill and leaning forward.

"When a bird hatches, she frees herself from the most suffocating imprisonment. She feels the sunlight wash over her featherless body, bathing in its glory— only to find herself in the next entrapment: the nest. The nest is cozier than the egg; there's no doubt about that." Theo traced the curved parameter of the windowsill before continuing, "Imagine laying in that nest, a bordered residence, looking up every day at the sky. The bird finally feels the constraints of her home, though the constraints had always been there."

"Is that how you feel?" Janus wanted to ask, but Theo's monologue was not yet over.

"But then, she learns to fly, a newfound freedom, no longer bounded by the sticks and twigs from before. The sky seems so endless..." Theo reached out his arm to touch the sky before returning it with a heavy thud to the windowsill, disappointed. His eyes locked onto the horizon, though most of it was covered by fog. "The sky, however, isn't endless. Everything has its limits. Every newfound freedom is simply the realization of a newfound cage. So it goes for the artist."

"And the critic?"

"The critic thinks his words are his freedom. He's satisfied in his nest, his prison, as long as no one restricts his singing."

Janus scrunched her face in protest.

"I disagree. The body is the most asphyxiating prison." She spoke slowly, as if in a trance. "And it doesn't discriminate among humans:

artists or critics. That's something a bird could never understand. It was trapped all along in its same-sized, feathered cage."

"Go on," he encouraged.

"I'd rather not."

"I knew you'd say that, and, ah, I'm so happy you did. I always trust you'll have the right words to say. Your predictability is endearing, my dear. Fine, you don't like the word predictable," Theo said, raising a hand in defense. "Reliable, then."

"Reliable," Janus confirmed.

"Reliable: another term I'd use to describe Demetrius," Theo said with a wink. "If you two see the world as black and white, is's and is not's, either's and or's, the good and the bad, then you make it easy for someone to see the world through your eyes. Why critically think when you can categorize? I have no trouble entering the wholesome mind of Demetrius: he must assume that I am tucked safely under the 'good' category. And if he received an invitation from me, why wouldn't he jump at the opportunity for a reunion?"

"Even after all these years?" Janus asked.

"*Especially* after all these years. Unfortunately, Demetrius was born with a heart of gold, one that couldn't grow cold if it tried. For him, I must be the same person now as he has always known me to be." Theo chuckled to himself. "I may be speaking hypocritically, for my sentiments toward the man haven't changed either."

"Why do you say unfortunately?" Janus asked.

An amplified *hoot* escaped from the corner of the room.

Theo paid no mind to the noise. He leaned over the edge of the window and peered below. Though the estate was mostly covered by trees and fog, a path from the front door to the main gate was visible from where Theo stood. His eyes traced the route until the moonlight revealed an oddity.

"Did G return outside?" Theo asked, seeing a man walking toward the main gate.

"That wouldn't surprise me."

"He should be resting. After the long journey he's had, I can't imagine he has any energy left."

"Is Demetrius' home far from here?"

"Far enough," Theo said, emptying his cup. "He didn't go all the way, for he met some lovely women where the forest—goodness, what's the name of that forest?— It doesn't matter. He met them where the forest meets the desert. It's easier to navigate the spaces you know and lovelier when those spaces overlap with wonderfully helpful people." He smacked his lips together in delight, and Janus followed suit. The cups clinked against one another as she grabbed them with one hand, keeping the shadowed hand from view.

"I'll get going then," she said. She pressed her lips together and paused uncomfortably for a moment before asking, "Would you mind?" She tilted her head toward the window, asking Theo to look away.

"My dear…" he protested, though surrendered. His shoulders fell as he exhaled deeply, turning his attention away.

She reached for the doorknob with her usually hidden hand. Her fingertips had just brushed against the cold metal when a shrilling squawk from the shadows caused Janus to shriek. Both cups shattered onto the floor. She pushed her back and palms against the wall as she peered into the darkened corner of the room.

The black covering which had enveloped the rectangular object had ripped in the center, and a small, round head emerged. She continued breaking free from her entrapment, rising like a blooming tower of terror, pressing her wings tightly against her body. The creature's head turned abruptly toward Janus.

Janus' eyes locked onto the creature's as the body expanded, growing until she was just taller than the once-seeming massive bookshelf.

Theo gasped in delight, instantly rising from his seat.

Janus quivered as the owl's wings gradually unfolded.

The dark brown feathers wrapped around the room, constricting and forcing Janus and Theo to move toward the middle. The wings circumvented the perimeter of the room until the new walls consisted only of feathers, swallowing Theo and Janus in darkness. Janus had noticed a shining silver color peeking through her feathers, but the creeping darkness extinguished the curiosity. Theo's smile couldn't be wider.

Emerging from the darkness were two round, golden eyes staring down at the captives. The burning yellow eyes with hints of scarlet around the pupil, like two round pyres, focused on Janus alone, piercing through her eyes to her very soul.

"Theo..." Janus whimpered, tears forming in the corner of her eyes. She trembled as she realized there was nowhere to hide. She couldn't remember the last time anyone had fully seen her. A tear fell down her cheek as the owl tilted her head and leaned closer to Janus. "Theo, please..."

Theo rose one hand toward the creature's eyes and the other toward the center of the owl's body, closing the gap between the two. The owl shrank until she was small enough to perch herself onto Theo's shoulder.

Janus gasped for air as she recoiled to the darkest part of the room. Her chest rose and fell rapidly as she watched Theo happily pet the bird, whose eyes were still locked on Janus.

"There, there. *Janus* isn't the enemy," Theo said softly to the owl. "See Janus, I told you she doesn't like strangers."

The owl again had hidden her body with her wings, but as Theo continued petting the creature, a soft clinking noise escaped her feathers. Janus closed her eyes to focus on her breathing, bringing her fingertips to her temples.

The clinking and jangling continued as Theo asked if Janus was alright. With a hesitant nod, Janus stood, leaning her body against the wall for support.

"I should go."

"Don't worry about the cups," Theo said, placing the owl on his forearm as he made his way back to the table. "I'll clean it up before Demetrius arrives. I forgot how fond of her I was." His voice trailed off as his fingers were lost in her feathers.

She stepped over the broken pottery and opened the door into the hallway. Before closing the door behind her, she poked her head back into the room, gripping the doorframe.

"Is there anything else you need?" She asked.

"Not from you, dear. Thank you. I just need Demetrius to arrive so I can finally give him his gift." Theo lovingly rubbed the owl's head as her cooing filled the room.

Janus shuddered and hurriedly closed the door.

A final *hoot* slipped between the cracks of the doorframe as Janus rushed down the spiral staircase.

Chapter

Ten

Demetrius' vibrant yellow shirt absorbed the sun's last rays as the towering trees cloaked them in darkness. The trees stood with threatening demeanors, hovering over the men in discontent. Their branches intertwined like disapproving crossed arms, and their leaves canopied the evening sky, selfishly challenging the travelers for their own amusement.

Fear lurked in the pit of Demetrius' stomach. The ruby ring bounced against his leg, comforting and reminding him the intentions of the journey ahead. From his periphery he noticed Damian stretching his neck out, waiting for a plan.

Demetrius' silence was unnerving and uncharacteristic. The ghastly silence trickled over them, amplifying the sounds of each horse's step and Damian's heavy breathing. Though they were surrounded by forestation, the air was less fresh and much heavier than before.

"How are we supposed to see—" Damian started to say, until a green glow emerged around them, showcasing an ecosystem that had never bathed in a spotlight. Demetrius pointed to the horse's hooves which shone bright shades of emerald.

The path before them narrowed, forcing Demetrius to take the lead. They rode without a word until they reached a fork in the trail, revealing four new routes. Each path looked identical, from the shrubbery on the ground to the branches sticking out.

"Now what?" Damian asked, anxiously rubbing his hands on his legs.

Beside each path was a tree with a rectangular mirror nailed to the center of it, no larger than the size of one's palm. Damian raised his wounded arm to block the green glow reflecting directly into his eyes.

"Which way do we go?" He repeated, eyes covered.

"The paths constantly change. The right path is supposed to choose us, as opposed to us choosing it." The four mirrors in front of them began rotating, reflecting more of the hooves' glow. Damian grunted in discomfort. With squinted eyes, Demetrius looked into each one's reflection until he saw a hint of yellow in the third mirror, the same shade as his shirt. "Follow me."

"I'll try," Damian mumbled, still shielding his eyes from the reflective antagonists.

"I didn't know the paths would be so narrow." Demetrius lowered his head and shifted his body significantly sideways, avoiding the intrusive branches.

"You sure you picked the right one?"

"Absolutely."

In the distance was another mirror evincing the emerald glow, then radiating the familiar yellow as Demetrius approached.

And so it persisted for Demetrius; he followed his own reflection, taking Damian with him. The two continued in silence, with Damian occasionally wincing in pain as branches scratched his bandaged arm.

Beneath the horses' hooves, the grim grass transitioned to solemn sand. The full moon above them highlighted the night's stillness and the sporadic assortments of tall, bare trees, twisted in unconventional positions.

"A direct path would've been nice, no?" Damian asked with furrowed brows, scanning the sand.

"We'll go straight until we reach the other forest."

The horses hesitantly moved forward, adjusting to the unfamiliar terrain.

The full moon hung dimly in the sky, as if cowered by the night's uncertainty. Shadows on the hilly sands marked the scattered bare trees, but their entities were barely visible against the midnight backdrop. The glow from the horse's hooves had little upon which to fall, masking the sand beneath their feet in a dull puddle of green.

"Tell me about Theo," Damian said.

"I wouldn't even know where to start," Demetrius confessed, sitting further back on his saddle, though he couldn't help but smile. "He's a man unlike any other. His abilities, his kindness, his imagination... We'd run out of time before we'd run out of words to describe him."

"It must've hurt when he left."

"I've never experienced a pain quite like it," Demetrius said, his smile fading. "It was a unique kind of pain, too. I thought the untimeliness of my father's death was one of the hardest realities to reconcile, but watching my closest friend *choose* to leave permanently, well, it wasn't any easier. To this day, I can't understand his reason for leaving. But that's love, Damian... love of any kind— it doesn't *seek* to understand. It just does."

An image of Gabriella flashed before Damian's eyes. He quickly pressed his palms to his eyes, rubbing the memory away, the same way he had rubbed the soil from his face.

"Ah, well, I'll have to take your word for it. I don't spend time contemplating the nature of love."

"Again," Demetrius said, a laugh escaping his lips, "love isn't something you contemplate. You *feel* it." Damian frustratingly raised his arms, immediately humbled by his stinging wound, forcing him to lower his arms in pain. Demetrius continued, "Theo's decision to leave couldn't have had anything to do with me, so how could I ask him to justify his rationale? What did he owe me? I think that's actually what hurts me most, Damian. That he didn't consider me when making his decision to leave."

"We can never enter the mind of another," Damian said, nostrils still flaring from the soreness, "but I, too, am curious as to what made him leave. I have my own theories about the man, you know."

"Imagine that! How can you have theories of a man you never met?"

"No one's really that unique, are they? I resonate with what I've been hearing about him. Not his magnitude of greatness, no. Don't laugh too hard! I meant more of the frustrations he felt, you know, with the Academy. Also, you must know he's famous. People refer to him as the ex-artist."

Demetrius twisted his neck alarmingly quick toward Damian.

"The... ex-artist?"

"You must know!" Damian insisted.

"Where did you hear such—such nonsense!" Demetrius' chest rose and sank as his mind whirled, searching for the answers he didn't have. Damian reached to put his hand on Demetrius' shoulder, though it only made him more tense.

"Where I've learned everything else in life, Demetrius. The Academy. He was a student of Leander's, no? Didn't graduate? Failed his final assignment? Caterina was telling me about him, though that's all she knew. She didn't seem too interested in the topic. In fact, I think she was slightly disappointed in my inquiry. Not sure why. And you, why do you look so surprised? Did you think she volunteered this information? No, I asked her about it. I had to!"

Demetrius' attention deterred to his memories.

"He was never, *ever* not an artist. The problem—not problem, the words escape me—he was more than... he excelled at every... ah, now

I'm just being repetitive, aren't I?" Demetrius rubbed the back of his neck harder than usual.

"You're saying he was more than just an artist?" Damian said, smiling from ear to ear. "That was my theory! He was a philosopher, or call him whatever you'd like but a lover of wisdom without a doubt, who just so happened to be skillful at the arts."

The green glow grazed the bottom of scattered bare trees, hardly standing like the limbs of forgotten skeletons. The slightest breeze would have fractured their formation. Damian's horse stepped on a fallen branch, snapping it in half.

"Theo's not one to limit himself to a definition," Demetrius said, scanning their transitioning surroundings, knitting his brows at the gradual expansion of the emaciated trees hovering over them. They eerily represented human figures, and though it was unfathomable, Damian sensed that they were slowly moving and changing shape.

"He'd consider himself your friend, no? That's a definition."

"I hope so. Sometimes I wish I could erase the last memories I have of him. But at the same time, we can't only recollect the good."

"You don't need to erase any memories. You need to erase the feelings attached to them. You talk about *feeling* this or that," Damian said, mimicking Demetrius' deep voice, "and look at what that does." He waved his finger in circular motions directed at Demetrius' sullen expression.

"Theo always said our emotions are what make us human, though I can't help but agree with you."

"Why don't you tell me about them? The final days?" Damian asked, suppressing his enthusiastic curiosity. "Maybe then I'll feel something. To a lesser extent. Hopefully." Damian jokingly crossed his fingers.

Demetrius inhaled deeply and slouched, weighted by memories and sadness. The trees around them bent further also, as though burdened by an inquisitiveness.

"It had been several days after we buried my father," Demetrius said quietly. "Several days— weeks, maybe a month? First my words escape me, now I can't remember exact dates..." Demetrius ran his hand through his dark curls as he looked up at the full moon. He had no indication of how much time had passed since they left, and waves of uneasiness flowed faster through his veins.

"Time is different for everyone."

"How could time be—nevermind, it's not important to the story. As you can imagine, I wasn't myself after he died. Believe me, Damian, and I can't stress this enough, without Aluna, Theo, and Leander, I wouldn't have overcome the grief." Demetrius' eyes stared blankly ahead, as though he watched his memories unfold before him.

"Theo had moved in with me and Aluna after that incident. Accidentally, of course. He was so worried about me— There would be moments, brief but prominent, where the sadness would destroy me. And Theo just couldn't leave my side."

"Aluna didn't mind?" Damian asked with a raised eyebrow.

Demetrius shook his head.

"I don't think she minded. Or if she did, she never told me."

"Interesting."

"I never knew the extent to which retelling bordered reliving," Demetrius said, his knuckles whitening. "Why is this so hard?" The horses started drifting further apart as they navigated the spaces between the trees, balancing along the hilly sands. The full moon, too, found its way between the branches.

"I was grateful for his company," Demetrius said, "but something in him had changed. Not toward me, not toward anyone. But the way he spoke, the things he said, were just... unintelligible. To me, at least. I remember he started drawing on the walls, and Leander was deeply troubled by this."

"You weren't?" Damian asked.

"My mind was preoccupied. Plus, in the beginning, he used pencils, so I believed it to be temporary. Once he started using paint, I had sunk further into my sorrow to care much about anything."

"Interesting," Damian repeated, frowning and rubbing his chin. "You said Leander was angered?"

"Something about the Artist Code," Demetrius said, waving his hand dismissively. "Leander approached me—why can't I remember when!—and told me Theo had to be stopped. Is it because I've never spoken these memories aloud that I can't recall them?"

Damian guided his horse to ensure close proximity to Demetrius, not wanting to miss a word. The number of trees surrounding them continued growing until Damian felt he had reentered a forest, this time rooted in sand. He winced as another branch scratched his wounded arm, but Demetrius persevered, focusing only on his recollection.

"I'd never seen Leander this serious, distressed, and genuinely, it seemed he was tortured. I'm not sure how he found a minute alone with me, as Theo was always by my side. But in that private moment, Leander shared with me that Theo could no longer continue drawing. It seems so minuscule to us, no? Drawing? How could it be dangerous? And similarly, how important could drawing really be? So what, if Theo stops drawing? But no, there was something more I couldn't understand—or I don't remember—no, no, I definitely couldn't comprehend it at the time. Leander told me that Theo's art comes from books, those which he'd read, and those which he'd written. I didn't even know he wrote! Do you see where I'm going with this?"

"Can't say I do," Damian admitted, clenching his teeth at what seemed like the hundredth scratch to his arm.

"I know Theo resided at my house to help take care of me. Never will I accuse him of ulterior motives. But one day, when I went to his room in search of him, Damian, you wouldn't believe... The *books*."

"What books?"

"Books were sprawled everywhere. Scattered across the floor, hanging from shelves, piled on his bed. And the walls— covered in sketches, or scribbles, I don't know the difference." Demetrius waved his hands around him and pointed in every direction, as if he had walked into that cluttered room.

"I'm guessing you didn't mind this either?"

"Ha! How could I pay mind to anything other than my father? But as Leander spoke, I recalled that visual, that mess I had seen only a couple days prior. It seemed like a storage room, where he could hide his things."

"So Theo used your home to hide possessions? From Leander? He had to hide books from Leander?" Two trees before them leaned against one another, creating an arch through which the horses traveled. The sound of branches rubbing against each other in the breezeless atmosphere unsettled Damian. He quickly returned to the conversation. "Your opinion of Theo didn't change, Demetrius? Not in the slightest?"

The glow from the hooves began to wane in and out, increasing Damian's uneasiness.

"It will never change. You'll understand when you meet the man."

"*If* we ever meet him," Damian mumbled, dodging another branch.

"My feelings for those I love don't change," Demetrius said, feeling the weight of the ring in his pocket. "I can't explain to you what it felt like when Leander approached me, pale and stern— more than usual, mind you— informing me of that which I couldn't see. Theo had indeed changed, but I didn't know for the worse."

"Only according to Leander," Damian added. "He only changed for the worse, according to Leander." Demetrius, for the first time since the recollection began, turned to Damian, raising a single eyebrow. The waning glow highlighted Demetrius' uncertainty and added an ominous aura to the facial twitch.

"Yes," Demetrius responded, slowly, "only according to Leander, Theo had changed for the worse. Leander needed to remove Theo from his own creative process, while I just needed to ensure Theo's health and happiness, in order to ensure my own." Demetrius returned his stare to the ever-growing amount of bare branches before him. "I know, without a doubt, that Theo's health and happiness were a priority for Leander as well."

"So what did you tell Theo?"

Demetrius squeezed his eyes shut and braced his muscles as sharp pains from the memories pierced his heart. He inhaled deeply, stretching his neck upward, letting the slivers of moonlight trickle over his tired face.

"I was in Aluna's garden one day. She had run to care for her new batch, again only for a moment, but in that momentary solitude, the sorrow strangled me, and I couldn't breathe. Theo had miraculously appeared. I don't know how long I had been struggling to breathe. He helped me back into the chair—yes, I had fallen to the ground! Have you ever felt the weight of pure sadness?—He sat beside me, distracting me with some tale or another. I saw the fire in his eyes as he brought this story to life. He would lose himself in those stories. I don't know what came over me, Damian. His monologue was illustrative, inviting, and so vivid, yet the more he spoke, the more I heard Leander's warning in my head. I couldn't stand it. Before Theo had reached the turning point of the story, his favorite part to tell, I interjected."

"So uncharacteristic of you," Damian said, a hint of sadness in his voice.

"It's funny you say that," Demetrius said, sighing defeatedly. "I think none of us were our usual selves during that time. I wish I could remember exactly what I said. My memory has never failed me to this extent." Demetrius dug his fingers between his dark curls, as if hoping to extract the details he sought. "I gave him a choice: stay beside me and reside in the world he knew and loved, leaving the dark stories and arts in the past."

"Or?" Damian asked, urgently. Demetrius' arms sank to his sides as his head fell, too.

"Or, leave."

"You made the man choose between his passions and his people?"

Before Demetrius could object, a wide shadow cast its presence before the two horses. Demetrius stretched his arm out immediately, commanding Damian to stop. The night sky masked the arrivers' identities; the moonlight only traced the three strangers with a silvery outline.

The horses neighed in protest, their fear echoing across the endless landscape. The figures simultaneously lowered the hoods upon their cloaks, permitting moonlight onto their silky, short black hair and pale faces.

Damian's eyes traveled from their smoldering eyes to their parted lips, cursing the cloaks that left the rest to his imagination. Their synchronous movements and appearances merged their identities into one, until the woman in the middle spoke.

"Hello," she said, her sultry voice sending chills down Damian's spine.

"Hello," Demetrius said hesitantly. The spokeswoman stared back and forth between Demetrius and Damian, before settling upon Demetrius.

"You are Demetrius?" She asked, tracing the lines of his yellow shirt and smiling. Demetrius straightened his posture and nodded, though his heart raced. The other two smiled at his confirmation before all three turned to Damian. "And you are?"

"Damian."

After a brief exchange of glances, their long, dark nails emerged from their sleeves like daggers, intimidatingly shining under the full moon.

"You have reached the end of your journey," the spokeswoman said to Damian. "One of us will escort you back to your forest. The other sister and I will help you, Demetrius, to your destination."

"Damian's not going anywhere," Demetrius said firmly. "Who are you?" The woman's lip curled, delighted by the inquiry.

"Why does that matter to you, hmm? We were instructed—"

"By whom?" Demetrius interrupted.

She tilted her head sympathetically to the side as the corner of her mouth continued to rise, humored by Demetrius' question. "We were instructed to ensure your safe arrival to the front gates."

"*Our* arrival."

She turned to her sisters. Their silent conversation amplified the silence of the desert surroundings. The trees above them leaned down, waiting to hear the final decision. Demetrius covered his chest to mute the pounding of his beating heart. Damian's hooded eyes and mesmerized stare returned as the trio faced them once more.

"We will take you both to the gates, then," She agreed. "But we will travel in silence. No more questions. Can you handle that?" Her lips remained opened as she awaited their response. Damian and Demetrius exchanged uncertain glances, though Demetrius ultimately nodded.

"Lovely," she said slowly, exposing her tongue as she enunciated each syllable. "Let's not waste another moment, then."

Damian bit his lip, fighting the urge to engage with their new guides. The radius of the emerald glow wasn't long enough to consistently keep the sisters in sight, and at times, only the snapping of branches guided them toward their destination.

A silvery fog emerged from the darkness, rendering the emerald glow useless. The twinkling grey mist wrapped itself around the five, swimming effortlessly throughout the surroundings. Damian glued his unblinking eyes to the back of Demetrius' yellow shirt as the fog gradually opaqued.

After a short while, though the passing of time was no longer measurable, a tower emerged from above the fog. Damian pointed toward it in awe, but Demetrius was too focused on remaining behind their guides. The sound of branches snapping grew distant, and the three hooded beings disappeared.

"Hey!" Demetrius yelled into the fog. Damian trotted alongside him and again pointed to the tower before them.

"I think we're here."

Demetrius relaxed his shoulders, hypnotized by the sight above him.

Chapter
Eleven

Anxious sweat drenched Leander's head wrap. The scarlet letter's pestering corners stabbed his lower leg, serving as painful, constant reminders of his greatest fears unfolding.

Mesa slowed down as they approached the stables, behind which the entrance to the Tracoses Forest awaited them. Leander envisioned Demetrius and Damian, full of excitement, preparing their horses for the expedition.

"Stay in the shadows," Leander whispered, holding his hood to ensure his privacy from the blaring light of the peaking full moon. Mesa moved accordingly toward the wooded area, where it met the grassland. Snores and shuffling escaped the stables' walls, but Mesa trotted, undistracted.

For a moment, Leander reconsidered his journey. Demetrius had left with the setting sun, and now the moon hung unapologetically in clear view, rendering it impossible for Leander to intercept Demetrius' journey. He suppressed several coughs, unwilling to entertain further deterrents.

"But I must protect him," Leander muttered to himself, lowering his chin and staring determinedly ahead.

They stood between two giant trees, parted by a single dirt path. Leander's hands, though shaking, tapped Mesa, encouraging her to proceed cautiously, and the full moon faded beyond the trees. The combination of his black cloak and Mesa's dark coat immediately erased their visibility, until Leander reached for his paintbrush, pointing it toward Mesa's hooves. A sapphire glow surrounded them, though its radius was short, prioritizing imperceptibility over utility.

The Tracoses Forest was just as he remembered from childhood, lifeless and still, the perfect maze to navigate with ease when equipped by knowledge of its patterns. This woodland was a collaborative effort between artists and botanists, ensuring the once-believed impossibility of intrusion or escape. Aluna should have received a signal that Leander had entered the forest, an unideal circumstance for Leander who prioritized his anonymity. Though he scowled at first, he relaxed his shoulders and faced the trees beside him, particularly the ones wrapped in vines.

"Please tell Aluna that I will bring Demetrius and Damian back," Leander whispered, not knowing entirely how the vines' communicative abilities worked. "Alone," he added.

He adjusted his sapphire ring as he repressed rising anger.

The two reached a diversion in the road: four paths separated each by a tree with a mirror nailed to the center of it. He remembered how his father had lifted him as he steadied the hammer. The two smiled at their reflections, nothing like the sunken scowl currently staring back at Leander in the second mirror. Mesa stopped, but Leander urged her to continue.

"Reflection doesn't require an abrupt halt," Leander whispered, raising his paintbrush over his head, though he'd already seen his reflection in that mirror. Its impression of the familiar sapphire blue was more comforting. "Reflection requires only self-recognition; otherwise, it is merely a dead-end, paralyzing our ability to move forward, or to act at all."

The mirrors were canvases, designed to guide those with the right intentions and puzzle the others. Drawing reflections was a skill of only the Greats, especially creating mirrors that reflected different images for different spectators. For those who have no business navigating the woods, the mirrors would reflect light to a blinding degree, complicating the explorer's ability to proceed or think clearly.

But for those who had a reason to leave, the mirrors could be used as guides, requiring one to only see the slightest bit of themselves in order to select the right path.

Leander peered over his shoulder before Mesa had completely proceeded onto the second of the four paths. The blue glow illuminated fresh prints of hooves on the third dirt path. Leander's heart sank as he shook his head.

"Of course we are not on the same path," Leander muttered to himself, lowering his chin as Mesa immersed them deeper into the forest. Leander's pulsing heart echoed in his ears as he thought back to the moment he had first informed Demetrius of the way the mirrors worked, when they were barely old enough to ride horses.

"The more time you spend in front of them," Leander had said, "the more you will overthink. You follow the one which reflects you."

"Aren't they all mirrors?" Demetrius asked. "How could one reflect better than the rest?"

"It is the secret of an artist! Like magic! Just follow the one that mirrors your bright personality," Leander answered, smiling with the last bit of energy which remained from the long day of helping his parents. "You will understand when you see it. And again, do not think for too long."

"All artists are just secret keepers! It's not fair!" Demetrius said, exhaling frustratingly.

"Become an artist, then! Join me and Theo."

Leander pushed the memory from his mind as he focused on his surroundings. The trees beside them were uncomfortably close, and the swatting branches restricted Leander from stretching out his arms.

Several childhood flashbacks later, the path and the spaces between the trees widened, causing more ambiguity in the path before them. Mirrors would arise every so often, and Leander, though still fully cloaked and hidden from the mirrors themselves, raised his paintbrush, pointing Mesa each time in the direction of the reflected sapphire.

"Do not be fooled by the ample space," Leander said as his eyes locked on the trees ahead. "Only one exit awaits us."

Chapter
Twelve

aterina flicked her pencil against the wooden table as she
contemplated her sketch. She tilted her head left and right,
turning the piece of paper upside down to visualize its every
potential. The candle's flame dance wildly, like the flow of ideas rushing
through Caterina's mind. Loose hairs from her braid fell on the paper,
adding to the dark lines Caterina had scribbled.

Her stomach growled as she dragged the pencil.

"Caterina?" Her sister called from the doorway, rubbing her eyes.
Caterina jumped, dropping her pencil. "What time is it? Why are you
still awake?" She walked into the small room, sat on Caterina's bed, and
patted the blanket. "You need to get some sleep."

"I'm not tired," Caterina said as a yawn fled her lips. Her sister patted
the blanket more aggressively; Caterina left her seat, clutching her
stomach to mute the second growling.

"You can't keep doing this," her sister said. "Every assignment of yours
results in total submission. You forget the world around you, and worse,
you forget yourself. Let me get you something to eat."

Caterina yelled a sentiment of gratitude as her sister's silhouette faded down the hallway. She returned to the sketch, holding the paper down with one hand as she traced a fainted outline of the animal she had been working on. The long ovals formed feathers, the abstract triangle defined a beak, and two large circles…

"Here," her sister said, handing her some water and bread, interrupting Caterina's concentration. "You shouldn't eat before bed, but if I had to guess, you probably didn't eat much today."

"Careful!" Caterina exclaimed, holding the water away from the sketch. "Thank you, so much, Safiya. I didn't eat much today, no, but I did have an apple."

"A whole apple! Come, sit on the bed. I need to get you out of that cursed chair."

Caterina sat beside her sister, taking a bite of the bread. Her sister pulled Caterina's braid to the side, untying it to revive its silkiness. Safiya's hair was dark and long like Caterina's, though she preferred styling her braids in two.

The candle flame flickered against the night's breeze that slipped through the open window as Caterina ate and Safiya braided her hair. She continued reminding Caterina of the importance of taking care of oneself, how impactful and detrimental one's unwavering focus can be.

"It's only six more days," Caterina said, wiping a crumb from the side of her mouth. "I'll sketch today, draw tomorrow, detail the next…"

"Your mind may tolerate these expenditures for a long period of time, but your body won't. What are you drawing anyway?" She stretched her neck over Caterina to peer at the graphite on the paper. "A bird?"

"An owl," Caterina said with a smile. Her sister tilted her head sideways and frowned. Caterina popped her head up to block her sister from seeing any further. "It's not done yet," she added.

"Why an owl?"

"I feel drawn to it," Caterina said. "The pun was unintentional— don't roll your eyes! Leander told me to look inward, that the idea was already inside me. At first, I was frustrated beyond words at his advice. He doesn't talk like that usually. It's an ambiguous thing to say, isn't it? I felt like I needed more direction, more assistance. Anything, really."

"It definitely looks like you need assistance," her sister joked, glancing toward the sketch again. Caterina playfully pushed her shoulder.

"But that's when I realized one of my biggest weaknesses, Safiya. My insatiability. My desire to know, to understand, everything, when it comes to art." Caterina brushed her hands together, wiping any lingering bits of bread. She reached for the cup and chugged the water as her sister finished braiding.

"And the owl represents something all-knowing? What is it, wisdom?"

"No, no," Caterina scoffed, holding the empty cup between her hands the way she held the apple earlier. "I'm not interested in such ideals or theories. That's too abstract for me. I envisioned the owl because of its ability to turn its neck and see everything surrounding it."

Safiya chuckled and nodded, taking the glass from Caterina's hands.

"If it's the practicality of the owl that interests you, then let me share a little-known fact about them," Safiya said, standing up and lifting the corner of the blanket. "Believe it or not, after an owl spends hours turning its neck around like a madman, it *rests*. It takes its time to eat and drink too. So come, my little owl, let's get you to bed. You can continue drawing in the morning."

"I'm not a child anymore, Safiya. You can't tell me what to—" But Safiya didn't listen. She blew out the candle and took it in her other hand to ensure Caterina couldn't work on the sketch. Safiya closed the window as Caterina tucked her legs under the blanket.

"Good night," Safiya said with a soft smile. "*Rest*, Caterina. Don't think about the assignment." After closing the door, Caterina listened to her sister's footsteps fading away again. She pressed her eyes shut in an effort to follow her sister's instructions.

The back of her eyelids presented her with a new blank canvas, but one much darker. She imagined her hand gliding across the black surface, layering the details of the owl. The harder she pressed her eyes to erase the imagery, the more vivid the shapes and colors would appear.

She sat up and leaned her head against the wall. As she tucked a hair behind her ear, she heard a rustling outside her window. She frowned, struggling to remember if the window was opened before. The sound emerged again, this time closer.

Carefully and quietly, Caterina pushed her blanket aside and approached her window. The midnight air grazed her skin and flowed through her hair as she removed the curtain. She looked at the moon, noticing two large, dark craters in the middle, like the eyes of an…

"Stop it!" Caterina said to herself, grabbing the windowsill. The swaying grass caught her attention until something red entered her periphery.

Caterina positioned herself against the wall, concealing herself while also feeding into her curiosity. The moonlight bounced off the stranger's tattered white dress and fiery hair, which messily lingered just beneath her shoulders.

"Gabriella?" Caterina whispered, sticking her head outside the window. Gabriella's dirty fingertips brushed the exterior wall, her uneven, long nails scratching off the loose dirt encrusted in the wall's hard texture. Her puffy red eyes met Caterina's.

"I…" Gabriella started. She dug her bare toes nervously into the damp soil beneath her. "I want to apologize."

Her greasy hair curtained her sunken cheekbones. The corner of Gabriella's mouth rose, just barely, enough to puzzle Caterina. It wasn't happiness or relief, but it wasn't anger or sadness either.

Gabriella's head shifted from side to side and nodded, as if entirely immersed in a conversation with herself. Though she had stopped twisting her ankle into the dirt, she nervously cupped both arms in comfort.

"You don't owe me an apology," Caterina said, keeping her distance from the window. "How did you know where to find me?"

"I was just walking," Gabriella replied as she pointed aimlessly around her, "and I heard your voice coming from the window. Was there someone else in the room with you? I didn't want anyone to see me, like this." Her shaky hand traced the rips of her dress.

"I understand. Well, thank you for—"

"I see what he sees in you," Gabriella interrupted. Caterina pinched the bridge of her nose as she sighed, though a feeling of sympathy immediately washed over her.

"It's really late, Gabriella…"

"Would you like to join me?" Gabriella stretched her grimy hand toward Caterina. "I feel at peace when I'm walking. There's so much to see when we look outside our paranoid minds, don't you agree?"

The moon returned to Caterina's focus as Gabriella leaned forward, extending a hand. The two craters protruded more noticeably than before, staring down at her. Caterina looked over her shoulder, gaging the improbability of a restful night while also half expecting her sister to be standing at the doorway, arms crossed disapprovingly. But her door remained closed, and as quietly as possible, Caterina slipped into her sandals and gripped the wall beside her for support.

Gabriella eagerly came closer, assisting Caterina in her escape. Gabriella's cold fingers wrapped around her hand, sending chills down her spine.

"Thank you. My name is Caterina, by the way," she said, formally extending her hand. Gabriella weakly shook it.

"I'm surprised you agreed to walk with me," Gabriella confessed as she hung her head and dragged her feet forward. "I wasn't particularly kind to you earlier."

"The world is full of surprises."

The full moon in the starless sky shone upon the two wanderers, as blades of grass grazed their feet, and the midnight air filled their lungs.

Everything reminded Caterina of her assignment: the curved leaves hanging outside the neighbors' homes looked like tiny green beaks; the layered bark on the trees rested similarly to those brown feathers she had begun sketching; and the two ever-present craters in the moon watched her walk further from her assignment.

Caterina subtly examined Gabriella's dress in an attempt to remove the assignment from her anxious mind. It had several textures. Laced material revealed itself through the holes of embroidered silk. A soft material wrapped snug around her waist and the ends of her sleeves.

"It was a gift," Gabriella said, noticing Caterina's stare. "It's not a gift anymore. It's a curse. A curse layered in memories, of what was, and what could have been. I should burn it."

Caterina's hands gripped Gabriella's worn shoulders. She gently brushed Gabriella's hair to the back and examined the dress unapologetically.

"You can't burn this," Caterina said, tracing the details. "We can fix it. Give it a second chance. Create something new."

"No, no, no, no, I don't think that's a good idea." She lowered her head to hide the snarl Caterina's kindness caused. She subtly stepped back, removing herself from Caterina's hold.

"I don't know who gave it to you, but—"

"Damian," Gabriella interjected as tears formed in her eyes. Caterina palmed her forehead.

"If he gave it to you, then it's *yours*."

A sudden burst of tears extinguished the impeding fire in Gabriella's chest as she fell to her knees and clutched the bottom of Caterina's legs. Caterina's eyes widened as she looked around in a panic, worried someone would hear them.

"Thank you!" Gabriella said, burying her muddied tears in Caterina's dress. "Thank you, ah, what a dear friend you are! I knew I wasn't crazy!" She burst into laughter before Caterina hunched over and pressed her finger against her lips, begging her to be quiet.

"You're not crazy."

Though maybe I am, Caterina thought to herself as she looked around to ensure their privacy.

"He gave me his heart," Gabriella said, stabbing her finger to her chest and staring blankly ahead. She wrapped her arm around Caterina's leg and leaned her head harder against it. Caterina tried to pull her up, but Gabriella remained grounded, if only physically.

"Let's keep walking," Caterina suggested with urgency.

"He gave it to me," Gabriella said as she started rocking. "He said he loved me. Many, many times. How many, you ask? More than anyone can count. That's all he said. Maybe that's all I heard. But he did say it, I swear! He gave me his heart. It was mine. It *is* mine. No one can have it. Not even..."

Caterina held her breath as Gabriella's blood-shot eyes looked up at her, the full moon glossing over the tears which had streamed down her cheeks.

In that moment of silence, the air seemed stiller. Not another sound was heard besides Caterina's heart beating and Gabriella's heavy panting as her chest refilled with anger.

"I don't want his heart!" Caterina insisted, raising her hands defensively. For the first time, she noticed how long and unkempt Gabriella's fingernails were.

"You reject it as if it was already offered," Gabriella said, rising. Her head hung lower than good posture would require, but her eyes tilted upward and unblinkingly at Caterina. She tucked her sharp nails into fists as she hunched over like a wolf gnarling at its prey. Caterina slowly stepped one foot behind the other.

"I'm not your enemy, Gabriella. You just called me your friend, remember? We're… friends." Caterina choked on the last word, causing Gabriella's nostrils to flare.

"Maybe I'm the problem. How could we ever be friends? I'm so quick to assert things. Ha! I don't even know you!" A crazy smile spread across Gabriella's face.

Caterina chuckled with fear, keeping her eyes glued to Gabriella's slow approach.

"I don't need to know you, however." Gabriella added, flipping away the hair that had fallen in front of her face. She brought her feet together and stood tall, stretching her neck back as she bathed her pale face in the moonlight.

"What I do know," she continued, tilting her head from side to side as if loosening the tensions which had formed in her upper body, "is that *Damian* will never get the chance to know you either."

Her head snapped back into position, eyes locked on Caterina. Caterina took off, running as fast as she could toward the nearest trees. The coarse shrubbery below her feet scratched her exposed ankles as she lunged into the woods. The lack of moonlight helped hide Caterina but hurt her ability to navigate. She kept her eyes forward until she fell. Her dirtied palms prevented her face from colliding with the soil.

A lingering branch had seized the bottom of her dress, tearing at the seams. With no hesitation, Caterina ripped herself free and continued running, her heart beating faster than ever.

She could hear Gabriella racing to catch up, screaming wildly, until suddenly, all was quiet.

Caterina held her breath as she pressed her back against the nearest tree. Sweat trickled to her chin. She looked up at the sky, enough to see those cursed craters peeping through the dark leaves above her.

She closed her eyes and directed her focus to her ears, though she was met with silence. She sighed in relief. She relaxed her shoulders as she opened her eyes, only to see the unwanted silhouette of the fiery fiend.

Caterina reached for the branch above her without hesitation, snapping it from the tree and pointing the jagged end at Gabriella.

"It's funny," Gabriella laughed, "how I've been walking for so long, but I can't remember the last time I ran, the last time so much energy flowed through me. Now, what should I do with this revived spirit?" Though she grinned, there wasn't enough light to see her teeth, giving the eerie appearance of a horizontal void slashed from ear to ear.

"Walk away," Caterina demanded. She planted her feet more firmly on the ground, steadying the branch that extended longer than her body. Gabriella clapped her hands in delight. "I mean it, Gabriella. Walk away."

"Oh, I plan to. When I'm done." Gabriella reached for a branch of equal length, closing one eye and pointing the newly-acquired weapon at Caterina's throat.

"No!" Caterina screamed as Gabriella approached with a content grin on her face. The smile fell into a scowl as Gabriella charged the stick toward Caterina's face. Caterina jerked to the side, shielding her face just in time with her branch.

The two, being of equal strength, pressed against each other's weapons, unable to push the other entirely off. Gabriella laughed and retreated a couple steps, pacing in front of Caterina, dragging her branch beside her as she calculated her next move.

Gabriella screeched as she charged once more, this time angling the branch upward as she aimed for Caterina's head. Caterina stuck her branch out sideways, blocking Gabriella's blow. The crossed sticks in the air looked like targets for either opponent, hovering over the other's face.

For every strike Gabriella forced, Caterina countered in the opposite direction, continuing to create these crosses as the hefty branches crushed against one another.

"Come on, friend," Gabriella chuckled. "How much energy do you have left? How much longer will you remain standing?" Caterina's nostrils flared as she caught her breath, keeping her eyes fastened upon Gabriella, who raised the branch above her head. Gabriella dramatically coiled her dirty fingers securely around the branch before jabbing it toward Caterina's feet.

Caterina instinctually jumped as the end of Gabriella's stick dug into the ground. Caterina aimed for the branch as she descended, pressing all her weight onto it, snapping it in half. While she steadied herself, Caterina kept her intact branch pointed at Gabriella, whose lips quivered in a growling manner.

Gabriella turned to find another stick, and while her back was turned, Caterina dropped her branch and fled deeper into the woods, not taking a single moment to look behind her.

She ran until the moonlight felt more present and the trees dispersed, surrounding her in a fuller silver glow. She was nearing the end of the wooded area, though she didn't know where she was. The sound of twigs breaking and leaves rustling behind her meant she had no time to contemplate her location. She continued forward until she reached an open field.

"Where'd you go, friend?" Gabriella called from the woods. Caterina's chest expanded and compressed as she scanned her surroundings.

With squinted eyes, she noticed a familiar ice-blue building atop the furthest hill. *Could it be?* She thought to herself. She quickly reached for another branch, this time for one that had already fallen and was easier to carry. She raced toward the building, adrenaline rising as she neared her destination.

Her feet met the recognizable soiled path that led to her beloved mentor's studio. She knocked on the door as she scrambled to find the words to explain what had transpired.

Her knocks went unanswered, and she could feel her heart in her throat.

"Leander!" Caterina called, knocking louder on the door. "Leander! Please! Open the door!" She pressed her ear to the door, awaiting footsteps. Tears congregated in the corners of her eyes as fear swam through her veins.

She locked her fingers around the doorknob, twisting it with all her might.

"Caterina?" A voice called behind her. Caterina screamed and turned around, her braid entangling itself with the branch she held in her other hand. She exhaled deeply as she saw the open door across the street, from which a woman had emerged.

"Quick!" Caterina said, tossing the branch to the side and grabbing Aluna's wrist as they raced through the front door. "We need to get inside." Aluna did not resist, and the two hurried through the doorway, closing the door behind them.

Caterina squatted, leaning her head beside the splattered mud on the wall before wiping the sweat from her forehead. Aluna returned from retrieving water, sitting beside Caterina on the poorly lit entryway floor.

"An introduction I'll never forget," Aluna said playfully. "It's nice to finally meet you."

"How did you know who I was?"

"I'm afraid our sweet Damian can't stop talking about you," Aluna responded, though her eyes glanced at the vines in the room down the hallway.

"Ah." Her smile quickly faded as she recalled Leander's absence in her time of need.

"Don't be sad about Leander," Aluna said, causing Caterina to sit up in surprise. "He isn't home. Neither is Demetrius." Aluna said the last sentence with a tint of sadness. "They'll be back by tomorrow. Until then, you're more than welcome to stay here. I can show you to Damian's room. I'm sure he wouldn't mind. I'll walk you back to your house in the morning."

"I need to be back before my sister wakes up," Caterina noted, bracing herself as she rose from the floor.

"I wake up with the sun. We can leave then, dear."

"I can explain what happened."

"No need," Aluna said, turning her back to the vines framing the closest window. She grabbed the nearest candle. "Let's get some rest."

Caterina rubbed the back of her neck as she followed Aluna down the hall. She noticed a door slightly ajar, from which an incredible amount of moonlight seeped into the hallway.

"What room is that?" Caterina asked.

"Just one of Demetrius' rooms."

Aluna closed the door as the candle's flame highlighted a large triangle engraved in the wood.

Chapter

Thirteen

emetrius arched his neck, tracing the body of the menacing tower looming over the trees. A semi-circle window with a golden glare faded in and out of view from the hovering fog. Vines hung in clusters beneath this window and wrapped the dark grey stone. The full moon shone brightly behind the tower, outlining it in an ominous silver.

"I don't remember Theo mentioning a tower," Demetrius muttered. His breathing quickened as his thoughts raced.

"I'd say twenty years is enough time to build a tower," Damian said, pulling Demetrius' sleeve forward.

"I don't remember a gate either."

Demetrius and Damian stopped their horses before their nozzles grazed the cold, iron bars. The metal structure extended beyond their visual capacities, creating the illusion of an endless barrier. Besides its grandiose radius, the gate itself stood peculiarly: some iron bars extended above the trees, poking from the ground like a crooked bottom row of teeth. The desert sand stopped where the iron bars began, protecting a long-awaited dark green terrain. The two dismounted.

"We don't have anything to tie the horses here," Damian said, twisting his body in search for something useful. He turned to Demetrius, sighing. Demetrius' body stiffened as he gripped two iron bars and pressed his face between them. The thick forestation and fog restricted his view of everything except a single path.

"Don't go anywhere," Demetrius mumbled to the horses as he pressed his fingertips against the gate's crooked latch and raised it. Damian shrugged his shoulders apologetically to the horses.

The momentum of the gate door opening parted some of the fog. In the newly found clearance, a long, dirt pathway led to a shadowed building. Fog swirled down the lane like the lingering remains of lost travelers, flowing mindlessly up and down the suggested route. The path was contoured by serpentine tree trunks, with branches sporadically splitting the silvery mist.

"Which way should we go?" Damian joked, eyeing the path.

Only two sounds met Demetrius's eardrums: his shortened breathing and his increased heartbeat. If another sign of life existed, its sound waves were lost amid the fog.

"Let's just find Theo and travel back." The weight of the pocketed ruby ring became more apparent with every step. "This wasn't the welcome I expected."

The two quietly began their journey down the path, coiled by the persistent fog. Demetrius' shirt no longer radiated as bright as before, contaminated by the ever-present grey.

Demetrius' attention never diverted from the tower, while Damian's head pivoted in every direction until he noticed the fog to their right fading. The opening fascinated Damian, particularly when a glistening object caught his attention. He grabbed Demetrius's shoulder and pointed.

The object of their focus was on the other side of a row of trees. Demetrius hesitated, but Damian, with his good arm, grabbed Demetrius and pulled him off the path.

Bending under low hanging branches and stepping over bulging roots, the two found themselves on the edge of a circular, grassy respite. A hundred square tombstones neatly arranged in a tight, even grid bathed in moonlight. Damian took the first steps, dubiously approaching the closest tombstone. Its speckled brown and rugged surface at first gave no indication of any inscriptions, but as his index finger traced the top border of the bumpy stone, he felt the engraving of two letters.

"*What* is this?" Demetrius yelled.

"*Who* is this?" Damian asked in a softer tone, continuing to glide his index finger back and forth across the lettering. *M.R.* "Are these initials?" He stretched his neck toward the tops of the other stones, all engraved as well. Damian grabbed his chest as nausea rose from the pit of his stomach.

"This is probably some artistic gesture," Demetrius remarked. "Theo came here alone."

"So you don't think people are really buried here?"

"Look how close these things are," Demetrius observed, pointing to the hand-sized amount of space between each stone. "How could anyone be buried here? At least not horizontally…"

Demetrius shuddered at the surfacing thoughts. Images of his father's tombstone flashed before his eyes, particularly the amount of daffodils Aluna had planted around it. Over the last twenty years, visitors would see more blossoming yellow petals than the tombstone itself, which is just how Demetrius preferred it.

The next thought was of Leander's sketch of his father's statue, the one to replace the tombstone altogether. Sadness overcame Demetrius as he pictured Leander working tirelessly on the project, unable to grasp the current state of Leander's mind. Demetrius leaned against the stone which Damian had observed, unintentionally placing his palm directly over the engraving.

"Are you serious?" Damian asked as he strolled to the other side of the grid, breaking Demetrius train of thoughts. "This is just some demented art statement? It serves no purpose other than… what? Aesthetics? It can't be. How? And *these*? Someone finds *these* appealing?"

"Yes, I suppose. Maybe." Demetrius slammed his eyes shut to pause his speculations. He squatted to get a better look of the tombstone's face. He exhaled deeply at the sight of his crooked reflection in the shiny, bumpy surface. He ran his fingers through his hair, using his perspiration to secure his pulled-back curls. "Theo's eccentric. I wouldn't be surprised if this was all his doing. For what, or perhaps for whom, we don't know. He'll explain what it means, I'm sure."

"What if he's not alone, though?" Damian asked as he continued observing the initials. "What if all the misfits come here?"

Demetrius looked back at his reflection, and his eyes widened. He sprang up to observe the other tombstones, failing to find a single speck of dirt in their jagged crevices.

And Demetrius knew Theo was not one to worry about cleanliness.

"We need to get Theo," Demetrius said insistently.

"Wait for me!"

As Demetrius rushed to the path, Damian's eyes locked on something familiar. His jaw dropped as he recognized the ornate "T" engraved on one of the tombstones.

"Demetrius, come back!"

Demetrius turned around to see Damian pointing urgently at a tombstone. When he saw Theo's classic stamp, he sighed a breath of relief.

"See? He clearly made this whole thing," Demetrius said, nodding to himself as his hand wiped excess sweat from his brow. "And we were worried for a moment there!"

Demetrius noticed Damian shifting uncertainly side to side, so he laughed to ease the tension, shaking his head at Theo's signature. "Like I said Damian, we can't let the paranoia get to us. Artists have a different way of seeing, a different way of being. There's no point in trying to understand."

"Right."

"It's all just art," Demetrius stated, pressing his lips together as he looked over his shoulder. "Nothing to be scared of."

Once they emerged from the row of trees and returned to the path, the fog quickly covered their previous entrance to the tombstones, swallowing the possibility of reentry. The journey along the path remained silent, while the two familiar sounds, his heavy breathing and increasing heartbeat, pounded upon Demetrius's eardrums.

The fog thickened as they traveled forward. Even the looming tower above them seemed more of an impression than a reality as the fog dismally opaqued. Damian waved his arms rapidly back and forth until he felt the pain from his wound. The swirling clouds of grey wrapped around his bandaged forearm, mocking his failure.

"Look!" Demetrius said. A reddish-brown outline of another person stood before them in the distance. Damian squinted his eyes but could not see to what Demetrius was referring. "Theo!" Demetrius started running forward, with Damian following blindly behind him.

Adrenaline rushed through his veins as his vision tunneled, unable to see anything except for the mystery figure.

As Demetrius got closer, the outline of the man doubled. Demetrius' brows furrowed as his brain rattled with the question of who the slightly shorter companion was.

Suddenly, Demetrius felt a burning pain in his right foot and the sound of metal rang in his ears. He had tripped over something and fell to the ground, clutching his foot in pain. Damian kneeled down immediately.

"What was that?" Demetrius asked, closing his eyes tightly to tolerate the pain. The fog was too concentrated for Damian to see anything, so he stretched his arms out and brushed his hands along the cold soil until something colder and slicker touched his fingertips. He crawled to the object and ran his hands over it.

"I can't see with all this fog!" Damian complained. As if on command, the fog in front of him vanished, and Damian gasped as another eye stared back at him. A man's head laid before him, staring blankly at the sky.

Damian screamed until he realized the head was made of bronze. Demetrius inquired about the discovery, and at a loss for words, Damian tried to show Demetrius. His face wrinkled as he used all his might to lift the object with his good arm, but it remained too heavy. He pulled his sleeves back and pushed on the chiseled object, rolling it to Demetrius for closer examination.

"Could this be part of what you saw in the distance, perhaps?" Damian asked, catching his breath and pointing aimlessly ahead of them. "A statue?"

Demetrius jolted his head backwards to see if the two figures were still there. The fog had evaporated in that direction, showing a statue of two men wrapped by a misty screen.

"I guess so," Demetrius said, still clutching his foot and keeping his head down to hide his reddening face. Damian rolled the head over and wiped off the excess dirt until he could see the details of the face.

"He's got your nose," Damian chuckled, raising the corner of his mouth. "And your eyes. And your mouth… wait…" His smile vanished. Demetrius's eyes widened.

"He made a statue of me?" Demetrius jumped up, forgetting the splitting pain in his foot. He stumbled toward the statue with intense curiosity. "He made a statue of *us*?"

The bronze statue portrayed two men standing next to each other, with one of them missing a head. Even without a face, the man stood in a powerful stance with his shoulders squared and arms casually, but confidently, resting on the sides. The body of the man next to him was twisted slightly to the left, while his hidden face looked over his shoulder as far back as possible, as if something behind him was more urgent. The left side of this second man's torso was missing. Damian circled the statue in search for more missing body parts, though he found none.

"We need to reattach my head," Demetrius said, causing Damian to stop in his tracks.

"We need to... what? Why?"

Damian watched as Demetrius limped to fetch the bronze item. Damian rolled his eyes and went over to help him, but the head would not budge from the ground. Damian, with the sleeve of his good arm still rolled up, kneeled to roll it like before, but this time the head remained anchored.

"We should just leave it," Damian grumbled as he restrained himself from kicking the cursed object. "It clearly doesn't want to be moved." Demetrius pursed his lips together, looking back and forth from the statue to the head on the ground.

"I suppose you're right."

"Let's just keep going. Like you said, Theo will explain it."

Damian took a final glimpse at the gleaming statue and noticed that the second man with the partly missing torso had a ring on his finger. He opened his mouth to ask something, but quickly decided against it.

The fog returned to ensure nothing would spark their imagination further.

The last thing Damian noticed was the leg of the second man in the statue was raised slightly above the ground, as if it was supposed to be standing upon something. The fog finished wrapping itself around the statue and removed its presence from the pathway.

After another small period of silence, the tower's glowing semicircle window burned through the night sky. Demetrius extended his arm toward Damian, stopping him abruptly. The fog began evaporating in slow waves, like a curtain parting to reveal the setting of a new scene.

The tower was made of grey stones, each a different size and protruding non-congruently. In a scattered spiral pattern, small, rectangular windows disturbed the stones, displaying the darkness within. Some of these windows were covered by strings of vines, falling haphazardly from the semicircle window to the ground.

Below the tower stood an average manor. Unlike its protruding addition, the manor's neatly arranged grey stones were visibly a lighter grey than the tower. The front part of the home protruded further than the left and right sides, creating a triangular effect.

Demetrius, still limping from the collision with his bronzed self, leaned on Damian to combat the front steps. As Demetrius reached the top step, he gazed toward the window of the tower. A set of fingers, protruding from a long, scarlet sleeve, slowly emerged from the windowpane. Demetrius held his breath, waiting for the familiar face to appear, but instead, the fingers glided around its edges before the flickering light vanished, indicating the curtain had closed.

"Theo!" Demetrius shouted, cupping his hands over his mouth. Damian grabbed Demetrius securely to steady his balance. As Demetrius inhaled deeply to call out again, two raindrops fell directly into his excited eyes. He blinked feverishly though the burning sensation only intensified.

Damian looked at Demetrius with a raised eyebrow.

"He's probably coming down to greet us," Demetrius said with a tight lip, rubbing his eyes. He pointed toward the front door, forcing Damian's attention away from his discomfort.

The front door was massive, large enough for the guests to have comfortably entered side-by-side. Chiseled on its wooden surface was the familiar and ornate "T." Its swirls and edges were deeply carved, highlighting the thickness of the front door. The bottom of the door was also engraved, though less intricately. A simple "welcome" was written. Strangely, or intentionally, only the e's in "welcome" were somewhat legible, appearing as two half-closed eyes unimpressed by the guests' appearances.

"We're definitely in the right place," Damian said with a smirk. Another raindrop fell onto Demetrius' face, right below his eye, rolling down his cheek.

Chapter

Fourteen

eander and Mesa reached the end of the forest, greeted by an endless desert and blinding full moon. Beneath Mesa were two parallel trails of prints, and Leander breathed a sigh of relief. Mesa followed the prints, accelerating as she adjusted to the new terrain.

The desert's stillness was prominent, amplifying Leander's paranoia. He looked to the moon, its perfectly round face freckled with dark craters around its rim, like the haunting sundial refusing to release Leander of its burning grip. Leander tucked his chin, hiding his face from the menacing orb of mocking light.

The bare trees scattered throughout the sandy hills looked like skeleton hands reaching out to capture the two travelers, and even though Mesa kept her distance, Leander unconsciously shifted away from the fragile figures as they passed each tree.

The trails of horse prints, once parallel, now separated as they winded between the skeletal obstacles.

Demetrius should never have taken this journey, Leander thought to himself. *Not for my own sake, but for his. He is not equipped mentally, physically, nor emotionally.* Mesa continued alongside one of the trails, dodging the trees that blocked their paths.

"Where did these come from? Trees were never planted in the desert," Leander said to Mesa, frowning. "Did the desert merge with the forest? No, what am I saying?" Leander eyed the nearest tree, grabbing Mesa in fear as what little color remained in his face disappeared. Twisted branches had formed two words: The End.

Leander blinked feverishly, but the words were clearly there. He raised a shaking finger toward the sign, but no words escaped his trembling bottom lip. A stinging sensation pierced his heart as flashbacks of Theo's writings surfaced.

He remembered walking into Theo's room to persuade him once more to take the ring and commit himself to the life of art. Theo was seated shirtless on the floor, his black pants proficiently hiding traces of graphite. He faced a wall with a pencil in one hand and a book in the other. His scribbles depicted the outline of three women with dark short hair standing in a triangular position. The setting sun sparkled across his perspiring skin, glistening.

"What is this?" Leander asked.

"I'm bringing this story to life," Theo said, paying no attention to Leander's presence, though he stretched out the book in Leander's direction. "Have you read this? It's a masterpiece, truly. And to think it remains buried between pages, flat and forgotten."

Leander rushed to Theo, snatching the pencil from his other hand. He stood over his former pupil, his former friend, fighting the single tear attempting to escape.

"You forfeited your right to create. Among many other things," Leander added in a lower tone.

"No," Theo said, standing to meet Leander at eye level. "I freed myself from creating under *your* conditions."

"These are not only my conditions. The Artist Code forbids you to recreate another's work, you know that. This is considered replication."

"Only artists live by the Artist Code."

"*Art* lives by the Artist Code," Leander corrected, raising a finger in the air. "Art is one's expression."

"Constricted expression, it seems." Theo crossed the room, carefully stepping over piles of books, to retrieve another pencil. The sun bounced off Theo's broad shoulders and black hair, but not as brightly as it bounced off his smile when he twirled the new pencil between his fingers. "Who would succumb to constricted expression?"

"Protected expression, Theo. If you could just—"

"If you could just leave me to do what I please, I would be so very grateful." Theo turned his back to Leander, raised his pencil to the wall and pressed the graphite onto the stone.

"Why has such a darkness overcome you?" Leander asked. Orange hues graced Theo's dark skin, accentuating the rich shadows along the curvature of his spine and arms.

"Darkness?" Theo scoffed. "Don't your eyes burn from constantly seeking the sun? Or do you feel as though you've become the sun itself?" Theo shielded his eyes from Leander, chuckling at his own mockery.

"If I am the sun, you, Theo, remain nothing more than the moon." Leander spoke through gritted teeth as the sun set behind Theo, gradually engulfing the two in caliginosity. "And let me remind you, the moon is *nothing* without the sun."

Theo amusingly snorted as he rose to face Leander. His height eclipsed Leander in his shadow; their profiles were so close, Theo need only to whisper. His intense stare never strayed from Leander's pale blue eyes.

"The moon was no *thing* to begin with." Theo's breath touched Leander's skin, and his words pierced Leander's heart. "The moon will always have a dark side, invisible to the high and mighty sun. My existence isn't contingent to yours, any more than yours is to mine. You're free now, can't you see? Free from having to shine your light upon me for others to see only the parts you permit. You can live by whatever code you choose, Leander. Choose protection, if that's what your heart desires.

Be the center of your own universe. Tell me though, if memory serves me correctly, you aren't permitted to destroy someone else's work. Correct?"

"Theo," Leander said softly though his clenched fists trembled, "will you *please* put the pencil down?"

"You didn't answer my question," Theo said, calmly returning to his drawing, rubbing his finger in a circular motion to spread the graphite in a shaded region. Leander exhaled defeatedly.

"I cannot destroy your work."

"That'll be all, then. You'll close the door on your way out, yes?"

The appearance of the memory transformed Leander's fear into anger. His heart continued pounding, but now fire pumped through his veins. His hand had stopped shaking.

"The end? We shall see," Leander said, his lips tightening. He pointed forward and, though Mesa resisted initially, the two continued, faster, toward their destination.

"His story has already ended," Leander asserted, "and I am here to finally close the book."

Chapter

Fifteen

emetrius banged on the door, competing with the sound of sudden pouring rain. The darkened clouds cloaked the top of the tower, right above the window. Rain streamed from the windowsill down the tower, like inconsolable tears, drowning the innocent hanging vines in sorrow. Demetrius tried knocking again, positioning himself close to the door to shield himself from the downpour.

Damian, protecting his bandaged arm from the rain, kicked the bottom of the door with all his might. The sound of howling wind consumed the space around them, muting their efforts.

"Theo!" Demetrius shouted against the roaring sounds of the atmosphere. His response came from the sky: a lightning bolt jolted toward them with such force that both men ducked. Without hesitation, Damian took a few steps back and charged toward the door, twisting the doorknob and slamming himself against the wooden surface. The weight of the door magnified the screeching sound it made as it dragged across the stone floor in the entry way. The two men stumbled into the manor, closing the door just as thunder struck.

The two stood in the eerily silent room as the storm outside grew louder. Stone walls and flooring added to frigidness hanging in the air. The windows in front of them showed the gusting winds forcing the shrubbery and its branches against the curtains, like skeleton hands clawing to escape their suffering. Water droplets dripped from their clothes as they looked around the dark room for a candle.

Lightening pierced through the tears in the curtains, providing enough light for the arrivers to see a large staircase leading to a second-floor balcony, where the outlines of multiple doors became visible. The stairwell was wider at the bottom than the top, with a carpeted trail flowing to the main door. Although Demetrius couldn't see every detail, the faded design was floral in theme, with hints of Theo's favorite color splattered throughout it.

Damian nudged Demetrius' side and pointed to the chandelier above them. Spiderwebs wrapped tightly around each candlestick like thin, coiled twine, restricting its utilization.

"It looks like the storm followed us inside," Damian whispered, making a cloud-like shape with his finger as he traced the outline of the chandelier. The webs and dust hid the chandelier behind a fog of greyness. "All that's missing is the rain."

As he finished his sentence, tiny spiders fell from their posts in the chandelier, winding down to get a closer look at the intruders. Damian ran to the closest corner, cowering down. Demetrius exhaled impatiently.

"Theo!" Demetrius yelled, limping toward the nearest pillar of the staircase and leaning against it. The echo in the room amplified the desperation in his voice.

"Where is he?"

Damian peeking from behind his hands to see if the spiders had returned to their giant nest. He covered his face again when he realized the critters remained in mid-air, some swinging in his direction, teasing his sanity.

"We'll just have to get him ourselves," Demetrius said, taking the first step as he gripped the railing with white knuckles.

The sound of a child's giggle startled both of them. They looked at each other with widened eyes as the sound of a baby squealing continued.

"Com-pah-nee?" the child squealed. The color from Demetrius' face faded as he retreated toward Damian, keeping his eyes in the direction from where the sound was coming. Damian separated two of his fingers and peered through them, staring at the floor ahead of him, expecting a child to crawl from the shadows. He knitted his eyebrows as he listened more intently, shifting his gaze from the ground to the nearest wall.

From where they stood, they could only see the protruding golden frame of a large canvas nailed to the wall, hiding the canvas. Another squeal confirmed the canvas to be the source of the noise. Avoiding the spiders dangling in the center of the room, the two walked alongside the walls until they stood in the spectator's view of this canvas.

"Com-pah-nee!" The boy giggled, clapping his hands together. He grabbed the wooden toy boat by his side and shook it, showing off his prized possession.

On the wall was a golden-framed canvas, large enough to portray a realistically proportioned little boy sitting on a carpeted floor with a toy boat now in his mouth. His sparkling dark eyes were partly covered by long, dark strands of hair, but nothing could hide the wide toothless grin on his face. The sleeve of his oversized white shirt fell off his shoulder as he raised his other hand to wave at the men. Damian raised his hand a little, making the boy gleefully smile and wave excitedly.

The canvas didn't show much else. Impressions of furniture could be identified in the background, but all the details and attention were clearly given to the subject.

"Nothing scary about a little kid, is there?" Damian asked as he relaxed his shoulders. A tear formed in the corner of Demetrius' eye.

"That's not just any kid," Demetrius said, sniffling. "That's Theo."

Damian held his breath as he cautiously approached the canvas.

"That's Theo, with his toy boat," Demetrius explained, hypnotized by the canvas. "And that boat... That boat looks just like the one my father had."

"I didn't know he had a boat."

"I remember the day my father took us on a boat ride," Demetrius said, tilting his head while maintaining an unblinking and unwavering stare. He stepped closer to the canvas. "Theo liked it so much, which was unusual considering he didn't enjoy the sea. My father gave him that toy for his birthday, but not when he was a child. I forget how old he'd turned... 15? Theo laughed at the gift, saying that it suited only his inner child, but he would keep the gift regardless. My father tried to explain the meaning behind sailing..." More tears congregated on his lower lashes as he tried his hardest to remember.

"I forget exactly what he said when he gifted it to Theo," Demetrius said, stifling another sniffle. "Something about how vast the world is. Look at him! He must have really loved that toy boat." Demetrius raised his hand, and in a mirror-like fashion, the little boy raised his hand too. Demetrius raised the other, and the little boy, though gripping his toy tightly, reflected his gesture.

"Demetrius..." Damian said, approaching him gently and putting a hand on his shoulder. "It's just a painting."

"I know, but it's so... realistic. Even that freckle on his nose." Demetrius bent forward until his face was almost touching the canvas. He pointed his finger at the boy's face. The boy reached out until his palm couldn't extend further, as if it had touched an invisible glass.

"That's odd," Damian said, examining the manner in which his little fingerprints squished against thin air. "Correct me if I'm wrong, but don't the live canvases at home come out of their canvases? Aren't we able to touch them? Caterina told me they wouldn't feel like the subject itself, just graphite or whatever it is artists use."

"Yes, remains of graphite would smear onto our fingers," Demetrius responded. "Or in this case, paint." He tapped the corner of the canvas, perplexed. "This appears to be an actual canvas, though."

"D- D- De-..." the little boy stuttered as he extended his boat to Demetrius. Demetrius' heart sank.

"Is he trying to say my na—"

"D... Dead!" The boy fell back in utmost joy at his minor verbal accomplishment.

Demetrius eyes widened, and the two quickly exchanged worried looks.

"It's just a painting," Damian repeated, placing an emphasis on each word. "Plus, even if this is a living portrait of baby Theo, how could he possibly recognize you as you are now?"

Demetrius waved again to get the boy's attention who bolted upright, staring happily at Demetrius.

"What's your name, little one?"

The boy shifted glances between the two spectators until he picked up the toy and put it back in his mouth. He crawled to the limit of the canvas, again stretching his arm as far as he could before his little fingers squished against the invisible restraint.

"It's not even a live canvas!" Damian asserted. "He's not real. Maybe this is the step before the artists bring the canvas to life? Maybe Theo just needs to finish the background? Maybe this is supposed to stay flat?"

"Maybe we should stop guessing," Demetrius said, shifting his focus from the canvas to the staircase. He opened his mouth to call for his friend, but instead, lightning and thunder struck. Demetrius heard whimpering but couldn't decipher from which of the boys it came.

The only light remaining in the room came from the little candle painted in the canvas behind the boy, sitting on the edge of an impression of a table.

"If only we could reach in and grab it," Damian commented.

"You won't be needing that," a woman's voice said from behind the staircase. The men immediately pivoted, waiting for their eyes to adjust to the darkness. A golden glow grew on the furthest wall until the side of a woman's face appeared between one of the staircase's railings. Her single eye darted back and forth between the two visitors.

"You said Theo lived alone," Damian whispered from the corner of his mouth.

"I think an introduction is in order," Demetrius said, raising his arms defensively as he breathed heavily. "Will you come out?"

"You must be Demetrius," she said calmly, eyeing his yellow shirt.

"Yes." Demetrius lowered his arms, extending one toward her though she remained tucked in the shadows across the room. "And you are?"

"Janus."

She placed the candlestick on the table beside the closest wall, creating a golden outline behind her while maintaining invisibility in the front. The recurring lightning sneaking through the ripped curtains highlighted her light hair tied in a tight bun and the slightest evidence of a narrow figure draped in oversized clothing. She positioned herself strangely, inorganically, intentionally, concealing the left side of her body. Her right side, however, showed the side of a high cheekbone, an elongated neck, and long, delicate fingers gripping a cup.

"Nice to meet you," Damian said, his voice deepening suddenly. "I'm Damian."

Demetrius shot Damian a disapproving look, but Damian's focus was elsewhere.

"We weren't expecting another guest."

Demetrius' ears perked up, and a wave of relief washed over him.

"We? You mean, you and Theo?"

"But of course," Janus said. Demetrius arched his neck in relief, grinning widely.

"If I may," Damian started, stepping forward. Janus immediately retreated, keeping her distance though she was as far as she could be. "Are you Theo's wife?"

"His what?"

"His wife."

"What is a wife?"

Demetrius returned his head to its normal position, his smile turning into a worried frown. He looked over at Damian, who had his hand on his chest and his lips slightly parted.

"I think I'm in love," Damian whispered.

The baby from the portrait cooed, waving his toy boat in the air. Angered by the lack of attention received, the boy threw the toy boat, only for it to land in front of him.

"I prepared one cup of water," Janus said. "If I would've known someone else was coming…"

"If I would've known someone like you would be here," Damian interjected. He hid his bandaged arm behind his back as he shot Janus a charming smile.

"Enough," Demetrius said, holding his arm out toward Damian. Lightning struck again, and Janus turned away, securing her face from the stark white light. In that instant, a blurred shadow ran past the windows.

Since Janus had turned away, she too had seen the figure. Her eyes darted toward the door in the corner of the room, and as it remained closed, she slowly exhaled.

"Could you do me a favor?" Janus asked.

"Happily," Damian responded.

"In the kitchen, that door right there, yes, there is still some fresh water in a large jug. You can't miss it. Could you pour yourself some? We'll wait for you here, before we make our way up the tower." Her voice was tender, yet ominous and distant.

"I'll go with you," Demetrius said.

"You don't need to," Janus insisted. "I have your water right here." She extended her arm and lifted the cup in proximity to her eye, securing Demetrius' glance. The orange glow from the candle flowed down her sleeve to the clay cylinder, highlighting the invitation.

"Thank you," Demetrius said, rubbing the back of his neck, "but I won't let Damian go anywhere alone."

"I think I'll be alright," Damian chuckled. "Where did you say the kitchen was, dear? Behind this door?" Damian pointed his thumb to the door past the canvas of the little boy, and Janus nodded.

"We'll wait for you right here," Janus repeated.

The candle from the canvas provided enough light for Damian to find the doorknob, and as the door closed behind him, silence fell over the room, with only the sound of pouring rain accompanying Demetrius' pounding heart.

Demetrius and Janus stood at opposite ends of the room, with the staircase directly between them and the spiderwebbed chandelier observing their standoff.

"He hasn't stopped talking about you," Janus said softly. "I feel as though I already know you."

A strong ping struck Demetrius' heart.

"You don't know how delighted I am to hear that," he said, wrinkling his forehead downward as he twisted his mouth to the side, showing anything but happiness.

"You seem nervous, Demetrius."

Demetrius lowered his shoulders and lifted his chin, forcing a smile. It quickly disappeared as his eyes traveled across the room, landing atop of the staircase. A defeated sigh escaped his nostrils.

"I wouldn't say nervous. I just… expected a different reunion."

"Expectations are the demise of existence," Janus said, sinking her body further into the shadows. "What are expectations but false senses of security regarding our understanding of the past? Why are we burdened with the desire to project what will be? Why are we never satisfied with what is? I'll tell you why, because we can't accept what *was* as what *once* was, and not what continues to be."

"I see you and Theo have gotten close," Demetrius said with a small laugh. "I hope this isn't too forward, but how do you know Theo? How did you end up… here?" Demetrius again scanned the room and unconsciously patted his sweaty palms against his pants as he braced himself, brushing against the ring in his pocket.

"That's a very good question. I feel as though I have always known him."

"A strange response," Demetrius noted with a frown, "for I have actually always known him."

"I never claimed to know him more than you do. I suppose for the duration of *his* life, you have always known him. In relation to *myself*, though, I hardly remember a life before him."

"Where were you before you came here?" Demetrius asked, stealing a glance at the closed kitchen door.

"I wasn't anywhere. Or if I was, I don't remember. Does that matter?"

Beads of sweat formed below Demetrius' hairline as his breathing hardened. Janus stood like an out of place statue, moving her head only in contemplation of questions before which she'd never been asked.

"Demetrius, are you alright?"

"Yes, of course," Demetrius said, choking on the last word. "Tell me more about you."

"I suppose it's only fair, as I already know *so much* about you," she responded. Demetrius closed his eyes as if trying to wake up from a nightmare. When he opened them, she was still standing in the same location. The candlelight only extended slightly in front of her, and he wondered if she could even see him standing in the shadows, until he remembered the miniature candle in the painting behind him.

Sweat dripped down his face as his eyes locked above him once more. He fought the urge to run, to find Theo for himself, to grab him by the robe and demand an explanation for this atrocious reunion. His blood boiled as tears converged in the corners of his eyes. Flashes of the disturbing fog, the eerie graveyard, the broken statue, the looming tower, and now Janus only infuriated Demetrius more.

He took a deep breath and relaxed his hands, believing that Theo's intentions had to be good. He again felt the ring in his pocket. He patted it and nodded to himself.

"I'm not sure it is I who you want to know about," Janus said. "I'll take you to Theo as soon as Damian returns. Would you like your water?" Though she offered the cup again, her feet remained grounded. A loud *bang* from the kitchen broke the momentary silence in the room. Demetrius whipped his head in that direction and called out Damian's name but received no response.

"I'm not thirsty, actually," Demetrius lied. *Maybe she's not moving toward me because she can't see me*, he thought to himself.

Demetrius gradually and discreetly tiptoed toward the kitchen door. Though he remained facing Janus, he felt for the doorknob behind his back. Once his perspired fingers wrapped around the handle, he pulled it down and leaned against the door to open it.

The locked door tested Demetrius' lucidity. He pushed his weight against the door as he fiddled harder with the doorknob, though nothing worked.

"Where did you send Damian?" Demetrius shrieked from across the room. The echo repeated his unanswered inquiry.

Lightning struck one final time, and in the flashing light, Janus had failed to hide the left side of her body. If any color had resided in Demetrius, it had completely disappeared as he stared in horror at the woman in front of him.

Chapter

Sixteen

Aluna peered inside Damian's bedroom, leaning her caramel curls against the doorframe as Caterina slid past her. Similar to the other rooms in the house, the furnishings were minimal. A narrow bed faced the doorway, and beside it was a window wrapped in viridian vines. Caterina hurried to the window and quickly closed the curtain. She moved some of the vines away from the frame, ensuring none of them perished in the process.

"We should make sure all the windows are closed." Caterina shuddered at the recollection of Gabriella.

Check the parameters of the property, Aluna told the vines. She smiled warmly at Caterina and nodded.

"I don't mind sleeping on the couch," Caterina said as she sat uncomfortably on the edge of Damian's bed.

"If that's what you prefer, so be it. Lately Damian hasn't been staying here though. The room wouldn't be so tidy if he had."

Caterina, too exhausted to theorize where Damian had been laying his head at night, collapsed onto the bed and groaned. Aluna crossed the room and sat beside her, patting her knee encouragingly.

161

The property is clear, the vines reported.

"You need to get some rest," Aluna said. Caterina covered her face, though she couldn't cover the soft sobs escaping from the gaps of her graphite-covered fingers. Aluna's bottom lip protruded "Unless there's something you'd like to talk about?"

"I don't understand what's going on!" Caterina cried, rolling over toward Aluna. "Nothing makes sense today. I knew I was going to be anxious for the final assignment, but this level of uncertainty I'm feeling— this *overwhelming* amount of uncertainty— can't be because of the assignment."

"Of course, it isn't. Nothing is ever isolated in that way."

Caterina tilted her head back, restricting the stream of tears.

"Why are you holding back, dear?" Aluna scrunched her brows together as she gently tipped Caterina's head to its normal position. "The cure to eliminating any overwhelming feeling is not to restrict its flow." Aluna wiped a tear from Caterina's cheek. "You say you don't understand what's happening, and that's because you are stopping yourself from immersing in the totality of each moment."

Caterina raised an eyebrow as she suppressed a sniffle.

"I remember when Demetrius was grieving over his father, how lost he was. He was barely sleeping, barely eating, barely talking." Aluna looked up at the ceiling, exhaling at the painful memories. "When he did speak, he would only ask everyone around him what he should do. I think he was just asking himself aloud, for his eyes glazed over every response he received. Leander, too, was of no help."

"What did you tell him?"

"Not much," Aluna said, frowning, "because what was there to say? His attention was on the situation, and of the situation, nothing could be said."

"What happened to his father, if I may ask?"

The vines bordering the window curled inward like perked, attentive ears.

162

"We still don't know exactly," Aluna said, placing her hands on her knees and shifting her weight forward as she shook her head. "It was the day of Theo's graduation, or at least it was supposed to be. I've never been to the Academy, as botanists study at the Atrium, but from my understanding there's a specific room where ceremonies are held, yes?"

Caterina nodded.

"It's called The Closing," Caterina said. "None of us know what it looks like until we've finished our program. Then all our friends and family are invited to the room on our last day. There's allegedly another room, behind it, where students meet with their mentors and receive an item that officially awards them with entrance into their respective fields."

"I suppose it was in this room the murder happened."

Caterina clutched her heart.

"*Murder?*"

"Myron, Demetrius' father, was laying there, face-down, with a knife in his back in this adjacent room."

The tears in Caterina's eyes vanished as she held her breath, paralyzed with fear and anticipation.

We've detected someone approaching the home, the vines informed Aluna.

Aluna, not wanting to alarm Caterina further, placed her hand upon Caterina's knee and nodded deeply.

"I'll return soon," Aluna said, rising. "I'd like to get some water before I continue. I sense we might not be getting much sleep tonight. But that's alright. Would you like me to bring you some, too?"

"I'll come with you." Caterina sprang up from the bed, but Aluna shook her head.

"No, no. Stay here, dear, and lay your head for a little. I'll be back before you know it."

The woman is getting closer, the vines said.

Lock yourselves around the curtain, Aluna responded. *Ensure Caterina can't open it.*

Aluna left the room but didn't close the door behind her. The candles in the hallway needed replacing, for the wicks barely stood beyond the rim of their holdings.

Who is this woman? Aluna asked as she paced the hallway, staring attentively ahead.

She walks unusually, taking great strides and bending to all sides with outstretched arms. She looks as though she is on the hunt.

Aluna stepped into the living room, where the window oversaw the front lawn and part of Leander's studio. There was no one in sight, yet Aluna's eyes remained fastened on the parametric hedges.

Can we close that gap, please? She asked. From the hedges spiraled new branches, quickly intertwining to form a protective barrier around the house. They proceeded to grow vertically, too, preventing anyone from peeking over them. *Thank you. Did I leave any of the windows open?*

Only the kitchen window.

The kitchen was immersed in moonlight as Aluna entered it. She retrieved the necessities to pour the water. From the window she saw the corner of the table outside, around which they had all discussed the arrival of Theo's letter. She sighed deeply, picturing Demetrius sitting in the chair, beaming with joy.

She balanced herself on her toes as she stretched her neck further, noticing for the first time the absence of the cursed scarlet envelope. Her eyes squinted as she recalled Leander's departure. *Could Leander read the letter?*

Indeed, the vines responded.

Her eyebrows rose. She placed her hand on the counter and crossed her ankles as she leaned to the side. Her curls hid her worried eyes.

Where did Leander go? Aluna asked.

In the same direction as Demetrius and Damian.

She turned her head back to the table outside.

She'd been tending to her garden when she received the news of Myron twenty-one years ago. Theo had rushed into their yard, trampling the nursery Aluna had just planted, screaming for Demetrius. Before Aluna could ask what had transpired, Demetrius emerged from the doorway and rushed toward Theo.

~

"It's Myron," Theo screeched through gasps and wails. Tears mixed with the blood oozing from a scratch swelling beneath his eye. "Quick! Hurry! Aluna, bring everything! We need to save him!"

Aluna rushed to the back of the garden where she stored her remedies, pocketing as much as she could before having to lift the crate of remaining supplies.

What happened? She asked the vines.

We do not know. They have silenced those of us in the vicinity of the Academy.

Silenced? Since when? How?

They painted coverings on our leaves, Aluna. On our eyes. One would not know we are painted; the layers are transparent to those looking at us, but through them we cannot see.

The vines closest to her wilted downward.

I'm sorry to hear that, Aluna said through gritted teeth. *We'll fix it.*

Aluna grabbed the paintbrushes necessary for every type of wound and stuffed them into her pocket. She paused briefly before pocketing a different kind of paintbrush, one that would assist in dissolving the abhorrent prison the artists had imposed onto the plants.

Are there any horses available? Aluna asked. *Or will we be walking to the Academy?*

All the horses are already at the Academy for the graduation ceremony.

Aluna shook her head as she gripped the crate of remedies and sprinted back to the men. As she turned a corner, the weight of the crate pushed her too far sideways; thorns ripped through her olivecolored sleeves, leaving several deep gashes on her arm. She winced in pain as she ran to her now-husband.

Demetrius had both hands on Theo's shoulders, shaking him for answers. Tears dripped onto Demetrius' shirt as Theo sobbed, unable to speak. Aluna placed the crate on the table beside them, tore off part of her sleeve, and with her other hand and teeth, wrapped the cloth tightly around the wound. Blood had trickled down her arm, staining not only her skin but the gold bracelets dangling from her wrist.

"Where's Leander?" Demetrius asked, clutching Theo's shoulder tightly.

"He's there, he's there," Theo said, shaking his head. "He won't move, can't move."

"Is he hurt?"

"Not physically." Theo covered his face and cried louder into his hands. Demetrius clutched the crate.

Theo, with hands soaked from tears, grabbed some of the jars to lighten the weight. Aluna hid her wound as she wiped the excess blood away and informed them that all the horses were already taken.

"No," Theo said, pointing to a black horse in the distance. He put his fingers to his lips and whistled, calling for the horse to approach them. The horse stomped unapologetically on Aluna's ruined nursery. "I rode this horse here. You take it back, and we will follow on foot. Don't wait for us, Aluna, go!"

"What kind of wound is it?" Aluna asked, tying her hair back. "I need to know what to bring."

Theo hesitated, looking at Demetrius.

"Well?" Demetrius asked with elevated eyebrows.

"Knife," was all Theo could say, patting his back over his shoulder. His tears erupted again, and he fell to his knees. Demetrius threw the crate into Aluna's arms as he immediately mounted the horse.

"We're going together!" Demetrius yelled, veins protruding from his neck. He lowered his arms to retrieve the container from Aluna and hoisted her in front of him. She leaned forward and ordered the horse to race toward the Academy, leaving Theo collapsed on the ground behind them.

The wind rushed past Aluna's eardrums, but not loud enough to drown the sound of Demetrius sobbing. She placed one hand on his knee as the horse sprinted down the dirt path. Her mind was oddly silent, as she had little information with which to ponder. The summer sun showed them no mercy, adding mystery in deciphering sweat from tears. His blurred, myopic vision erased the vivid, scenic route before them, as all he saw were his nightmares unfolding.

When they approached the building several minutes later, Zo stood in a black cape, cupping his hands firmly in front of his protruding stomach.

The Academy was a diamond-shaped building with tall pillars that touched the clouds. Colorful banners swayed gently in the breeze, tapping softly against the stone walls. Beside the building, several horses grazed along the grass. They looked up alarmingly at the arrival of Demetrius and Aluna.

Zo lifted his head and lowered his hood. The wrinkles around his eyes were sparkling with tears, and his nose was bright red.

"Demetrius—" Zo started, reaching for the crate in Demetrius' hands.

Demetrius dropped the crate into Zo's arms and pushed him aside, barging through the main doors. Aluna grabbed the crate back and raced behind Demetrius. Some of her paintbrushes had fallen onto the ground, only to be quickly swept up by Zo.

The lobby was circular with hallways and doors lining the inner walls. Above them was a giant glass ceiling. Aluna squinted as she noticed a ring of vines poking out from the corners of the roof.

I'll be back for you, she said.

"They're in the room down that hall!" Zo yelled, unable to run as fast as the two. Demetrius followed Zo's pointed finger down the longest hallway leading to the furthest room from the entrance. The walls were bare and grey, though had they been ornately designed, nothing could have diverted Demetrius' and Aluna's attention from the doors at the end of the hallway.

Sweat bled through Demetrius' yellow linens, gluing it entirely to his torso. His curls had flattened from the gusts of wind that drenched them in his tears. His nostrils flared and he breathed heavily as he opened the doors to the auditorium. The room was filled with people murmuring and whispering until they saw Demetrius: then, the crowd fell silent.

"The door… to your left!" Zo yelled from down the hall. He had placed both hands on his knees as he caught his breath.

Demetrius and Aluna crossed the auditorium avoiding the curious and concerned looks. Aluna balanced the crate in one arm with her hip as she slid a comforting hand on Demetrius' shoulder. He opened the door to the adjacent room.

The room was a perfect square, with dark grey walls that seemed almost black. A small square window in the ceiling caused a singular beam of sunlight to fall directly to the center of the floor, where Myron lay on his stomach; the handle of a knife protruded from his back. Demetrius ran to his father, slipping on the pool of blood. He fell onto Myron's lifeless body, wailing uncontrollably.

Aluna closed the door, though nothing could mute Demetrius' hysteria. As she bent down to place the crate on the floor, she noticed another body kneeling in the corner. His blue headwrap hid his sunken head, and his blue robe covered his body, running onto the floor like the waterfall of tears he couldn't muster.

"Leander?" Aluna whispered as she approached. At first, Leander couldn't respond. His sleeves trembled as his hands clenched in angered fists. Aluna squatted to face him. She reached for his arm, but he immediately pulled back.

"Where is Theo?" Leander asked, though Aluna could barely hear him over Demetrius.

"He told us the news," Aluna said. "I'm sure he's on his way back here."

As she finished speaking, the door opened, and Zo slipped inside, quickly closing the door behind him.

"Go to Demetrius," Zo whispered to Aluna, kneeling by Leander.

"It's too late to fix the wound," Aluna said as she wiped the oncoming tears. "He's gone."

Leander covered his face with his trembling hands, his sapphire ring glistening in the minuscule amounts of reflective light.

"But Demetrius is here," Zo said, helping Aluna wipe another tear away. "Go to him, dear." She looked at Leander whose gaze remained glued to the floor. Zo gave a single nod, wrapping his bear arms over Leander's shoulders.

Aluna approached Demetrius. Myron's tall and robust body, clothed in beautiful white linens, now saturated in scarlet blood, lied lifeless on the floor, as if he had been standing perfectly straight and fell without his knees buckling. Only his head had turned eerily to the side; his dark curls, identical to Demetrius', covered his eyes that hauntingly didn't close. His lips, too, remained partly open, as if desperate to utter one more thing before the end.

Through Demetrius' turmoil and lament, he had managed to cover himself almost entirely in the blood of his father. The brightness of his shirt and his spirit had vanished. Aluna sat cross-legged beside him. Demetrius instantly fell into Aluna's lap, holding her tightly and sobbing inconsolably. She held his head, mixing her tears into the blood and sweat which covered his precious curls. She looked up in despair, and once again, the tiny window seized her attention. Her hazel eyes traced the single beam of light that fell precisely onto the center of Myron's back, where the handle unapologetically glistened.

Her eyebrows furrowed as she observed the details carved into the steel handle. Thin, wavy lines extended from the center until it they all met at a curved tip, imitating the likeness of a feather. Somehow the handle hadn't incurred any of the blood, and as a result, it beamed mercilessly. She turned to Leander, who was still motionlessly hunched over and consoled by Zo. Aluna stretched out her neck to try and get their attention. Though she failed to do so, she noticed a rectangular item wrapped in a dark covering sticking out from behind Leander.

～

Water dripped onto the floor as Aluna blinked rapidly, returning to the present moment to notice she had tilted her cup too far. She grabbed the nearest cloth and cleaned the mess.

Did you hear us, Aluna? The vines asked.

No, I'm so sorry, what was it?

The woman has moved on. She is no longer in close proximity.

Wonderful, Aluna said, emitting a breath of relief. *Let's keep the hedges closed, please. Just in case.*

She wrapped her fingers around the cup and quietly tiptoed back to Damian's room, blowing out the candles in the hallway as she reached her destination. Through the open door she saw Caterina laying her head upon her clasped hands, her braid resting over her closed eyes, sleeping soundly.

Remain as you are around that curtain, Aluna said, *and please let me know as soon as she wakes up.*

Yes, Aluna.

Aluna walked back into the kitchen as though she was returning to the flashback, sitting at the circular table hiding in the corner of the room. Her eyes glazed over, choosing to observe the visuals playing in her mind. Her fingertip traced the rim of the cup as she placed her chin upon her other hand, staring wishfully at the full moon outside her window. She absentmindedly brushed her fingers along her arm where the scars of the thorns had almost faded.

Why are you not sleeping, Aluna?

I feel I am. Is this not a living nightmare?

Chapter

Seventeen

amian stepped into the small kitchen. A narrow, horizontal window ran along the ceiling's edges, shedding minimal light into the space. The kitchen was framed entirely by cabinets and counter tops carved from the stone wall's cold exterior. In the center of the room was an island, and a faint green glow emerged from its surface. To Damian's right was another door, slightly ajar.

The cabinets extended beyond the counter tops, leaving little room between themselves and the island in the middle. Damian scanned the room for the pitcher to which Janus had referred, but his eyes consistently returned to the glowing island. He leaned forward, pressing his fingertips against its corners. The surface felt cold and smooth, assuring him that he was in fact touching a countertop and not a canvas, but when he peered into the picture painted before him, he quickly removed his hand.

The painting was in a similar style to the one of the little boy, with its background portraying minimal detail as all attention and intention were evidently given to the subject. The environment depicted a night sky with twinkling stars washing over a swaying grassland. In the middle of

171

the field, and very close to the spectator, was a silver cauldron, engraved with rows of expressionless faces. The green glow escaped the rim of this round fixture, though its brewing contents weren't visible.

Behind the cauldron stood a skeleton, its body only noticeable above the waist. Bony fingers gripped the handle of a long silver spoon, with which the skeleton stirred the mysterious contents. The stars drifted and the grass danced in rhythm to the spoon, so the skeleton appeared uncannily still. Empty containers and bottles were scattered throughout the grass, lacking sufficient details to recognize the items. The silver faces engraved onto the sides of the cauldron reflected these multicolored vessels.

The skeleton's chin was lowered, suggesting it was staring into the cauldron, though eyes it didn't possess. Not a single sound migrated from the canvas as the skeleton slowly raised its head to face its spectator.

Damian peered over his shoulder to ensure it was in fact he who had the skeleton's attention.

"Hello," Damian said, reclining hesitantly. The skeleton stopped stirring, and the glow from the cauldron dimmed. "Sorry, didn't mean to interrupt. Do you know where Janus keeps the water?"

The skeleton opened its mouth to respond, but no words escaped. Instead, the now-static stars were visible through the gaps of the skeleton's opened jaw, for what needed to be said was clear as night.

"Right, well," Damian said, placing his on his hips. "I'll keep looking."

The skeleton's head rotated as Damian traveled around the island, peering through the darkness to find the water. Damian opened the cabinets closest to him, and the skeleton began stirring the cauldron again. As the stirring quickened, the green glow returned, brightening the kitchen.

"Would you mind stirring that a little more? Some light would be helpful."

The skeleton rested the spoon within the cauldron and stepped to the side. Its strides were strange, for the skeleton limped heavily on its left side. The fading glow from the abandoned cauldron bounced off the skeleton's sand-colored bony legs as it rummaged the empty containers hidden between the blades of grass. It made its way around the parameters of the canvas until its fingers uncapped a long, narrow bottle with liquid at the bottom.

"What's that?" Damian asked.

The skeleton limped to its original position and raised the bottle as far as its arm extended, pouring the contents into the mix. Gradually the glow returned, though the emerald green had become an earthy brown.

"Well, that doesn't help much," Damian mumbled.

He resumed his search for the water, approaching the last section of unobserved countertop, nearing the other door. He grazed his hand across the counter's smooth exterior. As he moved closer to the door, the color around him began to change.

What was moments ago a rich brown had grown redder. He froze, watching his hand bathe in a dark maroon radiance, then a rich ruby, and finally, a bright, scarlet red. Damian spun around, wide-eyed at the skeleton and the blood-colored light escaping its cauldron. The skeleton's attention wasn't on Damian. The door beside Damian creaked, solidifying his paralysis.

An old man's head emerged from the doorframe first, then gradually, as the door opened, Damian faced the stranger in totality. His long white hair was in stark contrast to his dark, wrinkled skin, and though it looked aflame in the scarlet light, it twisted and curled past his shoulders onto the exposed portions of his chest, covering the tears in his shadowed shirt. His pants, too, were severely ripped. Only his gloves seemed untouched. Though at first glance the man appeared ancient, the scarlet glow captured his toned arms and broad shoulders, a glimpse into a laborious past and present.

"Demetrius?" the old man said in a voice deeper than one Damian had ever heard.

"N-no."

The man bowed his head and pinched the bridge of his nose, sighing deeply.

"He dragged you along, then?" the man asked, crossing his arms.

"I'm Damian. In a way I dragged myself into this."

A nervous chuckle slipped from the corner of Damian's lips. The man uncrossed his arms and motioned toward what lied beyond the door.

"Come with me," he said.

"Oh, well, I— thank you for—er— the invitation, but I'm just here to get some water. Do you know where I can find it? I tried to ask this little fellow, but he's not much of a conversationalist."

"There's no water."

Damian felt sweat rising from his palms and congregating beneath his hairline.

"But Janus said..."

"Come with me," the man demanded.

Lines of concern bordered his mouth below his nose. His one arm rested gently by his side while the other leaned against the door. Damian ran a shaky hand through his hair, exposing his wounded arm.

Damian peered into the doorway as the cauldron's scarlet light flooded the darkness. Before him was a downward staircase with a flickering orange light at the bottom, radiating from the left.

"I think I'll head back to Demetrius now," Damian said. The old man shook his head.

"You're not prepared to go back out there."

"Not prepared? For what? For whom?"

"You say you dragged yourself into this mess, but have you considered why you've been permitted to do so? To accompany a man you barely know?"

"*Barely know*?" Another nervous chuckle left Damian. "I've known Demetrius my whole life."

"And yet you're surprised you ended up here, no?"

"Life is full of surprises."

"Listen to me," the man said, placing his gloved hand over Damian's shoulder. "You're not prepared for what lies ahead. The sooner you free yourself of the illusory foundations with which you've constructed this notion of excitement, adventure, and perhaps bonding with the man you think you know, the sooner you'll see what's truly unfolding here."

"Where's Theo?" Damian asked, leaning back toward the door from which he came, eyes darting side to side in fear.

"You would think he'd come down to greet a long-lost friend, wouldn't you? So either Demetrius is not long-lost, or...."

"This is ridiculous," Damian said, turning his back toward the man. "I'm going back to Demetrius. Allow me to learn the hard way, then, whatever lesson is at stake." Damian reached for the doorknob, but it didn't budge. He took a step back and with as much force as he could exude attempted to break down the door, causing nothing more than a loud *bang*.

"I know you have no reason to trust me," the man said, his voice deepening, "but at this point, you have no reason to trust anyone else either. I can answer some of the questions you have, for knowledge is a necessary tool and is its own weapon of defense."

"Who are you, then? How should I refer to you and your *omniscience*?" Damian joked.

For the first time, a smile broke the hardened lines of the man's face. "G."

"Your name is G?"

"A name is nothing but a word by which others refer to you. It's not for one's own reference. My isolated lifestyle doesn't require me to have a name."

"Does it stand for anything?"

"It stands for everything." His arm once more extended toward the descending staircase. "We don't have all the time in the world." With a great deal of hesitancy, Damian descended, and G followed.

Frantic knocking bellowed from the other door, but the two had already left the kitchen and closed the door behind them.

The room below was much colder, irrespective of the short staircase. Damian wrapped himself in his arms, cautiously with his bandaged arm, as he hurried toward the fireplace. Beside the fire were two wooden stools sitting patiently on an ornate blue rug. Damian tilted his head as he deciphered the imagery woven into the fabric.

"What is that?" Damian asked, pointing downward. G had been searching for something among the shelves across the room.

"I believe it's a lamb."

Damian frowned. The faintest resemblance of a lamb surfaced from the faded threads, though the details of its little head were worn beyond recognition.

"Now, what do I need to know?" Damian asked, taking a seat and resting his elbows on his knees, bringing his hands together as he awaited disclosure.

G found the item he sought, pocketing it before joining Damian on the second stool. In a more natural lighting, G appeared less frightening. His white hair trickled below his shoulders, the smaller strands trailing the wrinkles and scars on his face. The stubble on his jaw also hid more evidence of a tumultuous, scarred past. His blue eyes had hints of empty grey around the pupil, as though the youth in him had faded. His attire was the darkest shade of purple, only made apparent in the highlights of the creases.

"You must always be present," G said. Damian furrowed his brows and frowned deeper; he pressed two fingers to his neck, checking his pulse. G shook his head. "Not that kind of present. This kind." He tapped his index finger against his temple. "Observe this moment. You've traveled all this way, to an unfamiliar region, with a man you thought you knew."

"Let me interject, again, right there—"

"He doesn't know himself either," G continued, "and for that reason, he's brought both himself and you here."

Damian brought his lips to his clasped hands, pondering G's assertion. He thought back to the excitement Demetrius exuded at the beginning of the journey and how it had spiraled since then.

"Demetrius kept saying he didn't imagine things looking this way. The change in character I'm noticing must be from that disconnect, right? Expectation versus reality?"

"The mission isn't to know someone else in his entirety. We will never know anyone as much as we can know ourselves. We can never *trust* anyone as much as we can trust ourselves." G ran a hand through his hair and inhaled deeply. "We weren't expecting to see more than one guest. As soon as you informed me you weren't Demetrius, I feared for you. I thought I'd seen two figures treading down the path outside, but since I just got back from a long trip and haven't slept in a while, I thought my eyes deceived me." G's stare turned to the fire momentarily. He closed his eyes and hung his head, rubbing the back of his neck. "Rest isn't a luxury I'm afforded."

"Surely Theo gives you a break?"

"Why would he?" G asked, raising his head and his eyebrow. "He's not in command."

"He's... he's not? This isn't his property?"

"Not in the slightest. We all live here, the way we want to. At least, to the extent we can."

Damian buried his head in his hands, rubbing his hair frantically as he tried to piece the puzzle together.

"Why are you here, G? Wearing these mangled linens, depriving yourself of sleep? For whom? For what?"

"Again," G said, looking Damian unblinkingly in the eyes, "because I know myself. I know not only my potential, but also my reality, my actuality. This is where and how I reside. With that comes the knowledge of what awaits me as well."

A clear jar sat behind G, filled entirely of dirtied paintbrushes. Damian scanned the room in search of a canvas or easel but to no prevail.

"Is this how you usually speak?" Damian asked. "To such depths? I mean, potentiality and actuality... identity... these aren't typically the subjects of conversations when you first meet someone."

"I speak what I know."

"It's very deep, what you're saying," Damian noted, eyeing the depth of the jar as well. "And those brushes in the back, yes those, in that jar. Are those yours? Do you paint as well?" He steadied his breathing to contain his excitement.

"No."

Damian's mouth parted slightly as a wave of sadness momentarily washed over him. In a brief instant of desperation, he asked, "Did you used to paint? Would anyone consider you some sort of... ex-artist?"

"He's upstairs."

Damian jumped from his seat.

"I knew it! Wait... how do you know Theo is referred to as such?"

"We don't have much time," G said, reaching for the pocketed item. From his clasped hands he revealed the handle of a dagger, its blade glistening in the fire. Damian stepped back as G extended his arm. "Take it."

"What for?"

"Protection."

"From?"

"Not *from*," G said, standing up and grabbing Damian's hand, placing the knife in it. "*For*. For yourself. You may not need it, and in no way am I assuring you that you'll use it. But we act truer to ourselves when we feel we are protected and secure."

"Could you *please* tell me what I need to know? Any other day, I would love this ambiguity and mystery. Truly, G, you are a wordsmith, and I'd love to engage with you more. But I need to return to Demetrius before he begins to worry. And I feel this blade doesn't accomplish your mission of helping me know myself or feel protected. I feel quite the opposite, actually."

"You are now aware of a presuming danger," G said, returning to the staircase and directing his open palm toward the door upstairs. "The rest will follow."

Damian hesitantly climbed the stairs, concealing the blade in his back pocket. Its weight, though physically insignificant, increased Damian's heartbeat.

"Anything else you want to tell me?" Damian asked at the top of the stairs, turning his head. "G?"

Damian spun around, but G was no longer there. A breeze swept the room, shifting Damian's attention to the once darkened corner where a door leading to the outside was closing, and as Damian opened his mouth to call for G, the door slammed shut, leaving Damian solitary with only the sounds of a crackling fire and his paranoid thoughts filling his eardrums.

Damian looked up in agony before entering the kitchen. The red glow had subsided, replaced by the original emerald brilliance. The skeleton paid no mind to Damian's return, and before Damian could attempt to catch its attention, sounds of heavy knocking exploded throughout the room.

"Damian!" Demetrius' screamed. His voice sounded terrifyingly distant, as though he wasn't just beyond the other door. Damian circled around the kitchen's island, leaning on his wounded arm as he took grand strides toward the doorknob.

The glow looming around him faded into darkness as Damian turned the knob with ease, bumping into Demetrius, who pulled him by the collar into the main room.

"Where have you been?" Demetrius asked. Sweat condensed over his face, dripping beside his bulging, bloodshot eyes. "And where's your water?"

"I couldn't find it!" Damian lifted his hands defensively.

Demetrius released Damian from his grip. His chest expanded and collapsed quickly.

"Listen," he whispered to avoid the room's echoing. "Something's not right around here."

"You're telling me," Damian said, rolling his eyes. Demetrius grabbed Damian again by his shirt before quickly releasing him. Damian's eyes widened.

"I'm sorry, I just…" Demetrius ran his fingers through his sweaty curls, pulling at them in frustration. "We need to put all jokes aside and focus on getting to Theo."

"I can take you to him now," Janus said from across the room. Her velvety voice traveled across the darkened space as thunder struck in the background. Damian peered over Demetrius' shoulder. She had returned to a more reclusive position, hiding most of her body behind the staircase.

"That won't be necessary," Demetrius said, his voice cracking. "We'll find him."

"As you wish." Janus remained lingering at the bottom of the stairs.

"Why can't she come with us?" Damian asked.

"It… She… I'll tell you later." Demetrius reluctantly crossed the room with Damian following closely behind. Janus' eyes remained fixated on them as they approached.

"Sorry, did you say *it?*"

Demetrius brought a finger to his lips. He glanced toward the chandelier as they approached the center of the room, carefully avoiding the swinging spiders. Demetrius' sweaty palms gripped the railing of the staircase, opposite to where Janus stood.

"Here," she said softly. The two heard a clinking sound as she placed the cup on a hard surface. Her pale hand grasped the handle of a candlestick holder, extending it above the railing, shielding half her face. "You will need this. The staircase to the tower is the furthest door to your right."

The balcony atop the staircase was hidden in darkness. Damian patted Demetrius on the back and cautiously tiptoed toward Janus, bypassing the arachnids. Demetrius held his breath as Damian reached out his hand.

"Thank you, dear," Damian said. He grabbed the handle from her and flashed his charming smile, showcasing both dimples. He brought the light closer to her to examine the beauty he had imagined from across the room, but as the flame illuminated her features, Damian's smile was instantly replaced by terror.

Before him was indeed a beautiful woman, a beautiful blue eye skirted by soft lashes, a rose-colored cheek the same shade as her parted lips. Her delicate features weren't reflected on the other side of her face. A crackled and inflamed eye socket hid her second eye, surrounded by mounds of wrinkled, grey skin. That side of her nose was non-existent, like the chipped remains of a forgotten statue. Her mouth was in a permanent frown, weighed heavily by the sagging skin around her chin.

A tear formed below her blue eye as she ran away; her wailing faded into the distance as she moved into an adjacent room. Another round of thunder shook the windowpanes, cleaning the room of any sounds until silence enclosed them once more.

Damian stood paralyzed.

"Let's go," Demetrius begged.

"What... was that?"

"Only Theo can tell us. Let's go ask him. I have many, many inquiries."

The two walked beside one another, wordlessly agreeing to never leave each other's sides again. The flame ignited the space around them in an orange hue, and without hesitation or a morbid curiosity to investigate the remaining parts of the manor, the two approached the furthest door to the right.

Demetrius opened it as Damian raised the candle above their heads. The staircase began immediately at the foot of the door, and each step was made of uneven stone. Demetrius stuck his head in, frowning at its narrowness, as it only extended as wide as the single doorway.

"You're going first," Damian said, handing Demetrius the candle. Demetrius took a deep breath and nodded, wrapping his clammy fingers around the handle.

Demetrius turned, as if rethinking the entire purpose of this journey. He frowned as he stared at the ground floor, stretching his ear toward the main room.

The thunder and pouring rain had abruptly stopped. Demetrius' eyed the front door until Damian put his hand encouragingly on his shoulder.

"We're almost there," Damian said.

"I hope so."

Demetrius patted the ring in his pocket to remind himself of his beloved friend, erasing the pain of the horrific obstacles he had endured for this reunion. Damian nodded assuringly, feeling the weight of what resided in his back pocket.

The two ascended the winding staircase in silence; even their breathing was sparse. Once in a while a slender, curtain-less window, slightly bigger than one's hand, disrupted the stone wall, showing either glimpses of the full moon or total darkness. Some rain had trickled into the tower, gently dripping between the stones.

After what seemed an eternity, the two took the final step off the staircase and into a short, unlit hallway. At the end of the hallway was a door with a similar orange glow escaping its borders. A faint *hoot* greeted them.

Chapter
Eighteen

Leander pulled back his hood to gaze at the impeding tower that obscured the haunting brilliance of the full moon. Muffled horse nickering in the distance assured Leander his friend had arrived; he gently kicked Mesa's side, requesting her to stop. His momentary sigh of relief was interrupted by the anxious uncertainty of whether he was too late.

"We cannot let them see you," Leander said to Mesa, his eyes locked in the direction of the horses. He retrieved his paintbrush and pointed it toward Mesa's hooves until the sapphire glow faded. "We cannot let *anyone* see you. Stay here until I come back. This time, I will find you." As Leander dismounted Mesa, he felt a hefty branch snap in half, though no sound met his eardrums. With a raised eyebrow he bent to examine the branch. It weighed much less than he assumed it would, and with one eye closed, he peered into where the branch had broken. He repositioned himself for the moonlight's assistance, then gasped at its hollow inside.

"This branch... is nothing but a shell," Leander whispered. He lunged toward the nearest branch and snapped it across his knee, and again, it failed to emit a sound. Mesa stared at Leander puzzlingly and decided to follow suit. However, when she stomped upon the branch, a snap pierced the silence, causing the horses nearby to pause their grazing.

Leander ducked behind Mesa until the horses resumed chewing grass.

"The spurious are scattered among the sincere, I see. I should not be so surprised."

The discovery aggravated his chest, though Leander suppressed the cough. He rose, patted Mesa lovingly on the back, and carefully walked toward the tower until he faced the elongated front gate.

The fog waited beyond the iron bars like a patient hunter, eyeing its prey and tarrying perfectly still. Leander's sweaty palm grabbed the bar closest to him as his unblinking eyes scanned the eerie estate. The fog's opacity left little room for discovery, and the full moon, though blocked by the tower, reminded him that time was not an ally.

The moonlight washed over his pale hand and reflected the brilliant blue of his sapphire ring onto the lock of the gate door. Leander held his breath as he pushed the door open, watching the disturbed fog move in accordance. He adjusted his hood, concealed his presence, and tucked his hands under his oversized sleeves.

The aroma of damp soil filled Leander's nostrils, as though a thunderstorm had just passed. He detected the single, muddied path once the fog had swirled to the side, moving just enough for Leander to sense the colossal trees bordering the path.

"It seems I am at the mercy of the fog."

His hood restricted him from seeing any details until the fog decided to fade to his right. The moonlight shone brightly upon the hole which emerged from the masking fog.

He turned toward this crater and peered into what lied beyond the row of trees. His toes drifted toward the edge of the muddy path, remaining within its borders but still enabling his curiosity. In a spotlit area rested a grid of stones. The tops of these stones shone in a magnificent way, partially blinding Leander. A mental image of Demetrius' father's tombstone flashed before his eyes.

Had things gone according to plan, he would be in the Garden now, bringing to life the commemorative statue of the beloved man. He squeezed his eyes shut as memories of Myron's lifeless body surfaced.

Blurs of the moments surrounding the fateful incident accompanied this flashback: hearing Myron's piercing cry of agony, Leander bursting through the doors of the adjacent room and collapsing, feeling Theo's hand gently slap his cheek to regain focus, pushing Theo away with the metal end of his paintbrush, Zo's attempt to comfort and console him, and a hazy yellow blur rushing past him to embrace the bloodied body on the floor.

Tears surfaced as the heavy memories vanished. His gaze rested once more upon the gridded stones beyond the trees.

Leander clenched his fists as he directed his attention to the moon, the revealer of the graveyard, the unsolicited tour guide of Leander's uncontrollable thoughts.

"For what do you use your powers? To distract? To traumatize? The sun sheds her light on you every night, and this is how you repay her?" He returned his gaze to the imperceptible path before him and continued through the foe of fog, wiping away painful tears.

What did I just witness? Leander asked himself. *Did he arrange those stones? Was that another story of his? When will he learn stories are meant to be told? It is the art of storytelling, not storyshowing, that writing serves its purpose and remains secured on the paper.*

Leander's thoughts spiraled, rationalizing the arrangement of the stones, until he felt the bottom of his robe brush against something beside his foot. The fog thickened beneath him, and Leander exhaled frustratingly. He retrieved his paintbrush and rubbed the bristles together until a glowing blue halo appeared. He bent over and waved his paintbrush over the object.

Though the fog covered most of the details, Leander observed the bronze head, covered in soil, frowning at him. Leander pressed his palms to the wet soil as he peered below the bust's neck, and unlike the branch he snapped earlier, this object wasn't hollow. He brought his paintbrush as close to the object as possible without touching it, waving his free hand above the bronze object to clear the silvery mist.

In a matter of seconds, Leander recognized the face. His heart dropped to his stomach as he saw his cherished friend, though with much younger features, saddened eyes, and a prominent frown. Leander unconsciously mirrored this expression, suppressing the urge to lift his friend.

"This cannot be," he said to himself as he grabbed the end of his robes. He hastily searched for granite stains that would have been caused by the fabric rubbing against the object if the bust had risen from a canvas. The dark blue material, accompanied by mud splatters, minimal lighting and clouded mists, heightened the difficulty of detecting graphite stains, though he concluded that this part of the statue must be real.

"Has he abandoned the canvas completely?" A sharp pain pierced Leander's heart.

The momentary sadness disappeared as a branch snapped in the distance. Leander secured his hood and stood, firmly gripping his paintbrush. His heavy breathing marked the seconds of silence that followed. The disturbance emanated from the direction of the tower, though the fog shielded any possibility of identification.

"Demetrius?" Leander whispered, his eyes briefly falling to the bust below him. "Is that you?"

His inquiry was met with stillness, leaving Leander no choice but to abandon his bronzed friend and continue forward. His paintbrush remained in his grip.

How bizarre, Leander thought. *Why would Theo have created just the head of...* His thought trailed off as a shadowed impression of two figures parted the fog before him. Leander held his breath as the fog parted down the middle and off to the side, revealing the source of the detached head.

Leander recognized the headless man immediately. Adrenaline rushed through his veins as he stared at the bronzed commemoration of Demetrius. The adrenaline manifested as beads of sweat atop his pale skin, his layered attire soaking in the perspiration. His paintbrush gradually slid from his hold, forcing him to pocket it.

The level of detail was undeniably spectacular. Leander's mind frantically alternated between deep admiration and indescribable anger. His eyes wandered throughout the statue, noticing everything from the pores below Demetrius' eyes to the rough cuticles surrounding his nails.

Leander pressed his hand to his forehead, comforting his feverish mind. The moonlight again reflected off his sapphire ring, extending its brilliance onto the second figure beside Demetrius. He suddenly felt his throat closing, confining his ability to breathe.

The second figure was missing the left side of his torso and his head was turned inhumanly backward. Leander took small steps around the statue to examine the second figure, each step weighted by his pulsing heartbeat pounding out of his chest.

Leander's hands trembled as he stared at the profile of his younger self.

The moment felt like peering into a mirror of the past. His bronze double had straight hair that fell to his shoulders, curling only slightly at the ends. Part of his hair covered the left side of his face, the way Theo had once joked was the only unkempt and wild element of Leander's persona. Leander had always wanted to cut his hair until Theo expressed interest in it. Unknowingly, Leander slid his hand beneath his hood and touched the back of his headwrap, grazing his bare neck, once covered by those revered locks.

Next, he noticed his protruding collar bone and lean arms, both draped appropriately in loose, layered linens, an unachieved attempt in his younger days to hide his naturally thin physique. His long fingers, "like pencils wrapped in skin" as Theo would tease, were delicately sculpted beneath the large sleeves, and upon the fourth finger rested his artist ring. Leander held his hand beside the bronze one, and his lips parted as he admired the exact proportions.

"He thinks of me," Leander said, moving his outstretched hand to his chest. "He remembers me."

Leander's eyes darted side to side, trying to comprehend how Theo had executed such an exact replica. He thought back to his sketch of Myron and felt a minor sting in his chest knowing that although his recollection was reliable, the minuscule particulars had vanished from memory, deeming his portraiture incomparable to his mentee's.

"You, indubitably, are the greatest artist the world would have ever witnessed," Leander whispered under his breath, pressing heavily upon his beating heart. The moonlight bounced off the grey mist flowing through the cavity of his bronze self, emphasizing its emptiness. "Why did you have to cut out my chest? Surely you know what you took from me, and here you are, now, mocking that which I gave you. You may have kept your talent hidden from the world, but do you know where they hide now? In the four chambers of my—"

Another ruffling noise from the direction of the tower broke Leander from his nostalgic trance, and instinctually Leander reached for his paintbrush, sniffling away reemerging tears.

"Who goes there?" Leander asked, this time louder than before. "Do not make me ask again." The fog transitioned to its most opaque gradation yet. Leander waved his paintbrush pointlessly, as its light extended nowhere. He once more gazed upon the cursed moon.

"What use are you?" He left the statue, keeping his angry eyes on the abominable orb in the sky. "How do you expect me to find my way?"

Immediately after positing the question, the fog lowered, returning the tower to view. The semicircle window flickered its orange-gold glow from the nearest candle, giving the illusion of a blinking eye watching Leander from the heavens. Leander swallowed a pit of nervousness until a scarlet blur passed by the window.

Leander froze.

His heart pounded like a drum, pounding from his chest as if yearning and reaching for the scarlet subject itself.

A rejuvenated bolt of energy ran through his veins as he charged toward the tower, mud splashing beneath his sandals. Only by sheer luck did his headwrap stay fastened to his bald head. He held the edge of his hood as he stormed through the fog. He buried his cough in his sleeve, refusing to be deterred any longer.

His heavy breathing continued until he arrived at the front steps. Without hesitation he grabbed the railing and ran up the stairs, lunging at the front door. His determination blinded him from noticing neither the ornate engraving on the door nor the ominous "welcome" with its e's doubling as eyes. The door remained locked, no matter how hard Leander pushed against it. Like a mad man, he began pounding on the door, adrenaline supplying each knock.

His knuckles stung as he retreated, looking at the torn skin and fresh blood surfacing. His muddied sandals stamped the steps as he returned to the path. He shielded his eyes from the blaring moonlight, noticing for the first time the vines spiraling around the tower, conveniently to the desired window.

Throughout the vines were scattered small, narrow windows, through which a bouncing little flame ascended the tower. The windows were too modest to reveal who carried the candle, but the passing of two shadows following the flame answered Leander's inquiry.

"Demetrius!" Leander screamed at the top of his lungs. "Demetrius!" He waved his arms in the air, his hood falling from its position and revealing his face to the moonlight. *I have arrived just in time*, he thought to himself ecstatically. His sleeves, too, fell, displaying his thin, pale arms. The orange glow within the tower continued ascending, and without hesitation, Leander sprinted to the lowest arrangement of vines. He interlocked his fingers with the leaves and pulled himself up, shoving his soaked sandals into the thickest portions of the vines.

"Demetrius!" Leander shouted a third time. "Please! Wait!"

He grunted as he shifted his weight, reaching for a higher string of vines. As his sweaty palms secured himself, Leander felt a forceful tug on his cloak, choking his neck. He gasped for air as he fell onto his back, mud splattering across his face.

Above him stood an older man with luminous, tangled white hair, dressed in dark, tattered clothing. The wrinkles in his face accentuated his angered brows and thin lips as his chest expanded and collapsed, his fists risen as he loomed over Leander. The moon emphasized his physique, tracing the curves of every muscle and scar. His gloved fingers wrapped around the handle of a small blade.

Leander coughed in an attempt to catch his breath.

"Please," Leander said with a strained voice. "I come peacefully. A friend... I am a friend." His face tensed as he mustered the energy to point in the direction of the statue as identification. "Please..."

"Who are you?" G asked.

Leander's eyes fluttered as he stared at the moon above him, witnessing the bouncing candle's glow fading through the final windowpane before reaching its destination.

"Please..."

"Get up!" G ordered. "Who are you? How did you get here?" G intentionally kept the blade in view. Leander groaned as he leaned on his shaking arm, propping himself onto his knees before wobbling to his feet. He adjusted his headwrap and faced the man of equal height.

A moment of silence passed as Leander's eyes met G's. They were strangely similar. Leander peered behind his shoulder to gage how far he had fallen and how hard he must have hit his head.

"I asked you some questions," G reminded Leander hesitantly, since he, too, had noticed the unmistakable affinity.

"I have come to rescue Demetrius," Leander said, coughing as his lungs failed to retain enough air.

"From?"

Leander stared at the blade in G's gloved hand.

"Perhaps the same thing from which you protect yourself."

Leander secretly reached for the paintbrush in his pocket. He held his breath as his fingers grazed two separate, wooden pieces. He pressed his lips together and closed his eyes momentarily, dropping his hand to his side defeatedly.

"I'm not going to ask you again," G said, stepping forward. "Tell me who you are."

In closer proximity, the two immediately recognized the shapes and colors of their eyes were identical. Their scrutiny shifted toward their opponent's hands.

"You're one of the Greats," G said, pointing to Leander's sapphire ring with his blade. Leander raised his eyebrows in surprise.

"How do you know about the Greats?"

"Though I'm nothing more than a groundskeeper, I'm afraid there's a lot I know that I can't explain." G removed his glove to show the faintest circular imprint upon his third finger, the scarring of a suffocating ring.

"I see," Leander said, consciously controlling his breath as panic ensued. "I do not have the answers you seek, and furthermore, I believe you already know who secures your revelation." Leander put his hands defensively in the air. Pain traveled down his spine as he inched to the front door.

"I do," G said, following suit, "But I don't seek answers to my questions. I seek why these questions consume every waking moment of my existence!" G lunged toward Leander, who had turned to run but could not escape. G grabbed Leander from behind, wrapping one of his enormous arms across Leander's chest and with his other hand held the tip of his blade into Leander's neck.

Leander squirmed as he unsuccessfully tried to pull away from G's grip.

"You turned him into a mad man," G whispered into Leander's ear through gritted teeth. "You pushed him too far. You couldn't just let him live, could you? And as a result, I'm here, forced to live my deathless life."

"A deathless... life?" Leander said with limited breath. His eyes widened as his heart raced. "What— What do you mean? You cannot... possibly be..."

"You know exactly what I mean!" G said, pressing the blade into the first layer of Leander's skin, watching a single drop of blood roll down his neck like a tear of pain. "And I refuse to let you make him madder!"

"How... dare you... blame... me for what... happened!" Through a revival of adrenaline fueled by fear, Leander grabbed G's hand as it held the blade, pulling it away from his neck. In the same motion, Leander pushed G's hand to where he supposed G's neck would be, as the two were of equal height. He heard the blade pierce through flesh, and G released Leander from his hold.

Leander spun to face his identical adversary, who gargled blood.

"Forgive me," Leander said as his fingers delicately coiled around G's wrist, shoving the blade further into G's neck until he began staggering, "but no one is stopping me from getting to Theo." At the sound of Theo's name, G fell forward, directly onto Leander. The two collapsed into the mud, dirt and stillness washing over them before Leander struggled to free himself from G's lifeless weight.

There Leander stood, covered entirely in mud and blood. For the first time, not a single thought crossed his mind. He silently returned to the wall of vines, interlocking his hand once more with the dark green leaves. The scarlet red blood on his hand brushed against the leaves, and Leander watched as it dripped to the soil below.

He rotated his hand in a circular motion, watching as the blood flowed in accordance. He swiped the blood onto the index finger of his other hand, squeezing it tightly with his thumb. He brought his fingers to his nose, expecting the bloody smell of iron.

Instead, the most familiar scent of all rushed through his nostrils.

Leander was covered in red paint.

PART THREE

PART THREE

Chapter
Nineteen

D emetrius handed Damian the candle before proceeding down the darkened hallway.

Though a dim light escaped from the corners of the doorframe, the shadows persisted, amplifying the night's presence in the short hallway. Demetrius' heart pounded harder with each step until his breath reached the door. He turned to Damian, who gave a single nod.

"Remember," Demetrius said in a whisper, "we're here to bring Theo home. Whatever oddity lies beyond this door," Demetrius shuddered as his imagination spiraled, "is just art. No diverges, alright? No curiosities. We can ask him whatever we'd like on our way home. But right now, we must persevere. And leave."

Before Demetrius knocked, a familiar voice slipped through the doorway.

"Is that who I think it is?" Theo asked, his voice sounding distant.

Demetrius pushed the door open. Before him was an expansive and cluttered bookshelf spanning the extent of the wall opposite him, and directly in the center stood his childhood friend, his bare chest curtained by a scarlet robe trailing onto the floor.

Theo shook his head in disbelief, beaming at the sight of his old friend. The full moon was now positioned outside the window, highlighting half of Theo's face, sinking into the crevices of his wrinkles and illuminating some white streaks of hair whisking by his ear.

Though the man before Demetrius had indisputably aged faster than Demetrius thought he would, his intense, warm eyes remained unchanged. Theo raised his arms like spread wings and locked Demetrius in a tight embrace. Damian stepped to the side, shielding his wounded arm and watching Demetrius press his arms against his body, unable to move. Damian blew out his candle once he noticed another glowing below the window.

"It's really you," Theo said, releasing Demetrius and patting him heavily on the shoulder. Demetrius nodded, unable to hide the sigh of relief and a smile emerging from the corner of his lips. Even his eyes regained their usual sparkle.

"You have no idea how happy I am to *finally* see you," Demetrius responded, holding his head in his hands. Theo kept a hand on Demetrius' shoulder and nodded.

Damian coughed under his breath, catching Theo's attention.

"Who's this handsome boy?"

"I'm Damian," Damian said, twisting his mouth at Theo's description but shaking his hand regardless.

"Don't tell me you were afraid to take this journey alone, Demetrius!" Theo laughed, pushing Demetrius' arm playfully. "You were the one who wished me well upon my departure, no? Surely you wouldn't knowingly let me go anywhere too treacherous."

The candle by the window crackled throughout the room. The change in Theo's tone clung to the air, weighing heavily upon the atmosphere.

"I asked Demetrius to tag along," Damian said, "and he was kind enough to permit me to do so."

"Is that right? How kind! And what did you think of your tagging along, Damian? Come, both of you, join me at this table." Theo pointed toward the table by the window, where the candlelight spilled onto three books stacked orderly against the wall.

"Where will you sit?" Demetrius asked hesitantly, pointing at the two chairs.

"I have too much adrenaline to be stationary. Two decades of waiting for such a moment! I'm not sure the excitement will ever cease." He limped across the room to close the door, after which he reclined against it. Demetrius' brows knitted together.

"Are you alright?" Demetrius asked. "Are you limping? I'm limping a little, too." He felt the pain in his foot as images of the bronze head resurfaced.

"We have no control over our aging," Theo chuckled, shrugging his shoulders dismissively. "But does that mean time must be so aggressive in reminding us? I say not! Don't clutter your mind with worries of me, Demetrius. Sit down, ease your leg. Please, I can't wait any longer! You *must* tell me all the details of your travels."

"We can share with you the— what's the word for it— *tumultuous* journey we had," Demetrius said, rubbing the back of his neck. "But it's such a long story. Wouldn't you agree, Damian? It would best be told on our way back home."

"That sounds like a fantastic idea," Damian agreed, also refusing to take a seat. "It was an interesting journey to say the least."

"Tumultuous? Interesting? I beg you to share it with me as you regain your strength for the expedition back. Have you had anything to eat? Drink? I wonder where Janus is."

At the sound of her name, Demetrius fell into the chair behind him, palming his face at his sudden lightheadedness. Damian rushed over, shaking Demetrius shoulder.

"I'm alright," Demetrius groaned, pressing his hand harder against his forehead as he squeezed his eyes shut. Images of Janus' distorted proportions and features burned the forefront of his mind. Theo tilted his head and frowned.

"This isn't the spirited Demetrius I remember. Let me get a better look at you, in this candlelight."

Theo closed one eye and squinted the other, framing Demetrius' face with his outstretched hands. He snickered. "I see those wrinkles by your eyes have stretched almost to your temples! Good to know the laughter inside you is as present now as it was then. And those lines, from your nose to the corners of your mouth, a smile is no stranger to your face. So why is it that you sit here, frowning?"

Damian removed the window's curtain, inviting the midnight breeze into the room to relieve his friend's migraine. Demetrius inhaled deeply.

"She's so beautiful, isn't she?" Theo asked, pointing to the moon. "I'll admit my envy toward her. Yes, Demetrius, envious! Imagine what it'd be like having the surest sense of self and being surrounded in total, blissful silence. The moon simply *is*. She *is*, and she *shines*. And look at us! Well, at least just you and me, Demetrius, two old men, aging, changing, without a say in the matter. I will add, however, you were always a source of light for me."

"And you, for me," Demetrius said, leaning his tired head on his hand, staring at Theo with glossy eyes.

Demetrius squeezed his temples with his hands, begging his migraine to vanish. Waves of sweet nostalgia and crippling anxiety washed over him. Damian continued patting his back, eyeing Theo suspiciously.

The candlelight accentuated the embroidered details of Theo's robe; the orange glow ignited the scarlet threads, magnifying their fiery appearance, in complete contrast to the rest of the cold, poorly lit room.

"Don't hang your head like that, Demetrius. Gravity won't spare you for much longer. When we're young, we act against gravity, don't you think? Head in the clouds, strolling through life with nothing weighing us down."

"Is it not age," Damian interrupted, "but knowledge, that has the power to weigh us down? I can imagine a young child retaining his innocence and blissful ignorance into adulthood as long as he's not tainted by acknowledging the harsh reality."

Theo crouched and touched his folded hands against his lips as he contemplated Damian's question. His robe pooled onto the floor, surrounding him in a sea of scarlet.

"Ignorance is not innocence, nor is it happiness," Theo said softly as he shook his head. "I spent years, here, studying the aging process, specifically the phenomenon of dissimilar maturing, why some people are more accepting of change than others though they exist in the same context. And the answer, my friend, is not a matter of happiness versus dismay, but of acceptance versus resistance."

Demetrius leaned his head against the wall, covering his eyes with this hand. Theo continued.

"You may ask what inspired this. I'm sorry to recall this memory, Demetrius, but it must be shared. And you must admit how different we all were during that time, the time of grieving."

Demetrius lowered his fingers for a single, tired eye to reveal itself, though he remained silent.

"We were all affected by the same event but in entirely different ways."

"How so?" Damian asked, crossing his ankles as he leaned against the windowsill.

"Demetrius, for one, you were entirely mute. The most boisterous and energetic individual had become a shell of a man." Theo gripped his heart as he continued. "I don't think I've witnessed a more heartwrenching, painful sight. Then there was, of course, the Great man himself, who had cut his hair—"

"He *lost* his hair," Demetrius muttered. Theo froze. He squinted his eyes as his eyebrows drew together. Demetrius, surprised by the sudden silence, removed his hand and stared questionably at Theo. "You didn't know?"

Theo shook his head.

Damian shifted his weight uncomfortably as the room grew quieter.

"How?" Theo asked as his voice cracked. "How did he lose his hair?"

"He's a private man, you know," Demetrius said. "He never shared with me the cause of his sickness."

"Sickness?" Theo and Damian said in unison. Demetrius looked bewilderedly at both men. Genuine uncertainty illuminated from the two as Demetrius exhaled deeply.

"It's not my story to tell," Demetrius said, readjusting his seating. "But yes, Leander has been sick for many, many years."

Theo staggered to the bookshelf, bracing himself as he felt the weight of the news.

"He's alright," Demetrius assured him. "He's always persevered."

"You say he's a private man," Theo said, eyes glued to the floor, "but in reality, he's secretive. There is a difference, let me tell you. A private man withholds information pertaining only to himself. A secretive man hides the truth that others have the right to know. Another diversion of aging, no? How some become more reclusive the more they experience?"

Demetrius returned to his slouched position as the mental exhaustion grew. As he leaned his head back, he noticed for the first time some markings on the wall. Though they weren't legible, an intentional pattern ran through the indecipherable lines.

"I became consumed with this question of self," Theo continued, "of how much we shape ourselves, as opposed to how much the world contours our identity. I always thought it was a mixture of both, but after such a traumatic event, well, it seemed you two had no control over yourselves." Theo again placed his hand over his heart, this time hanging his head as well.

"You changed too," Demetrius objected.

"No, my dearest friend. I cannot say I have ever changed, at least not in the sense of deterrence. I became more of who I was already becoming."

Demetrius inhaled deeply, his sweaty curls rubbing against the wall behind him. He immediately turned to the wall and noticed his head had smudged the drawing behind him. Theo waved a dismissive hand toward Demetrius' widened eyes, accompanying the pardon with a slight smile.

"If anything changed about me, I'd have to say it was the desire to focus on one particular thing, as opposed to everything and anything. And thus, gentlemen, I return to my original posited investigation about aging."

Theo strode to the center of the room and cleared his throat.

"My only means of witnessing the tribulations and effects of life was to create a life, well, multiple lives, and see how they interacted with one another, given that this environment is indubitably controllable and static enough to perform such an exhibition."

"*This* environment?" Demetrius asked with raised eyebrows, pointing feverishly around him. "This environment is controllable and static? Ha! Theo, you wouldn't believe the difficulty, the *peril*, we faced, and what it took to walk through that door right there."

"Let me rephrase that," Theo said as he brought his hands together apologetically. "Don't look so panicked! You were never in any danger once you stepped through that gate. No one is here to harm you. I have created this setting, the ideal setting, for no reason other than to explore this question of identity."

Theo waved his hands as he spoke, and outside, the fog creeped into view before vanishing downward, mirroring Theo's gestures.

"It didn't take as long as you might think it did, to raise a functional tower like this from a canvas," Theo added. "I'm sure another artist would tell you the same. Did you know the Academy is a risen canvas as well? Quite a collaborative effort, isn't it?"

Damian blinked frantically, recollecting the familiar hallways, rooms, and details.

"That can't be," Damian said. "I'm sure I've touched the walls plenty of times and never felt a smudge of graphite or paint, or anything else artists may use."

"It's a secret," Theo responded. "Many generations ago, the Greats collaborated on creating the ideal learning center. I can only imagine how inconvenient traveling to each student was, or even simply searching for students."

Damian dragged his hand across the wall beside him, testing Theo's remarks. He rotated his palm toward the candlelight, searching for any indications of lingering mediums.

"Since everything here is of my own creation, I hope you see, Demetrius, that you have nothing to fear, for I would never put you in harm's way. You shouldn't categorize anything in this vicinity as a threat to you. Surely you don't doubt my caring nature? Have I ever showed any bit of hostility toward you?"

Demetrius hesitantly shook his head as he searched his memory for a proper response. After a moment, he slammed his fist on the table.

"Why weren't you the one to greet us?" Demetrius asked as the candlelight burned his glossy eyes. "If you cared about our friendship and our reunion, why weren't you eagerly waiting for us at the door?"

"I wasn't at the door, no," Theo said, smiling from ear to ear, "but I most certainly was in the room with you. Did you not see my portrait? Yes, it's a much younger version of me, but I hope you could still recognize me."

Demetrius' jaw dropped.

"Of course I recognized you!" Demetrius asserted, recalling all the painting's details. He shot a glance at Damian, wagging his finger assertively. "I told you the child—er, Theo?—the portrait was trying to say my name."

Damian shook his head, extending his wounded arm toward Theo.

"How could the child version of Theo recognize the adult version of you?"

Theo's smile widened, his white teeth glistening in contrast to his dark, mischievous eyes.

"One of my realizations was precisely that—our actions are extensions of ourselves, unable to live irrespective of our current condition. You see? Creating the child version of myself means creating a child of my *current* self. I cannot erase what I have endured, or with whom I have met. Stuck like glue, I tell you! I have no identity independent of that. I was a student, an artist—I shudder at that thought—a friend…"

"That's why… That's why I'm surprised you chose to leave," Demetrius interjected, "if you really considered yourself a friend."

Demetrius held his breath, and even the candle's flame stiffened. Theo quietly walked over to his bookshelf, his robe trailing behind him. Though his head remained still, his eyes scanned the shelves. He reached for the furthest book to his right, tapping the top of its spine to remove it from its place.

"Do you remember what you said to me?" Theo asked, keeping his attention on the books.

"When?" Demetrius asked. A delicate *hoot* traveled from a covered object propped against Theo's bed. Damian gripped Demetrius' shoulder as the side of Theo's lips rose.

"What was that?" Damian whispered.

"When?" Theo continued. "The day you asked me to leave."

"I never asked you to leave!" Demetrius rose from his seat. Damian's hand fell off Demetrius' shoulder, and he stepped behind Demetrius in fear. "You were given a choice!"

"Let me share with you something about choice."

Theo's eyes rested upon the book for a moment before facing Demetrius. He stretched out his hands to both chairs, asking his visitors one final time to sit. Demetrius, with a frustrated exhalation, sat down, and Damian followed, hurrying around the table to his chair.

"There is choice," Theo proceeded, holding up one hand, "and there is the illusion of choice." Theo extended his other hand, positioning himself as a weighted scale. Demetrius pressed his lips together, weighing his elbows onto his knees as his clasped hands bounced impatiently before him. Theo rose the second hand above his head. "Choice, *real* choice, is not a question of doing *this* or *that*. It is a question of doing *something*… or doing *nothing*."

"Interesting," Damian said, rubbing his chin as he leaned against the wall. "And what do you mean by this, doing nothing? What does that look like?"

Demetrius shot Damian a disapproving glare.

"Complacency," Theo said. "Stagnancy. Passivity. Suppression. Oppression, even. Either we act of our volition, or we do not. You see, Demetrius, ultimatums don't exist."

Demetrius buried his head into his lap as he once more recalled the day he shared Leander's ultimatum with Theo. Images of Theo's animated storytelling flashed before his eyes as he remembered how he had interrupted, how Theo had his arms in mid-air, similar to the way he stood now, with his mouth agape and his eyes wide.

"It wasn't *my* ultimatum," Demetrius mumbled.

"This was the problem," Theo said, nodding slowly as he lowered his hands. "You chose to be the mouthpiece of another. You chose to reiterate the words of another. You chose one friend over the other."

"How dare you!" Demetrius cried, rising again from his seat. His eyes bulged from their sockets as he approached Theo pressing his index finger against Theo's chest. "How dare you accuse me of anything except having your best interest at heart."

"You said it yourself," Theo said as he gently removed Demetrius' finger from his robe. "The ultimatum was not yours. The choice, however, to approach me, your beloved companion, with the words, the *threat*, of another man, with little context as to what those words even meant, was all your doing. Am I wrong?"

"But Leander…"

"Ah, yes, Leander. Let me guess. He approached you frantically, deer-eyed, even, as you were still mourning the death of your father, to share… what with you, exactly?"

Damian lifted a finger in the air and tilted his head toward the two.

"You said something about Theo drawing on the walls?" Damian reminded Demetrius softly.

"Yes," Demetrius said. "Leander informed me you were breaking some code—"

"Some code!" Theo laughed and clapped in delight. "*Some* code? You only continue to prove my point! Do you not see it?"

"How could I've seen anything at the time?" Demetrius cried, aggressively jabbing his fingers beside his eyes. "I was mourning! I'm still mourning! And you, standing here now, with no empathy..." Demetrius paced back and forth, adrenaline rushing through his veins as he rethought everything. Damian hopped from the chair and hurried to Demetrius' side.

"Calm down," Damian said.

"Yes," Theo nodded, "sit back, Demetrius. You didn't let me finish. You chose to utter the words of another man, forcing me to make a decision based on this man's terms."

"*This man*? You speak of him as if he meant nothing to you! I won't let you talk about Leander in this way!" Demetrius yelled as he released himself from Damian's grip. "If you don't think Leander cared about you, you're... delusional!"

Another *hoot* hit Demetrius' eardrums, diverting his attention to the shadowed corner of the bedroom. The covered object moved in an unnatural manner, like something stuck under a blanket, unable to find the edges to escape.

"Delusional," Theo said, frowning. "A provocative word choice."

"What would you call it?" Demetrius asked, his eyes darting between Theo and the concealed object. "I've proudly cherished our friendship my whole life, Theo. But you and I both know, no one cared for you, understood you, the way Leander did." Theo scoffed as he shook his head.

"Demetrius, Demetrius, Demetrius. Enlighten me, won't you? On your concept of care. How was it, exactly, that Leander showed he cared for me? Actually, you'll excuse me for changing my mind, won't you? I can better demonstrate how I know for *certain* that Leander never cared for me at all."

Demetrius reached for his chair and dragged it to the center of the room, positioning it directly in front of Theo. He sat on it backwards, propping his forearms on the top rail of the chair, resting his head on his palm.

"I can't wait to hear this," Demetrius said with fiery sarcasm. "Go on, prove it. Prove Leander never cared."

"Look who sits before me… and look who doesn't."

"But the letter was only addressed to me. Only I could see the ink."

"No…" Theo said, tilting his head slowly to the side. "Was the letter delivered to only you?"

"How was it delivered, by the way?" Damian asked, though no one paid any mind.

"The letter was delivered to the Triangle Room," Demetrius said, though he felt a tightness in his throat as he pictured the third abandoned seat at the table, "when both Leander and I were just about to leave."

"Help me understand, Demetrius. What makes you sure that only you could see the ink?"

"Well," Damian said, putting a hand on his hip, "I, for one, was not able to see what was written."

"And by the time I opened the envelope, Leander had already left. But wait," Demetrius said, rising slowly from the chair. "Do you mean to tell me…"

A muffled groan escaped from the windowsill. The three turned their attention to the open window, where bloody fingers had entered the frame, stretching toward the midnight sky. Ruffled vines accompanied the agonizing groans as a full hand drenched in blood gripped the windowsill. A dulled sapphire ring grabbed everyone's attention as the intruder's second bloodied hand shakily hung onto the window's edge.

Chapter
Twenty

Leander mustered the energy to pull himself over the ledge. Moonlight trickled down his bloodied cloak, highlighting the fresh stains, particularly the cut on his neck. Though its depth was minimal, its pain magnified with each cough.

Someone grabbed him by the arm and helped Leander into the poorly lit room. Leander collapsed onto the floor, unable to see who had helped him as his cough echoed against the stone walls.

The reddish-brown mud on Leander's cape had streaked down the wall where Leander had fallen, wiping away the graphite markings. Leander gasped for breath, pressing his hand against his heart as he finally observed his surroundings.

Before him was Demetrius, crouching at eye-level to rub Leander's arm, partly to comfort, though mostly in disbelief at his friend's presence. The candlelight amplified Demetrius' deep, worried wrinkles. To his right stood Damian who covered his mouth in disbelief.

Leander detected Theo's presence though only the scarlet streaks of his shadowed physique penetrated Leander's blurry, unfocused vision.

Leander's heart raced as the room around him faded, mesmerized entirely by the scarlet robe.

With shaking arms, Leander failed to lift himself to his feet until Demetrius wrapped his arm around him, stabilizing his footing. Leander gave a single nod as he readjusted his headwrap.

"What are you doing here?" Demetrius asked. Demetrius tried brushing off the mud that had transferred to his yellow shirt, but the more he rubbed, the more his shirt soaked in the mess. He frowned as he noticed the splotches of red mixed in the mud. "What happened, Leander?"

Though his muscles ached, and his nerves felt aflame, Leander stepped forward, passing Demetrius and gluing his twitching, pale eyes to Theo. The silence in the room weighed heavily upon the four men.

A teeth-bearing smile emerged from Theo's lips as he stretched out his arms, then quickly retracted.

"You've made a warm embrace a moral dilemma," Theo joked, pointing to his mud-covered former mentor. Leander studied the man in front of him, squinting without saying a word. Theo pursed his lips together. "Let me at least offer a heartfelt welcome. I didn't think you'd make the journey, but uttering any form of disappointment about your arrival would be the furthest thing from the truth."

"Why don't you take a seat?" Demetrius asked, reaching for his chair. Leander didn't move. His eyes wandered the dark perimeters of the room. His heart stung and his nerves tensed at the familiar, chaotic arrangement of books. Demetrius pressed his hand onto Leander's shoulder, shaking him gently. "Leander, you look…"

"Unwell," Theo finished. "Frighteningly unwell. There's not an ounce of color in your cheeks. Why, you look like a canvas of a man." The corner of Theo's mouth rose to emphasize his joke. Leander frowned as images of blood gushing from G's throat flashed before him. Theo turned his head. "Where's your sense of humor, Great One? Did it drain out of you too?"

Leander rolled up his sleeve, exposing his pale and fragile arm from beneath the dirtied, navy fabric. He wiped his face with the back of his hand, removing specks of dried dirt. The red residue remained on his cheeks, like an artificial blush of an embarrassment to severe to bear, contrasting the pale blue eyes above it.

Theo's mouth opened as he recognized the source of the redness. Their dissimilar shadows vanished as Theo closed the distance between himself and Leander. His dark, intrigued eyes traced every inch of Leander's cloak and robe, observing everything except for the tears which had begrudgingly congregated near Leander's lashes. Theo reached for Leander's other hand, covered entirely by the dulled navy sleeve. Leander prayed Theo couldn't hear his rapid heartbeat.

"Did you…" Theo asked, focusing intensely on Leander's reddened hand. Leander pulled his hand from Theo's grip.

"You said I look unwell?" Leander mumbled coarsely, his throat aching as the words left his lips. "You have become the prime illustration of all that remains unwell." His disapproving frown deepened as he breathed heavily. "My external presentation may be soiled, but let these stains mark the unruly obstacles *you* placed in my way. Obstacles which *I* overcame."

Theo chuckled, shaking his head. Damian and Demetrius had returned to the table by the window, unsure of how to proceed.

"Overcame?" Theo asked, folding his arms. "Or destroyed?"

Leander's knees trembled as Demetrius scrambled to his side, pulling the chair alongside him. Though he refused to sit, Leander propped his hand on the top of the chair, leaning his weight against it. His sapphire ring, now dulled by grime, clanked against the chair, asserting its presence in the exchange, reaffirming who stood, weakly, before Theo.

"Destruction," Leander muttered, "is no small accusation, and yet, this… place… seems to be grounded in nothing but destruction and extinction." Theo raised his eyebrows and clapped joyfully.

"Is that what you see?" Theo asked, gesturing around the room at the sea of books and sketches on the wall. "Destruction?"

"Was there not a graveyard beside the entrance?" Leander retorted.

Demetrius and Damian exchanged nervous glances, though Theo remained poised. His gesturing hands transitioned to pointing at Leander's red stained fingers.

"It seems that a burial is quite necessary now, doesn't it?"

"What does he mean, Leander?" Demetrius asked. "Theo, what are you referring to?"

"The floor is yours," Theo said to Leander, unable to hide his grin. "I am curious as to who met your unexpected wrath."

Demetrius' heart sank as he gripped Leander's arms in anticipation.

"Wrath?" Demetrius asked. "What wrath?"

Damian's eyes widened as he remembered G dashing out the door into the yard. Janus wouldn't risk the full moon entirely exposing her. Unless there was someone else living in the estate about which he didn't know, G was the only person with whom Leander could have interacted. Damian's stomach turned as he traced the red splotches on Leander.

"Don't say it was G," Damian whispered, feeling the weight of G's blade in his back pocket.

"Who?" Demetrius asked, spinning around.

"Go on," Theo encouraged. "Tell them how you broke the Artist Code." His attention returned to Leander's sapphire ring until Leander pulled his sleeve over it, averse to revealing what had transpired. His vision blurred again, and though he blinked feverishly, he couldn't stop the room from spinning.

"Sit, Leander," Demetrius said, pushing onto Leander's shoulder until his knees buckled. Leander's notorious posture was replaced by sagging shoulders and a weighted head. The room felt colder as the orange candlelight dimmed, allocating lighting responsibility to the moon. Leander groaned, wrapping his arm around his stomach.

"The thought of violating the Code," Leander started, "I... I cannot... No." Though he remained slouched, his tired eyes pierced through the shadows of his headwrap, glaring at Theo. "Violating the Code is never my intention, though intentions vanish when one doesn't have the knowledge to comprehend his context, restricting his ability to act in accordance to anything. Perception... Perception is a mirror. Since we only see that which we have already come to understand, when we are greeted—no, seized—by something unfamiliar..."

"We destroy them?" Theo suggested. Leander straightened his spine, displaying his tightly pressed lips.

"When we are seized by something unfamiliar, our vision alters, beyond our control, and though our eyes will always remain the same, we never perceive the same way again," Leander said. The breeze from the window whirled into the room, reigniting the flame until it swayed feverishly. Its dance bounced dull hues of yellow and orange across the walls closest to it, gracing the remaining graphite on the walls and grabbing Leander's attention. "In fact," Leander added, "we must really ask ourselves if we have ever had the ability to see anything, or anyone, in his truest form."

Theo clapped his hands together, each louder than the previous. He bent down to Leander, resting his elbows on his knees as the ends of his scarlet robe overlapped with Leander's. Theo pressed his fingertips together as he leaned closer, speaking in a tone only Leander could hear.

"It's good to see you, Leander," Theo said, staring intensely and unblinkingly at his mentor. Leander held back the tears that formed at the sound of Theo saying his name. "But, it's even better to see you break the Code, permanently ridding yourself from the title of Greatness."

Leander's heart dropped as Theo reached for Leander's hand, and in one swift motion, removed Leander's ring.

"What are you doing?" Demetrius asked, mortified. Leander, fell back into his chair, his now bare hand falling limp to his side. He looked up at Theo with glossy eyes and a parted mouth, too depleted and appalled to rally the energy to defend himself. Theo limped across the room with Leander's ring secured tightly in his fist.

"You're right, Leander," Theo said, his back turned toward his company as he approached the bookshelf. "We will never, ever, know anyone in their purest form, their absolute intention, their moral totality. And do you know why that is? I'm sure you do." Theo pivoted to face his mentor, grinning from ear to ear. "Come on now, why must you continue looking at me that way? You're an artist, no? Tell us, what would you say is the difference between a man and a canvas?"

Theo dragged his finger across a row of books until he stumbled on the right one. Propping the book above his fist with one hand, he flipped through the pages with the other, licking his finger to expedite the process.

"That's a silly question," Damian said.

"It's an important one to ask," Theo stated. "For Leander either broke the Artist Code or…"

"Or what?" Demetrius asked, looking between Leander and Theo. "Or *what*?"

"Or he's a murderer. Which will it be, Leander?"

A gust of wind entered the room once more, this time extinguishing the single candle and any lingering light-heartedness. The cold, silver moonlight seeped into the room, highlighting each man's reaction to Theo's assertion.

Damian had backed himself into a corner, pressing against the blade for reassurance. Demetrius had released his grip from Leander's shoulders, as though he'd burned himself from holding something ablaze; his eyes traced the red, muddied splotches on the back of Leander's robe, all of which eerily glowed in the moonlight. Leander hid his depleting appearance in the shadows.

Only one side of Theo was visible. He patiently awaited Leander's response, tapping rhythmically on the corner of the book. The moonlight spilled into a perfect curve before Leander. He grimaced under his cold spotlight, for though he was cast in the shadows, his secret was brought to light. The weight of his actions burned his posture.

"What do you consider yourself to be?" Leander asked, his voice dried and drained. He stood to face his mentee with gritted teeth. "Have I reached your rank? The graveyard you have, what—who— did you destroy to create it?"

"Ah, why am I not surprised? You continue to see us as equals, as two halves of some unfortunate whole." Theo slammed the book shut and slid it under his arm, with only a corner of its spine sticking out. Damian's face grew pale as he noticed a single, gold "G" engraved. "Let me explain to you our differences, then. Have you missed my monologues?"

"Please," Demetrius begged, sweat dripping from his forehead, "if either of you have ever cared for me, show me, show me *now*, by telling me what's going on. I deserve to know. *Please.*"

"I would be happy to enlighten you, my dearest friend." Theo pocketed Leander's ring and interlocked his fingers as they fell in front of him. He tilted his head in the direction of Leander. "And you, you'll save me the lecture of the Artist Code, I hope? I can't be held to something with which I don't agree. I'm not an artist."

Leander clutched his heart, further abandoning his posture.

"Someone once said that all men are merely characters," Theo began. "Did I read that somewhere? I can't remember. But let me assure you of the falsity claimed here. Men are not characters, nor are they canvases, nor are they anything else stagnant. Both characters and canvases, even though they may be flawed—and how fascinating it is that the flawed ones are most intriguing—they both are presented to the spectator as already complete. Objects on display. Someone else, the author or the artist, what have you, tells you about the characters. You can't witness them for themselves. They are produced and exhibited."

Theo reached for another book and threw it across the room to Damian, who quickly snatched it as it whirled past Demetrius' alarmed face.

"You're familiar with this text, I assume?" Theo asked Damian. Damian stared at the cover and nodded. "Very good. It ends so tragically, does it not? Though we are informed in the beginning the trajectory of events, we observe his attempts to divert his fate. A horrible, horrible fate. Killing one's father? Marrying one's mother? His efforts are exemplary; he left his family, friends, and city, everything he ever knew, to protect them and himself from this horrific fate." Theo scanned the room, stopping at each guest before turning his attention to the full moon. "And we, the spectators, the mere observers, feel the *agony* upon the revelation that he had indeed *fulfilled* his prophecy, rendering all his intentions useless."

"What's your point?" Damian asked.

"Two points, actually," Theo said, holding two fingers in the air. "The first is that the difference between man and character is indubitably knowledge. We know as much, if not more, than the character undergoing his own life. How absurd would it be to experience such a phenomenon? To look you in the eyes and say with certainty that I know your *entire* life's story, and more. No, man is not granted such luxury."

Leander pressed his lips together and gripped the back of the chair, stabilizing himself as he stood. He winced in pain as he faced Theo.

"Knowledge is not that of all or nothing," Leander said, lowering his shoulders with difficulty. "I do not have to know all of you to recognize an affinity. We know as much about a character as a man, for a man created the character."

"And what would you call a man without character, Leander?" Theo crossed his arms and leaned against the bookshelf, continuing to hold the book marked "G" under one arm.

"I would not call him a friend."

"I have to admit something to you," Theo said, limping toward Leander. "You're right. Everything we create, characters included, is an extension of the self. I discovered this through great trial and error, more than you'll ever know." Theo pointed at the book in Damian's hand. "I must have read that story thousands of times. I refused to blindly accept how his story ended. So, I painted him. Yes, Leander, one of your biggest nightmares: I brought another man's work to life."

214

"You… met him?" Damian asked, placing the book on the table and shifting uncomfortably as though the book had suddenly become dangerous. Demetrius stared at the book, imagining characters crawling out from the cover, stretching their pleading arms from the pages and desperately stumbling and staggering forward.

Meanwhile, Leander's reddened eyes burned as he observed the entire collection of literature before him, imaging each cover as a tombstone for a terminated character.

"No," Theo sighed. "Unfortunately, I did not meet him. I couldn't. I could only meet my interpretation of him. I brought him out of his sandy, miserable context into this… well, less sandy environment. But since I created him, he only met my expectations. How could he do something beyond which I had drawn him to be?"

"When he no longer served your curiosity," Leander said as he tightened his bottom lip to prevent it from trembling, "how did you…"

"No, no, no," Damian interjected, waving his wounded arm in the air before pointing at the book under Theo's arm. The gold "G" shined in the moonlight, imprinting its gleam onto Damian's vision. "You mean to tell me, that you can just bring whomever to life?"

"How else would you define a creator?" Theo asked.

Damian's jaw dropped, as did his ability to verbally express his shock. Theo gripped the book, raising it beside his head.

"Let me repeat," Theo continued, "that I can only bring *my* thoughts and interpretations to life. That's the true tragedy. An exploration of any character is an investigation of myself, for it is a *relation*ship which we experience. Not a man himself."

Demetrius slammed his hands against the table. The veins in his forehead and forearms protruded as he balled his hands into fist.

"I'm tired of this!" Demetrius yelled, saliva spewing from his mouth as he shouted. "This is what you've been up to, Theo? This is what you left us for? I don't care about these technicalities! Man! Character! I can tell you what the real tragedy is!" Demetrius stormed past Leander toward

Theo, pressing his finger against his own pounding heart. "You left your real friends for imaginary ones. You forfeited friendship for... for what! Is this what you wanted?"

Demetrius snatched the book from Theo and threw it behind him. Damian ducked as the book hit the wall and fell to the floor. He immediately crouched to retrieve it, eyes widening with curiosity. The sound of Demetrius' uninterrupted shouting faded as Damian opened to the first page.

The book was written in a similar style to a journal. The first page had a single sentence written in the center:

"What if he hadn't changed?"

Damian wrinkled his face as he turned to the next page, finding a list of attributes. He ran his finger down the page, reading as fast as he could until he recognized about whom he was reading. He slowly looked up, his eyes meeting Leander's worn and worried expression. As he parted his lips to speak, Theo had pushed Demetrius to the side and hurriedly approached Damian, retrieving his book. He put a finger to his lips and winked at Damian before turning back to Demetrius, who was still breathing heavily from overwhelming emotions.

"Your words carry validity," Theo assured Demetrius. "This brings me to my second point. If you remember, my first point was that knowledge separates man from character. You can disagree all you want, but once I share the second point, I'm sure you'll finally understand." Theo walked to the center of the room, facing the full moon. His three guests, though they stood significantly apart, stared anxiously at Theo. "Knowledge itself," Theo said, pausing for emphasis, "cannot be created or destroyed, only discovered. It is knowledge, not art, that is eternal. It's not the canvas that lives on forever but the knowledge it carries."

"No," Leander said, though his emerging cough prevented him from saying more. Demetrius helped Leander back into the chair.

216

"Yes," Theo said, "and it is for this reason, that creation itself is an illusion." Theo stepped backwards, removing himself from the moonlight. "What we create has already, in fact, been created. That which you sketch onto the canvas is an extension of what has already existed in your mind. You're doing nothing more than illustrating your thoughts, your knowledge. Isn't that fascinating? You, the Great, have never actually created anything."

"No," Leander repeated. He gasped for air as sweat trickled down the side of his face.

"Yes! And in the same respect, you've never destroyed anything either. Does that not bring you some respite, some relief?"

Leander leaned forward, ensuring his whisper reached Theo's ears.

"The Code..." Leander said as he coughed again. "Art is... Immortal... Once the subject is alive... You cannot..." Demetrius kneeled beside Leander, gently placing one hand upon Leander's shoulder and one on his knee. Leander's gaze remained firmly on Theo.

"You face a severe predicament, in that case, Leander. I'm sure you realize this already, but there's only one question left to ask you." Moonlight traveled across Theo's extended arm as he pointed to the red stains on Leander's cloak and robe. "I know what you've done. You know what you've done. So, tell me, are you a breaker of the Code, or are you a murderer?"

The weight of Theo's question was too much for Leander to bare. He slid off the chair, clutching his heart as his knees hit the ground. He crouched over as his attire created the appearance of a darkened puddle spilling onto the floor.

"You should've taken the relief I offered you earlier," Theo said, lowering his outstretched hand and moving further into the shadows until he reached the corner of his bed, where a covered object patiently waited.

"Stop it!" Demetrius yelled from across the room. "Can't you see you're hurting Leander? Where's your sympathy?"

"I don't have sympathy for the Code, or anyone who lives by it," Theo said, his voice abruptly lowering to a menacing tone. "Living by the Code would've restricted my subjectivity. I could never have explored so many lives, relationships, stories, perspectives. Once I made that realization, that nothing could be created or destroyed, well, then, I was free to explore as much as I pleased. Why do you think I started wearing these scarlet threads before I left you all those years ago? This discovery is not new. You always said I could use a splash of color, Demetrius, remember? Scarlet suits me well, I think. The stains are far less noticeable. Perhaps now you'll join me, Leander?"

Demetrius violently rustled his sweaty curls as he faced Leander. He leaned down, resting his hand on Leander's back with more pressure than before.

"Who did you hurt?" Demetrius whispered to his friend with bated breath.

Before Leander could answer, a bellowing *hoot* traveled along the stone walls, robbing everyone of their thoughts. Leander's head sprung up as he faced the direction from which the sound emerged. Though his eyes stung from copious tears, he could faintly recognize what looked like the stolen object from his room at the Residence.

With an incomprehensible resurgence of energy, Leander sprang to his feet, ridding himself from Demetrius' touch. He lunged through the shadows, collapsing as he reached for the covered object. Theo stomped his foot right before Leander's face, blocking Leander's reach.

"Theo," Leander begged, "what has become of you?"

"What have you forced me to become?"

Leander's outstretched hand trembled and tears ran down his face as he watched the cursed canvas come to life.

Chapter
Twenty-One

Caterina sprung from her slumber, gasping for air as she clutched her chest. The vines hanging around the curtained window turned to her, like the curious eyes of bystanders. She hoisted herself to the end of the bed, dropping her head into the palms of her hands. Her bare toes pushed against the cold floor, sending a chill down her spine.

The girl has risen, the vines informed Aluna, who rushed to Damian's room.

Sweat dripped down Caterina's forehead, mixing with the graphite smeared on her delicate fingers as she pushed her hair back. Grey smudges trailed under her eyes as she wiped away tears.

"What's wrong, dear?" Aluna asked, joining Caterina on the bed.

"What time is it?" Caterina leaned toward the window to check the outdoors, but the vines quickly grasped the edges of the curtain. Aluna gently moved Caterina's hair off her shoulder, reverting her attention.

"I believe it's around three in the morning," Aluna said.

"I can't bare this night any longer," Caterina said, weaving her fingers through her hair before gripping it. "I just woke from the most terrifying nightmare. I knew I was dreaming, but I couldn't wake up. It was like…"

"A living nightmare."

The vines drooped as if watered by Caterina's tears that Aluna helped wipe away. Aluna placed the candle on the nightstand, freeing her hands to comfort Caterina.

"You really should get some rest," Aluna suggested, rubbing Caterina's back.

"No, no, I can't do this anymore. The nightmare… Leander… He was sick and unable to move. His hands," Caterina continued, extending and examining her own hands, "they trembled violently. He couldn't even hold a paintbrush." A tear fell onto Caterina's hand as she clenched them.

"I think that's a nightmare we all share," Aluna said softly. "Watching our loved ones suffer."

"Is Leander…?"

"Is he what, dear? Suffering?" Aluna felt Caterina's hands' tremble as the silence grew. "He is resilient," Aluna assured her.

"I have to get back to drawing."

Caterina charged for the door and rushed down the unlit hallway.

"Caterina, wait!" Aluna yelled, leaving the candle to chase Caterina into the darkness. Aluna continued to call for her as she saw glimpses of Caterina flash through the slivers of moonlight escaping the edges of the closed curtains from adjacent rooms. When they reached the main entry, Aluna rushed toward the door, sprawling her body across its frame. Caterina squeezed her feet into her dirtied sandals and turned to Aluna.

"Let me go," Caterina said. "Please."

"If you leave, you're not going alone." Aluna's curls fell onto her face, hiding everything but the stern shape of her lips.

The room echoed two increasing heartbeats as Caterina considered the ultimatum. She sighed, agreeing to subside. Aluna slipped into her sandals as well, and the two entered the cool-aired midnight landscape.

Part the hedges, please, Aluna said. Caterina jumped behind Aluna, clutching her arms as she watched the plants behave accordingly. Aluna smiled. *Thank you.*

"Am I still dreaming?" Caterina asked, pinching her skin. Aluna shook her head. Caterina looked over her shoulder at the hedges as the two stepped onto the main path. The bench upon which Caterina would wait for Leander came into view. Caterina traced the outline of his studio, fighting the urge to knock upon the door.

"We shouldn't stay in one place too long," Aluna whispered as the hedges intertwined once more. "I'm following your lead."

Caterina walked slowly past Leander's home, unable to keep her eyes off his door until it was no longer feasible. She avoided the full moon above her, scared to see the haunting, eye-shaped craters.

The path before them twisted and turned throughout a residential region. Houses of different shapes and sizes basked in the moonlight. Their off-white exteriors glistened, occasionally blanketed by emerald vines. Accompanying their soft footsteps was the sound of curtains swinging against the houses' walls, greeting the nighttime travelers. The two walked in silence, mindful of the sleeping neighbors.

Beyond the houses, the path continued winding through the hillside, with a new residential area lining the horizon. The grass around them grew taller the further they walked, and Caterina aimlessly trickled her fingers through them.

"It must be so nice," Caterina said, watching the moonlight shine upon the swaying grass, "to always feel connected to something. To never feel alone. How long have you nurtured this relationship with plants?"

"I graduated from the Atrium a little over twenty years ago, though I don't remember a time when plants haven't been a part of me. It's not quite a connection."

"Why not?"

"A connection implies a link between two separate entities. I don't believe separating myself from the greenery is even a possibility." Aluna shuddered at the thought. "I still experience loneliness, though, believe it or not."

Caterina waved her arms at the scenery around them, the acres of grassland leading to forestation in the background. "How can you be lonely when you are so intimately part of all this?"

"That's like asking how one can be lonely when she is so intimately attached to all her thoughts," Aluna said, smiling wearily as she also ran her fingers through the grass. "Though we internally extend ourselves to great lengths, we may still long to extend ourselves to the touch of another. Fulfilment is less about how far we can extend ourselves, and more about to whom we reach via extension."

A rustling in the grass nearby seized Caterina's attention. She grabbed Aluna's arm as she stood paralyzed.

Do not fright, the grass said, *for it is nothing more than an adventurous nocturnal creature.*

"There's nothing to fear," Aluna said, patting Caterina's back.

"Suddenly everything terrifies me," Caterina said with a sigh. "And I need to apologize to you, for keeping you up so late and dragging you along into my mess."

Aluna stepped in front of Caterina, placing her hands gently on Caterina's shoulders.

"The only person you owe an apology to is yourself. You are extending yourself too far at the moment."

"It's the uncertainty. Without Leander," Caterina said, choking on Leander's name as tears reemerged, "I'm not sure which direction to go in. So, I'm just… going." She flexed her fingers as they longed for the familiar grip of a pencil. Aluna shook her head and grabbed Caterina's restless hand.

"Can I share something with you? From my experience, I can assure you, knowing oneself is more vital than knowing anything else, including the likes of others. So many people spend their time trying to understand the world around them without ever understanding themselves."

"How does that relate to me?" Caterina asked with a raised eyebrow. "Art is a very expressive field. Everything I will create will be an extension of me, to some degree."

"Or will it be an extension of a version of you, one perhaps you've fabricated to meet the expectations you think Leander demands?" Caterina opened her lips to object, but Aluna shook her head. "I understand the dynamic, and as your mentor, of course you rely on him to achieve your goals. But tell me, what has he assigned for your final project?"

"That's just it," Caterina said, dropping her arms defeatedly. "The assignment wasn't clear. It was a blank prompt. Well, not blank, essentially. He told me to use my imagination, which I can assure you is never void, but I'm afraid the overwhelming whirlwind of thoughts has a blurring effect, and I can't pinpoint an individual thought. I asked him for more clarity, but he insisted that the sketch already exists within me."

"Is that right?" Aluna grinned. "Leander always surprises me. But Caterina, don't you see that he's advising you to do the same thing, to look within? We all develop a method of seeing and comprehending the world around us, and I'm sure your skills have proven to Leander your mastery of this task. It's apparent to me, through this assignment, that Leander has challenged you to now navigate a whole new world: yourself. I'm not an artist, but I suppose Leander's understanding of himself was through exploring the breadths and depths of his own imagination. Your final assignment, then, seems fitting."

Caterina paused, contemplating Aluna's interpretation. She pursed her lips together and twisted them to the side. Her anxious fingers returned to the tall blades of grass. Aluna's grin remained, content with Caterina's momentary silence and self-reflection, until Caterina ultimately shook her head.

"You see, my imagination... Hmm... What is my imagination if not a combination, a collection, of that which I've come to know? Is it really my own? I mean, I've spent years studying the works of others, learning their techniques, seeing their visions. How can I detach myself from any of that?"

"There's a light in you," Aluna assured her, "which can only be ignited by one thing, or one particular sequence of things. You gravitate toward the arts, no? Why is that? Why couldn't you, for example, study philosophy?"

A visual of Damian immediately invaded Caterina's mind. His enticing eyes, charming smile, and most importantly, his appetite for curiosity. She gently touched her lips, remembering the sensation of his lips on hers. In her memory, she pictured herself resting her head in the crevice of his neck, tracing the lines of their interlocked hands.

"I don't particularly enjoy idealism," Caterina said, blinking feverishly to rid herself of the images of Damian. She turned away, hoping Aluna wouldn't notice the color flooding to her cheeks.

"Philosophy is more than just idealism," Aluna noted, "but I understand your aversion. And botany? Have you ever considered being a botanist?"

"No, no. I've always wanted to be an artist."

"Then you're already familiar with the candle within you. Some search their entire lives for the source of their spark, and unfortunately, they may never find it. One reason for this, I believe, is because they're too focused on others, or the world around them. And if your focus remains on Leander, though he shares your spark and love for art, you will never be the artist you are destined to become. You're not the next Leander. You are Caterina."

Caterina looked up, and the full moon met her gaze. Its two giant craters, earlier a terrifying reminder of her doubt and anxiety of her current work of progress, suddenly provided her some comfort. She stared into the round, owl-like eyes of the moon, seeing for once a surface upon which she could create something spectacular. A chuckle slipped from her lips as she smiled at Aluna.

"Thank you," Caterina said, squeezing Aluna's hand. "I think I finally know what to submit for the final project."

Aluna returned the smile. Caterina's eyes remained glued to the moon, outlining its details until they were firmly imprinted into her memory.

There appears to be an intruder, the grass said to Aluna. *Someone is waiting outside your home.*

Aluna watched Caterina from her periphery to ensure she didn't sense a change in Aluna's demeanor.

Who is it? Aluna asked.

There was an elongated silence as the inquiry traveled to and from Aluna's home. Her mind raced with theories.

His face cannot be detected, the grass informed her.

His?

Yes. He first knocked on the door of the studio across the street. Upon dismissal and with concern, he approached your door. He now sits perplexed on the bench.

The grass around them gradually declined into sparse patches as they approached Caterina's community. Aluna looked around for signs of greenery through which she could continue the conversation, but to her dismay, the grassland stopped a couple steps in front of them.

Caterina quickened her pace, adrenaline fueling her determination to invest herself entirely to the final project.

I will be back shortly, Aluna said, following behind Caterina.

He has returned to your—

Aluna halted, tempted to retreat to hear the statement, but Caterina was too far into a trance to be interrupted or slowed down. Aluna sighed and hurried after Caterina.

They turned down a slimmer path, and Caterina pointed to the third house.

"I have to sneak in quietly. Otherwise, my sister will have a fit. But Aluna," Caterina turned to face Aluna, who had hidden her concern, "I cannot thank you enough. For protecting me, for caring about me, for teaching me. Though we just met, I feel as though, in some strange way, I was meant to meet you." Caterina wrapped her arms tightly around Aluna, who returned the embrace.

"Be safe," Aluna said, rubbing Caterina's arms as she stepped away. "And protect your spark."

Caterina beamed and nodded, waving as Aluna turned to leave. She sped as silently as she could to her house, peeping over her shoulder to see Aluna at the opposite end of the path.

Caterina tip-toed around her house until she approached her bedroom window, still open from hours before. She sighed in relief, gripping the wall as she hoisted herself into her room. She immediately slipped off her sandals and sat at her desk. The room was dark, except for a beam of moonlight shining through the swaying curtain. She frowned, remembering her sister had confiscated her candle.

She reached for her nearest notebook and placed her sketches on its cover. Pulling the curtain back entirely, Caterina sat beside the window, resting the sketch in her lap and bathing the paper in the light of the full moon. She sacrificed her posture as she traced the curves of her original drawing, darkening the outline with certainty. Her long, black hair spilled over her shoulder, like an added curtain to shield the sketch from the eyes of another.

The moon continued her journey across the sky as Caterina sketched, crouching over the piece of paper until her nose smeared the graphite. She had just finished shading the beak when the sound of someone clearing their throat broke Caterina's focus. She gasped and turned to see Safiya leaning against the doorframe, arms crossed behind her back.

"I can explain," Caterina said, raising her graphite-covered hands defensively. Safiya shook her head and approached Caterina. Without a word, she revealed the candle she had been discreetly holding. She placed it on the corner of Caterina's desk.

"I see there's no stopping you."

Caterina's eyes sparkled as she smiled, rising from her chair to hug her sister. Safiya lit the candle.

"This will be the last time," Caterina said, staring unblinkingly at Safiya to convey her seriousness, "that an assignment will consume me. My approach has changed. I've had… a revelation."

Safiya furrowed her brows and placed the back of her hand against Caterina's forehead. Caterina playfully pushed her sister's hand away. As she turned to leave, Safiya noticed Caterina's muddied sandals below the window and raised an eyebrow at her younger sister.

Caterina brought her hands together and scrunched her face, asking silently for forgiveness. Safiya applied pressure to her temples, inhaling and exhaling deeply.

"Don't worry about me. I'm alright," Caterina assured her. "I'm more than alright, actually. I'm an artist."

Caterina dragged her chair back to the desk and immediately returned to the task at hand.

"Let me know if you need anything, my dear little artist." Safiya closed the door behind her as she left the room.

Caterina observed the sketch before her: a majestic owl with a beautifully patterned arrangement of dark and light feathers, soon to be brown and white. Its round face, though horizontally elongated, was perfectly symmetrical. Beside its little beak remained two, unfinished circles.

Caterina tapped her pencil against the desk, biting her bottom lip as she focused on her imagination.

"The eyes," she said to herself. "They need to be more than just for seeing." She stared around her darkened room looking for answers. "No! Look inward, Caterina." She took a deep breath and closed her eyes. She sat silently, noticing that her breath had slowed down as she immersed herself in her imagination.

For the first time, she noticed an arrangement of indescribable shapes and colors which she had never seen before. They flowed in and out her vision like the clouds on a windy, summer day. She sat back into her chair, enjoying the spectacle before her.

She had leaned too far and instantly opened her eyes as she steadied herself from falling. After a brief moment of reorientation, she returned her focus to the owl. She frowned as the shapes and colors now seemed flatter. She ran her fingers through the colored pencils beside her, sighing as she realized she couldn't recreate or reflect the shades she saw in her imagination.

Her eyes widened as an idea struck her. She snatched a regular pencil and leaned over the paper, tilting her head to allow the candlelight's full glow onto the paper. She closed one eye to ensure this last detail was added with precision.

In the space reserved for each eye, Caterina delicately wrote "mirror."

Chapter
Twenty-Two

Demetrius bent toward Leander until a *hoot* sent paralyzing fear through his veins. Two round, inferno eyes appeared from the shadows, their brilliance blinding the men. Demetrius stumbled backwards, retreating as the eyes enlarged before him. The golden glow extended onto the creature's beak and its closest feathers. Though her wings didn't expand, the owl settled into her newly acquired space, spanning from floor to ceiling. A clinking sound trickled through the ruffling of her feathers.

Damian, too, withdrew from the creature. He pressed his back against the wall, and the blade in his back pocket made a similar noise to the sound emerging from the owl's rumpled feathers. Damian's eyes widened as he inched toward the door.

"Theo…" Demetrius started to say.

"Don't be afraid," Theo responded, unable to mask his gleaming grin. The bird tilted her head in curiosity, her eyes now vertically aligned glaring at Demetrius. A soft whimper escaped from Leander, diverting the bird's attention to the ground.

Leander propped himself up, though his shaking hand assured him no stability. His head hung low, and though no one could see, a tear fell onto his muddied apparel, adding to the pooling puddle of misery Leander emanated. Theo crouched to Leander, resting his elbows on his knees and repeated himself to his old mentor.

"Don't be afraid."

With closed eyes, Leander sat back, bringing his arms into his lap. He exhaled deeply and faced Theo. The fiery light accentuated Theo's utmost delight, his black eyes ablaze with excitement. Leander's vision blurred as more tears surfaced, and to prevent them from falling, Leander had no choice but to look up.

The owl's pupils dilated when she recognized Leander. Silence seized everyone's breaths.

Everyone's unwavering attention to the owl permitted Damian to gradually reach the door. He twisted the doorknob behind his back. The owl screeched, and everyone covered their ears in agony. Damian immediately released the knob, but it was too late. The owl expanded her wings, circumventing the room the way a snake coils around its prey. Her wings covered the men in complete darkness, blocking the full moon entirely.

Her eyes were the only source of light, like two fiery moons blazing down on the men. For the first time since the beginning of his journey, Demetrius' shirt, though dirtied by the endeavors, shone its familiar bright yellow. Theo's scarlet threads, too, shone brightly in this new, vibrant lighting. Leander, however, remained as dark as ever, and even his sapphire ring, though mostly covered in grime, failed to radiate a single sparkle.

"She's beautiful, isn't she?" Theo asked, his dark eyes sparkling with excitement.

"B-b-beautiful?" Demetrius asked. Damian, feeling a similar sentiment, rushed to stand behind Demetrius.

"What are those?" Damian whispered to Demetrius, eyeing the glistening metal peeking beneath the feathers.

"I'm glad you asked," Theo said. The ends of his robes brushed past Leander's fallen composure as he approached Demetrius and Damian with a smile. He placed a heavy hand on Demetrius' shoulder. "She was originally a gift."

"For?"

"You."

Demetrius peered over Theo's shoulder hesitantly, awaiting an indication of pleasantry a gift usually embodies. He furrowed his eyebrows. Leander grimaced as his body weakened, restricting him from standing.

"She was made to protect you, Demetrius," Theo assured. "Surely you know what an owl represents?"

"Wisdom?" Damian asked with a cracked voice.

"Perhaps," Theo responded with a shrug, "but more specifically, I chose it for its nocturnal nature. You, Demetrius, are our constant ray of light, with a smile that beams from miles away, an energy that warms an entire room and blesses even those with cold hearts, but I'm afraid even your own brightness restricts you from noting the shadows and those which dwell in them."

Leander turned toward his friends and reached out a hand for assistance. Theo, noticing Demetrius' eyes shift to the floor behind him, immediately turned and grabbed Leander's hand. Stinging pain traveled down Leander's arm as he felt Theo's skin wrapped around his. Though Leander gripped Theo's hand with all his might, Leander's eyes clung harder. Before he could savor the momentary physical contact, Theo released his hold.

"I'm tired of these grand gestures and metaphors," Demetrius said, wiping his hands down his face. "Please... Please tell me how this was supposed to be a gift?"

"Don't tell me you don't like her! I will save you the theatrics, my friend. You can't deny, however, that you are indeed too optimistic for this world. Hmm? No?" Theo turned to Leander and crossed his arms. "Don't you think Demetrius is too optimistic?"

231

Leander mustered the energy to cross his arms as well. His nostrils flared as he breathed heavily, though he remained silent. Tears awaited their release on his bottom lashes, stinging his eyes as he stared defeatedly at Theo.

"I hear no objection," Theo said, returning his attention to Demetrius. "Shall I continue then? Optimism, one of the strangest gifts one could possess, provides temporal moments—seconds, minutes, hours, days, eras—their perpetuity and brilliance. Consequently, your optimism is a reward to those around you, for who doesn't find its nature refreshing? But, to be in a constant state of optimism? To be in a constant state of anything, really, is…" Theo looked over his shoulder at Leander, "sad."

The owl's eyes focused once more on Leander, showering him in burning radiance. His appearance was strangely like a permanent shadow, for no amount of light could illuminate his presence.

"What's more strange," Theo continued, "was that I never wanted you, Demetrius, to change. I do treasure you, more than you know. You are a rarity. But, it is a sort of sickness to remain constant. So this gift was created to be the missing part of you. A remedy, so to speak."

Theo approached the owl's body and gently glided his hands across her feathers. The shiny, elongated strands of metal between the feathers became more prominent, and Demetrius stood paralyzed as they swung back and forth. Damian crouched behind Demetrius, peeking only slightly from the side.

"Are those… knives?" Damian asked.

Theo brushed his hands across the feathers once more, showcasing the feather-shaped reflective metal swinging beside the natural brown feathers.

"Technically, no," Theo said, though he chuckled at the idea. "What you see are mirrors." Demetrius held his breath. He looked over at Leander, who had covered his face with his bloodied hands.

"Mirrors? Shaped like knives?" Demetrius asked, his heart racing. "When did you make this gift? When were you planning to give it to me?" Demetrius clenched his fists as he anticipated the answer. Damian rose from his crouched position, feeling Demetrius' energy shift from fear to rage. Theo smiled, extending his palm from across the room toward Demetrius to calm him.

"This was supposed to be a gift of gratitude, I assure you. Your unconditional support, patience, trust, and most importantly, your friendship, meant more to me than can ever be expressed in words."

"I think a simple 'thank you' would've sufficed," Demetrius said.

"Words only suffice when one desires to express an idea. But not a feeling." Theo shifted to his right, where Leander squeezed his lips together to suppress a cough. "Isn't that what you taught me? Yes, yes that's exactly what you said to me when you realized I was slipping through your fingers."

"No," Leander said weakly. Theo cocked his head to the side. The orange light slid between his angered wrinkles, amplifying his disdain for Leander's retort.

"No? It was the day you bribed me with the ring!"

Demetrius held his breath as he felt the ring in his pocket.

"You told me there was nothing more liberating than expressing one's soul, and the highest form of expression was only achieved through art," Theo continued through clamped teeth, approaching Leander until he could speak in a lowered, condescending tone. "Words could never satisfy a stoic like yourself, could they? But forget the words of others! After being in this tower for so long, I often wondered, do you hear the words *you* say? Or does their worthlessness only heighten your pretentious devotion to art?"

"Leave him alone," Demetrius warned Theo. Theo stepped back, though his gaze remained locked.

"If you were truly able to express yourself through your art, why is your loneliness so prominent, Leander? Could it be that through your highest means of expression, no one resonates with you? Or perhaps, you've never truly expressed yourself? Well? Which one is it?"

"Stop it!" Demetrius yelled. He rolled his sleeves and crossed the room, pushing Theo further away from Leander. Though the push was not severe, Theo rocked back, pressing his robe against the owl's brown feathers. The clanking noise echoed throughout the room. Damian, discomforted by the sound once more, crept toward Demetrius, positioning himself between Demetrius and Leander.

"I was born to create," Theo said, pressing his finger against his chest, "to learn, to travel, both physically and mentally. And you!" Theo turned his pointed finger toward Leander. "You forced me to shrink myself, to glue myself to the pencil and canvas, to mute myself and my vision. For what? For whom? No, I couldn't let you do that to me. I had to tell you, using your language, how wrong you were about me."

The owl closed her eyes, extinguishing light from the room. Damian gulped at the sound of the mirrored feathers brushing against one another. In the darkness, he reached into his back pocket and retrieved G's blade, gripping the handle tightly and squeezing his clenched hand subtly behind his back. When the owl opened her eyes, a bead of sweat ran down Damian's face as he realized Leander was right behind him.

Damian peered over his shoulder with pleading eyes, silently begging Leander to not say a word. Leander's eyes traveled from the blade, to Theo, then back at Damian. When Damian gave a single, subtle nod, Leander returned a discrete shaking of the head. Damian pressed his lips together and turned his head around. There was no way for him to return the blade to his pocket without being seen, so he had no choice but to wait for another moment of darkness.

Theo gently patted the owl, smiling as he focused on Demetrius.

"You see, my friend, I was provided a unique opportunity, one which not only allowed me to create something to show my gratitude for you, but also one that would teach that man behind you who I really was. Why was I so desperate to shatter the ideal he had of me? A question for another day."

"I still don't understand," Demetrius said, "how this terrifying creature would be a gift to *me*?" The owl squinted, disapproving Demetrius' description. Theo wrapped his fingers around the handle of one of the elongated, pointed mirrors, tilting it outwards for everyone to see.

"She was much tamer, I promise you. Let's not forget she was trapped and hidden away for how many years? Too many. She would've been like a pet, though there'd be no need to domesticate her. She would've been trained to recognize the people of our community, and in the presence of someone who you'd need to examine more closely, she would spread her wings to showcase her mirrored feathers. If you weren't able to see the bad in them, well, let's just say she wouldn't be afraid to show the person his or her true reflection."

Theo brushed his finger against the tip of the mirrored feather, and although the cut was minimal, a scarlet drop of blood bubbled on his skin. The owl looked at Theo's finger, bringing its face closer to the blood as though fascinated by it. The intensified glow near the mirrored feather stung the men's eyes. Though he squinted defensively, Demetrius recognized the detailed carvings in the reflective blade.

This was the second time in his life he saw those curved, feathered lines on a handle.

"You..." Demetrius said, pointing a shaking finger at Theo. "You..."

"Now, now," Theo said, raising his hands in defense. "You didn't let me finish. This creation was originally intended to be my final submission for the Academy, my final attempt to show my beloved mentor who his student was, or more accurately, who he wanted to be."

Demetrius spun around to face Leander, pushing Damian out of the way.

"You allowed him to make this?" Demetrius asked Leander, his lips trembling as he breathed heavily.

"I did not. I forbade it from the moment he showed me... the first sketch." Leander coughed, patting his chest. Demetrius pivoted his head between his two friends, unsure of who to blame or question.

"Yes, yes. I remember all those silly requirements you tried to impose. Complete freedom and trust weren't the preconditions I was given for the assignment," Theo scoffed, "which only made me want to prove myself more. That requires freedom, don't you think? Freedom to go beyond one's expectations, soar past the parameters. My mentor here feared the idea of his favorite Theo rising."

"Theorizing what?" Demetrius asked. Theo shook his head, but before he could clarify, Leander coughed and spoke.

"The Code," Leander said softly.

"Forget the cursed Code! 'One does not create to destroy,' is that right? Is that what you're trying to say? My piece is inherently destructive? You couldn't be further from the truth. She only reflects the destructive nature already existing in others. Were you scared to see your own reflection?"

"No," Leander said. "Never."

"Never?" Theo said with raised eyebrows. The corner of his lips rose in delight. "If that's the case, why don't you share with Demetrius that which he has yearned to know for the last twenty years?"

Demetrius slowly faced Leander, tears of disbelief stinging his eyes. His mouth was open, unprepared for, yet already shocked by, what Leander was about to disclose. Leander inhaled deeply. His cough worsened, as did his ability to conceal the truth he'd swallowed for years.

"Theo brought me the canvas on the day of his graduation," Leander said, forcing himself to watch the tears run down Demetrius' face. "I refused to let him on stage with a project that broke the Code."

"It always comes back to the Code, doesn't it?" Theo said. "You said it was a canvas like you'd never seen!"

"I had never seen anyone break the Code as much as you happily did," Leander said, squeezing his lips together to suppress another cough. "Standing here is validation enough that I read you right."

"What did you just say to me?"

"Enough!" Demetrius yelled, saliva spewing from his mouth as he wiped tears from his face. "No one will make another move or say another word unless it pertains to what I need to know." Theo threw his arm in Leander's direction, pursing his lips together as he waited for Leander to continue.

"I had no choice but to ask Theo to permanently leave the Academy," Leander said, lifting his chin. He stared blankly to the side, watching his memories unfold before his eyes. Though he sporadically coughed, he continued his retelling. "He fought me on this, but my obligation to the position and the discipline superseded any counterargument. He desired to retrieve the canvas, but this I too refused. My trust in him had been broken, and I no longer thought it safe to permit him the acquisition of the weapon he had finished creating."

"*Almost* finished," Theo corrected. Leander winced, experiencing more mental pain than physical.

"Theo had failed to tell me the piece was not entirely complete," Leander said, his eyebrows lowering as more tears ran down Demetrius' face. Leander hobbled to Demetrius, reaching for his hand. "I was in a panic, Demetrius. Upon realization that my one student would not be graduating and had just stormed out of the room with a promise to never see me again, I was distraught." Leander's hand shook violently as he gripped onto Demetrius, pleading for him to understand.

"You forced me to leave, Leander!" Theo exclaimed, his voice roaring over the room.

"But I *never* forced you to kill!"

No one spoke.

The owl's wings circled closer around them, her feathers hanging like bars, imprisoning the men in their cold truth. The lump in Demetrius' throat grew as rage boiled in his stomach. Demetrius released Leander's hand and glared at Theo as his eye twitched uncontrollably.

Damian, who was still hiding his blade, stepped toward Demetrius; he discretely lowered his hand behind Demetrius' clenched fist and shoved the handle into the center of his hand.

Demetrius perplexedly felt the newly acquired object. Leander, standing behind the two, watched the transaction in silence.

"Demetrius," Theo said, shaking his head, "your friend has yet to tell you the full story. I was forced to leave the Academy, remember? How can an absent man be accused of anything?"

"An absent-minded man is often guilty," Leander said. "We had been in the adjacent room to the auditorium. Once Theo left, I had covered the canvas and placed it in the corner. Your father…" Demetrius squeezed his eyes shut, bracing himself. He heaved violently as the flashbacks returned. Damian placed a consoling hand on Demetrius' shoulder.

"Go on," Theo said from across the room, arms folded.

"Your father had entered the room, informing me the time had come for me to take the stage. I… Demetrius, I am so sorry."

"Just tell me!" Demetrius pleaded, swallowing the tears that ran down his face into the corners of his mouth.

"I had asked him to stay with the canvas, to ensure Theo would not retrieve it while I was away." Demetrius lowered his head and sobbed harder, using his free hand to wipe away the sweat and tears. "He had come to support Theo, and since Theo was no longer in attendance, I assumed he would not mind guarding the piece. As I mentioned, however, I was not informed the piece was incomplete."

"I would've told you had you given me the chance to explain myself," Theo said unapologetically. "The one part that remained unfinished was the training. I had yet to teach her what to detect, outside of someone's potentially positive projections. At the time, however, she was only familiar with my face and Leander's."

"Wait, wait, wait," Damian said, raising an eyebrow. "The implication here is that you were to somehow train her to see someone's true intentions?"

Theo grinned and nodded.

"I was young, then. Naive. She would have been the first of her kind, a canvas that truly goes beyond the essence of a canvas, one that can acquire skills not sketched in its footprint." Theo exhaled a disappointed sigh. "It's a shame, really, that she never got the chance. I had planned to showcase this skill for the first time on stage."

"What happened instead?"

"Myron's curiosity must've gotten the best of him," Theo said, uncrossing his arms and sighing.

"All I remember was the yell," Leander said, his voice trembling. "I rushed off the stage and found the owl had risen from the canvas on her own. And your father... your poor father..."

"There was a mirror protruding from his back," Theo said, shaking his head. "Leander was clever to have had someone guard the canvas, for I had stayed in the shadows of the auditorium waiting for the opportunity to sneak back into the room. But Demetrius, I swear to you, I don't know how the incident occurred."

"Canvases do not possess minds of their own!" Leander yelled. His risen voice resulted in a coughing fit, and Leander stumbled backward, unable to catch his breath. Damian looked worryingly at Leander until he saw Demetrius stiffen his posture and calmly wipe the remaining tears on his face with his free hand. He stepped toward Theo but said nothing. Damian's eyes widened.

"*Your* canvases don't possess minds of their own, Leander!" Theo argued. "Your little waterfalls and lambs are pathetic extensions of your already surface-level understanding of existence and expression!"

Demetrius took another step toward Theo.

"What is it you want, Theo?" Demetrius asked, his jaw clenched beneath a deep frown.

"All I've ever wanted," Theo replied with a deep breath, raising his chin, "no— all I've ever needed is to understand, *why*? Why is it we are the way we are? Why are *you* the way you are? And more over, you were the one, Leander, who commanded to keep Demetrius in the dark as to what had transpired, preventing him from healing and understanding. You fell to your knees in agony, remember? Or does your memory conveniently escape you? Yes, remember! I dare you to remember! You fell to your knees as soon as you covered the canvas. Was that not your first priority upon entering the room? I saw you, Leander. You rushed toward the owl before you rushed toward Myron."

"To prevent further destruction!" Leander cried, shaking his head as he pressed his hands to his hollow cheeks. His eyes wildly darted back and forth as his fingers trembled against his skin. "Prevent further destruction... and protect... what was left." His cough seized his rebuttal.

"Say what you will, but the truth remains. You covered the canvas and fell to your knees. You should be grateful I was there to quickly close the door and protect your reputation. I even listened to your command, to go tell Demetrius what had occurred, but 'spare him the details for now.' You remember now, don't you?"

Leander stopped shaking and slowly lifted his head to meet Theo's gaze.

After a heavy moment of silence, Leander wailed in uncontrollable anger, charging toward Theo and snatching the blade from Demetrius' hand in one quick motion. He grabbed Theo's shoulder, dug his fingertips into the scarlet fabric, and pierced Theo directly in the heart.

The inferno lighting trickled over the sparkling blood pouring over Theo's red robe, blending seamlessly into the embroidery. Leander's unwavering eyes stared deeply into Theo's as he pressed the blade deeper into his former student until only the handle remained visible. His once teared-stained cheeks were now reddened with anger as veins protruded along his forehead.

An eerie smile spanned across Theo's face as the familiar scent of lead filled Leander's nostrils.

"We're not so different now, are we?" Theo whispered into Leander's ear before his knees buckled and his body collapsed onto the floor.

Chapter
Twenty-Three

Trickles of scarlet oozed onto Leander's pale fingers as the blade glistened in unapologetic victory. Demetrius cried out and rushed to flip Theo over. Leander, paralyzed, held the blade vertically, permitting the scarlet residue to stain the stone floor. A screech filled the room; the owl covered her head with her wings as she shriveled, flattening herself onto her canvas. The two inferno eyes that had glared at the men from above, now peered through the flat graphite from below.

The full moon, though no longer visible from the window, shone its silver light into the room once more, its cool tones adding to the chills of the heavy silence. Damian quietly retrieved the black covering crumbled on the opposite side of the room and veiled the canvas, tucking the fabric tightly around the corners.

Theo's blood had gushed downward from the wound over his heart, freeing his resting face from any tainting. Demetrius cupped his hands around Theo's bearded face and sobbed.

"Why?" Demetrius cried out. He pressed his forehead against Theo's, gasping for air as he sobbed harder. "How could you do this?"

"Demetrius—" Leander started.

Demetrius gently put down Theo's head and glanced at Leander with tear-stained cheeks. He shook his head with a disgusted frown.

"How can you stand there now, covered in your friend's blood, and not say a single word?"

Leander kneeled beside the body and grabbed Demetrius' shaking hand.

"This," Leander said, eyeing the redness that now covered Demetrius' hands, "is not blood."

Demetrius drew back his hand and furrowed his eyebrows. He shook his head as he raised his hands to his temples.

"What is it then, hmm?"

"It is paint."

Demetrius frowned, scanning Theo's still body. Damian propped the covered canvas against the bed and carefully approached Theo, also curious as to Leander's observation.

"Paint?"

Demetrius' eyes wandered from the ends of Theo's robe back to his covered eyes when he noticed in his periphery Leander's trembling hand. Leander sniffled back tears, though he could no longer restrict his cough.

"This… was not… Theo. It seems this canvas… remarkably existed with the conditions of the dead, and… died with the characteristics of existence." Leander turned away as he continued coughing, his energy depleting rapidly. Demetrius' eyes darted back and forth along Theo, searching for indications of falsity. He patted the sleeves and twisted the robe's fabric.

Demetrius sprung to his feet and frantically looked around the room, expecting the real Theo to appear from the shadows. He paced anxiously, burying his head in his hands as he processed.

A heavy book from the shelf had fallen, frightening the three. Its collision rocked the bottom shelf, causing an avalanche of books to join the fall, like a final round of applause for the last chapter of a beloved tale.

Damian's eyes widened as Leander's discarded weapon reflected upon his pupils. He fought his nausea as he inspected the red fluid, the fresh layer coating the parts which had already dried.

"Does that mean…" His voice trailed off as his bottom lip trembled, remembering what G had said about protecting oneself.

"I never knew his skills would develop to this extraordinary level," Leander confessed, interrupting Damian. "There has never been a time where art existed to this degree. The owl is closer to the art we know, one that returns to the canvas, as its existence is dependent on its creator's presence or direction. Theo has somehow found a way for the art to survive independently. I am afraid I cannot tell you what is real around here and what is not."

"What about G?" Damian asked, closing his eyes. "The man you met outside? Was he…"

"A canvas," Leander said, nodding and shuddering. "An extremely intricate, detailed, and complex portrait."

Demetrius continued pacing and pulling at his hair.

"No, no, no," he repeated to himself with every step. "Then where's the real Theo?" Demetrius dashed to the window, sticking his head into the night's sky. The fog had cleared, and he desperately scanned the parameters.

Damian reached for Demetrius' shoulder, pulling him back into the room for his safety. Demetrius fell into the chair beside him, slamming his head into his folded arms on the table. His dark curls fell onto the three books which had remained on the table. Engraved on each spine was a single letter: "D," "L," and "T."

Demetrius reached for the one on top, engraved with his first initial. The cover was a dusted yellow, with marks of wears and tears along the edges. A red, braided string hung loosely from the middle. He rapidly flipped through the pages, landing at the blank, marked page.

"What is this? A journal?" Demetrius asked.

"What does the first page say?" Damian asked, recalling the strange first page of the "G" book.

"This handwriting is difficult to read. I think it says, 'What if he knew?' What does that mean?"

Demetrius turned the page to find a list of characteristics. The further he read, the closer his eyebrows knitted together.

- a gentle soul, too fragile for the ultimate horrors of life
- a contagious smile, permanently etched into the corners of his mouth
- an unfathomable sense of unconditional devotion and loyalty, of which no one deserves yet ultimately receives
- an unbreakable trust, to which reciprocity never tests or hinders its endurance
- an inability to process that which is devoid of any goodness
- a persevering idealism, one of which has yet to be broken
- an infinite amount of good intentions, all of which are meaningless when accompanied by ignorance

"What *is* this?" Demetrius repeated, banging his fist on the table. "Who wrote this? Theo? You'd know his handwriting, wouldn't you Leander?"

Damian reached for the next book, the one marked with an "L," and extended his arm out to Leander. Its faded blue cover reflected hints of shimmering sapphire as it passed through the moonlight. Leander remained paralyzed across the room and shook his head, so Damian opened the book himself.

"Put it down, please," Leander asked. "I need not know what was written about me."

"About *you*?" Demetrius asked, putting his book down and staring once more at the spine. "And what, this book is supposed to be about *me*?" He reopened the book to the descriptive list and read aloud. "'A persevering idealism, one of which has yet to be broken.' What does that even mean?"

"You always see the good in everything," Damian said, shrugging.

"Not anymore." Demetrius threw the book across the room. It spiraled into one of the shadowed corners, disappearing.

The last book was marked "T," and Damian couldn't take his eyes off it. His fingers itched with curiosity, and he looked at Demetrius with pleading eyes. Demetrius waved his hand dismissively, leaning defeatedly against the back of the chair.

The book was in perfect condition. Its scarlet cover lacked even the faintest scratch. The pages were off-white, and most were covered in writing from top to bottom. Damian looped his finger around the red thread, intentionally placed in the middle of the book, separating the only two blank pages.

He raised an eyebrow as he flipped from the first several pages to the last ones.

"The handwriting shifts dramatically," Damian noted. "Could it be that two people authored this?"

Leander's heart sank. He inhaled deeply before holding his breath, crossing the room hesitantly. Without a word, he reached for the book in Damian's hands, to which Damian didn't argue. Leander observed the cover for himself, his index finger lingering a little longer on the spine's embroidered gold letter.

He exhaled and opened to the bookmarked, blank pages. He turned to the page prior to the separation and read quietly to himself.

> "… though I can't say for certain what will become of him.
> Our resemblance is uncanny, but there's a darkness in his eyes
> I can't place. Perhaps I will never know what makes a man,
> nor will I know what belongs solely to oneself. But engaging
> with a replica of myself is entertaining, an amusement I
> would recommend everyone to experience at least once.

These thoughts may be too fresh, as he has only experienced life for an hour or so. I will show him our home, the land, and the graves. How morbid! But he must know. Once he is familiar with his setting, he can meet the rest.

It may be through the eyes of others that I will learn what is truly mine, what cannot be duplicated, negated, or extended. For someone to say my twin has everything in common with me but one thing, that will be my ultimate discovery. Once I learn this, I will write to D & L, for I will have a better sense of who I am, not only who I've wanted to become."

Leander squeezed his eyes shut, refusing tears from falling. He slowly turned to the next written page, the one with the different, less legible handwriting.

"I am unsure if the original self could have predicted what would become of him, but I am certain that having an answer to his burning question supersedes the unfortunate yet inevitable predicament in which he finds himself, buried under those layers of soil, guarded by his dense, manifested fog.

He lives not only through the question he posed but also through me. Upon reading his earlier entries, I find myself agreeing with him, that only through the eyes of another, by stepping out of one's own imprisoned being, could the riddle be solved.

It has been several days since the stone was placed upon his buried self, yet neither Janus nor G have noticed the original self has been misplaced. Is this a testament to our affinity? Or are Janus' and G's eyes too familiar with the sight of the original self?

I have no choice but to write to those who knew him from the past and see how their expectations compare to reality."

Leander slammed the book shut, clutching it with white knuckles as he failed to stabilize his shaking hands. Demetrius hurriedly approached Leander, dragging the chair with him, forcing Leander to have a seat. Leander's pale face had turned a more transparent blue, deepening his elongated, sunken cheeks, until he resembled a skull.

"Tell me," Demetrius demanded desperately, crouching beside Leander and placing a hand on his friend's knee. "Please, just tell me. What did he write? Did he say where he can be found?"

"Yes." Leander hunched over, coughing into his sleeve. He gasped for air as he continued, though his voice was thin. "Yes, I know where he is."

"Where?"

Leander paused, unable to stop the oncoming sobs.

"He is buried outside."

Demetrius fell to the floor, clutching his chest with his available hand. The two sat for a moment, crying together. Damian rushed to the window and peered in the direction of the graveyard. His heart stopped as he recalled the stone with the ornate "T" engraving. His head snapped around, eyeing the bloodied body on the floor.

"When was he buried?"

"I do not know," Leander said. "The different handwritings derived from the two..." Leander's voice trailed off as he recomposed himself, gripping the book tightly. "The first half of the journal was written by... Theo, and the second half was written by his portraiture. I have little to no reason to believe that it was his own portraiture that buried him."

Demetrius pounded the ground.

"It can't be true," Demetrius said, his cries carried by the echoes. "Tell me it's not true, Leander. You know him. He wouldn't create something so vile. Why would he paint himself a killer?"

Leander brought the journal close to his chest, closing his eyes as he pondered Demetrius' question. The pristine journal was now entirely covered in mud and red paint.

"Though I have theories, I am afraid you and I will never know," Leander said. "I do not think he considered himself a killer, but I believe he had a *dying* desire to understand and learn, and this intensified passion was poorly translated onto the canvas. We experience inexpressible sentiments and dispositions throughout our lives, and unfortunately, this one in particular seemed too consuming."

"Which one is that?" Damian asked.

"Again, I can only make assumptions. There was a conversation I had with him, a couple days after the incident of your father's."

Demetrius' nostrils flared as he clenched his fists.

"You knew," Demetrius said with a frown. "You knew this whole time what had happened to my father."

"Yes… Choosing to protect Theo was the second hardest decision I have ever made."

"And the first?"

"Deciding to see him again," Leander said, turning to the fallen portraiture. The moon outside had shifted more, resulting in dark shadows now covering the body except for a single hand stretched out across the floor in the direction of the three remaining men.

"I can't believe you watched me suffer for years and never considered telling me what really happened. I would've understood."

"I can explain," Leander said, though the return of his cough suggested otherwise. "After the incident, Theo paid me a visit to my studio. I had not seen him since that day, and to say I was fully recovered and functioning regularly would be no small lie. His appearance startled me, and his threatening demeanor, though understandable upon reflection, restricted me from thinking clearly."

"What'd he say?" Damian asked eagerly.

Leander heaved, leaning against the back of the chair to free his lungs from the pressure of his hunched posture.

"He needs water," Demetrius said, looking anxiously at Damian. "Could you?"

"Are you serious? You want me to go back down there, alone?"

Leander attempted to speak, to dismiss Demetrius' suggestions, but a raging coughing fit emerged, leaving Damian no choice but to rush to the kitchen. He entered the dark staircase, leaving the door behind him open. The moonlight trickled through the narrow windows of the tower, permitting Damian enough light to not tumble down the stairwell.

Meanwhile, Demetrius had grabbed Leander's fragile hand.

"You're going to be okay, you hear me?" Demetrius said, panic striking his vocal chords.

"I have not been well for a very, very long time. The weight of my actions and choices has led me here, and though I have carried this pressure for the majority of my life now, never has it felt heavier." He dropped the journal onto his lap as he pressed his free hand to the center of his chest, near his heart.

"I forgive you," Demetrius said, squeezing Leander's hand. "I do, I really do. I don't know the full story, and you don't have to tell me, but I know you prioritized me, acting in my best interest. You were only trying to protect me from the truth."

Leander slowly shook his head.

"If you forgive me for anything," Leander said, "please forgive me for prioritizing Theo."

The room was silent. Demetrius softened his squeeze on Leander's hand.

"Why'd you prioritize him?"

Leander clasped his hand over his heart but remained quiet.

"If you don't have the decency now, after everything we've been through, to be honest with me, then no, I can't forgive you."

"He wanted to tell you," Leander said, avoiding Demetrius' glaring gaze. "He graced me with the opportunity to tell you first and even offered to approach you together. I informed him once more that we could not share with you what had transpired, for the Code states that art created to destroy would not be tolerated, and as a result, Theo and I would face the most severe punishments from the Academy."

"So, you cared more for your reputation?"

"No, of course not. One's reputation is fabricated, built entirely off the perception of others. There would be no perception to have, however, without the individual himself."

"I don't understand."

"I live for art," Leander said, his bottom lip quivering. "If I was stripped of everything I have acquired, the title, the studio, my students, the Academy, yet I was still allowed to create and abide by the Code, I would have everything I need. My work was never about my reputation. This lifeline of mine, fueled solely by art, was an affinity I recognized in… Theo, though his extended beyond art, and unfortunately, into a much darker side of reality. How could I create knowing that… Theo's… means for creation would forever be taken away? "

Demetrius crossed his arms and scoffed.

"And you really believe I would've told a single soul what you'd done? Leander, I don't even blame you for what happened! I simply can't understand why you wouldn't tell me."

"The Code," Leander said, looking up at Demetrius with glossy eyes. "I never wanted to break the Code."

Leander turned once more to the lifeless, outstretched hand. He wrapped his arms around himself as he hunched over and unknowingly began to rock back and forth. Demetrius rubbed his friend's muddied back in an effort to comfort him, though he couldn't hide the anger on his face.

In the distance, the two heard approaching footsteps followed by mumbled profanity. Damian came into view several moments later, stopping at the door.

"What happened?" Damian asked Demetrius. Demetrius jaw remained clenched as he reached for the cup of water, giving it to Leander. The more Leander drank, the harder he cried, the harder he coughed.

"Your secret is safe with me," Demetrius said after relaxing his muscles, finding it impossible to remain upset during Leander's distress. "When we return, I promise not to tell anyone what happened. We have quite some time to come up with a story."

Leander fell onto Demetrius' shoulder, grabbing his neck with one hand as he cried inconsolably. Demetrius and Damian stared at each other in shock, neither of them saying a word.

"The Code is a matter of principal," Leander said, wiping his tears as he returned to his chair. "I was foolish to think Theo keeping a secret had any relevancy to my very being and my abidance. I was more foolish to think his departure provided me a second chance. I was most foolish to believe I could control my fate. Now, my friend, I cannot make the same mistake again."

"Don't talk like that. We'll return home safe and sound, like we promised."

"You will," Leander said. "I can never show my face again."

Demetrius rose once more, wiping his hands down his face in utmost frustration.

"I forgive you, Leander. I do. Please, I can't lose you too."

Leander held out his hand, and Demetrius helped him to his feet. Leander held Demetrius' shoulder, his bottom lip quivering as he spoke.

"Thank you," Leander said, "but I will never forgive myself."

Leander approached his fallen mentee and reached into the pocket to recover his soiled sapphire ring.

"No," Demetrius said, his voice cracking. "Don't do this to me."

"I may not have the right to ask anything of you, but please, if you could, return this to Zo." Leander wrapped Demetrius' fingers around the ring.

Demetrius dug his fingers into his palm, imprinting the ring onto his skin. He turned toward the window and fought the urge to toss the ring through it, finally understanding how Theo felt all those years ago.

"Is this goodbye?" Demetrius asked.

Leander threw his arms around his dear friend but said nothing. Demetrius shook his head as he squeezed Leander with all his might. Leander fell back into the chair, his remaining energy speedily dwindling. Demetrius held onto Leander's hand one last time, shook it with his might, and pocketed the sapphire ring, patting it as brushed against the ruby one.

Damian nodded toward Leander, the corners of his mouth weighed with sadness. He was the first to walk into the darkened hall, waiting for Demetrius.

Demetrius' head fell as the sobbing returned. Through his blurred vision he glanced upon Leander, who had turned toward the window and rested against the back of the chair, his still hands folded in his lap. His skin appeared translucent and matched the blue tones of his ruined attire, especially the areas draped in shadows.

Leander heard the door close behind him, and silent tears poured down his hollow cheekbones. His eyes burned as they fell upon the book engraved with an "L." He reached for it and as it lay in his lap, the blue cover blended perfectly with Leander's robe.

He raised his arms and loosened his head wrap, curling his fingers around the fabric soaked with paint and sweat. A tear fell, bringing Leander's attention to the faint details painted on the cover. Thin line drawings of owls were delicately and subtly painted in a checkered pattern. Leander flipped his fabric over and ran his hand over the inside design. His fingertips rubbed against identical owls stitched into the material.

"He remembered," Leander whispered, opening to the first page.

Leander hunched over as another coughing fit surfaced. This time, small splatters of blood dripped onto the page. He felt time running out, so he held his chest with one hand as he frantically turned to the last page of the book.

> "...and the saddest aspect of this man's life is that he had frozen himself, in time, in space, in mind. His inability to face the truth masked him forever in darkness. Though I'm not one to believe in good and bad, how can I ignore the reality that a man in darkness will never deliver light to the world, and more importantly, to himself. He will inevitably do once more what originally led him down the unlit path.
>
> Only he who dives into darkness can escape from its murky grip, from its opaque, shadowed depths. Obstacles arise when his eyes grow accustomed to the night, for then the shade suffices and the sun stings.
>
> We will only meet again when he's ready to face the light."

Leander's heart burned, and he gripped his chest harder. He coughed, wincing as his throat felt aflame. The coughing wouldn't stop, restricting Leander from catching his breath. Blood trickled from his mouth, mixing with the tears that had accumulated under his chin.

With his last ounce of strength, Leander clutched Theo's book to his heart. His head fell back, and his face turned a final shade of blue.

Leander's hand dropped to the side, releasing Theo's book onto the floor beside him.

The full moon had now entirely faded from view, leaving Leander in the shadows.

Chapter
Twenty-Four

The night air was filled with the soft sounds of tall grass swaying, accompanied by the whispering vines updating Aluna of the unknown man's whereabouts. Paper curtains gently tapped along the stone walls as the breeze flowed through them, solidifying the rest of the world's peaceful sleep. Aluna quietly turned the corner and squinted toward the risen hedges surrounding her home. A cough in the distance diverted her attention to a man sitting on the bench.

His beard met his folded hands which rested upon his protruding stomach. He gazed at the moon, tapping his fingers as he twisted his mouth sideways.

"Zo?" Aluna asked.

Zo clapped his hands together as he rose to greet Aluna. His concerned expression faded immediately into a smile, beaming from ear to ear. He hugged her tightly, then stepped back, taking a moment to admire her.

"Aluna! My dear, how long has it been? Too long, too long. You look lovelier than ever."

"That can't be true."

"Your glow supersedes everything else," the old man said, pressing his hand against his cheek. "I do worry why I'm seeing you at such a late hour? Or an early hour, I should say."

Aluna sat on the bench and tied her curls back, permitting the moonlight to wash over her face. The bags under her eyes had darkened, as did the wrinkles beside her eyes and lips. Her weary eyes were half-closed, though Zo's presence ignited a sparkle.

"I had no plans of sleeping tonight," Aluna said. "Demetrius has embarked on a journey from which he should be returning by sunrise."

"Oh, no! He really left? Tell me, did Demetrius leave before seeing Leander?"

Aluna's eyebrow rose.

"How did you now Leander was looking for him?"

"My dear, who do you think advised him to do so!"

Aluna stretched her neck to look both ways, ensuring no one could overhear them. She inclined her head to her home, and Zo nodded, following behind her.

Please open the hedges, Aluna asked.

Zo gasped as the greenery obeyed unpromptedly. The hedges separated perfectly like interlocked fingers releasing their hold. The hedges met once the two reached the front door, intertwining themselves with ease.

Aluna lit the nearest candle and gestured Zo toward the living room which bathed in moonlight. The room filled with a warm, orange glow as Aluna lit other candles one by one before closing the curtain and asking its circumventing vines to secure the curtain's placement.

"What a wonderful home you have," Zo observed, sitting exactly where Leander had been only hours previously. He traced the parametric vines and nodded. "Very unique."

"Thank you. I share every waking moment with the plants. Often even in my dreams. It may seem strange to most, but every botanist lives relatively similarly. I'm sure that's not the same among other artists."

"Definitely not!" Zo said laughing, slapping his knee at the thought. "I can't imagine such a world! Our similarities stem from *what* we do, not *how* we do it. It appears artists may have something in common with botanists as well, which I never knew." Zo cocked his head toward the window. "How did the hedges act on their own will?"

"Would you share with me how a canvas rises?" Aluna asked with a smirk. Zo laughed once more and shook his head. Aluna reclined on the opposing couch, crossing her legs as she cupped her knee, smiling at Zo. "It is good to see you, Zo. It truly bothers me, that we haven't seen each other since those awful circumstances. I'm sorry, I'm not sure how I could've lost track of time."

"Oh, my dear," Zo said, wagging his finger, "you are not to blame! None of us were the same after that day, were we? I, for one, retired from the Academy immediately. Yes, I know! Shocking! I resorted to another part of the land, and there I've stayed for many, many years. You couldn't have found me if you tried!"

"You didn't have any students?"

"Between you and me," Zo said, lowering his voice and leaning closer to Aluna, "after Leander, I had stopped mentoring entirely. He would occasionally seek advice, especially regarding his own experience as a new mentor, but he was such an incredible student that the thought of training another was unfathomable. I had experienced greatness, and I couldn't settle for anything less."

"You could've mentored Theo?" Aluna asked hesitantly. Zo chuckled.

"Now that would've changed everything, wouldn't it? But no, I couldn't do that to Leander. He was so excited to work with Theo. The two already had such a personal connection, prior to Leander achieving his status. However, the level at which Theo worked, the two seemed more like equal partners. From what I heard, Theo grasped every lesson immediately, leaving very little need for a mentor in the traditional sense."

"Did that drive Leander mad?"

"Mad? No! Well, perhaps in a great, sensational way. A true mentor desires to dissolve his title, which can only be done once the mentee matches his talent, though ideally the mentee should supersede his mentor one day."

The flames flickered before them, wax racing to the base of the candle as if time had sped forward.

"Where did their relationship sour?" Aluna asked. The leaves of the vines turned inward, eager to hear Zo's response.

"I don't think it was ever truly sweet," Zo said. "Leander is a very private person, but as a mentor of his for many, many years, I know that Leander held Theo in too high esteem, which would be the downfall of any relationship."

The orange flames illuminated Zo's nervous hands rubbing against each other.

"My dear, I would love nothing more than to tell you everything I know, but I hope you can see why I can't do that. In fact, there is a lot I wish I could do now, but it seems much too late."

"You're protective of Leander," Aluna said, nodding, "and I completely understand. It's for Demetrius' sake I wonder what happened, since now I realize I've been kept in the dark about so much. You know, today was the first time I'd spoken with Leander, just the two of us. We've of course exchanged pleasantries and never has there been tension between us, but at the same time, I had never spoken solely to him."

"And?" Zo asked, grinning wildly. "Quite a man, isn't he?"

Aluna chuckled softly.

"Today was perhaps one of the worst days to share that moment with him. But in our brief conversation, I saw the pain in his eyes, the fear, the loss, yet I don't know why he felt that. Moreover, Leander, who, in my mind, is attached to Demetrius at the hip, couldn't have had a more contrasting reaction to the appearance of Theo's letter. And I wonder, Zo, why their views on Theo differ?"

Zo huffed as he rose from the couch and walked over to the vines. Using the nearest candle, he illuminated the leaves which had pressed themselves against the wall in defense. Zo gently caressed one of the leaves, lifting it from its collision with the others.

"Look at these leaves, Aluna. They all stem from the same vine, they require and undoubtably receive the same amount of care and nourishment, and yet, their shapes and sizes vary. In the most perfect conditions, we will always see variance. And in non-perfect conditions, well, I'm sure I don't have to tell you the extent of variance then."

Aluna rested her chin on her hand as she gazed dreamily at the vines.

"I know you want to help Demetrius as much as I want to help Leander, if not more," Zo said, "and I need you to know that you *are* the help Demetrius needs. Leander couldn't have saved Demetrius from himself."

Aluna lifted her head to meet Zo's eyes, hers glossed with exhausted tears. Zo hurried to sit beside her, cupping her hands into his.

"When Myron died," Aluna started, sniffling as she refrained from weeping, "I no longer recognized Demetrius' eyes. They were two dark holes that led to an empty, midnight abyss. Something in him would ignite around Theo, which I never understood. Let that be the case, for I only wish him the best. But if Theo meant so much to Demetrius, something treacherous must have occurred between Leander and Theo for Leander to wish Theo a permanent disappearance."

"Yes, yes, it does seem that way, doesn't it? But Aluna, don't you see? You are Demetrius' lifeline. When Theo left, Demetrius didn't perish. Leander's presence didn't save him, for when the letter arrived, Demetrius left against Leander's will. Ah! It breaks my heart to utter those words, but it's the truth. But you see how the only constant in his life is you? Without you, my dear, well, there'd be no Demetrius."

Aluna pressed her forehead to Zo's cupped hands, sobbing quietly under the curls that shielded her face from view.

Zo lightly raised Aluna's chin and smiled endearingly.

"Love is a beautiful thing, and what you two share is like nothing I've ever seen. Please believe me when I tell you, Aluna, that Demetrius' only need in this world is love. Love is the only thing that keeps him living, which means love could be the only thing to kill him. A lucky man, he is, having but a single weakness."

Aluna rose, wiping straggling tears from her cheeks. She straightened her posture and released her curls from their hold. Zo placed his hands over his heart.

"I just want him to come home," Aluna said.

"And he will, my dear. He will. I hope Leander joins him in his return too."

"Why would he not?"

Aluna waited patiently as Zo dismissed his pessimistic thoughts.

"He wouldn't miss the ceremony tomorrow," Zo assured himself. Aluna closed her eyes, tilting her head back at the weight of the reminder.

"The ceremony… I'd forgotten about it completely."

"Will it be postponed?" Zo asked. Aluna's throat tightened. She looked over her shoulder at the unlit hallway behind her.

"Would you like some water?" She asked. Zo heaved as he stood and followed Aluna into the kitchen.

The large window removed the necessity of additional candlelight. The silver glow transitioned into a more golden hue, and Zo rushed to the window to watch the yellow light escaping from the horizon. Zo turned to Aluna and frowned as he noticed the reemergence of tears.

"He'll be home soon," Zo said, placing his hand on her shoulder. "He said he'll be back by sunrise, no? Demetrius is a man of his word, especially to you. And Leander, well, there's nothing I can do but hope. He's his own worst enemy. Surely you're not shocked to hear that? Yes, yes, Leander rarely voices his troubles, and when they aren't solved, they magnify. I hadn't seen him in quite some time mind you, and when I did see him, the hollowness in his cheeks, his hair completely gone, of course I said nothing."

Aluna's gold rings clanked against the cup she held firmly.

"Why did you come searching for Leander?"

"He's not well, Aluna," Zo said, crinkling his nose. "A man can only carry so many burdens, both mental and physical. I've seen other artists slouch lower and lower over time as the boulder upon their shoulders expand into unmanageable weight."

"Wouldn't the additional weight strengthen them?" Aluna rubbed her arm where the scars from the thorns failed to fade.

"There will always be a limit. I feel Leander's is slowly approaching if it hasn't already. Let's not think about the worst, shall we?"

The paper curtain, though folded at the top of the window, tapped lightly against the edges and the vines. The leaves adjusted themselves, restricting further collisions.

Has Demetrius reached the forest yet? Aluna asked.

No, Aluna. We will immediately inform you of his return.

They sat at the table, watching ripples form in their cups of water as they anxiously tapped.

Please come back safely, Leander, Zo thought to himself.

～

Caterina rubbed her smallest finger along the lines of the sketch, blending the graphite into the paper. Her fingers held the loose hairs framing her face, restricting any deterrence from her concentration. She gently blew the excess graphite away, brushing away bits of broken eraser.

The peeping golden light seeped through her window, traveling along the bare walls and onto Caterina's graphite-smeared hands. She rolled up her sleeves and slouched into her chair.

The sketch depicted an owl facing the spectator with its wings stretched to the paper's edges. Its feathers were delicately detailed, overlapping one another in a synchronous pattern. Its dark beak drew the immediate attention of the spectator, guiding the eye to the two, round circles beside it.

These circles were left softly shaded with a white streak crossing through the center, indicating a reflective surface. Caterina pinched the edges of the paper and tilted the paper back and forth, smiling at how the graphite shimmered in the light of the rising sun.

The canvas upon which she had to transfer the sketch rested beside her desk. A yawn parted her lips, so she walked to her bed, satisfied with her progress. She passed her mirror and stopped for a moment.

"The answers to your unasked questions reside within you," Leander had said to her. "Trust yourself."

She pressed her hand against the glass and stared deeply into her brown eyes. A ray of sun beamed across her dark eyes like a blindfold, basking them in glimmering gold. A pearly-white smile spanned across her face.

Leander loves the sun, she thought to herself. *He wasn't so wrong: I look like a painting in this light.* She closed her eyes as she absorbed the sun's warm presence.

A sudden stinging pain pierced her heart as she reminisced her mentor, and gruesome images surfaced before her. She saw her cherished mentor covered in blood, his face thinner and paler than a canvas.

She immediately opened her eyes and cried out, gasping for air as she settled on the floor, holding herself upright with one hand while the other pressed upon her forehead. Her door swung open, and Safiya rushed to her sister's side.

"Something's happened to Leander," Caterina said, unable to catch her breath. "I just know it. Something terrible has happened."

The image intensified in her mind, of Leander alone in the center of a room, his headwrap sprawled on the floor beside his chair. The morning sun reflected off his exposed head, blinding Caterina from seeing other details.

A gentle breeze flew through the room, sweeping Caterina's sketch until it teetered onto the floor beside the torn ends of Caterina's dress.

"What's this?" Safiya asked. "What happened to your dress, Caterina?" Safiya pulled at the edges of Caterina's dress, observing the dirt stained into the ripped linen.

"How can I sleep now?" Caterina responded dismissively, springing to her feet. "I must go back."

"Go back? Go back where? What you need is sleep. *Now.*" Safiya lunged toward the doorway and blocked Caterina from leaving.

"You don't understand," Caterina said with wide eyes as she feverishly braided her hair. "Without Leander..." Caterina couldn't finish the sentence. She snatched the sketch from the ground, carefully bringing the edges together, creasing the paper.

"Where do you think you're going?" Safiya shouted as Caterina slipped into her sandals and adjusted the strap of her canvas bag upon her shoulder. Caterina pressed her hand against the wall, leaving a graphite-smeared handprint behind. She pulled the curtain aside and looked apologetically at her older sister.

"Please forgive me," Caterina said, tiptoeing out of the window. "I'll explain later."

Caterina landed once more outside her bedroom window. Though the sun wrapped Caterina in its warmth, she felt chills run down her spine. Tears burned her eyes as she rolled down her sleeves, protecting her skin from the sun's constant reminder of her mentor.

The sketch fit safely between the notebooks in her bag, and she flung her braid behind her as she faced the long road ahead.

She raced toward Leander's studio; adrenaline rushed through her veins.

Aluna said he'd return soon, Caterina assured herself.

Chapter

Twenty-Five

The two rings in Demetrius' pocket clanked against each other as he stormed down the spiral staircase with Damian trailing close behind. Rays from the rising sun pierced through the small windows, blinding Demetrius as he passed them. Echoes of their footsteps bounced off the walls and lingered, matching the tumultuous storm of thoughts racing in Demetrius' mind. He unclenched his fists to push open the door.

Damian caught up, catching his breath as he placed his wounded arm upon Demetrius' shoulder and observed at the entryway below.

"Wow," Damian said, blinking rapidly. "This room is almost unrecognizable with just the tiniest amount of sunlight. Still not welcoming, though." Damian swallowed his thought as he gazed upon the webbed chandelier.

The once darkened and greyed main room was now glossed in dusty yellow as the sun attempted its intrusion through the dirty windows. The flowered carpet along the staircase showcased more details, particularly the scarlet petals. Demetrius snarled as he gripped the railing and silently descended the stairs.

"Should we find Janus?" Damian whispered as he scanned the room. "I couldn't find her when I came for the water. We should tell her, right? Shouldn't she know what happened?"

Demetrius stopped in the middle of the staircase and turned to Damian with fire in his eyes.

"She'll find out the truth the way we all do," he responded through gritted teeth. Damian's eyes widened as he watched Demetrius storm toward the main door.

"Come on now," Damian said, remaining on the staircase. "We can't do that to her."

Damian squinted as a beam of light traveled across his eyes; he lifted his wounded arm to shield himself from the sun, as he heard the turning of a doorknob and felt a gust of fresh air travel past him.

Damian peered over his shoulder, wincing as the sun directly hit him.

"She's probably hiding somewhere anyway." Damian followed Demetrius, closing the front door behind him.

The sound of a child whimpering filled the empty room.

The front lawn, no longer cloaked in unforgiving fog, reflected the morning hues of a peaceful sunrise. Leaves gently rustled against one another, whispering to each other as Demetrius rushed down the path. Though a brilliant, warm orange glazed the land, Demetrius only saw red.

"Demetrius, wait!" Damian yelled.

"Why are you taking your time and wasting mine? It's time to leave." His chest rose and fell quickly as his nostrils flared. "What are you looking around for? Are you looking for a souvenir to take with you?"

"I'm not sure I'll need something to remember this night."

"Ha!" Demetrius exclaimed. "And you think I'll ever forget it?"

"You need to collect yourself, Demetrius. Otherwise, we'll never make it home. The worst is over."

"Maybe for you," Demetrius gruntled with a clenched jaw, "but now this misery is permanent." Damian retreated carefully, but Demetrius

266

refused the space between them to grow. The breath escaping his widened nostrils hit Damian's face, emphasizing the rage accompanying each syllable. "Do you understand loss, Damian? Have you ever felt the weight of agony? Of course, you haven't. The last thing I need from you is to tell me how to feel. I'm the only one ever guided by sentience."

The memory of Gabriella throwing dirt into Damian's eyes flashed before him as he unknowingly brushed the invisible dirt from his face. He felt his heart race the more he watched Demetrius' face redden with anger. Damian lowered his chin and continued stepping backward, until he tripped over something behind him. The intense aroma of lead paralyzed him.

Damian shrieked as his fingers landed in a tangled mess of bloodied white hair.

G laid on his back, his darkened apparel reflecting reddish tints in the rising sun. Very few strands of hair remained white, as most of them, thickly coated in dark red, fell messily across his face. His exposed neck showed the fresh wound.

"That's G," Damian said, his voice cracking as he stumbled back, distancing himself from the body. "That's the reason Leander arrived covered in bl—er—paint."

Demetrius flinched at the sound of Leander's name. He bent his neck, tracing the height of the looming tower, noticing that the window was still open. His muscles tightened as he briefly waited for his friend to pardon him farewell once more. Damian's eyes fell to the grass beside him, unable to face G.

"I know he wasn't real, but—" Damian started.

"Real!" Demetrius scoffed. "What *is* real, Damian? What's the point of even wondering? How do I even know if *you're* real?" Saliva spewed from his mouth as he pressed his finger against Damian's chest. Damian defensively rose his hands.

"You don't need a knife to confirm my existence," Damian muttered. Demetrius had already turned away, adrenaline and rage fueling his accelerated pace toward the main gate.

The sun trickled through the leaves above them as they walked, adding speckles of light onto the splattered blood and mud absorbed by Demetrius' once-yellow shirt.

They passed the statue of the two men.

Demetrius saw his bronze head had remained discarded to the side. The other bronze man had returned to its original form, showcasing a man with a bald head, though Demetrius paid no mind to the second man. He momentarily considered a final attempt to reattach the severed part, but instead, he kicked dirt upon it and persisted down the interminable path.

"You might as well bury me too," Demetrius mumbled.

Since the fog had vanished, their whereabouts were clearer. The skytouching trees that bordered the path were fairly dispersed, permitting insight into what existed between the trunks. In the near distance, the gravestones reappeared.

"Do you think he's buried here?" Demetrius asked, breathing heavily and feeling gravity pull the pocketed rings. He stepped in the direction of the stones before immediately turning away and proceeding toward the gate.

"Don't you want to find out?" Damian asked. His inquiry was met with silence, leaving Damian no choice but to abandon his interest.

By the time they reached the gate, the sun had emerged from the horizon, setting the sky ablaze. Demetrius heard the horses neighing; he quickened his pace until he was practically jogging, ecstatic to see the asymmetric iron bars before him.

The horses rushed to the men, attempting to squeeze their nozzles between the bars. Demetrius yanked the iron door open and rushed to mount his horse.

"Wait!" Damian yelled. "Wouldn't Leander have come by horse? Shouldn't we search for his horse instead of abandoning it?" Damian stretched his neck in the direction of the desert, waiting to hear another horse, but no such sound emerged. Demetrius grabbed Damian by his shirt and glared into his eyes.

"This will be the last time you speak either of their names in front of me. Do you understand?"

"No," Damian said, furrowing his brows. "No, I don't understand this change in you. I've never seen you so angry, and I don't think it's warranted. Sadness seems more appropriate, no? Who are you angry with?"

"Who am I angry with?" Demetrius repeated as he slapped his chest. "Who's left? Is there someone to direct my anger toward except myself? No! I tortured myself with the illusion of brotherhood. This myth of the perfect trio, of unconditional love, loyalty."

Demetrius released Damian's shirt and breathed heavily. The tower in the distance reflected upon his glossy eyes as he stood, paralyzed by agony.

"Demetrius…"

"It's incomprehensible," Demetrius whispered, clenching his fists and tightening his muscles. For a moment he considered sprinting toward the castle, feeling the lingering connection toward Leander and Theo. Instead, he latched onto the iron bar beside him.

"What is?"

"All these memories I have… was any of it the way I remember? I feel like I've fallen from a dream. A dream where I was loved, not forsaken. Appreciated, not despised. My stomach's in knots, churning from all my misinterpretations, my ignorance. I've fallen from a dream… into a nightmare." Demetrius gripped another bar and shook the structure furiously. "No, I haven't fallen, I've *woken* from a dream into a nightmare."

He clutched his heart, digging his fingertips into his chest as he battled the stinging pain.

"That's not true," Damian said. The leaves above them swayed as a gentle breeze encouraged them to face the sun. "Think about Aluna. She's not part of this nightmare. There's still something… dreamy left for you."

Aluna, Demetrius thought to himself as tears resurfaced and burned his eyes. He felt the grass tickling the exposed parts of his feet, lightly gliding upon his skin, as soft as Aluna's touch. The momentary relief vanished as his heart sank once more.

"Time has rid me of choice, Damian. I didn't decide how things would end, nor did any of my actions play a role in preventing this... this... tragedy. Yet *I* am the one hurting most now. Why has their grief been bestowed upon me? *Why*? I'll never know!"

Demetrius grabbed his hair, pulling at his sweaty curls. He screamed toward the sky as the veins in his face, neck, and arms burst from his skin. Sweat dripped from his forehead onto his dirtied shirt, which had already clung tighter to his skin from the sun's heat.

"You, sun! How do you shine brighter and brighter, regardless of the days? Ha! You *are* the days, aren't you? Is that how you stay golden? Unaffected? Undeterred? Show me your hidden shadows! Share with us your secret powers, instead of rising and mocking us with your happy glow! Why must you glisten while we dull? I'll never know!"

He seized his collar and in a single motion tore his shirt down the middle, crumpling the yellow linen into a disheveled heap of fabric. He threw the remains over the gate. Demetrius caught his breath as he glanced toward the shredded remains of his shirt. It suddenly felt foreign to him, the memories sewn between the threads.

"Let's go," Demetrius said softly, as he lowered his head.

"But Leander's horse..." Damian whispered, though Demetrius paid no mind.

The two rode between the desert trees, which no longer depicted any particularities. They rose from the sand like the deserted bones of once esteemed architecture, barely framing the landscape before them. Though the sunlight added warmth to their presence, the spaces between the branches seemed magnified, emphasizing their hollowness.

The pink sky washed over the hilly terrain, painting its surface in gradations of warm tones. Streaks of vibrant orange emerged from the sun, patterning the sky with dreamlike colors around the two travelers. The sand absorbed the heat and danced freely in the subtle breeze.

The sun brightened everything it touched except for Demetrius and Damian. Tears joined the accumulation of sweat dripping down Demetrius' beard. Another stinging sensation jolted from his heart down his arms as he held onto his horse.

"Look," Damian said, swallowing his nervousness, "I know we just witnessed something traumatic, but I need you to hold on, okay? We'll be back soon."

"Back to what?"

"Aluna, Demetrius," Damian said, shaking his head. "I'm the last person to prioritize another person, but even I know there isn't a soul out there who loves you more than Aluna. And look how easily you've forgotten her!"

"There is no forgetting Aluna. Not now, not ever," Demetrius assured him.

"She consoled you after your father's death, and she'll console you now."

"What I feel is beyond consolation. I don't even know if I can face Aluna in this condition."

The trees around them bent inward, creating a crooked arch under which the horses trotted. Prints from their previous journey, accompanied by a new set of prints, were faintly pressed onto the sand, though the breeze gradually erased their presence. Demetrius sighed, wishing he could mimic the motion with his memory.

A tree before them extended its branches, causing both travelers to stop in fear. The trunk twisted and turned as its branches spiraled and intertwined, shaping itself into the body of a particular man. One arm rested on its hip while the other waved, and the branches around its face parted to depict a familiar and never forgotten smile. Though the figure had no eyes, Demetrius felt it looking directly at him. The color from his face faded and his neck bent backward completely as he stared at the enormous structure before him.

"Is that your—" Damian started, but Demetrius had drowned out the sounds around him as he immersed himself in a memory of his father.

∾

Myron had taken young Demetrius to a house he was building for a growing family. Men and women gathered around the site, preparing the timber and mud to be pressed into bricks. The new family was there too, weaving strands of thin papyrus to eventually curtain their windows. The space was boisterous and lively, though in his father's presence, Demetrius was focused only on his hero.

They greeted everyone with smiles and pleasantries. Myron's closest friends would ruffle Demetrius' hair, complimenting him on his handsome face and affinity to his father. Demetrius observed in awe how his father could accomplish every task and help everyone in need. He'd follow his father around like a shadow.

"Look around, son," Myron said, squinting as the midday sun warmed the community's work in its golden glory. "What interests you, hmm? What do you want to learn?"

"You know everything, so I will know everything too!"

Myron chuckled and shook his head.

"I don't know everything, Demetrius. All I know is how to offer myself to others. I may not be the best at any one thing, but I can always help. That's something you must learn, and I will teach you. You see that bearded man over there? The one molding the bricks? Two days ago, he didn't want to get his hands dirty. He asked how he could help, though he had that one condition."

"I like getting my hands dirty!" Demetrius giggled.

"As do I! As does the other man beside him. He came to me and shared how he failed to make the mud solid enough for bricks, because his mind was elsewhere. He recently lost a brother, and the sadness makes everyday tasks a challenge."

"But… He looks so happy now…"

"Why do you think that is, Demetrius?"

Demetrius tilted his head as he watched the two men mold bricks. They'd pause every now and then, slap their knees as they hollered, wiping tears of laughter with their biceps to avoid their muddy fingers.

"Are they friends?"

"They became friends faster than you can imagine! The one who lost a brother stopped going out; the other refused certain work. But with a common goal, something so simple as readying bricks, they came together and reshaped their minds, and maybe even, their hearts. Isn't that something, Demetrius? Now they'll lay the bricks not only for the new house but for the foundation of a new friendship."

"Should I make bricks?" Demetrius asked, tilting his head to the other side. Myron lifted Demetrius onto his lap.

"You should make friends, my son. Don't give me those sad eyes! Look again at those two friends over there."

"You're my friend, páppa."

"Always and forever! But why would you limit yourself to just one? Isn't that young boy over there a schoolmate of yours?"

A few yards away, a boy with dark hair and white linens sat in dirt, using his finger to trace shapes into the soil. He used one leg to pivot, trapping himself in an unevenly drawn circle. He smiled at his minor accomplishment. In his lap was a book his mother had left him, keeping him preoccupied as she attended to building the home.

"Yes," Demetrius said hesitantly. "His name is Theo."

"Why don't you go over there and say hi?"

Demetrius pressed his lips together, his eyes darting side to side with uncertainty. Myron lifted Demetrius from his lap as his little feet hit the soil. He crouched down until he was at eye-level with his son.

"Listen to me, Demetrius," Myron said in a low tone. "We have three places we can put our faith and trust: in ourselves, in others, and in the universe."

"The universe?" Demetrius asked, looking up at the clouds.

"That's right. That's where I choose to put my faith. The other two options are dangerous. You know why? You and I, we're going to mistakes, some worse than others. But, can you imagine the universe making a mistake?"

Demetrius rubbed his chin and shook his head.

"That's because in the grand scheme of things, there are no mistakes. We are too small to see the bigger picture, though. All we need to know is that there *is* a bigger picture. Now, you don't know if Theo is meant to be your friend, but would it hurt to try? What if years from now, you find yourself sitting and laughing beside him, like those two new friends over there?"

The two men had taken a break from their responsibility and washed their hands of mud. They walked toward a group of neighbors who were sharing fruits and bread, asking if they could join. Although they entered the circle of friends with ease, it was evident they were still entirely consumed by their own conversation, as they shared bread and laughs.

"What if he doesn't like me?" Demetrius asked, turning his head to Theo who had starting drawing with both hands on opposite sides of him.

"Keep an open mind and an open heart, Demetrius," Myron said, giving a single nod. "The universe will do the rest."

~

Demetrius stared at the prints in the sand, resisting the urge to scream at the clouds above him. There was no one left for him to trust. Pain spread from his heart through every nerve of his body. He gasped for air as he leaned over his horse, squeezing his eyes to minimize the pain.

Damian screamed in a panic, reaching for Demetrius' shoulder to pull him up. Demetrius caught his breath, panting as the pain faded.

"Don't do that!" Damian yelled. "You scared me. Look, up ahead! It's the forest, finally. Please, just hold on a little longer. We've almost reached Aluna. What happened to you just now?"

Demetrius shook his head, his locked jaw preventing him from voicing his overwhelming thoughts.

The forest appeared just as it had before the two set off for their journey. Leaves of emerald green greeted them as trickling sun rays sprinkled the entry. The last grains of sand fell off the horses' hooves as they stepped onto the grass. Though the tall trees canopied most of the light, there was enough to prevent the two from traveling in complete darkness.

"We're looking for mirrors, right?" Damian said, swiveling his head back and forth. Demetrius nodded, his shoulders sunk, and he hung his head.

"Follow the mirrors that are hung as pairs, not the single ones. It'll be difficult to spot them now," Demetrius said in a lowered tone. "Neither of us particularly stand out as we did before."

"Come on now," Damian said, puffing his chest and grinning. "You act like your yellow shirt embodied your entire personality. Chin up! We're nearly home."

"Why don't you lead the way? The paths won't change anymore, as long as we follow the double mirrors. There's one—two now."

Damian patted Demetrius on the back, thanking him for the find.

"I really suggest you cheer up," Damian said, speaking over his shoulder as Demetrius trailed behind. "Don't take this the wrong way. I'm just worried about Aluna's reaction when she sees you."

"One day the world will understand the cost of sentience," Demetrius muttered to himself, "and its restrictive inability to be anything else. I can't feel something I'm not."

The horses trudged along, dodging bulging roots and outstretched branches. Damian had no problem finding the double mirrors and staying on the right path. Every so often he would lean his head back to ensure he could still hear Demetrius' horse close behind him.

Their only sign that a significant amount of time had passed was the position of the sun when they emerged from the forest. The sky was freshly painted a tranquil blue with not a single cloud to disturb its brilliance. All the colors shined vibrantly around them, causing at first a burning sensation to their eyes. Once their eyes had adjusted to their recognizable surroundings, Damian closed his eyes and exhaled a sigh of relief.

Horses neighed faintly in the distance as the roof of the stable entered their view.

"Let's return the horses later," Demetrius said, pressing his lips together as the brief immobilizing pain surged through his body. "I need to see Aluna."

Demetrius ordered the horse to accelerate, which was easy to do now that the terrain wasn't made of sand. They soared through the grasslands, gusts of wind wiping away Demetrius' tears. He braced himself for his return home, for he knew he'd pass Leander's studio. He felt the energy in his body decrease, realizing what little strength he had left to endure more pain.

"Damian," Demetrius said loud enough over the horses' hooves, "you'll tell Caterina about Leander, alright?"

The agony Demetrius reflected inhibited Damian from arguing.

"Of course," Damian said.

The two traveled the remainder of their journey in contemplation of sharing the tragic news.

They reached the end of the grassland, where an outstretched path led through a neighborhood of houses, Demetrius' at the furthest end. They looked at each other for a brief moment, observing how the tolls of their expedition had manifested on their minds and bodies.

"Thank you," Damian said, "for letting me come with you. It might not mean a lot to you, especially at this moment, but I need you to know, this has opened my mind to a lot more than I could've ever imagined."

Demetrius winced as Damian's words triggered his father's advice to always keep an open mind. Demetrius instead smiled the weariest smile and patted Damian's unwounded arm.

At the end of the path stood Aluna and Zo, eagerly awaiting Demetrius's return.

Aluna rushed to Demetrius at once with a smile on her face. As she neared, horror consumed every facial muscle. Her frown deepened and her lips parted, struck by worry. The sight was too much for Demetrius to bear, for he knew the pain in Aluna's eyes would only deepen.

The last thing Demetrius heard was Zo shouting as to Leander's whereabouts; his eyes rolled back as he fainted off his horse, collapsing to the ground.

Chapter
Twenty-Six

emetrius's eyes fluttered open cautiously, adjusting to the scorching sun. Gravel stung and scraped his bare back as he propped himself up, recognizing three concerned heads floating over him. The sun shone directly behind them, circumventing their heads in golden halos. His eyes locked first onto Aluna's, since she was closest. Her gentle hands brushed against his beard as she wrapped them around the back of his head.

"Aluna," Demetrius muttered, tears immediately forming on his lower lashes. She touched her finger to his lips.

"I told him to hold on until he saw you," Damian said, shaking his head. "I didn't think he'd take it so literally."

"You're safe now," Aluna assured Demetrius, brushing away a sweaty curl from his forehead. Her hazel eyes glistened from the tears she refused to cry. Demetrius buried his head in her lap, unable to constrain his wailing misery. His back expanded and compressed as he hyperventilated.

Aluna buried his head further into her lap to prevent alarming the sleeping neighbors. Zo circled around Aluna, kneeling beside Demetrius as well. He peered over his shoulder, squinting, hoping to see a familiar blue robe somewhere in the distance. He coiled his bottom lip, bracing himself for an unbearable truth he already understood.

"Let's get him inside," Zo insisted. Aluna lifted Demetrius chin and wiped his tears, though they fell regardless. The two of them helped Demetrius to his feet, swinging his arms around their shoulders for support.

Though the sky had turned prominently blue, none of the neighbors had yet stepped foot outside, granting the group privacy as they relocated. They stopped abruptly as they reached the hedges, hearing someone in the distance running. Zo eagerly looked up, though his excitement quickly transitioned to confusion when he saw a young woman with a long braid and tattered dress rushing toward them, securing her tote bag over her shoulder.

Damian's heart skipped a beat as he took a couple steps forward, stretching out his arms in anticipation. Caterina approached the group, staring at Demetrius in shock.

"Hi Caterina," Damian said, biting his lip. Caterina swiftly pushed past him, rushing over to Aluna.

"What happened?" She asked, her eyes darting from Aluna to Zo. Demetrius' head hung between the two as tears plopped onto the soil below him.

"Damian will tell you," Demetrius said, his voice hoarse.

"Where's Leander?" Caterina asked without hesitation, clutching her chest. Zo squeezed his eyes shut as Demetrius wailed louder. Aluna tilted her head toward the home and Zo nodded. The hedges separated, allowing the trio to enter the home, leaving Damian and Caterina in the sun.

"Where is he?" Caterina repeated, grabbing and shaking Damian by the shoulders.

"We should probably sit down."

Caterina seized Damian's wrist, bolting toward the bench beside Leander's studio. She sat facing Damian, placing both hands on his knees, impatiently anticipating information. The ripped ends of her dress brushed against Damian's exposed legs, igniting a curiosity within him. The intensity in her eyes, though sometimes masked by an adamant stray hair, prevented Damian from diverging from the topic of Leander. Damian used all his might to focus on her brown, frantic eyes. He placed a comforting hand on one of hers.

"He's not coming back," Damian said.

Caterina's breathing accelerated as she shook her head. Damian tried holding her cheek, but she firmly slapped his hand away.

"What do you mean? What happened?"

"Does it matter? He decided not to come back."

"I don't believe you!" Caterina yelled, rising from the bench. Damian stood, facing her. A few neighbors stuck their heads out their windows. Even the plants hanging from the windowsills swung in the breeze closer to the conversation.

"You wouldn't believe me if I told you what happened, Caterina! *I* don't even believe what happened. In such a short amount of time, I mean, how long has it been since the two of us were sitting right here? Happy as could be? Excited for what's to come?"

Caterina lowered her risen shoulders and observed Damian. Muddied sand accompanied fresh rips through his linen shirt, while the bandage, too, appeared hanging by its final thread.

The bags under Caterina's eyes were extremely prominent, and the lines around her lips were gravely deep, indicating the severity of her anxiety. The tiny hairs around her face spiraled uncontrollably in the morning breeze, refusing to take part in the unkempt braid she'd made.

Damian reached for Caterina's hand once more, and this time, she didn't pull away.

"I'm sorry," he said. "I don't mean to upset you. It's just, I don't know how to tell you what happened because I can't comprehend it either. Just give me a minute, will you?"

The two sat again on the bench. Caterina dropped her tote to the ground, not realizing some of her pencils had rolled into the soil.

"We met Theo," Damian said. Caterina's eyebrow twitched with the slightest interest. "Well, we met more than just Theo, but he was indubitably the main event. Demetrius and I had spent several minutes talking to Theo before Leander surprisingly showed up, crawling through the window!"

"He climbed through a window?"

"Oh, did he *climb*! Can you imagine? I don't blame him. I can assure you that the front door and the main room were furthest from welcoming."

"This is too much." A single tear traced her jawline to her chin. "Can you please just tell me why Leander's not coming back?"

Damian leaned forward to check around them, ensuring no one would hear him. The words left his mouth like a meager bird afraid of leaving the comfort of its nest.

"He… broke the Artist's Code."

The color in Caterina's cheeks immediately vanished as she looked at Damian in utmost horror.

"W-w-what?" Her fingers trembled as she grasped her knees and leaned forward, rocking back and forth as she shook her head. "This can't be happening. This can't be real."

"Ha," Damian chuckled. "Reality."

"How? How did he break it?"

"I'm not quite sure of the Code's hierarchy of rules, so he may have broken more than one. Artists are hard to understand. He destroyed something Theo had created, I'll say that. Two things—er, two people? Two canvases?"

But Caterina couldn't hear him. A ringing in her ear grew louder as the visual of Leander returned. She felt as though she was in that room, standing directly behind him, fighting the urge to retrieve his fallen head wrap and tie it for him, to place his fallen hand back into his lap. In this vision she stared more intensely at the fallen hand and noticed he no longer wore the sacred ring.

Her eyes burst open as she turned urgently to Damian.

"The ring," she said with a shortness of breath as she scanned Damian. "His ring! Where's the ring?"

"Hey! Don't look at me like that! I don't have it! He gave it to Demetrius with his sincerest apologies."

"He apologized to Demetrius?"

"I don't remember exactly. And who knows if Leander was even in the right state of mind at that point."

"Don't you dare question Leander's integrity," Caterina said, lifting the tote bag onto her shoulder as she turned her back toward Damian. "I've heard enough here."

"Don't despise the messenger! You look like you haven't slept either. Come on, Caterina. I know you're upset, but let's stay practical here."

Caterina turned on her heel and faced Damian with flared nostrils.

"There is nothing practical *here*. I'm going inside to see how I can help."

"Well, I'm coming with you!"

The hedges permitted their entrance as they gently opened the front door. The sound of overwhelming grieving bounced off the walls, paralyzing the two at first.

"He's gone forever," they heard Demetrius cry. "They both are."

Caterina and Damian tip toed into the living room to find Aluna and Zo sitting on either side of Demetrius, the three of them sobbing though Demetrius most violently. The vines surrounding the curtain grasped onto it more securely than ever, ensuring the roaring cries remained in the room, though this only amplified them internally. A few candles burned on the table as the curtain restricted most of the natural light from gracing the room.

Aluna gestured toward the opposing couch, and Caterina and Damian quickly took a seat.

"Demetrius," Zo said through his tears, using his sleeve to wipe away those which had dripped onto his mustache and beard, "They will always be with you." Zo patted Demetrius over his heart, but Demetrius pushed him away.

"They were never with me," Demetrius replied, pulling his hair and spitting as he spoke passionately. "Don't you see? I'm not sure if they cared more for each other or just for themselves, but regardless, no one cared for *me*! My brothers…" Demetrius slammed his fist on the table, cracking the wood down the middle. Aluna reached for his fist and caressed it in her palms. His other hand clutched his chest as the piercing stings traveled throughout his entire body.

"They loved you, dear," Aluna said, rubbing her palms together.

"Yes of course they did!" Zo added. "Everyone loves differently, you know. And Leander, well, not much of a sentimental man, is he now? He came to me, Demetrius, are you listening? He came to me before he crossed the desert to see you. Protecting you was the only concern he voiced. I told him not to let anything prevent him from protecting you. There could be no other motive. He felt defeated though, and he thought Theo's word meant more to you than his."

Demetrius clenched his jaw and frowned, shaking his head at the statement.

"Did he tell you the truth from which he protected me?" Demetrius asked, using his muddied forearm to wipe his face. Aluna and Zo exchanged nervous glances and said nothing.

The candles on the table burned brighter as Demetrius lifted his head, his tear-stained face glistening in the candlelight. He stared blankly ahead of him, barely moving his mouth as he uttered the horrible revelation.

"Theo killed my father. And Leander knew."

Silence fell over the room as Demetrius grew eerily still. The tears had suddenly vanished as he spoke the truth into existence. Zo stood, placing his hands over his head as his mind spiraled to process this information.

How could Leander keep such a secret? Zo thought to himself. *Why did he protect a monster?* Bits and pieces of what Leander had told him over the years flashed before his eyes: Leander's refusal to let anyone else mentor

Theo; his devotion and admiration toward his mentee; his determination to keep Theo by his side under any condition; the ruby ring.

"Leander blamed himself," Demetrius continued. "It was Theo's canvas that produced the cursed blade. An accident, I was assured."

"How is Leander to blame?" Zo asked, sliding his hands from his head to his cheeks, holding his face in disbelief.

"He asked my father to guard the canvas while Leander administered the graduation ceremony. No one knows what happened except that the blade ended up in his back."

The bags under Demetrius' eyes deepened, as did the wrinkles on his forehead and around his eyes.

"Speaking of which," Demetrius said, "we must prepare for the ceremony."

Aluna looked alarmingly at her husband, pressing down on his shoulder to assure he remained seated.

"It can wait, my love. You're in no condition to prepare for such an event."

"I'm as ready as I'll ever be," Demetrius said, choking on his words. He gently lifted Aluna's hand from his shoulder and rose from his seat. "Will you come with me? I want to see the Garden before anyone else arrives." Aluna nodded, though she couldn't hide her frown.

"I'm coming too," Zo said, pressing his fist to his lips to stop himself from crying.

"And me too," Damian stood. "We've come this far."

"I want to help," Caterina said in almost a whisper. "Did Leander already make the commemorative statue?"

Demetrius tilted his head and smiled wearily at Caterina. He shook his head.

"There won't be a statue," Demetrius said. "But thank you, all, for coming with me."

"Let me get you something to wear before we go," Aluna said. Demetrius nodded as he walked toward the nearest wall and pressed his exhausted body against it. Zo turned to Caterina quietly and took her hand.

"You are Caterina?" Zo asked, mustering a smile through his tears. Caterina nodded. "I'm Zo, Leander's mentor. I wish we weren't meeting under these circumstances." Without a second hesitation, Caterina flung her arms around Zo, sobbing into his chest. Zo held the back of her head and tilted his towards hers, as they cried together.

"I'm sorry, I'm sorry," Caterina said, pulling away.

"No, my dear, sorry for what? The stars have aligned in such a way that this, unfortunately, is where we find ourselves. You must know, Leander spoke so highly of you. I haven't wanted to meet a student in a very, very long time, but when he spoke of you, well, I almost considered mentoring again."

Caterina buried her face in her hands, unable to respond.

"That's alright, dear. You don't need to mask your emotions with me, or anyone for that matter. You're an artist! And now, by the Code, I am your new mentor, and I will make this my greatest honor. We didn't choose this, but we won't resist it either, alright?"

Caterina nodded, though her head was weighed by overwhelming sorrow. Zo put his arms around Caterina once more, embracing her in a hug.

Aluna returned and helped Demetrius carefully put on a faded yellow linen shirt. The shirt met no resistance as she pulled it down his back, having cleaned his chest and back before they sat on the couch.

She lightly tapped his heart and stood on her toes to gently kiss him. He gave her a big hug, closing his eyes as he breathed in her neck. His hand traveled to her back as she turned to the hallway, and he followed. The others followed as well, Damian trailing furthest behind.

Their eyes readjusted to the sunlight as they left the poorly lit home. The Garden wasn't too far on foot, so they left the horses and traveled on foot. Aluna held Demetrius' hand and rested her head on his arm. The only sensation preventing Demetrius from feeling entirely numb was her fingers intertwined with his.

People had started their days, tending to their yards and engaging with their neighbors. Expressions of worry and confusion followed Demetrius as the group walked past others. Bystanders whispered and some pointed, but Demetrius stared blankly ahead. The world continued spinning while Demetrius remained completely still, at least in his mind. His periphery was blurred by the traumatic flashbacks he couldn't erase from his vision. His heart hurt with each pump, and he clenched his freed hand to resist the pain.

Behind him and Aluna, the three reacted differently to the stares of others. Zo met everyone he knew with an apologetic smile, placing his hand on his chest to assure them he would return to exchange proper greetings later. Caterina brushed some of her loose hair toward her eyes, blocking the strange stares from her vision. Damian continued unbothered, though he would stretch his neck over those in front of him every once in a while to gage how close they were to reaching their destination.

Soon they approached a large, wooden archway covered in tangled greenery and bright flowers. The Garden seemed endless to the naked eye, its grid-like pattern extending to the horizon. The sun was now directly above them, shining brightly upon each green square.

Animated statues of those who passed greeted them. Some smiled and waved the way they did in their waking lives; others merely nodded or turned away. Demetrius kept his head down as they passed two loving partners holding hands, occasionally gazing into each other's eyes. They each had a paintbrush behind their ears, perfectly balanced. Zo held his breath, unable to fathom how those two would've reacted to the news about their beloved son.

The group walked along the middle pathway until they reached the section where Myron rested.

His allotted plot had a square stone protruding from the center, his name engraved on its flat surface. Detailing the perimeter of this grassy section were beautiful yellow flowers, like miniature suns brightening the area. A butterfly landed on the flower closest to Demetrius' leg, its bright orange wings flapping softly. Demetrius placed a heavy hand on the stone's edge. He hung his head as he gripped the stone with whitened knuckles.

"Can I have a moment?" Demetrius asked under his breath. Aluna approached Demetrius and gave him another kiss before rubbing his shoulder and walking away. Without a word, the remainder of the group followed her, walking back to the archway.

Demetrius sat in front of the glossy stone, resting his arms on his risen knees and staring at his reflection. His father's name was written across his eyes.

"You told me to trust the universe," Demetrius whispered, as a throbbing pain pierced his chest and rain down his arms, "and though I love you with my all my heart, Father, I don't think you've given worse advice. Or if this guidance was ultimately true, forgive me for misunderstanding."

Demetrius reached into his pocket and retrieved the two rings. The debris from Leander's had transferred onto Theo's, and the two rested in Demetrius' palm as ancient, forgotten relics. The gems no longer sparkled, nor did the metal bands glisten. He pinched the band of the sapphire ring and held it before his face.

"I trusted you for your wisdom and your reasoning," he spoke to the ring. "Your level-headedness, though sometimes at odds with the rest of the world, encouraged me to rely on you. Most people think emotions and reason are mutually exclusive, but I thought together, we were undeniably strong. I didn't know that this whole time, there was someone who had fortified a wall between us."

Demetrius placed the sapphire band upon Myron's stone and looked down at the ruby ring. It had the metal cross on it, just like Theo had left it, though now its surface was scratched.

"And you," Demetrius said, his bottom lip quivering, "I don't have the words. I truly don't. If my father's death was an accident, why couldn't you tell me? If it wasn't, why? Just why? What did I do that made you take my greatest joys away from me?"

His fingers wrapped tightly around the ring and he brought his fist to his lips. Tears streamed down his face as he squeezed his eyes shut.

"You were my best friend," Demetrius whimpered. "I would've forgiven you, Theo. My heart wants to believe it was an accident." His heart experienced a sharp jolt of agony, seizing his breath momentarily as he clutched his heart with his other hand. He could barely open his eyes as he hyperventilated. He forced his eyes open to stare down at the bloody ring.

"How could I expect you to care about me when you couldn't care for yourself? You became your own worst enemy. When? How? *Why?*"

Demetrius gasped for breath as he leaned forward, a mixture of sweat and tears watering the grass below him.

"I showed you nothing but love, nothing but care, and did any of that reach you? Ever? It couldn't have, for if it did, you would've never chose to leave me!"

The pain traveled from his heart to his fingertips, giving his hand a burning sensation as it held the ring tighter and tighter.

"And even now, with all the truth I've finally been given, I want nothing more than to see your stupid face laughing at me as I suffer here, sharing with me some supposed wisdom about the unfairness of the world. Do you see this ring, Theo? I kept it, after all these years. After all these years… and what have you kept from me? You left me. But again, you left yourself, and to that, is there anything more to say? In leaving yourself, you left everyone, yet only *I* am truly left with the heaviest weight, the burden of abandonment."

Demetrius stretched his hand toward the stone as he winced in pain, placing the ruby ring beside the sapphire one. His head spun as he observed what remained of the three fundamental figures in his life.

"What am I to do without you?" Demetrius asked as tears traced his frowning lips. "The desertion, the depression. This is *torture*! Why is it the harmless who are harmed? I would never wish this upon you, yet here I am! If you were brave enough to betray me and leave me, be bold enough to take me with you!"

Veins bulged from Demetrius' neck as he yelled at the stone before him. His planted his palms in the grass, leaving barely any space between himself and the top of the stone where the rings were.

"Is this what you wanted to see, hmm? Is this who I am without you here? Is this what pure hatred feels like? My heart can't stand it, no... no..." Demetrius fell onto his back as his breath failed him. Excruciating pain traveled through his body like lightening, restricting him from a moment of respite. He grasped at the flowers beside him in an attempt to lift himself, but the nerves in his fingertips stung with torment, permitting him nothing more than uprooting the plants beside him.

His lungs didn't hold enough air for him to scream for help, and after a minute of struggling, his body became still, as his drenched face collapsed to the side, covering it in the fresh soil. Demetrius, an enemy to no one, lied beside his father's grave, like a sleeping child, but with the heart of a grown man who has loved and most certainly has lost. His tall stature, now covered in sweat, tears, and dirt failed to accurately depict the extent to which his spirit was soiled. The world to him was no longer a perfectly painted masterpiece as he rested in his final position, immersed in a bed of torn, bright yellow flowers, reunited with the greatest men he'd ever known.

THE END

CPSIA information can be obtained
at www.ICGtesting.com
Printed in the USA
LVHW030715261221
707138LV00024B/2700